I0823715

ILLUSIONS OF FIRE

ILLUSIONS OF FIRE

NISHA SHARMA

UNION SQUARE & CO.
NEW YORK

UNION SQUARE & CO. and the distinctive Union Square & Co. logo are trademarks of Sterling Publishing Co., Inc.

Union Square & Co., LLC, is a subsidiary of Sterling Publishing Co., Inc.

ISBN 978-1-4549-4777-6 (hardcover)
ISBN 978-1-4549-4778-3 (ebook)
ISBN 978-1-4549-4779-0 (paperback)

Library of Congress Control Number: 2024948054

For information about custom editions, special sales, and premium purchases, please contact specialsales@unionsquareandco.com.

Printed in the United States of America

2 4 6 8 10 9 7 5 3 1

unionsquareandco.com

Cover art by Kushiaania
Cover and interior design by Marcie Lawrence

For the *Buffy* fans, the *Supernatural* nerds,
and the monster geeks who always knew the truth:

South Asian babes do it better.

Content Warning

Some elements of this story, specifically fight scenes, may be triggering to readers. Please be mindful that this text includes on-page murder (possessed human and paranormal entity), including dismemberment and decapitation. There is also grief and reference to dead family members (mother and aunt).

THE ORACLE HAS SPOKEN.

"When flowers will be begot within flowers, and fruits within fruits, then will the [world] come to an end. And the clouds will pour rain unseasonably when the end of the [world] approaches."

Book 3 of the Mahabharata

1. LAILA

Mauritius

Ten Years Ago

Laila threw up seawater. Her belly tightened as she heaved, and the salty ocean gushed out of her. When she could finally breathe again, she rubbed the grit out of her burning eyes. The pretty dress that Mama had bought for her eighth birthday was scratchy and stiff, clinging to her trembling body. Her long black hair that she'd learned to put into a braid all by herself was unraveled and tangled in wet clumps.

And she was all alone.

The beach stretched in either direction and dipped into an angry sky swirling with gray and black. It shifted above her, rumbling and cracking, threatening to swallow her in quick gulps.

"Mama?"

Laila climbed to her feet and looked around for her mother. Moments passed, and no one responded to her call.

Laila slowly turned in a circle. When she and Mama used to go to the beach, there were brightly colored beach umbrellas that she loved to count, and striped towels stretched out on warm sand. This beach was so different.

"Mama?" she said again, and her voice echoed in the silence. There wasn't even a caw of a seabird to respond to her coughs and cry. She flexed her toes, and the sharp white grainy sand was frigid beneath her bare feet. She felt the cold to her very bones.

To her left was an ocean that stretched as far as she could see. On the right was a monstrous jungle brush that was so wild and dense that Laila couldn't squeeze through the branches.

She was never allowed to go in the jungle anyway. It was far too dangerous for a girl born from fire. Too many monsters waiting for her to be alone and unprotected. At least that's what Mama told her.

Her mother. Where was she? Why wasn't she here? How did Laila get here?

"Mama!" she screamed. Her Creole felt like rocks in her mouth. "Mama, where are you!"

Her chest tightened. She started gasping between the chattering of her teeth.

It was Friday. The last day of school. She was supposed to go to a birthday party for her best friend.

Her feet sank deep into the wet dunes and her arms were so heavy as she tried to use them to propel herself forward. She struggled down the beach, looking for someone, anyone.

"Mama!" She tried to run now, her wet dress slapping against her legs, as she looked for help. But the faster she ran, the louder the crashing waves and the more scared she became. Where were the people?

When the clouds darkened to soot black and encased the beach in dark shadows, Laila stopped running. She was crying, sobbing, begging.

"Mama! Please! Anybody!" she screamed as she hugged herself.

In the distance, she heard a faint jingle from the trees. She whirled away from the waves that grew higher and higher. Was someone coming? Were they good people? Would they help her?

Through tears, Laila saw the large straw hat peek through the ominous jungle leaves. Then, a lady in a long blue dress stepped out from behind a tree trunk. She grew closer and closer, until Laila recognized the face that was partially covered by big black sunglasses.

"Usha Masi!" Laila ran toward the woman, who tossed aside her glasses and hat and dropped to her knees. Laila catapulted her body into the familiar embrace.

Once she was in Usha Masi's arms, the tightness in her chest loosened and her whole body relaxed. She was with someone who loved her. She was safe. Usha Masi said a few pretty words and hugged Laila even closer. Soon the magic made Laila warm again. Her clothes were no longer scratchy. Her hair felt dry, and she had her favorite red sandals.

"I was so scared," Laila sobbed against Usha Masi's shoulder. Her Creole came out in hiccups and bursts. "Mama isn't here. Where is Mama, Usha Masi? Did you find her?"

Usha Masi pulled back and cupped her hands around Laila's face. Her red eyes looked sad as she scanned Laila from head to toe.

"My darling princess," she said. "I thought we'd lost you, too."

"Lost me?" Laila said. "I'm right here! But I want my mama. Usha Masi, can you take me to her?"

A single red tear traced down Usha Masi's cheek. Because she was different, because she lived forever, the water from her eyes was like blood. But now as she cried, Laila felt scared all over again. Something was still very, very wrong.

"Laila, you're in a dream."

Laila looked around at the forest behind her, quiet and still. It felt so real to her. The sand, the fear, the crashing waves. She touched Usha Masi's arm, her skin warm and smooth under her hands. "A dream? A scary one? Then all I have to do is wake up, right?" She'd be back in Mauritius, striped umbrellas and people all around them again. She'd be on her way to a birthday party, and she'd sit in the back seat of their tiny vehicle and listen to her mama's beautiful, musical laughter.

Usha Masi ran a long black nail over Laila's cheek. She continued to cry, her voice turning into that raspy demon sound she sometimes made when she wasn't in her human body. "Yes, my darling. All you have to do is wake up. Your masis and I will be waiting for you."

Her masis. The four rakshasi who came and visited her every summer. Who told her stories and taught her how to use a bow and arrow. "Mama too, right?"

More red tears. "No, darling. Your mama won't be there. Not anymore."

Laila's throat began to burn again, and her stomach churned like the roiling sea. "Why not? Where is Mama?"

"Your mama is no longer with us, darling," Usha Masi said. "I'm so sorry."

"No," Laila sobbed. There was no way that it could be true. She and Mama were a team. "No. Mama is here. She's somewhere."

Laila spun on the heels of her sandals and stumbled before righting herself.

"Mama?" she shrieked. "Mama!"

Usha Masi touched her shoulder, but Laila pushed her away. "You're lying, Usha Masi! Mama can't leave me. She can't!"

Laila felt hot—her skin was starting to burn. In the distance, she watched as the ocean began to bubble and steam.

"Mama!" she screamed.

"Laila. Laila, take a deep breath. You're going to hurt yourself." Usha Masi came forward again, as if she was going to grab her and wake her up. As if she was going to show her an even scarier dream.

"Don't touch me!" she shouted, shaking off her masi's touch. "Mama! Mama!"

She was scared again, but this time she couldn't control it the way she was supposed to. Fire shot from her palms and the sand rippled under feet. Laila couldn't stop screaming. She ran down the beach as the world around her began to burn.

Then the beach turned to glass and her nightmare began.

2. KARAN

Lombok, Indonesia: Mount Rinjani National Park

Seven Years Ago

Karan was thirteen years old when his father told him that he was ready for his first kill. Karan was less certain about his skills and abilities, but he'd boarded the flight from Delhi to Bali first, then the one to Lombok, with his dad and his dad's best friend.

He'd sat in a middle seat behind both adult men, whom he'd looked up to his entire life. They were professors in military history, mythology, and the occult at the University of India, Delhi, and they talked the entire trip about asuras and other monstrous and godly beings. But then, they always talked about the supernatural. That was their life's work and they lived and died for it.

Both Karan's father and Satyapal had also trained Karan since he was old enough to walk: he learned how to hold a bow and arrow, to wield a sword, and to use all his senses. They'd taken him on hunts through the jungles in India between their college semesters, and they had patted his back when he threw up after seeing his first celestial being murdered.

And his second.

Okay, and maybe his third.

As the son of the son hundreds of generations removed from Karna, a great warrior in the Mahabharata, it was his destiny to uphold truth and justice. His lineage had been asura-hunters ever since the Great War spilled so much blood that the soil in Kurukshetra was still red to this day. It was time for him to accept his destiny, to do his duty, and prove that he had what it took to be an asura-hunter too.

That's what they told him, anyway.

"Are you doing okay, beta?" his father said as he patted him on the back. His hand was heavy, and strong. He was in his thirties and because he practiced with his Asi every day, wielding his sword with precision, he looked as young as his college students sometimes. He also walked like a soldier even though he'd never been in the military. He told Karan once that he didn't believe in what the army fought for.

The only unruly part of him was his hair that grew thick and black, just like Karan's. His eyes were the same deep brown too. Karan was still growing, but hopefully by the time he was his father's age, he'd be just as tall, topping six feet, with broad shoulders and long limbs.

"Leave the boy alone, Vasudev," Satyapal said. He clapped Karan's shoulder with a bit more force and enthusiasm, sending Karan swaying forward. "His training will kick in and he'll make us all proud. He's already so tall. So strong. He'll be fine."

Karan always wondered why Satyapal loved the hunt. He didn't have to be here. He didn't have a sacred lineage, but he'd grown up with Karan's father, studied in the same graduate program, and even trained at the same local archery studio in Delhi. He'd been the first person to hold Karan as a baby after his parents and grandparents. He'd been trusted with family secrets, and because of his specialization in the South Asian occult, he planned most of their trips.

"Thanks, Satya Uncle," Karan said as he hoisted his bag onto his back. Doubts continued to swirl around him like a fog he couldn't control. There were many times when they'd gone on a hunt and come back with nothing. They'd chase rumors up and down mountains, hearing elderly couples yelling from their homes about the wicked and the damned. The townspeople pointed fingers at mostly women, accusing them of being a demon in the skin of a human. So many expeditions had ended early after they discovered in their research that the evil entity was just a man. Karan prayed this was one of those times.

Earlier that week, they'd checked into a lodge, a small place in Senaru at the base of Mount Rinjani at the national park entrance. There they interviewed a dozen townspeople about bloodsucking demons prowling the dense rainforest. Then they met with the local religious leader who had been the one to call Satyapal for help. Karan shuddered when the old man said the word *rakshasa*. Because the locals were primarily Hindus, they attempted to bless the forest, pray to the gods, do anything in their power to fight back. Lombok had been hit hard with natural disasters, and tourism was an important part of their economic recovery plan. A rakshasa would not only destroy their tourism, but it could also kill their local population.

"It's just a short ride into the heart of the forest," Satyapal said as they got into the small red rented vehicle that was barely large enough to fit one driver, let alone three men and bow bags.

This was his legacy, Karan thought as his heart began to pump heavily in his narrow chest. This was what he was meant to do. Every man in his family conducted their first hunt alone at thirteen, and they'd survived to tell the story. He would do the same, then continue hunting for the rest of his life.

He wished he had a friend the way his father had Satyapal to share all his secrets with, though. They were Indian Indiana Joneses in real life, except they dealt with much scarier beings. If only he could share this with someone his age, maybe he wouldn't feel so . . . freaked out about it all.

As the car drove into the dense foliage following a small, barely cleared path, Karan swallowed hard. He could do this. He'd seen monsters before. He'd done his homework. He memorized all the texts his father made him study. He'd survive this and make his family proud.

They sat in silence, not wanting to share their secrets with the driver, who was also their certified guide, a mandatory companion for all hikers who wanted to enter the park. All he knew was that they were from an Indian university looking for wild pigs in Lombok at night. He had reluctantly agreed to drive them when he was offered a ridiculously high fee. His one stipulation was that Dad and Uncle Satya didn't tell anyone that he stayed in the car. That worked out in everyone's favor.

No one was supposed to know about Karan's legacy. It was too dangerous to draw attention to their mission and their duty.

Uncle Satya was the exception, of course.

The car came to a halt, and Karan got out along with Satyapal and his father. Their driver, a skinny man who trembled at the sight of the looming trees, pulled forward into a small clearing and waved at them before rolling his windows up.

They stood on the road, three asura-hunters staring at each other.

"Are you ready?" his father asked as he removed his bow from his bag.

How could he not be? Karan thought about all the prep work they'd done that week. Just like every hunt, after their interviews, they spent a considerable amount of time canvasing the area in the daylight.

"I'm as ready as I'll ever be, Dad," Karan said. He straightened his custom-fit Kevlar gear that still felt so heavy and clunky on his reed thin frame.

"We'll be right behind you," Satyapal said as he adjusted his night-vision scope. "If we go together, then there is a chance they'll hear us, but you'll never be alone out there."

"I understand," Karan said. His fingers trembled as he attached the small cylindrical metal scope to his own bow. "I got this."

"Maybe it's too soon," Karan's father said to Satyapal. "He's only thirteen."

"You were too," Satyapal said softly. "And this is a real rakshasa sighting! Rakshasa have been rumored to be extinct for centuries. This may be our only chance to see one in person. My intel is good, Vasudev."

Karan's father looked doubtful, but he nodded. "Fine. Karan?"

"I can do this," Karan said again. He repeated it over and over again in his head. *I can do this. I can do this.*

He put on night-vision goggles, and then after one long hug for each man, he pulled out his small machete and began cutting his way into the thick brush.

The night swallowed him as he went deeper and deeper into the forest. He heard hissing, buzzing, and the soft huff of animals. He felt the hard prickly ends of branches, the thick wide faces of leaves against his cheeks. Then his training set in and he followed the path that he was supposed to take by the red glow from his compass.

The last sighting was near the waterfall deep on the southeast side of the forest, so that's where he'd go.

Fifteen minutes later, he was sweating, his bow slipping out of his grip from his damp palms.

He stepped into a clearing covered in moss and surrounded by bowing sinuous banyan trees before he took off his goggles. Karan looked up at his first view of the full moon. It shined down on him, as if taunting him. Even though it was night, he knew he wasn't alone. There was the hum of insects, the flap of wings from birds in the treetops. The random hoot of an owl or the grunt of monkeys swinging above. He had to filter all of that out and focus on the noise that *didn't* belong.

Just as he was able to pick up the sound of water crashing on rocks in the distance, he felt a sharp chill behind him.

He spun, bracing his feet as he strained to see if there was an animal or an intruder. His research told him that there were predators in these woods. The question was, which kind was he dealing with right now?

The trees rustled overhead.

A branch snapped.

Karan rushed to put on his goggles so he could see into the dark. His blood was pumping hard in his chest as fear and perspiration pricked the back of his neck.

Nothing. He saw nothing but infinite black and the neon lines that highlighted foliage as he stepped into a small clearing on a game trail.

Another sharp gust of cold air gripped him by his throat.

And then a voice. The deep, raspy sound of tortured souls surrounded him.

Little boy. Are you lost?

Have you come out to play with me?

No one will hear you cry, you know.

Karan swallowed hard. So it was a mythical rakshasa, out in their true form. Karan could feel his heart pounding. He kept his bow steady just like his father taught him as he turned in a circle, looking for any signs of movement. He didn't know if it would come at him with magic, or force, so he had to be prepared for both. He had a satchel of herbs in his pocket in case he needed protection.

You are in my woods, little boy. Leave or I'll tear open your belly and suck the meat off your bones.

"There isn't much there," he said loudly into the forest. "I work out with my dad."

When a scream came from his left, he knew he was about to be attacked.

His destiny pounded in his blood, in his soul, and pumped through his body as he braced himself for his first kill.

The monster came out of the forest in naked red and brown flesh. It had long black claws, curved fangs with sharp points, and matted black hair that hung around a cocked head. It screamed again, and spittle steamed as it hit the soil.

Karan didn't even have time to raise his machete before it lunged forward. He dropped his bag and stumbled back to avoid the slash of claws and fangs as the rakshasa advanced with speed and power. He retreated, gripping the machete in one hand as they continued to rotate through the clearing.

Karan had to lock a single hit and buy himself a moment to catch his breath.

Keep calm and focus on shifting from defense to offense. His father's voice echoed through his head even as the monster slashed at his face and pushed him back until he hit the edge of the clearing, outside the perimeter of the moonlight.

Its red irises were filled with fire, and they entranced him long enough for the monster to grip his arms and get close enough for its spittle to drip off the tip of one fang. It fell on Karan's shoulder and burned like lava.

He kicked the monster's abdomen, then dove to the side, frantically crawling until he could retrieve his bag. After a fumble, his crossbow was in his hand moments later. The monster stayed back, circling as Karan adjusted the bow against his shoulder.

It didn't attack him. Something felt off about the way it waited.

Ready to be eaten, little boy?

"Not really!" he shouted back. His shoulder burned, and when he reached up to touch the new hole in his shirt, his fingertips came away wet with blood.

Okay, that's a first, he thought. His mom was going to be so mad.

He shook his head, desperate to regain focus as he shifted into fighting position again.

Who are you? the creature asked. It was as if they saw him for the first time, taking him all in from head to toe.

"I am Karan Singh," he said in Sanskrit. "Son of Vasudev Singh, and descendant of warrior and demigod Karna." His bloody fingers slipped over the tip of the arrow as he loaded the crossbow. He cocked it and took aim at the rakshasa's heart. "And I'm here to have your head."

The rakshasa screamed with its clawed hands outstretched between them. Its cry almost sounded like *no* before the arrow punctured its chest.

Karan quickly jumped to his feet, strapped his bag on his back again, cocked his crossbow a second time, and readied his machete with his other hand.

The rakshasa screamed again, and the torturous sound echoed through the forest as it gripped the arrow with both hands and collapsed to the ground. Steam billowed from the wound, and a light blue glow radiated from its skin before the creature changed.

"What the . . ."

The shape of the rakshasa—fangs, teeth, and leather skin—shifted until it was a naked woman. She was young, even younger than his dad, and she had a gaping wound in her chest where the arrow was still buried deep. A shadow began spreading from the center of the wound, creating black sliver veins that spread across her skin.

"You need to stay away," the woman whispered, gasping for air.

Karan knew he should keep his distance, but this wasn't a monster anymore. He came closer, weapons still at the ready. He'd memorized all the rules, all the steps on what he was supposed to do at the end of the hunt, but the monster wasn't acting the way it was supposed to. He began to tremble, the humid air weighing hot and heavy on his skin. "Y-you're not a rakshasa."

The woman writhed on the ground, her head thrashing back and forth. "*Rakshasi.* I am Usha, guardian of—"

The woman's voice cut off as she coughed up blood.

Karan fell to his knees. *No*, he thought. No, this wasn't right. This wasn't what was supposed to happen. Their bodies were supposed to smoke, then disappear.

"Guardian of who?" he demanded. "Who?" Karan stuck his machete in the ground and gripped the end of the arrow. He yanked hard until there was a resounding pop as the tip released from the bone, muscles, and tissue.

The black veins continued to spread across her skin. "It's not healing," she gasped. "You're from the son of the son of Karna. He was a strong soldier. He fought valiantly."

"You know who I am?"

"I know who you came from."

Karan had to fight back tears. "My ancestor? How? Are you . . . are you immortal?"

She nodded. Her hair began to turn white, and her skin began to wrinkle. "Little boy," she said, and despite the demon in her voice, it sounded almost like she was trying to comfort him. "You are not . . . evil."

"N-no, ma'am." That's when he realized that he was shaking. Tears blurred his vision and fell hot and fast down his cheeks. He'd made a mistake. He knew in that moment that he'd made a terrible mistake. Monsters weren't supposed to make sense. They weren't supposed to suffer and be . . . kind.

"Please," she whispered now. "Stay away from her. Don't touch her."

"Who—who are you talking about?"

The woman shook her head. "She is . . . divine."

The rakshasi gasped and gasped. Karan went to press the palm of his hand against the hole, but she screamed. "Your blood! Your blood."

"Okay. Okay, I won't touch you." The blood from his wound. The one that had made it onto the tip of the arrow. That's what had caused this. But how? How could his blood kill a rakshasi so quickly?

His father was wrong. His uncle was wrong. They shouldn't have come here.

"I—I am so sorry. I had to . . . I have to kill asuras. That's my legacy. But not you. I should've never come here."

Shock, and then what looked like understanding, crossed the woman's face. It glowed down in the moonlight even as the black veins crawled up her neck and over her cheeks, spreading like ink dropped in water.

"Satyapal," she hissed.

Satyapal? How did this rakshasi know his uncle?

"What can I do?" he cried. He was sobbing now, and he couldn't stop. "What can I do to fix this?"

"Don't trust him," she hissed. "He's . . . dark magic."

The sound of screams echoed through the trees. It was far away.

Run, she mouthed with ghosted words. Her voice no longer worked. The black veins reached her eyes and turned them black. "Run now before they catch you."

"No." He brushed a tear off his cheek. "No, I can't leave . . . You're dying. I did this. I did this, and I didn't know—"

"Shhh." Her skin was completely black now and illuminated in blue light. "You are . . . forgiven. Go. Now."

She closed her eyelids, and the sound of screams echoed closer than ever.

Karan scrambled for his bag, his weapons, his night-vision goggles, and ran as fast as he could through the cut path that he'd made in the forest. He didn't stop to think, didn't stop to turn around and look over his shoulder now.

He practically ran into his father's chest. Those strong, familiar arms wrapped around him, comforting and sure. "Karan! Are you hurt? Are you—"

"Move!" he yelled. And then his father and uncle were hot on his trail back to the main road. They kept running until they got to their guide's car. He must've seen them running, because he turned the car around and sped down the road the minute they dove into the car.

"What happened?" Karan's father asked. "Are you okay?"

"It's gone," Karan said, gasping for air. He tugged at the neck of his Kevlar vest. "I shot it. It's done. B-b-but the body . . ."

"Did you speak to it?" Satya Uncle asked. He sat in the front passenger seat and twisted around to look at Karan's face. "Did it talk to you?"

There was a frenetic energy in Satya Uncle's voice. His gaze zeroed in on the blood oozing from Karan's shoulder. "You hurt?"

"I'm fine," Karan said softly.

"*Did it talk to you?*" Satya Uncle insisted.

Karan was quiet for a moment.

I forgive you.

"No, it didn't talk to me. It just sort of screeched."

Karan watched his uncle and father glance at each other, before his father wrapped an arm around his shoulders and pressed a handkerchief to the wound. He winced, but leaned against the warmth of his father's side, smelling the familiar sweat from a man he'd only wanted to make proud.

It was the first time that he'd lied to his father and uncle. He'd trusted them with his life, but in that moment, he felt like he had to keep the rakshasi's words to himself. He wasn't ready to share them.

The vehicle had barely driven half a mile down the road before they saw the flames in their rearview mirror. The driver shouted in what sounded like multiple languages and pressed his foot on the gas so hard that everyone in the vehicle jerked back in his seat.

The forest behind them ignited in an inferno, an explosion of bright yellow. Karan's father and Satya Uncle saw the blaze and began cheering, then hugged Karan and gave each other high fives. An asura that bursts into flames is an asura that has died. Thankfully the flames began to die out as soon as they appeared, but the fact that they'd happened was proof that Karan had killed his first monster.

Karan knew the truth. The flames weren't the end, but the beginning.

The conversation he'd had with her played over and over again in his head as he listened to his father celebrate his initiation as an asura-hunter. All he could think about was the sound of the rakshasi's screams.

3. LAILA

Finger Lakes, USA

Present Day

Laila woke in a cold sweat. Visions of fire and the heavy weight of loss pressed like stones on her heart. It had been ages since both her mother and Usha Masi died, and months since the last time she'd had a nightmare where she remembered the days they left this world. Her trembling fingers reached for her phone, and when she tapped the screen, the bright light nearly blinded her.

It was four a.m. on the first day of her freshman year in college.

That was, if she was going to college. The reality of her life made it difficult for her to suck in a deep breath. This was another kind of nightmare.

The few online classes she'd registered for didn't really count as the same experience she'd once hoped to have herself. Not when she was comparing her fall semester with that of her friends who'd graduated from high school and went off to start their lives. Laila could pretend all she wanted that she was normal. Taking classes, working behind the information desk at her aunts' winery, driving to archery practice at the local studio.

But she was not normal. She was raised by three demon aunts and had a bloodline from a mythological being. A bloodline that required her to have a child before her twenty-fifth birthday. She was eighteen. Seven years to go.

Laila reached across the bedspread to touch the tattered pages of her most beloved novel: Kate Chopin's *The Awakening.* She'd been forced to read it in AP English two years ago, and she'd read it hundreds of times since.

A protagonist who refused to be defined as a mother-woman. By her ability to conceive children. To escape her fate, she stripped naked on a beach and tried to swim away from her problems during a storm. She drowned in the ocean.

Morbid, but definitely familiar. Laila had no intention of drowning, and she'd long ago accepted that her reality was different from that of Chopin's protagonist.

She tossed the phone aside, and heard a loud, irritated meow.

"Sorry, Billi," she whispered in the dark. Laila pushed her thick comforter away and shivered when her feet touched the icy-cold floor.

"Descended from fire, my ass," she muttered to herself as she brushed her long, frizzy hair over her shoulder and crossed her bedroom to her private bath. The motion-sensor lights turned on, and the large white marble room glowed. She might as well get ready, she decided. There was no way she was going to go back to sleep now.

Laila didn't even bother looking in the massive mirror with the touch sensor as she put her long hair up in a messy topknot. It was way too early to care about appearance. Not when she didn't have to be at the vineyard until noon for her afternoon shift.

She paused as she mentally reviewed her schedule in her head. Damn, she had practice at night. The fall season started today as well, which meant that she'd have to pack her workout clothes and change in the office. Reviewing her familiar routine helped slow her racing pulse, and she slowly began to relax as she finished washing her face and brushing her teeth.

When she finished in the bathroom, Laila crossed her bedroom suite to her large walk-in closet. She pulled out her duffel from her bag cabinet and dropped it on the marble-top dresser island. The white glittered under the gaudy chandelier her aunts insisted she needed. Then, after tossing some clothes and her shoes in the duffel, she went back to getting dressed for the morning.

Upstate New York was muggy and humid in August, but her ferocious adopted aunts, her masis, all preferred to keep the haveli as cold as possible. That meant she had to wear layers: T-shirt, jeans, and a hoodie with the vineyard logo on the front.

By the time she was walking down the double-wide marble staircase to the main level, her phone read 4:30 a.m. She fed the cat in the butler's kitchen, the small alcove space her aunts used more for storage than actual food prep, and poured herself a cup of chai from the automatic dispenser in the industrial-size main kitchen.

She sat at the twelve-foot-long island and was halfway through her tea when she realized that the house was eerily quiet. Laila checked the time again.

The masis woke and did their yoga practice at four a.m. By now they should be online shopping, or slurping chai like it was blood . . . which they often preferred to chai.

"Masis?" No one responded.

She put down her cup and walked through the corridors to the pink and gold living room, the mudroom, and the offices used for the vineyard.

The house was empty.

It wasn't the first time she was left on her own, but fear still tickled the back of her throat. She hated being alone.

Laila slipped on a pair of Chucks, knotted the laces, and opened the front door to the balmy early morning. Fog snaked through thick tree trunks in the heavily wooded forest surrounding the home. A private lake that emptied into one of the many rivers in the area lay just beyond the tree line. Exotic cars lined the long driveway that wove its way down to a main road in the distance.

At the base of the hill was the winery surrounded by manicured shrubbery.

The view was so different from what she'd grown up with in Mauritius. She was born on an island with crystalline waters. White sand and island life. A speck in the Indian Ocean. Then her masis had moved them to the dense rainforest in Indonesia. When Usha Masi died so soon after their move, they immigrated to the cold forest in Germany before her aunts decided it was time to go to America.

Now? Upstate New York was her home.

"Hello?" she called out into the dark.

She stepped off the expansive porch and onto the black soil. The night was slowly lifting so she could see more than just shadows in the distance.

"Masis!" This time she shouted for them.

A high-pitched shriek. A whisper of laughter on the wind.

The hair on the back of her neck raised.

A cackle echoed through the trees. Laila spun in a circle, trying to pinpoint where the sound was coming from. Her pulse sped up. She glanced at the front porch and realized that she'd stepped far from the house.

"Little girl," a gravel-rough voice said from the distance. "Covered in flesh. Delicious blood to drink."

"Oh, gross," Laila said out loud. "Seriously?"

The attack came from the back. It always did. Laila ducked and moved in the dance-like fighting form that she'd been taught since she was eight. She barely escaped the red limb with long black fingernails that swooped out to grip her by the throat.

She spun, facing the rakshasi with elongated canines and blood-red eyes. "It's not even five yet!"

Laila blocked the first combination of punches, and the hard, unyielding strength of the attacks strained her muscles. She dropped to sweep the legs out from underneath the rakshasi, but she wasn't fast enough, and she felt the graze of talons against her ribs and knew that she'd just lost another sweatshirt. That fueled her anger as she jabbed forward, going for a throat punch all while avoiding nails and teeth.

"Too slow," the rakshasi hissed, spitting acid with each word. The spittle hissed and steamed as it touched the ground.

"I think you're just mad because your ancient India fighting technique doesn't approve of throat-punching."

The rakshasi shrieked, legs spread, knees bent, naked red and brown flesh. She held up her hands like bear claws, and a long, forked tongue licked at her canines.

Laila centered herself, cleared her mind, and waited for the next attack. She was not going to take the bait. She was not going to lose her cool. That would only make this impromptu combat routine longer.

After finally losing her patience, the rakshasi lunged. Laila took a running leap and put all her power into a roundhouse kick that had her losing her balance and toppling over. Her knees sang in pain as they hit the ground. Her palms burned as pebbles and rocks cut into her skin.

The rakshasi cackled, and the sound was echoed by more voices coming through the trees. Great, now she was going to have an audience.

She jumped to her feet seconds before a large foot almost crushed her skull.

"Unoriginal, Masi," she taunted.

The fight continued, and she kept retreating, working on the defense, blocking, punching, landing one hit for every three she received in return. The forest floor filtered with light as the sun began to lift over the horizon. Sweat beaded across her forehead, and her back ached as she held herself rigid and firm, just the way she'd always been taught to fight.

She used to look forward to these surprise attacks. They were a game when she was a child, and she would be so proud of herself when she beat her masis. But now, on the verge of losing the freedom she pretended she possessed in her life, Laila was over it.

When she fell to the ground, feeling a jolt of pain in her hip from the impact, her frustration mounted. She hadn't even eaten breakfast or finished her first cup of chai. It was the first day of college, something she'd never experience as a normal eighteen-year-old in the United States, and all she wanted was to be left alone to work and go online and head to the studio. But no, she had to fight one of her aunts. As the attacks mounted, and she moved back in defense, her anger grew until it burned in her palms.

"Can't we stop?" Laila cried, stumbling to her feet for the umpteenth time.

"Fight me!" the rakshasi hissed. Her throat was full of hisses, and she deftly blocked elbow jab, kick, punch, and blow.

"I want to stop, Rashmi Masi!"

"No!"

Laila blocked another combination and felt the sting of talons against the flesh on the outside of her thigh.

"I said enough!" For the first time in seven years, the tight leash on her emotions snapped and fire burst from her palms and scorched the forest floor. The force of it flung her back until she hit the ground. Her head banged against a rock, and the shearing pain was the last thing she remembered before the fire died again.

"Is she up?"

"Shhh! Give her some space."

"Rashmi, you were too hard on her. When she said stop, you should've stopped."

"How else is she going to learn to defend herself?"

"We have been guarding the Daughters of Draupadi for centuries, and the biggest enemy they had to defend themselves against were human men."

"Well, if that's not reason enough to teach her how to kill in one hundred and eight ways, I don't know what is."

"But the *fire*."

"She just turned eighteen last month. It's always more intense by the eighteenth year."

"But not like this."

Laila cracked open one eye and then the other. Her three masis surrounded her, hovering over her prone form as she lay on the large kitchen island. They were back in their human forms—their dark brown skin luminescent, luscious thick black hair swirling around their shoulders, almost as if it was alive and shifting on its own. Their faces, frozen at twenty-eight years old thanks to the magic of immortality, did nothing to hide the centuries of living that reflected in their golden-brown eyes rimmed with a thin red line.

Laila lifted her head and winced at the pain. She smelled the herbal pack Rashmi Auntie must have made for her. It sat in a warm wet towel at the base of her neck.

"Seriously? You could've put me on the couch."

"She's awake!" Giri Masi shrieked. She shimmered with glitter and the jewelry she preferred to wear as she wrapped her arms around Laila's waist and squeezed. "Darling, I'm so, so sorry."

"It's fine," Laila said, and sat up. She took inventory of the burns and pain that often plagued her after a sparring match. Her hip, her leg, her neck. They had already healed, even though her clothes remained ripped. Laila picked up some more of the scent of the rich herbs that made up Rashmi Masi's special mix, which she packed into a paste and smeared on her skin to accompany magic incantations. "How long was I out?"

"Twenty minutes," Vika Masi said. She stood at the end of the island with her arms crossed over her signature blue dress. Her long fingernails, sharpened to points, tapped against her slim collarbone. "Are you okay?"

The fire. It was brief, but powerful.

When Laila was a kid, she would put her hand in front of a fan in her mother's bedroom. The fan was so strong, it would push her hand back. Laila would lean into the air, loving the resistance of the forced cool breeze. She looked down at her palms now. The smooth skin was soft and unmarked. Even though it had happened before, on the day of her mother's death and then again on the day Usha Masi died, it still felt brand-new.

She remembered her history. She knew why she was able to produce fire. Draupadi, the mythological woman in the Mahabharata, was formed from fire. When she produced her offspring from blood and fire, a happy by-product was the inherited ability to shoot flames like a character from *Dragon Ball Z* in times of great stress.

"I wonder why I'm lighting up like a candle now," Laila said as she continued to flex her fingers. "My family, all three of you, are with me, so it's not like someone died. My life is the same as it's been for the last five years. Did something shift in the stars or the universe or whatever?"

Three heads shook in unison.

Laila swung her legs over the side of the island and hopped down. Her rakshasi masis would be the ones to know something was wrong in the stars. They'd been alive during the Kurukshetra War, had met Draupadi herself, and were entrusted with the safety of the Daughters of Draupadi in exchange for protection and immortality.

They towered over her now at six feet and watched her in silence as she bent her knees to test for soreness.

"Now that I'm sweaty, I'm going to shower," Laila said. "I had hoped to have chai first, but you guys decided to *jump me.*" She glared at them, and three demonesses averted their eyes in guilt. Laila knew that it wouldn't last long. They'd be nagging her into more Sanskrit lessons sooner rather later.

"Laila," Vika Masi said, her voice firm as she continued to stare Laila down. "Is it stress? That may trigger some erratic behavior."

She thought about Kate Chopin's mother-woman in *The Awakening* that she'd left on her bed that morning. "No, everything is the same as it always is," she said.

"I think we still need to check the books," Vika Masi said.

"Yes, yes!" Giri Masi said, clapping her hands together.

"The library should have something for us," Rashmi Masi said. She pointed to the hidden panel between the large great room and the kitchen. It led to a lower level underneath the house that held an endless cavern of books, a vault with texts that were centuries old, blessed and protected by a god so they could remain preserved forever in their original condition.

"If you want to check the books, go ahead," Laila said. "But your girl has a work shift. As do most of you."

"Wait," Vika Masi said. Her command was so parentlike that it reminded Laila of Vika's older sister Usha Masi. Vika Masi had the same bone structure, the same commanding presence, the same smothering tendencies. "Darling, I want you to try and call the fire again."

"What?" Laila sputtered. She clenched her fists. "You know it just happens. I can't call it like a dog."

"Dogs are delicious," Giri Masi whispered before Rashmi Masi slammed her elbow in her sister's gut to shut her up.

Laila rolled her eyes. "No eating dogs," she said. "You promised. Household animals going missing makes people suspicious."

"You're not supposed to have that kind of fire, Laila," Vika Masi persisted. "Stop changing the subject."

Laila started to back away from her aunts. "I don't know what you want me to say. I'm a descendant of Draupadi, the wife of five mediocre demigods who somehow managed to save the world and their kingdom after winning the Kurukshetra War. The fire is in my blood!"

"Yes, but not like *that*," Vika Masi said. "You're different. This is a mystery that we should focus on."

She wanted to shout, to yell that she'd learned her lesson. Hell, she'd spent years of her life trying to find the person who killed her mother in the hit-and-run accident. She'd spent even longer obsessing over her Usha Masi's death before her aunts told her she was making herself sick. "The only mystery I need to focus on today is how I'm going to stay off social media so I can stop obsessing over my friends' college pictures," Laila said. "Maybe this is the universe trying to make up for being stuck here by giving me pyrotechnic skills." She turned and waved over her shoulder. "We'll figure it out later!"

Before her aunts could stop her again and tell her that she wasn't needed at the winery, she made her escape. If the winery was all she had, if her job behind the information desk and her training at the academy was the only chance at human interaction she'd be able to enjoy, she'd take it.

As she left the kitchen and jogged up the marble stairs, she swallowed the lump in her throat. The fire had her worried too. Maybe when she came back from work, she'd look at the books herself to see if there was an answer to the surge of power. Because if there was one thing that she was sure about, it was that if it happened again and she was in public, she'd be even more isolated than she was now.

4. LAILA

VIKA MASI: Darling girl, we haven't found anything this morning in the books, but we'll look again to see if we can find something.

GIRI MASI: Tomorrow is the new moon!!!! We will be hunting!!!! For sport!!!! We won't see you with our eyeballs, but we love you with our hearts!!!!

RASHMI MASI: Your meal kit is unpacked in the human fridge, and you left your protein shakes in our blood fridge again, so we moved them back over.

VIKA MASI: Don't forget to do your Sanskrit homework.

LAILA: You are all buzzkills, but I love you anyway.

It took some time, but Laila had managed to stop thinking about the fact that fire had ejected from her palms that morning. It helped that work was chaotic. August was still peak season in the Finger Lakes, and even though it was a Monday, a steady stream of people came through the winery information center and kept her busy.

Laila imagined that one day, after her baby-making responsibilities were finished and her kid was a functioning human being who understood the responsibility of their legacy, she'd travel to different vineyards and wineries before settling down to run Divine Winery.

It was a medium-size vineyard, with a winery, tasting room, and gift shop, located off the main highway next to one of the larger lakes in the region. It was an ideal location for tour buses and locals, both of which were the bulk of her customers today.

When her watch beeped to remind her that it was five, Laila took advantage of the lull at the end of her shift to clock out and run to the back offices to change. She shoved some of the storage boxes aside so she had room to maneuver. The space was a glorified junk room since her aunts had never visited. To manage the business, Laila's aunts had a team of people who worked for them, managing everything from the grapes to the distribution center to the tasting room. Most of the employees didn't even know that the company was owned by Vika, Rashmi, and Giri Masi. Their paychecks were signed by the company, and the general manager was responsible for all the administrative details. Lucy, the GM for the last five years, got most of her directions by email from an accountant and a lawyer in New York City.

Lucy knew that Laila was related to the mysterious owners, so thankfully she didn't say anything when Laila used the office to change into her workout gear, a fitted tank and matching high-waisted leggings in lilac.

"Have a good practice," she said as they passed each other in the hallway.

"Thanks," Laila replied. "I'll see you tomorrow for my double shift."

Before she could make it out the door, Denise, one of the gift shop attendants and her archery teammate, stopped her. "Hey!" she said as she stepped in Laila's path. Her thick corkscrew curls were tied in two space buns on the top of her head. She was still wearing the winery uniform of T-shirt and jeans. "Any chance you can give me a ride to the studio? My boyfriend dropped me off and he was supposed to get me too, but he's running late."

"Sure," Laila said. "I'll meet you out by the car."

With a grin and a quick thanks, Denise ran off to the employee restroom where she'd have to change. If Laila knew her better, she might've offered her aunts' office. It was just that Laila didn't know anyone well enough to entrust them with information about her personal life. It wasn't that she didn't want to get super close to her friends. It was just that it was too dangerous to try. No one was supposed to know about their secret. Laila's aunts could be hunted by religious extremists, and Laila would be dissected by Hindu fantasists interested in her blood. There was also a chance that she could be locked up because people thought that she was insane.

As she walked to the car, she thought about her relationship with Denise. Like the rest of the friends that she'd spent time with in high school, Denise had always been a great asset on the team, and she was always fun to hang with during team dinners. She wasn't going to college for a year because she needed to save money for the expenses. But soon Denise would be gone too. Then Laila would be alone in the Finger Lakes, the last of her friends moving on with their lives while her destiny was a decidedly different path.

She tossed her bag in the back seat and was ready to get inside, when she felt someone watching her.

The hairs on the back of her neck prickled, and she froze. Without making any sudden or jerky moves, she scanned the parking lot around her, casually looking for someone or something that didn't make sense.

There were a group of bachelorettes who were still chatting next to their car with their hired driver. Across the gravel drive, there was a couple taking pictures of each other. A van with Divine Winery's logo painted across the side was parked in the back row.

Her heartbeat sped up, and she quickly opened the driver's-side door of her Audi and slipped inside. It was nothing. She was still on edge, unnerved from that morning, that's all. After starting her car, she let out a deep breath, and then almost jumped out of her skin when someone knocked on her window.

"Holy shit, you scared me," she said to her friend Denise when she rolled down the window.

"Sorry about that," Denise said. She motioned to her canvas bow bag. "Okay to still ride with you?"

"Yeah, of course. Hop in."

"Thanks, Laila." Denise squeezed her huge bow bag into the back seat and climbed in on the passenger side. "I owe ya one."

"The next time I need to switch a shift I'll let you know."

Denise laughed. "You're on. I'll take whatever extra shifts I can get. Hey, have you seen the posts online from Sarah, Josie, and the rest of our former teammates? It's like all our friends started college today and they're living their best life. I'm so jealous."

"That's exactly what I woke up thinking about," Laila said with a sigh. "I'm happy for them."

Denise snorted. "I wish I was. Now that they're officially gone, we're going to have a whole new crop of team members we'll have to deal with at the studio starting this week."

Laila winced. She hadn't thought about that. "That's just what we need."

"It gets worse," Denise said as she checked her lipstick in the visor mirror. "I overheard Ben talking and he said that the studio got some more sponsors, so some of the Olympic trainees have relocated from the Dakota training facility to here. We might be stuck with douchebags all season."

"Ugh, that just makes today so much better," Laila said with a scowl. She turned onto the main road and headed toward the studio. She muttered a curse in French, one of the first languages that she'd learned, and glanced over at Denise, who giggled in response.

"What?"

Denise shrugged. "You hide your accent so well that sometimes when it comes out, it's a little surprising. Then when you switch into like the fifteen languages you know, it's a reminder that you're . . . I don't know, not from here."

No matter how much Laila tried to blend in, tried to maintain some sense of normalcy, she'd never be like everyone else. It took her a long time to accept that, and she was okay with it now, but it still amused her when other people told her that she was "not like other girls."

Understatement of the year.

Unless of course other eighteen-year-olds were tasked with becoming a woman-mother and could shoot fireballs out of their hands.

"You were the coolest person in high school," Denise said with a sigh. "The rest of us were either rich kids of winery owners or kids of farmers."

"I *am* a rich kid of winery owners," Laila mused.

Denise waved a hand as if to brush her words aside. Her chipped purple nail polish sparkled. "But most people don't even know that about you. You're cultured, you know? You've lived somewhere else besides the Finger Lakes."

"And now our friends will get that opportunity," Laila said.

There was a long, awkward pause before Denise spoke again. "Hey, can I ask you something? Why aren't you going away to college?"

"It's just not the right time," Laila said smoothly. It was the same excuse she'd been giving people since she was a junior. College? Just not the right time. She couldn't be away from her masis because they were tasked with protecting her, and a college environment would make it impossible for them to hide. They'd have to move, and rebuilding their compound, creating their library again, was a huge undertaking. Then there was her deadline. Obviously, college would've made dating and sex easier, but it wasn't worth the risk of exposing her masis. And from what Laila was told, she came from a lineage of women who made terrible decisions about men. Draupadi's biggest weakness had been her husbands, her love for Arjun specifically. That's why the women in Laila's family were forced to live alone.

She pulled into the studio parking lot and motioned to the large warehouse-style building. "Well. Here we are."

Denise grinned at her, her metal retainer flashing in the light, her dimples winking.

"Let's go shoot some arrows."

Laila tapped her fist with Denise's and got out of the car. She retrieved her bow from the trunk, along with her small workout bag holding her shoes and her armguard.

They entered the studio to the whizzing sound of arrows cutting through the air and the sharp thud of tips slamming into targets. Targets were set up in a U shape around the inside of the building, and the exit corridor to the left led out to the field targets.

"Looks like the team is over there," Denise said, pointing to the target area on the left.

"Are you ready?"

"I'll meet you in a bit. I'm going to say hello to Ben."

Laila waved at some of her team members who were waiting for their turn at the targets, then crossed to the other side of the room where she'd spotted the familiar bald head. Ben was surrounded by what looked like the national men's team that had come over from the Dakota training facility. That made sense considering he owned the facility and was head coach of a winning team for multiple national and international competitions over the years.

As she headed over to say hello, some of the men's team members watched her approach, their eyes lighting up with interest.

She knew she was beautiful and attracted attention. She'd probably have a long-term relationship if she wasn't trying to prolong her independence. Dating to her always felt like she was shortening the freedom she had. It's not like she didn't want to date. She was attracted to women and men, and she'd gone out a few times with both. But dating meant there was more of a chance she'd find the one. The person who was supposed to give her a child.

When Ben realized that he'd lost the focus of most of the team, he turned to face her.

"Laila! My favorite student." He held out his arms, and Laila embraced him. His brawny grip practically cut off her airways for a hot second before he let her go. His shiny head glistened in the overhead light.

"Where have you been?" he said in his deep, boisterous voice.

"You mean since I saw you last week? Working. Sorry for interrupting your meeting, but I needed to talk to you before you leave and I start practice. I came to ask you if you still need help with the ten-year-olds tomorrow."

"From you?" Ben asked. "Always. What changed your mind?"

Ben had been asking her to work at the studio since she was sixteen, but she'd been too busy training back then. She was still busy training now, but in the winter, when the winery would be slow and her shifts would be cut in half, she didn't want to be stuck at home in her own thoughts. "Now that I'm no longer in school, I could use the work," she said. Then she leaned to the side to look at the guys, who were still staring at her. "Hi."

"Oh, let me introduce you," Ben said. He turned to face his students as well and dropped an arm around her shoulder. "Laila, this is our new crop of students. Some are from the Dakota training facility and others made it through tryouts last week. Gentlemen, this is Laila Bansal. The best student at the academy, if not the entire state. She was on the varsity high school team, and if I can convince her, she'll be on the national team before you know it."

"Not likely," she said. She waved at the team. "Nice meeting you. Good luck." She made a move to go when a deep husky voice stopped her in her tracks.

"What makes you the best?"

Laila slowly turned on her heel to see who'd spoken.

The small cluster of players parted. In the back stood the only other South Asian student in the room. His T-shirt, armguard, and athletic shorts were all incredibly . . . fitted. Laila had to wonder if he had human legs or tree trunks for thighs.

"Karan!" Ben said. "You made it to practice."

"Sorry I'm late, Coach," he said. He had an accent like the Bollywood actors her masis preferred to watch. It was a mix of Indian city and British boarding school. His eyes remained locked on Laila. "So? What makes her the best student?"

"'Her'?" Laila said. There was that strange prickle on the back of her neck. She'd felt it that morning right before her sparring session, and she'd felt it in the parking lot. "*Her* doesn't owe you an explanation as to how I earned my title. Ben? Thanks for the time."

"I'd like to see you prove it," Karan said.

Laila practically rolled her eyes into the back of her head. "Really?"

He nodded, the corner of his mouth twitching up in a small smirk. "You have some of the national team practicing here now.

If you're the best, you should at least be able to keep up. And if you can't . . . well, this place has seriously oversold the skill of their instructors."

The national team *oooh*ed as if this *boy* had just delivered the mother of all burns.

It was one thing for someone to come for her. She couldn't care less. But it was entirely different for someone to come for Ben. He'd been like a father figure to her since she'd started training at the studio. His patience and generosity were unmatched. More important, he was almost as good as her aunts, and they'd had a little help from centuries of practice.

"I don't do showcases," Laila said. "They bore me."

His full mouth quirked in amusement. "Then a competition. Come on. You can't be opposed to hitting some targets."

"Showmanship isn't my thing either," she said.

"That's sort of the point of competing, isn't it?"

A few of the other teams from the surrounding target areas closed in. They'd started to gather a crowd. Probably because the men's team were acting like idiots every time someone said something. Her heartbeat sped up just a little.

"And who am I competing against?" she asked, arms crossed over her chest. "You?"

He shrugged. "I am one of the best on the team."

When none of his teammates challenged his statement, Laila knew he was probably telling the truth. That did nothing to intimidate her.

She looked over at Ben, who raised a brow. It was her call.

"Okay," she said with a sigh. "Fine. Speed and accuracy. A set. Three targets, varying distance. The highest score, declared winner."

"Are you sure?" Ben asked. His voice pitched low, and there was a hint of worry. That alone was interesting since Ben was always confident in her skills. Maybe the South Asian dude was as good as he thought he was after all.

"I'm sure, Ben." She turned back to the team. "Any chance some of you can help set up the targets?"

They ran, practically bumping into each other in the process. Laila had to control her eye roll at their puppy-dog eagerness. Meanwhile, Karan raised a brow in her direction, then walked toward the rack of recurve bows. She watched him lift one of the larger ones. He definitely handled it like a pro.

Ben leaned closer to her. "He gets impatient," he whispered. "Rushes the first target instead of the last. That's where the money shot is, though. Don't you rush too."

"When have I ever?" Laila whispered back. She shrugged the canvas bag off her shoulder and began to unwrap the bow that her aunts had given her.

Some of the junior coaches and her old varsity teammates came over to ask what was going on, and when they found out it was a competition against the men's national team, she was instantly surrounded by her teammates. The familiar faces, people she trained with and spent time with on a regular basis, gave her words of encouragement.

Not that she needed it. Laila had been trained by rakshasi.

By the time the targets were set up, and the quivers next to each starting point were filled with arrows, the entire studio had picked a side. Ben looked like he was enjoying the locals versus nationals impromptu competition, so he pulled out his blowhorn and had two of his staff keep time.

"Are the competitors ready?" he shouted.

Cheers thundered in the hall. Laila shook her head. Her aunts would be so irritated that she was bringing attention to herself. She was supposed to keep a low profile for her safety and theirs, but when had a little competition become such a big deal?

In minutes everyone was focused on Laila and the new guy.

She looked down at her bow and adjusted her armguard. Should she pull back her performance? She didn't want to call attention to herself if she was *too* good.

Ben approached them with a quarter. "Call it," he said, and flipped it.

"Tails," Laila said, just as Karan called heads.

"Heads-side up," Ben said, showing the coin. "Karan, you're up first."

He gave her a cold look that startled her.

What was that about?

Then, as if he hadn't sneered like he hated her, his mouth curved into an easy smile and he took his position at the starting line. Laila stepped back and waited for his time to start. For someone who'd challenged *her* to a competition, he sure as hell looked like he was thinking his circumstances were her fault.

"Karan from the men's national team," Ben shouted. "You're up first. And your time starts . . . now."

Without hesitating, Karan pulled an arrow from the quiver, strung his bow, and with a quick flex of his wrist and those long-tapered fingers, released the arrow on a breath at the first target. He hit the second ring. He strung the bow again, released on a breath, and hit the second to center ring. Moving down the line, he twirled the arrow between his fingers, strung the bow a third time, and, waiting for almost thirty seconds, nicked the bullseye.

The hall was quiet now. He was playing at an expert level, and he'd just proven his skill.

"Your turn," he said quietly.

Laila thought about her aunts, and what they'd want her to do.

Don't draw attention to yourself, Laila. You're too precious to risk.

But then again, her aunts were literal man-eaters. If someone challenged them, there was a good chance that they'd suck blood first, inhale the intestines next, and then ask questions.

Yeah, screw it, she thought.

Laila passed Karan and gave him a wink. His eyebrows shot straight to his hairline.

Weren't expecting that, were you?

"Laila, same rules apply," Ben shouted into the blowhorn. "Ready?"

"Ready," she said. She centered herself and repeated a mantra three times over in her head for focus.

"And your time starts . . . now."

She picked up the first arrow and shot it within the next breath. She strung the second arrow with more patience, centered, then let go. She did the same with the third arrow. When she finished, she dropped her bow to her side. "Done!"

The studio was pin-drop silent now. She looked at her targets.

Two just nicked the bullseye while the third hit it dead center.

"Holy shit," she heard someone whisper.

Denise was the first one to start cheering. Then the room erupted. Laila accepted a hug from her team, and a high five from Ben. She hoped no one took pictures and posted or anything. Her aunts would flip out, they'd be so upset.

When she looked over her shoulder at the men's team, she saw Karan standing by himself, looking from her targets back to her.

She wasn't sure if he was a sore loser or not, but she wasn't above being a sore winner.

She crossed over to him and waited for him to acknowledge her presence.

"You're really good," she said. "But I'm better."

Karan nodded. "You are."

Laila turned to leave, but he called out her name.

"Are you South Asian too?"

She shrugged. "Technically, I'm Mauritian, but culturally South Asian. My mother was Indian, from India. Father was Indian from Africa. And yes, it's weird that the two brown kids are the best at archery."

"You remind me of one of those South Asian mythology stories my dad used to tell me."

There was that prickle at the base of her neck again. She'd *never* heard anyone mention her holy text outside of her aunts.

"Why, because I'm a brown woman?"

"No, that's not it," he said with an easy grin. "There is something about you that makes me think of this woman who is said to be formed out of fire and is the prize of an archery competition. I was just thinking that if you were in her shoes, you'd probably want the competitors to fight you to prove their worth instead."

The reference to Draupadi had her spine stiffening. The hairs prickled on the back of her neck in warning. She knew the scene well. She'd read it over and over again as a child, and had raged in frustration at her aunts. And then she'd found peace in the fact that her ancestor was a resourceful woman, a woman who held a grudge often and sought justice and vengeance whenever she was wronged.

But Karan was right. If Laila had been passed over like a prize, if she had a *choice*, then she would've fought for her freedom.

His words hit way too close to home in that moment, while the rest of the archery academy buzzed around her. This had to be a coincidence. "I have to go," she mumbled.

"Wait," he said, and held out a hand. "Thanks for humoring me. Did Ben really teach you how to shoot like that?"

Laila looked down at the gesture, then back at his face. She thought about it for a second before pressing her hand against his. "My aunts," she said. "They're demons. At archery."

The lights shut off, and the sound of a transformer blowing echoed through the academy.

Her hand burned, and she could almost see the light glowing from between their palms.

Then there was a zap—an electric bolt that jolted up her arm and down her spine. She jerked back at the same time Karan did.

Seconds later, the lights turned back on. Laila gasped and looked down at her palm. A glowing Sanskrit symbol glittered on her skin, then faded. She looked up at Karan. He had the same expression of shock on his face.

Without waiting another moment, Laila grabbed her bag and ran.

5. KARAN

Karan was not expecting the witch to be a beautiful eighteen-year-old on the archery team with insane target skills. But then again, his uncle's intel hadn't exactly been specific. It came in bits and pieces. If it wasn't for his cousin helping him put those pieces together, and steering him toward upstate New York, he would never have found Laila Bansal.

He checked his watch, then the rearview mirror in his car. He was parked in the back of the gravel parking lot in front of a trailhead that was supposedly the closest access point to the witch's compound. According to his drone footage, that was the best way to describe it: a fucking compound.

Karan leaned back against the headrest and closed his eyes. His plan was insane. Thinking about it made his heart race. He was supposed to sneak up on a witch, slice off her head, put it in a cooler he'd stored in his trunk, and call his Uncle Satyapal. No big deal. Once he'd made the kill, then Uncle Satya would barter the head for intel on his parents' location.

They'd been missing for three months. Three long, lonely, frightening months, and this was the closest he'd ever gotten to finding them.

He was supposed to start his third year at Oxford, but with his parents' disappearance, he had no choice but to take the semester off so he could look for them. His father would've hated that he'd chosen a hunt over finishing his degree in South Asian military history and mythology, but this was about family.

He jolted when his phone buzzed in his pocket. He read "Badhuri" on the screen and answered the video call from his cousin.

"What is it, Boo?"

His cousin sat in front of a wall of books. She leaned closer to her phone screen and narrowed her eyes behind thick-framed lenses. Her hair was tied in a severe French braid, and her mouth pressed in a thin line. She somehow looked both eighty and sixteen at the same time.

Since she was unaccompanied by her bodyguard or mentor, that meant she was alone in her apartment in a rare moment of independence. The think tank that hired her a year ago liked to keep a close eye on their investment.

"Karan. As the cool kids say, 'How's it hanging?'"

"Boo, no one has said that for like thirty years now."

Boo tilted her head, her brows furrowing. "I am spending time with millennials lately. Whatever. I'm just calling to see if you're in New York."

Karan sighed. "Yeah, I made it."

"And?"

"And what?"

"And have you seen the witch yet?" Boo burst out. The mix of British and German accents colored her voice. "Is she more like that old show *Charmed* or the wicked witches in *Wizard of Oz*?"

More like Charmed.

He looked down at his palm, remembering the electric current that zapped him when they'd touched. "I ran into her at the archery studio. She's a student on the archery team."

Boo's shoulders slumped. "That's not . . . evil witch–like."

"She beat me at target archery."

Boo's jaw dropped. "You're lying."

"No. And it wasn't even a close score, either. She straight up annihilated me. If we were looking for confirmation that she's an evil spirit, then we just got it." There was no way that a normal human could beat him, the descendant of a mythological figure that was the greatest archer in the universe and the bastard son of a queen. Not unless they were also superhuman in some way.

"What happened after she beat your score?" Boo asked.

Karan didn't know whether he should mention it, but Boo was resourceful, and it didn't hurt to see if she could find some more intel. "I shook her hand, and there was some sort of . . . power surge." He looked down at his palm. "My skin felt like it was on fire, and this strange symbol glowed on my skin before it disappeared."

Boo's eyes widened. "Do you remember what the symbol looked like?"

"No, not really. I can try to draw whatever details I can think of and send it to you."

"Of course. I'll look into it. I wonder if she marked you with a curse. We don't know anything about her, so we can't take any chances. The fact that we found an Indian witch in the Americas is incredible. In India? There is one in most villages. In the rest of

Asia? Absolutely. Europe, less so. But America? Mind-blowing. We should do some more research."

"There is no *we*, Boo," Karan said. "I need you to stay as far out of it as possible. You're still new to this."

Boo snorted. "I'm a genius, and a descendant of the same demigod as you. I may not have the legacy, but I make up for it in intelligence."

She talked like a robot sometimes, Karan thought. It was as if she was programmed to be stubborn. Truthfully, he'd had this conversation with her time and time again, but she refused to listen to him. Refused to hear reasons why she needed to keep her distance. He'd been trained to find and fight asuras since he was a child. He'd studied and trained and harnessed his legacy with the focus and intention of a soldier. When Boo had reached out to him a few years ago, both Karan and his father were stunned at the revelation that there were more descendants from the Mahabharata. Uncle Satya was less so, since he'd spent so much time focused on lineage and family trees as part of his dissertation. Either way, both adult men in his family had welcomed her with open arms. Karan had been more skeptical. But now he needed her, and Boo wanted so badly to be a part of his mission that she had no clue how she could get hurt.

"You don't have to do this alone." Her voice was soft now. Soothing.

"Boo," Karan said with a sigh. He scrubbed a hand over his face. "I have to hike to her compound to see if there is a way I can get close to the witch tonight. My plan is to do a sneak attack on her own land."

His cousin's expression became solemn. "Be careful. Your parents' lives are important, but you can't help them if you get hurt yourself. If she's truly the asura that Satyapal said she is, then according to folklore and mythology, she has the ability to shape-shift, cast spells, curse your soul, drink your blood—"

"I got it, thanks."

"There is also superhuman speed, agility, witchcraft, which is a misnomer for beings described in the vedas—"

"Boo, I said I got it. I'll be careful. I promise."

The last thing he saw before he signed off was the doubt in his cousin's eyes. He peered through the windshield at the faint shape of the moon that was starting to peek out between the tops of the trees. "I never thought I'd have to do this without you, Papa," he said in Hindi.

Since his first solo monster kill, he'd hunted over a dozen asuras. He knew one day he'd have to leave his father behind, but this was too soon. Going from India to Oxford to the United States, then driving to the Finger Lakes on the wrong side of the road, was overwhelming. It would've been comforting to have Papa's solid hand resting on his shoulder in support.

"You have a mission," he said to himself, just as his father would tell him. He'd kill the asura, get back to Uncle Satya, then bring his parents home alive and safe. After that, he'd return to his schooling. He'd teach, train, and fight, just like all the other members in his family had, generation after generation after generation. He believed in his legacy and Karan hoped that the belief alone would carry him through.

He stepped out of his car, locked it, and tucked the keys in a discreet box underneath the bumper. He waited to see if there was any sign of vehicle traffic coming up the road before he pulled his crossbow, a quiver of arrows, and a machete out of the trunk. He strapped everything to his back. If he had to engage in hand-to-hand combat, he'd just have to pull one strap and all of it would fall to the ground.

He put on night-vision goggles and, after taking a deep breath, began cutting his way into the thick brush. He felt the echo of memory from his first hunt. He'd rarely remembered that first kill, though. His uncle told him it was probably because of the adrenaline.

He'd remember this one, though.

Two miles to the compound. Two miles was nothing if he was going to save his parents. They were all he had. Along with Uncle Satya and Boo, his parents were a critical part of his life.

Karan fell into the rhythm of slicing through brush. He stepped on the roots of snarled trees and vines, only clearing what he absolutely had to so that he could move forward.

The silence, the humidity that sprouted beads of sweat on his temples and down his back, the hum of the cicadas and the birds overhead. There was something eerily familiar to that night that he couldn't shake.

He'd walked a mile when he saw light through the thick brush. There was the soft sound of water lapping at a shore. Karan had reached the lake. He remembered seeing it through the small screen on his drone device. It was relatively large for a private body of water, and there was a clear path up to the house.

Since he didn't see anyone else coming in and out of the property in the hours of surveillance he'd completed, he figured that it would be safe to take the path. If he ran into the asura, then he'd cut her head off right then and there.

When he reached the edge of the forest, he scanned the lake for any signs of movement. Just as he was about to step out into the clearing and head for the path around the opposite side of the lake, he saw a sleek black head pop up out of the water. There was a heat signature.

A person. No, a woman.

Karan watched through night-vision goggles as Laila Bansal swam in easy strokes across the lake toward the dock. She gripped the rungs of a ladder and hauled herself out of the water. Rivulets traced the lines of her body. She turned to face the moonlight, her face tilted up toward the glittering stars in the sky.

That's when he realized that she was naked. Her black hair fell in a waterfall down her back and wrapped around her hips. Her skin glistened, and even as he pulled his goggles away, he couldn't avert his eyes from the figure in the distance. She was like a flame in the night, stretching her arms over her head and seeming to enjoy the easy strength of her long, lean body.

Was this how she captured her victims? By entrancing them with her beauty? He'd never read about an asura quite like her. He'd never encountered anything or anyone like Laila.

That's when he heard another woman. He froze, straining to hear the voice.

"Laila! It's late! Come inside, beta."

The asura bent down to pick up her towel that she must have left on the dock and wrapped it around her body. "Coming, Masi!" she called back.

Masi? She lived with her aunt? There was nothing in his research, nothing in his notes, that indicated she had family of any kind. Sure, there were rumors that the winery she worked at belonged to her aunts, but Boo's research showed that the business was owned by a shell corporation who listed Laila Bansal as the true owner.

Would an asura really use the respectful term *masi* if she was evil?

He thought back to Satyapal's message. That he'd received word from a contact that there was a disturbance of energy in the Finger Lakes region. Satyapal said that the message referenced great power, which could be used as a bartering chip for more information from occult collectors. Could all his surveillance, all the intel he'd gathered about Laila Bansal, have been wrong?

He watched her step off the dock and walk up the path into the woods on the opposite side of the lake. That was the path that he'd intended to take, the one where he'd hoped he'd find her alone.

She really was beautiful, even if she was an evil asura.

With the image of Laila Bansal imprinted in his mind, Karan backed away from the edge of the clearing when the lake was silent again and followed the same path to the car he'd parked at the trailhead closest to her home. By the time he slid into the driver's seat, he was soaked with sweat and grime, breath heavy and heart pounding from the exertion.

He closed his eyes and rested his head against the seat rest. He'd hoped he didn't have to keep up the pretense of being one of the newest archers on the men's team for long, but he'd have to continue the ruse until he figured out his target.

That meant he had to practice first thing in the morning. When he was done, he was going to find Laila Bansal again. This time, he'd get her alone somewhere far from both the studio and her home. That was the only way he'd have a chance at killing her.

6. LAILA

"Usha Masi!" Laila called out as she ran through the hallways of her new home. "Usha Masi, where are you?"

She ran to Usha Masi's room first when the nightmare woke her up, but no one was there. Laila knew that wetting the bed was only for babies, and a nine-year-old shouldn't be doing something like that. She just wanted Usha Masi to hold her first. She wanted Usha Masi to tell her she was safe again. She was way too old to be having accidents, but the fear and the night terrors were impossible to escape.

"Usha Masi!" she screamed again. Her pajama pants felt wet and heavy, and shameful, as she sobbed out her aunt's name. She turned a corner and reached the heavy basement door with all the gold locks on it.

"Are you there?!" she screamed now. She began pounding on the door.

It flung open, and her aunt's red-rimmed eyes, wide with shock, looked down at her. "Laila? What's wrong? Why are you awake? It's the middle of the night."

Laila threw her arms around Usha Masi's waist and pressed a cheek against her abdomen. She could barely get the words out, her tears hurt so bad. "I had a dream, and I thought you were going to die!"

Usha Masi crooned in that soothing, musical voice of hers, almost like a lullaby. Laila felt like her hurt was slowly disappearing, evaporating under the warmth and the sound of her aunt singing. She squeezed her eyes shut and held on to the one woman who made her feel safe after her mom died in the accident.

Usha Masi ran a hand down her back, then used her talons to scratch her scalp like a really nice massage.

"Dreams can be scary, Laila," Usha Masi said. "But you're stronger than dreams. You're stronger than all your fears."

"But I need you," Laila said. She sniffled and lifted her head to look up at her masi. "I couldn't find you when I needed you. You weren't there when I woke up!"

Her demon aunt smiled, and her eyes twinkled. "Darling, I'll always be there for you. When you're dreaming or when you're awake. You may not see me, though. But I'll always be here, okay?"

"Promise?" Laila whispered and sniffled again.

"Promise. Now come. Let's get you out of these wet clothes."

That morning, Laila had lain in bed for over an hour after her alarm went off. She stroked her fingertips against her palm. The electric current she'd felt the day before in the archery studio had jolted through her body. She'd brooded for the rest of the day. She'd even gone down to the library to see if she could find some reference to what had happened to her. When she felt her body tensing up, anxiety twisting around her spine and tightening her muscles, she decided to take a short dip in the lake.

Her copy of *The Awakening* lay next to her, tattered and spread open. She'd underlined and tabbed the moments of Edna Pontellier in Louisiana, reading the words and feeling Edna's responsibility deep in her soul.

She thought of both Edna and Draupadi as she got dressed and ready for the day. The zap, the feeling between herself and Karan, was . . . unsettling.

There could only be one reason for their connection, and the more she dwelled on it, the more anxious she became.

There were rules, specific guidelines when it came to having the next descendant in Draupadi's lineage. Some of those rules had been put in place by Draupadi herself. Others were learned over time. A rule that had not changed was that the second parent to a daughter of fire had a magical connection.

That meant that the electricity she felt with Karan had to be a sign that he was her man. There was no other explanation. He was the future father of her child.

"I think I'm going to be sick," she muttered to herself as she pressed a palm to her abdomen. She was always told that she'd know the minute she found the person who she was supposed to have a family with. The person who would leave her or who she would have to leave. The zap through their touch, the brief symbol she saw on her palm, was most likely the symbol of her fate and her destiny.

It was too soon, she thought. She had hoped to put it off as long as possible, but here she was, just a few short months after her eighteenth birthday, facing her future.

Laila thought about her dream, about how she missed her Usha Masi and her mother terribly. If her mother was here, then she'd be able to tell her for sure that the zap meant she'd found her sperm donor. She wouldn't have to guess.

She petted Billi, who sat on a textbook that she'd purchased for the online South Asian history class she was taking, then went down to the main kitchen. After dumping cat food into the dish, then taking care of the garbage for the week, Laila went in search of her masis. She came close to telling them what happened with the new guy at the archery studio the night before but decided against it. Telling them felt like she was accepting the inevitable and she wasn't sure yet if that's what she wanted.

Just as Laila was about to go into the library to check for her aunts, she received three messages in rapid succession. Pulling out her phone from the back pocket of her jeans, she smiled at the sequence of texts.

VIKA MASI: We smelled human on the property when we were doing surveillance. We're out in the woods near the lake.

GIRI MASI: There is herbal tea!!!! For strength!!!!

RASHMI MASI: Don't forget, training tonight.

The unease she felt at being alone in the house dissipated. They were on the property. That was close enough, she thought as she grabbed a to-go cup from the main kitchen, poured herself some chai, and walked out of the house. She had to get to work.

Laila had forgotten about destinies, prophecies, and the rest by the time she was five hours into her shift. Her boss needed her to reorganize the stockroom and review all the inventory because of a few big parties that were coming in on the weekend. She didn't mind the work, especially if it kept her in the back storage rooms for most of the afternoon.

The winery and vineyard were how her aunts were able to afford the luxuries they preferred. There was a long history of the rakshasa race hoarding shiny things, and her aunts were no different. They preferred to surround themselves with diamonds and jewels whenever they could, and in the twenty-first century, they needed money to keep up their expensive habit.

But the work felt good. It felt *real.* Laila liked getting her hands dirty, doing the mundane. It helped her stay grounded in reality.

With Taylor Swift blasting through her earbuds, she was halfway through alphabetizing the Divine Winery merchandise on the overflow shelves when she felt someone touch her shoulder.

She reacted before she could process that the touch wasn't a threat. Her elbow hit her intruder hard in the chest. Her fist dropped to hit the person in the gut, and before they could take another breath, she'd flipped their positions until their back hit the shelves with Laila pinning their wrists next to their head.

Her eyes widened when they met Karan's surprised pale golden-brown ones. "What are you—"

Karan gripped her wrists, and in seconds, Laila was the one pinned to the shelves. He held her wrists in each hand above her head. Her earbuds fell out and hit the wooden floorboards with a soft click and rattle before they rolled to a stop next to a discarded box.

In her next sharp intake of breath, she took in his rich, clean woodsy scent mingled with musky aftershave. She felt the hard edges of his belt buckle brush against the exposed strip of skin from her T-shirt riding up over her navel. The hard strength of his hold had her muscles trembling.

"If your opponent is heavier than you, take him to the ground, not against a wall," he said softly. Their lips were inches apart, and every deep breath that Karan took brushed their chests together.

Laila did not like to be pinned, especially by someone she didn't trust. With a slight shift of her hips, she brought her knee up in a quick jerking motion. She stopped millimeters away from crushing his crotch.

Karan was wheezing even before she made contact.

"Didn't anyone ever tell you not to sneak up on someone like that?" she said conversationally.

His hands immediately released hers, and he backed away a few steps with his hands up in surrender. "I'm sorry, I didn't mean to scare you."

Laila didn't say anything for a few long minutes before she reached down to pick up her earbuds. She kept him in her line of vision the entire time. "You aren't supposed to be back here. This is for employees only."

Karan rubbed the back of his neck. "Yeah, sorry about that. Your friend Denise was the one who said I could come back here to see you."

Of course. Denise was probably playing matchmaker. That was the last thing she needed right now, especially since she could still feel the tingle of his touch against her skin.

Laila nudged one of the empty boxes with her sneakered foot. "Where did you learn to fight like that?" she asked.

He shrugged. "I went to a military academy in the UK. Boarding school education."

No wonder his accent was hard to place, she thought. Hers had pretty much faded to an American accent in the last five years she'd been stateside.

He brushed a hand against a stack of T-shirts that she'd just folded. "What about you?" he said casually. "Where did you learn those moves?"

"Please," she said. "I'm a woman. Self-defense is almost a required skill these days."

And I have been training with rakshasi since I was old enough to walk.

"That's the unfortunate truth," Karan said with a smile.

"So?" she asked, then rubbed her palms against her jean-clad thighs. She had to be imagining things, but she swore that her palm felt itchy. "Why did you come to see me? Interested in getting your ass whooped again?"

When he grinned at her, that crooked, easy and confident smile, she felt a flutter in her chest. "*Interested* is a good word. I'm definitely interested."

She thanked the gods for melanin, because if she was as white as Denise, then he'd for sure know that she was blushing.

He crossed his arms over his chest, his biceps and triceps flexing in the fitted Henley he wore, and leaned against the shelving unit across from her. "How is such a talented archer like yourself not on the Olympic team winning medals?"

Because it would draw attention to me.

Because it's not fair to compete against normal people when I'm so abnormal.

"I'm not interested," she said. "My life is here in upstate New York. I don't really want to go anywhere else."

He watched her with an intensity that made her uneasy, but she refused to let it show. Not with this . . . stranger. No matter what role he was going to play in her life.

"Go out with me," he finally said.

"Excuse me?" That was not the response she was expecting.

"Go out with me," he repeated, ignorant of the uneasiness fluttering in the pit of her stomach. "You're talented, obviously smart, and beautiful. I want to get to know you better."

The storage room was spacious, but in that moment, she felt like the walls were closing in on her. Her chest tightened, and the itching on her palm intensified. "I don't think that's a good idea." She should keep him as far away as possible, as long as she possibly could. That was the only way she could preserve her freedom.

"Okay."

It was as if every word that came out of his mouth was a surprise. "'Okay'? Just like that?"

Karan shrugged. "I mean, if you're not interested in me, I'm not going to push. But I came out here because I want to get to know you better. I figured that maybe we can go for an easy night hike or something after class."

"A night hike?" Now she was just repeating everything he was saying. It was like she'd never been around men before or something. She tried to feign disinterest as she reached out to brace herself against the shelves. It took her two tries before she touched the unit. "Most people are afraid of the forest at night. We have bears and other wild predators out here, you know."

He grinned again. "With your moves? I'm pretty sure I'll be safe."

"Ha ha," she said, and smiled for the first time since seeing him again. She tried to mimic his pose. "Are you just asking me out because I'm the only other Indian here? Because I beat you in archery and you have some fetish where you have to have the girl who is better than you, or because of some ulterior motive?"

Karan tilted his head to the side. "Maybe a little bit of all three," he said.

There was a sound outside the storage room, a series of voices discussing payroll and some other details about the business. Laila straightened, then motioned to the door. "I think you'd better go before I get in trouble."

"Wait, don't you have family that owns the winery or something?" he asked.

Laila froze. "How do you know that?"

"Oh, your friend Denise told me . . ."

Denise. She had to remind her friend that she didn't want people to know she was related to the owners. "It doesn't matter. I'm not going to take advantage of my role and bend the rules."

His amused expression turned pensive. "You are not what I expected," he said.

There was something about the way he said those words that had her pausing. His expression grew serious, and she swore if she looked hard enough, she could see the coldness she'd glimpsed in his eyes during their competition. "What does that mean?"

He shook his head, then pushed off the shelving unit with his foot. "You'll just have to meet me tonight. Let's say eight? At the red trailhead parking lot. I'll have the flashlight if you're afraid of the dark. If you decide not to show? No big deal. I'm sure I'll see you around the archery academy."

Without another word, he turned to leave her alone with her thoughts.

She looked down at her palm and swore she saw the faint outline of the symbol taunting her.

This was her destiny, dammit. This was her calling, and he was making it so easy for her to like him. Maybe it was time to accept the inevitable. The faster she completed her duty, the easier it would be for her to get on with the rest of her life . . . right?

She shoved her earbuds back in, and turned to the shelf she was organizing. She still had another hour left of her shift, which meant that she could overthink all her life choices before practice. Then she'd overthink what she had to wear for her date with destiny tonight.

7. LAILA

Laila didn't bother going home. Practice ended at seven, and she knew that if she set foot in the compound, she'd lose her nerve and stay inside with her aunts. Instead, she worked with the junior coaches one on one for thirty minutes and let off some steam until it was time for her to meet Karan. Thankfully, Ben and the rest of the staff were oblivious to the fact that each time she let go of an arrow, the target steamed, as if she'd set it on fire.

She replayed her encounter with Karan in her head over and over again with every draw and release of an arrow. To be honest, Laila was surprised that when he'd touched her again, when he'd pinned her to the shelving unit, there hadn't been more sparks, but the thought of him now had her smoking. Maybe it was just a one-time thing?

Her nerves continued to rachet up a notch with each passing minute until she left the studio to meet Karan at their designated spot. Thankfully, the fire was under control by the time she got there.

As she parked a few spaces over from the only other car, a Toyota sedan at the trailhead, she wondered why there wasn't any information in the diaries of her ancestors that clued her in to how they found their potential matches for a child. It would've been helpful to know what she was supposed to do. Or was it a straightforward one-night hookup? Once she sorted out her destiny, she was going to make a checklist.

Step one: try not to incinerate the sperm donor of your child.

She opened the door of her car when she had waited long enough, and Karan stepped out from the driver's side of his vehicle at the same time. His tall, muscled frame was now in jeans and a short-sleeved shirt. He'd left an hour before she did from the studio, so he must've gone home to change.

What she wasn't expecting was the bag of fast food from her favorite burger place in town, and the soft drinks on the cardboard tray in his other hand.

"I got you your fries," he said, smoothly. "I know I said a hike, but I figured you might be hungry."

"Starved," she admitted.

He flashed her a quick grin. "I took a walk down the trail a bit, and it looks like we can eat down by the water. I have a flashlight, so it won't be too dark. Unless you'd rather something up here out in the open?"

He was testing her boundaries, she thought. A warning whispered in the back of her brain from all the viral murder mystery videos she'd seen on social media. *Don't meet with strangers alone. Don't accept food from strangers. Make sure people know where you are at all times.*

But she was a Daughter of Draupadi, adopted by demons and trained in ancient military science. If anyone could handle herself, it was Laila. But just in case, she had a knife tucked in her clutch. She hoped that her instincts were right, and she could trust him.

"I'm fine down by the water." She took one of the sodas from his container. "Ready?"

"Yeah." His jaw flexed, as if he wanted to say something more, but he tucked a flashlight into his back pocket from inside his car, then locked the door. "Let's go." He motioned toward the wooden gate that led down a stone path to the edge of the falls.

"So, what else is in the bag other than fries?"

"I got you one of the veggie burgers," he said. "When I asked around at the archery studio, one of your team members mentioned you don't eat meat."

She couldn't hide the fact that she was impressed by his attentiveness. "That's very . . . thorough of you."

They stepped under a canopy of trees and dense foliage. She felt at home in the dark, embracing it like a comfortable sweater that draped over her. A cool breeze filtered through the leaves and brushed gently across her skin as they moved down the path.

"You're not creeped out that we're meeting at a secluded hiking falls in the dark for our first date?" There was a touch of humor in his voice. And maybe some condescension?

"I like the forests around here," she said. "And it's not every day I'm asked out to dinner in the woods."

They found a perfect flat rock to sit on at the base of the small waterfall. As the water crashed into a pond and filtered into a wide, shallow creek, Laila had to thank the gods for its beauty and the peace it brought her.

"I never pictured an archer from the *men's team* having a romantic side, but this is gorgeous," she said.

Karan laughed as he stretched out his long legs and opened the fast-food bag. "You say 'men's team' with some serious disgust."

"The misogyny in our sport is real," she mused.

"Fair enough. I promise you won't get it from me."

"That's good to hear," Laila said with a laugh.

The clouds shifted in that moment and Laila looked up at the moon shining brightly into the open glen. "This is one of my favorite falls in the area. In the summer people come out here to swim, but the later it gets, the quieter it is. There are a few others that are just like this one, too."

"I'll have to check them out."

He handed her a burger container, a sleeve of fries, and some napkins before he flipped on the flashlight and propped it up between them. It emitted a white glow that illuminated the entire rock and half the falls.

"Thanks." Laila hesitated for a moment before she took a bite of the veggie burger. The cheesy and spicy flavor combo was bomb, and she couldn't help but let out a moan. She should've been more wary about taking food from him, but the flavor was worth the risk. "This is . . . great."

"I'm glad," Karan said as he ate his own burger. He looked so much more approachable. Not like the grumpy older person she assumed he was when they first met.

"Can I ask you something?" she said.

"Shoot."

She dabbed at the ketchup at the corner of her mouth. "Why did you challenge me? At the archery studio?"

He grinned at her, and a small dimple formed in the middle of his chin. "I couldn't help it," he said. "I like to be the best, and Ben kept talking about how you're the one to beat."

"When did you start? Archery, I mean."

"When I was a child," Karan said. He bit into a fry and chewed. "I was born in India, and as soon as I was strong enough to draw an arrow, I was enrolled in classes. My father played too. It was the one sport we did together."

"It's just, you don't see a lot of South Asian archers outside of the US. You know?"

"I'm not from the US, remember?" Karan said. He bit into his sandwich, then after a moment, spoke again. "South Asians have a history of archery. It is such a huge part of our mythology, you know? My parents used to tell me these wild stories about it, and I loved it. That's why I kept practicing until I was recruited for the men's team here in the States."

"Wild stories?" Laila said. There was something about the easy way he mentioned mythology that had her cocking her head.

"I'm sure you've heard of them from family," Karan said, rolling his eyes. "Gods, demons, wars. The Mahabharata is a great example. The greatest archers in our folklore come from that epic."

"I don't know it," she lied. "What's it about?"

His eyebrow twitched as if amused by her answer. "What, the Mahabharata? It's . . . well, it's an epic poem really. There are eighteen volumes of mythology about families, gods, and demigods that culminate in this war that lasts for eighteen days where cousins fight against cousins for a kingdom. It's supposed to include lessons about life, and a philosophy for humans."

Laila shrugged. "I wouldn't know. My aunts raised me, and they never mentioned it."

There was a long pause, as if Karan were debating whether she was telling the truth. "You've heard of the Bhagavad Gita, right? I mean, everyone's heard of that now."

"Totally," she said, trying to hide her smirk. She could recite passages by the time she was twelve. "That's the one in *Oppenheimer*."

"Right," he said slowly. "The Bhagavad Gita is the most famous volume in the Mahabharata. I'm guessing your aunts weren't religious, huh?"

"Not at all," Laila lied again.

They finished their food and talked about their childhood. Archery. Their teams. It was easy conversation. Easier than she'd had in so long. He was poking at her, prodding for information about her past, but she started to wonder if that's because he was just trying to get to know her and any uneasiness she felt from his questions was just nerves because they were on a date.

It wasn't the first time she'd met a guy who was interested in her family. She'd dated before. Casually, of course, but she'd had experience fielding some of the same questions. As long as she didn't reveal too much, she'd be safe. Regardless of his role in her destiny, she'd never put her aunts' safety in jeopardy.

Half an hour later, Karan tucked their trash back into the fast-food bag. "So?" he said. "Is there a chance that I can see you again?"

"Yes," she said. She'd genuinely enjoyed his company. He was sweet, and wanted to know about her in a way that didn't make her feel like she was an outsider. "But maybe next time you can ask without the manhandling outside the studio."

He winced. "Yeah, sorry, love. Training sort of . . . kicked in."

The endearment had her shivering. "Yeah, I know what you mean." The sun had set, and the falls sounded louder than when Laila could see to the top. Her skin began to tingle as she grew more and more aware of how close she sat next to Karan. It was . . . thrilling.

Wanting to know if they could recreate their electric chemistry, she reached out and closed a hand over his.

The rumble of thunder sounded in the distance.

And then there was darkness.

Laila pulled away. She could barely make out the shadows of his face.

"Damn," he said. A second later, his cell phone turned on, emitting a small rectangle of light. "The batteries must've died in the flashlight. Stay here for a second. I'll run up and grab my spare. I should have one in the trunk."

"I can come with you," she said, getting to her knees.

"Nope, don't worry about it. I'll be right back. I don't want you to trip on the way up with just cell phone lights. I'll be quick."

He was already moving, climbing over rocks, heading toward the stone path. And then the light was gone, and she was left with the sounds of the waterfall.

"That's just dandy," she murmured. Laila reached behind her back for her clutch where she'd left it.

Except it wasn't there. She carefully passed her hand over the entire rock, and that's when her heart started to pound in her chest.

She was alone in the dark without her keys, her cell phone, or her knife.

Dammit, had he taken it? No, she must've just dropped it. There was no way that Karan was trying to harm her. Not when they saw each other regularly at the archery studio.

Her aunts were going to kill her for this.

Laila got to her feet when she heard a twig snap. Her anxiety ratcheted up another notch and her hands began to glow. Between the moonlight and the firepower within her, the glen became visible again.

"Karan?" she called out.

There was no answer. Her voice shook but she called again.

She began backing away from the rock where they'd sat, and her Converses were instantly submerged in the shallow creek.

She felt a whisper of air to her left. Laila dropped to her knees just as a shadow launched at her. Without a second's hesitation, she punched out with the heel of her hand, straight at Karan's crotch.

He jumped back just in time. His splash was exactly what she needed to hear. She ran in the opposite direction, stumbling over rocks and creek bed. Her eyes began to adjust to the shadows as she cursed herself for misreading all the signs.

But she could handle one man. Especially when she was pissed.

An arm looped around Laila's neck before she made it past the creek bed. The chokehold was strong enough to have her eyes bulging.

Laila forced herself to focus as she struggled for breath. She tugged and gasped and her mind went hazy, then she felt her palms heat again.

Thank you, ancestors, for the firepower.

She pressed her palms against the arm wrapped around her throat. Laila fully expected Karan to jerk away at the heat, but he continued to squeeze as if he felt nothing. When he began to drag her back into the water, she went to plan B.

With all the strength she had in her, she jumped, and used her entire body weight to flip him over her shoulder. She almost fell to her knees underneath him but managed to complete the move. He landed with another splash. His groan was louder than the waterfall.

"So much for a first date," she said hoarsely between gasps of air.

"I knew you were a witch," he said.

"What did you just call me?"

She didn't have time to sidestep. The water was making it too difficult, so when he tackled her around the waist and pushed her under the surface, the only thing she could do was brace herself against jagged rocks and hold her breath.

Laila boxed his ears and felt the eye gear he wore over his head.

Night-vision goggles?

She tore them off and threw them as far as she could as she struggled to keep her head above water.

"Hey!" he snapped.

She spit water in his face, then bent her knees and flipped them so that she straddled his chest. Laila's ponytail fell like a wet rope around her shoulders as she pulled back and punched Karan across the jaw.

His face was much softer than a demon's but pain shot through her knuckles as she scrambled back, tripping twice until she was knee-deep with the waterfall at her back.

She heard him get up, splash, groan, and stumble.

"What do you want?" she called out over the roar behind her. "Why all the drama?"

"I'm here to kill you," he said simply.

Karan was moving closer. Laila tried to remember which side of the falls had rocks she could climb over, and which side had a flat wall. She shifted, praying that she was moving in the right direction.

She didn't answer as to not give away her position.

"I have to give it to you," he said, his voice echoing around her. "You're the most humanlike asura that I've ever met. I hate to cut off your head."

What the hell was this psychopath talking about? Cut off her head?

And to think that she'd resigned herself to him being her intended baby-daddy.

She paused, just a little too long. Before she could move, her knees were knocked out from behind her, and her head was underwater.

This time, he pressed a booted foot against her abdomen to keep her underwater and gripped her shoulders so she couldn't lift her head up for air. He was stronger than she'd anticipated, and her fingers slipped as she tried to grip his foot. Her lungs began to burn, her nose on fire from water rushing up her nostrils, and she squeezed her eyes shut to focus.

She realized, somewhere in the swirling panic in her brain, that all her training wasn't enough, wasn't *nearly* enough, when the person she was fighting was actually trying to kill her.

That's when she felt the valve pop off her control, and the warmth rushed through her. The flames spread into her chest, and just as she was beginning to lose consciousness, she straightened her arms, breaking the surface, and a funnel of fire shot out of her hands into the sky. Everything was illuminated, and she could see Karan's expression as clearly as if the water were just a sheet of glass between them.

He stumbled back, giving her just enough time to lift her head and gasp for air. She choked, heaved, and the power rushed through her as it shot straight in the sky as blue and white flames tipped with burnt orange.

"Oh my god," she heard Karan whisper, crystal clear, as if he were speaking in her ear instead of five feet away next to a waterfall. "Laila, stop! You'll burn us both alive!"

She submerged her hands, but the fire came faster and faster until it formed a cyclone straight into the sky. She felt it shredding her apart, and she knew she was crying as the fire poured out of her.

As the fire destroyed her thoughts, leaving nothing but fragmented words of terror behind, she vaguely recognized Karan's large form, dripping wet as he reached out to grip her shoulders. His touch was like a switch. The fire immediately died, and both Karan and Laila were plunged into darkness once more.

"Wh-what?" she gasped, heaving for breath. "What are you?"

He hauled her to her feet. The lines on his face were harsh and carved in stone. "I've never seen an asura do that before. What *are you*?"

She swayed in his arms, her head hanging back as if barely held together. "I am no asura. I am Laila Bansal." She gasped, then coughed up water again. She closed her eyes, feeling her knees give out underneath her. "I am the Daughter of Draupadi, and when I wake up, I'm gonna kick your ass."

With her hands fisted against his chest, Laila took one deep breath and succumbed to the darkness.

8. KARAN

An hour after Laila passed out in his arms, her head rolled to the side and she let out a long, painful groan. He almost fell to his knees in relief.

He needed her awake and responsive.

He needed answers. That's why he'd dragged her back to his cabin, and out of precaution, tied her to the one chair in the room.

She was going to hate that.

"Laila?" he said as he sat in a chair in front of her, his arms crossed over his drying shirt. "It's time to wake up."

The sound of his voice had her jerking in her seat. Her clothes had mostly dried, but her hair remained a thick damp rope over one shoulder with puffs of frizz at her temples. Her blurry eyes cleared and focused on him, bloodshot and swollen. "What—You!"

She jerked forward as if she was ready to make a lunge at him, but all she managed was to inch her chair forward. He'd tied her wrists with paracord behind her back. The rope extended underneath her seat and wrapped around her ankles in a precise knot that required two hands to untie. He'd learned how to do it in his brief stint in the Boy Scouts in India.

"You can always fry your ropes," he said evenly. "But since we're secluded out here, I can't guarantee that we won't die in the fire, since it doesn't look like you have a lot of control over your power."

"Don't try me!" she roared. She looked around at the shabby, sparse cabin that he'd rented in the campground close to the archery studio, then tilted her head back as if to let out a scream to bring down the entire structure, but Karan had fortunately anticipated that move. The second her mouth opened, he shoved a clean handkerchief in it.

She gagged, her eyes going wide as he held it in place until she stopped struggling and began breathing in fast, shallow breaths through her nose.

"I'm sorry," he said. He didn't know why he felt the need to apologize since there was still a very good chance that he was going to cut her head off, but he couldn't take it back now.

"I was told that you're an asura," he said. "That you're not human. I don't want to hurt you if you're the wrong target. I won't have an innocent death on my conscience."

She glared at him, but she'd stopped struggling.

"Throughout dinner," he continued as he leaned his elbows on his knees, "I kept trying to gauge your reaction to my questions, but you seemed so . . . normal. Cagey, but normal. It wasn't until I left the clearing that I saw your hands glow. Then there was that fire." He motioned to the cut on her cheek and held himself back from touching it. "But, Laila, you bleed crimson."

When she rolled her eyes, his confusion grew even more. It was as if she was saying *No shit.* That meant if she wasn't an asura, and she wasn't human, then she fell somewhere in between.

Like him.

"One conversation. Five minutes. Then if I'm satisfied that you're not an asura come to wreak havoc on humanity, I'll drop you off at your car so you can go home."

He waited for her to nod before he slowly pulled the handkerchief out of her mouth. There was still so much fire in her eyes that he was afraid she'd become engulfed in flames, and they really would burn together before he had a chance of finding out if he could save his parents.

"Look, maybe we should start with this." He moved his chair aside, turned, and then lifted the hoodie he'd changed into so that she could see his tattoo. It was a crisp black ink that stretched from one hip to his shoulder, like a permanent quiver. The text was in Sanskrit, and no wider than three inches.

"I don't know what you're showing me," she said evenly.

"I didn't have any tattoos before we entered that clearing," he said.

"Okay," she said evenly. "What does that have to do with why you attacked me and then kidnapped me?"

"Laila, it matches yours."

"I don't have any tattoos," she replied.

Her response was so quick, and she leveled him with a gaze so direct that he believed she didn't know she had a tattoo either.

Karan knew without a doubt it had appeared at the same moment as his. When he'd seen her naked at the lake, he remembered the smooth, unmarked dark brown of her skin. Except that when he'd carried her to the car, her shirt rode up and he saw the markings at her waist.

"You do now," he finally said. Then he retrieved his phone from his pocket, walked behind her, pulled her shirt up at her hip, and took a quick picture. Then he showed her the screen. Her eyes went wide.

"What did you do to me?" Her voice had taken on a high-pitched edge. She struggled against her ties with enough force for the rope to create burn marks against her wrists.

"I'm asking you the same question," he said. The fact that they had matching markings had to mean something. More important, there was a chance that if he killed her now, it could in some way hurt him. Then he'd never have a chance at saving his parents.

"Why would we have a matching tattoo after fighting? A fight that proved you have some training of your own. You're not exactly a normal eighteen-year-old from upstate New York, are you, Laila Bansal?"

"Normal is overrated," she said flippantly. Bitterly.

"I'm not fucking joking, Laila," he said. "What happened to me? To us?"

"I don't know! Look, do you think I want to have a matching couples tattoo with a guy who tried to *drown* me before trying to cut off my head? And there I was thinking that you just wanted to get in my pants."

His anger burned some of his patience away. "Then are you a witch or something?"

She scoffed. "No, of course not."

"Holy hell, Laila, just tell me if you're fucking human."

"Yes!" she roared, tugging at her bindings. "Yes, I'm fucking *human*—happy? Now the question is, who are you and what are you doing in my town?"

It was too late for pretense. He had to be just as forthcoming if he expected the same from her, and he was running out of time. He sat back in the chair, his muscles heavy with fatigue. "My name really is Karan," he said. "I was born in India. My family comes from a long line of military heroes turned scholars. We specifically study South Asian mythology and the occult."

Laila gaped at him. "So what, you're *witch*-hunters?"

The truth wasn't that far off, he thought. "We have a responsibility to keep the balance between the natural and supernatural. It is my legacy as a descendant of Karna."

Her eyes widened, her jaw dropping. "*Karna?* The legendary bastard son in the Mahabharata?"

The word *bastard* had his spine straining. "He was also the best marksman in the Kurukshetra War, a man of dignity and loyalty, and my namesake."

"What you're telling me is that you're a supernatural ghost hunter without a job," she taunted. "Boy, do I know how to pick 'em."

"What I am is a third-year student at Oxford University," he said tersely. "I have the highest marksmanship score in the South Asian subcontinent, and three gold medals in the junior Olympic team for my country."

"With that kind of fancy lineage, I'd hope so, otherwise you'd be a disgrace," she spat out.

Karan was ready to launch into his pedigree when he realized exactly what she was doing. He was usually so controlled, so measured in his response. He'd learned patience from the best, and for some reason, this woman crawled under his skin in a way that no one ever had before.

He got to his feet and rested his hands on either side of her chair before leaning close enough for their breaths to mingle. He watched her pupils dilate. Her chapped lips parted in surprise.

"I thought you didn't know about the mythology," he said softly. "Daughter of Draupadi, what is a lie and what is the truth?"

She pressed her lips together into a thin line.

"Yeah, see, this is when you start talking," he replied before straightening. Then he flipped his chair around and straddled the seat. He folded his arms across the back of the chair. "If you're not an asura, then who are you, Laila Bansal?"

She shook a frizzing curl off her face, then tilted her chin up. "Are you going to torture me until I tell you my sob story?"

"No," he said softly. "But I can't let you go until I know."

"I'm human."

"It's not enough," he said. "What's with the fire?"

"Yeah, that's not your business."

Karan felt like his teeth were going to crack from how hard he was clenching his jaw. Dammit, she was stubborn, but he'd told her the truth. He wasn't going to torture her or hurt her. Not now. "What if I told you that I'm here because my parents went missing?" he said.

There was a long pause. "What does that have to do with me?"

Karan hedged his bets before he told her the rest of the story. "A few months ago, I got a call from a family friend. My father didn't show up for work. He went to their house, and it was empty. Both my father and my mother were missing. I was in Oxford, but immediately jumped on a flight to go home. My parents had vanished without a trace."

He looked up to see that Laila was listening intently. Her face remained cool and expressionless.

"My uncle and I looked everywhere. They're nowhere to be found. That's when we devised a plan. We know where we can get more information, but to barter for it, we need the head of an asura. There is a collector who deals with the occult that would make the exchange with us. Through my uncle's network, he found information about an asura living here in the mountains. I arrived a week ago for surveillance."

Her eyes went wide. "You were spying on me. I *knew* I felt someone watching me."

Karan nodded. "It's protocol for every hunt. Canvas the area, complete interviews with locals, and observe the target." He'd talked to so many people in town and they'd all pointed to the strange family that owned the winery with the beautiful daughter who was unnaturally gifted at archery. The first time he saw her, he was sure that Satyapal was mistaken. She radiated carefree confidence that was so different from the demonic nightmares he'd often chased. And she was beautiful. How could this person be an asura, an evil being? They were supposed to be demons in the night that were like the stories of the devil from Western myths.

He'd hesitated, and used unorthodox methods of getting her alone simply because he wasn't sure that his hunch was correct. There was blood on his hands, on the hands of his ancestors as far back as Karna himself. But damn if Karan was going to be responsible for the death of an innocent. He had a hazy memory of hurting someone once, and even if it was just a dream, he wasn't going to chance that dream becoming a reality.

"I genuinely liked you," she said, cutting through his thoughts. She said it with such an easy, open honesty that cut him off at the knees. "I actually thought we had . . . chemistry."

"We do," he said before he could stop himself. "But that fire isn't human—"

"No, you don't," Laila cut in. "You don't get to judge me for that. I'm not some asura, and I'm not a key to whatever you're looking for with your parents. Look, I'm sorry they're missing, but your intel is wrong. I'm like you, but different. Which is why you need to go."

Like you, but different. A descendant? As far as he knew there was only Boo and himself, and neither of them could do anything beyond archery or nerd-math.

He watched her closely, the set lines of her face, and knew that this was as much as she'd say about the matter for the rest of the night.

Karan had a choice. He could keep her, or he could let her go. There was no way she would call the authorities on him, not if it brought attention to herself. And if she disappeared from her regular routine, people would talk.

The other possibility was that she'd panic and make a mistake, even though he had his doubts that she was the panicking type.

"I'm not leaving town until I find out who you are and why we're both marked, Laila. You're going to see me at the studio and when you're at the winery. I'm not going anywhere."

"I'll take that chance," she said.

He stood from his chair, hoping that this was the right move. "Come on, I'll take you—*Umph*."

The ropes dropped, disintegrating around her chair, and she socked him so hard in the nose that blood sprayed like a fine red mist across the cabin floor. Pain exploded over his face, and a starburst of light blinded him.

She would've kneed him in the balls, too, if he hadn't jerked back. He turned away from her, his hands still covering his throbbing face.

"News flash, asshole," Laila called out. "Your ancestor has nothing on mine."

Before he could stop her, she snagged his keys and her clutch, which he'd left on the small console table next to the cabin door, and bolted out of the room. He rushed after her, leaving a blood trail, but when he grabbed the handle of the door, it singed his palm.

"Son of a bitch!" he shouted, jerking back. She'd done something to heat the metal until it burned him. He was still seeing stars as blood dripped down his face. "Laila!"

Seconds later, he heard his car starting up and speeding out of the small parking lot within his section of the campground. Then she was gone.

"Son of a bitch."

It was going to be a pain in the ass getting his car back, but he'd worry about that later. First, he'd fix his nose, then he'd call his cousin. Regardless of whether Laila was going to be able to help him, that didn't change his mission. He had to figure out a way to save his parents, and if killing another demigod wasn't happening, he'd find something else that the collector wanted so that they could make the exchange.

There was no other way.

9. LAILA

Laila had finished crying by the time she drove back to the trailhead where she'd parked her car. After she chucked Karan's keys into the trees, she wiped her eyes, fanned her face, and climbed into her own vehicle before she sped out of the lot and toward her house.

When she got on the single-lane highway that snaked through the dense evergreens in the inky black night, she took a few deep testing breaths to make sure that she could control the flames inside her. She didn't think it would be a problem, because she felt . . . cold. It was as if she was an empty vessel and regardless of how hard she'd try, she was spent.

Laila replayed her conversation with Karan in her head. She was infuriated that she could've ever believed he was her destined match. How embarrassing, how *ridiculous* could she have been? The signs that she'd read as interest were actually signs that she should stay away from him. She had made the same ridiculous mistake about men that her ancestors made before her.

Picking bad partners was really a genetic trait in her family after all.

But had anyone ever picked someone as terrible as she did? Karan hunted asuras! She'd never encountered someone like him before, considering her aunts had always been so protective and sheltered her from any potential threat. But in the diaries of the women who came before her, there were references to being hunted.

Karan, her intended baby-daddy, just happened to be a descendant of Karna, too. He'd intended on beheading a witch but found Laila instead. Now they had matching tattoos as if they were destined to carry the physical reminder of their mistake for the rest of their lives.

"The masis are going to kill me," she whispered to herself.

She relaxed her death grip on the steering wheel to reach over her shoulder and touch the top of her tattoo. She had to figure out what it meant before they saw it. Damn, most of her clothes were belly-baring workout attire, which meant she had to work fast. If they realized what had happened between Karan and herself, they'd be out for blood.

"I doubt the other women in my history had to deal with getting in trouble over a tattoo," she muttered as she pulled into the long driveway leading up to the front of her house. All her aunts' cars were parked in their respective spots, one after another.

Great, she thought. If she tried to run to her room without explanation, they'd know she was hiding something. What was she supposed to tell them about where she'd been? About why her hair and clothes were damp?

When she pulled into the small space next to the front entrance, she could feel heat from the fire inside her coming back. She took a few testing breaths and realized that instead of overwhelming her, suffocating her, she felt warm. The brisk chilly air and her damp clothes didn't seem to bother her at all.

Her aunts were still going to fuss.

"Just suck it up and accept your fate," she murmured to herself as she exited her car.

A few seconds later she was walking barefoot through the wide marble and stone hallways with their vaulted ceilings. "Is anyone home?" she called out.

Silence was her only response.

Laila's voice echoed through the house one more time as she walked to the staircase and headed up to her room. Maybe she needed to take a quick shower to cool down and change into clothes that weren't stiff with river water. Then she'd find the rest of her family and they'd tell her what to do.

Laila entered her dark bedroom and had just flipped on the light when she heard the long, low moan. Her heart clenched at the sound. It wasn't a battle cry she was used to hearing.

Her skin tightened with goose bumps as she dismissed any plans for a shower and ran out of the room, following the sound.

"Masis!" she called out as she raced through the halls, down the stairs, and into the main kitchen. "Masis!"

The low moan started again, and she heard it from the hidden panel next to the living room. The library.

She punched in the code and bolted down the spiral stairs into the underground training studio and study space that her aunts had spent years building into the mountain. She passed the two-story library, the desks littered with leather-bound texts and scrolls, and ran down the hall through a second set of double doors into the temple. The white marble room glowed with small diyas flickering with tiny flames.

She came to a screeching halt when she saw her three masis wearing white saris, sitting on the floor facing each other in a triangle. They held hands, and their hair, a riot of frizz that was normally styled in shiny waves down their back, was streaked with white. It covered their faces as they rocked forward and back and side to side.

"Oh my god," Laila whispered.

The sound cut off as if someone flipped the switch on a stereo system. Their heads turned to her in unison, and she gasped before stumbling back into the wall.

They had all aged. Their flawless dark brown skin, frozen at twenty-eight years old for centuries, was now marred with creases and spots. They had wrinkles at the corners of their eyes and mouths. Their necks had jowls and their eyes reflected the centuries that they'd been alive.

"What happened?" she whispered, her heart pounding in a rapid staccato. "When did this start?"

"This morning," Vika Masi said, her voice almost hysterical. "Shortly after you left for work. It started with our hair. I thought my Dyson was too strong . . ."

"I put some herbs in my shampoo!" Giri Masi panted. "But nothing is working."

"The wrinkles!" Rashmi Masi moaned.

Laila had started walking toward them but stopped at Rashmi Masi's words. "Wait a minute," she said. "Have the three of you been down here in the temple moaning for like the last fourteen hours?"

They looked at each other, guilt in their expressions.

"And not one of you thought it would be a good idea to call me? You'd rather just sit here having a moan-fest that you all look decrepit now instead of twenty-eight?"

"We didn't want you to worry," Vika Masi whispered.

"And we had to meditate to find out what we have to do," Giri Masi said.

"I don't think you can pray away the gray," Laila snapped. She crossed the rest of the distance and sat on the cold marble floor between Vika and Giri Masi. She scooted forward and then held out her hands for them to take so that she was part of their circle. "I should have been here with you. I'm a part of this family—"

"The most important part," Rashmi Masi said. Her lips were thinner than they'd ever been, and they practically disappeared when she pressed them together. "Our entire existence has been to protect you and your ancestors. But if we are aging . . ."

"You won't be around long enough to protect me," Laila finished with a whisper. The truth of what was happening hit her like a fist to the gut, as strong and as fast as one in a sparring session. She still had some of the bruises from her go-round with Karan, but they were nothing compared to this moment of realization.

Laila would be alone without these women. She'd have no one. Panic fluttered in her throat, a quick burn.

They sat in silence for a moment longer before Giri Masi's head dropped back, her mouth opened wide enough for her sharp canines to show, and she took a deep breath as if she were going to let out another moan.

"No," Laila said, squeezing her hand. "I think we're past the moaning part."

Giri Masi's mouth closed with a quick click of her teeth.

Vika Masi was the first to speak, her voice low and aching. "I am not ready to die. I am not ready to leave the one Daughter of Draupadi who has felt like our daughter out of all the daughters. My sister Usha would've known what to do, but I feel like we're failing you."

Laila's heart clenched, and her eyes watered as Rashmi and Giri both nodded as if sharing the sentiment.

"I refuse to be left alone on this earth without you," she said, the grip on her aunts' hands hard. "I don't know what's happening, but we can figure it out, right?"

"We have to focus on your safety first," Rashmi Masi said. "You're the most important—"

"If you die, then none of this matters." Laila squeezed their hands, hoping her voice remained steady even as her thoughts raced to figure out what was happening. *First Karan shows up and now this?* "Has this ever happened before?"

The masis looked at each other. Rashmi Masi was the first to speak. "Once. About five hundred years ago."

Some of the tension in Laila's shoulders eased. "Okay, it looks like you recovered from that. What happened?"

"Our youth and immortality are dependent on your survival," Vika Masi said. "Your ancestor became very ill. She was dying, and so were we."

Okay, not as comforting as she thought. "I'm not dying," Laila said. "I'm healthy as a horse!"

"That is why we're so scared," Giri Masi said with a shiver. Her white hair shifted over her shoulders. "Because there is no danger toward you now, but it could be coming."

Laila thought of Karan. If he was the reason her aunts were aging, then she'd personally eviscerate him. Her increased firepower, the electric current between them, his fascination with her. All of it was leading to this.

She looked up at their faces and realized they were watching her, as if expecting Laila to assure them that she was fine. She should've told them about Karan in that moment, but if they didn't focus on themselves and their immortality, then it was possible they'd die before they could get a chance to kill Karan. Laila refused to lose the last of her family. Maybe it was selfish of her, but she didn't want to be alone again, and that meant protecting these rakshasi as much as they protected her.

"There is no danger," she finally said. "Maybe it's a cyclical thing. Every five hundred years or something you have to re-up your subscription to immortality. What did you do last time?"

Vika Masi spoke. "We went on a pilgrimage to Bhalka in Gujarat."

A religious pilgrimage to the town where the god who had once blessed them had taken his last breath. Laila's mind was already racing with juggling real-life responsibilities and her supernatural ones.

"Fine. We're going on this religious pilgrimage in India. I'll take an extended leave of absence from the winery. Archery can wait too, and my online classes are easy to keep up. I haven't been to India before, and I just have to make sure that my passport—"

"Laila," Rashmi Masi interrupted. She squeezed her hand back. "You should stay here."

Laila's jaw dropped. "What? Absolutely no way. I'm coming with you—"

"There is a protection spell on the property that we put in place when we first moved here," Vika Masi said. "It'll be difficult for us to protect you in India, where there are so many sages who may recognize you for who you are. We can't complete our pilgrimage if we also don't protect you. You will stay here while we are gone, so we know that you'll still be safe."

She wanted to argue. She wanted to push back and tell them that she could help them, she could protect them, because she had been training for it all her life. But there was a part of her that knew this religious pilgrimage was something that she'd never be able to be a part of. These were rakshasi. They were demonesses that were warriors who fought side by side with the Pandavas. They had seen more wars, famine, and change in the world than any other beings in existence. Their journey to salvation was a different one from what she would've had to do. And if they had to focus on her the entire time they were there, then there was a chance that they were right, and she would cause more harm than good.

"Fine," Laila said quietly. "If you think it's safer for me to be here, then I'll stay. But I want us to be able to communicate regularly.

That means you have to keep your phones on you at all times and pick up when I call you."

"We will do our best," Vika Masi said.

"Do better than your best," Laila said fiercely. "You're all I have left. I need to know you're safe—otherwise I will come after you myself."

The masis looked at each other again to communicate silently, then nodded.

They sat for a moment longer, and Laila felt her heart ache the same way that it had when her mother died, and then more recently, the moment she'd discovered Usha Masi's death.

"Laila?" Rashmi Masi said.

"Yes?"

"Be careful." Then she said something that sounded so much like Usha Masi. "You may be the Daughter of Draupadi, but you are human, too. You can make mistakes. But in your case, those mistakes can be the end of the world."

End of the world.

That's right. The very existence of her lineage meant that humanity had a fighting chance of completing the circle of life.

"Okay," she said softly. "Don't worry, I got this."

"When we're gone," Rashmi Masi continued, "we need you to remember everything we taught you, because it may save your life."

Laila had come to accept her fate a long time ago. Grow up, learn mythology and folklore, train to protect herself, and have a child to pass on the knowledge.

But in that moment, when a destiny that she hadn't agreed to was hurting the people that she loved the most, she resented it all.

She resented being a Daughter of Draupadi. She resented that she'd never have any normalcy and that she couldn't go to college and parties and date. She resented Karan showing up and upsetting her life. She resented that her decisions and choices, her interest in Karan, may have hurt her family.

Karan. He was so screwed. No one messed with her family and got away with it.

"I'll be fine," she said, her voice hard. She squeezed her masis' hands, then swallowed the lump in her throat when they trembled in hers.

While her aunts were away, she was going to figure out what the hell was going on with her connection to Karan, and how to get rid of the tattoo on their backs.

It was almost an hour later before they stood to leave the temple. The diyas had mostly diffused and all that was left was cold white marble.

"Beta, why are you wet?" Giri Masi asked.

She looked down at her drying clothing, then shook her head. "I went for a hike and got hot, so I jumped in the water. Don't worry about me. Let's get you packed."

10. KARAN

When Karan's parents went missing, the first person he called was his uncle. They'd searched everywhere together. The school, the safe house, the gym. Then Uncle Satya had used his contacts, a network of resources that he'd never shared details about, and told Karan to go after Laila. His solution wasn't ideal, but in the moment, Karan knew they were out of options.

Now that he'd gotten more intel on Laila, he wanted to call his uncle once more to ask him what to do. Except, this was something he wasn't sure he could share quite yet. There was a strange familiarity to the mystery behind Laila that had the hairs on the back of his neck lifting in warning.

After she'd left his cabin, he'd performed his cursory security sweep before going to bed with an ice pack on his face. He'd dreamed of monsters and blood-tipped arrows. A familiar voice haunted his dreams, and he woke up hearing the echo of her rasping speech.

She is divine.

Do not trust him.

You are forgiven.

He wrote down the message, even though he didn't understand the significance of it yet. Karan was going to trust his instinct on this one and wait.

To maintain close contact and anonymity in town, he decided to go back to training the next day. He had a bruised nose, and a purple smudge under one eye, but his team didn't press him about it. Once he told them that he was sparring as a cardio workout, they accepted his answer and moved on.

It helped that his skill and performance didn't waver.

Laila was still on his mind as he headed to the locker room that night after practice. He quickly stashed his things, and then pulled his shirt off from over his shoulders. He'd take a quick shower and then call Boo again when he returned to the cabin. Hopefully his cousin would come back with information that could help him develop a backup plan.

The locker room was eerily quiet, but that was because most of the national team had left an hour ago. There were members of the cleaning crew who were busy scrubbing mats, replacing targets, and refreshing bathrooms, but he had been the sole student left. Thankfully some of the junior coaches vouched for him so that he could practice on his own.

He wrapped a towel around his waist, the same ratty one that he'd have to go and wash that weekend at the laundromat, and stepped into the open showers. After turning the knob on the faucet closest to the door, he waited for the steam to start filling the room before he stepped under the spray. The hot water beat down on his aching muscles and his still-bruised face like a salve.

He closed his eyes and dunked his head under the spray, praying for some relief from this nightmare. When had his life gotten so off track? Was he the descendant of Karna that would fail his legacy? Karan had always been honored by the responsibility that rested on his shoulders. Now, he wished all of it away.

There was the soft hush of a door opening that had Karan's head jerking up. He wiped the water from his eyes and stepped back from the spray so he could listen. When there was nothing, he called out.

"Hello? Someone's in here."

There was a scraping sound against the tile floor. Then a soft creak of a locker door. It was barely audible, but enough for him to realize that he was not alone.

He turned off the water and quickly wrapped the towel around his waist.

There was another sound, this one coming from the left. Then the locker room was plunged into darkness. If it was just a member of the cleaning crew, they would've called out. There would've been noise by now.

Then someone began to whisper.

A soft, gentle melody in a language he didn't understand echoed off metal and tile.

It sounded like a young girl.

Then it giggled and spoke in English.

"Come out, come out, wherever you are."

Oh hell, no.

Nothing terrified Karan more than dead children. He'd take eight-foot-tall monsters over a singing dead demon child any day.

His fingers clenched on his towel, when there was a clang of a locker door closing.

He hunkered down and padded softly out of the showers and around to the right side of the room to hide behind a row of lockers.

There was the soft brush of clothing. His heart was pounding too hard for him to identify what it was. He held his breath, and after a few seconds of silence, he peeked around the corner. He saw the wispy trail of white flutter over the tile heading in the opposite direction. An ethereal glow illuminated off the being.

Karan's heart began to pound. He had to get to his bow. Even if he wasn't entirely sure it worked on ethereal beings, it was the only form of protection he had in the moment. He waited for the hint of another sound, then rolled to the left to hide behind the next row of lockers.

There was that giggle again. Childlike. Soft.

"I like to play games," it said in a singsong voice. It was close. Too close. "I've come to take your soul, but would you like to play a game with me first?"

The soft singing resumed, echoing louder and louder.

Karan couldn't stay seated in his position any longer. He was unarmed, and a sitting duck wearing a thin towel. Sending up a brief prayer, he got to his feet and made a run for the exit. Right before he reached the door, it swung open and almost slammed him in the face. The last person he expected to see stood on the other side.

Her eyes were wide in shock, and she held up her hand where a Sanskrit symbol glowed in the center of her palm. "What . . . Oh my god."

The childlike giggle came from behind him, and then the singing. He watched as Laila's eyes went wide as she focused on the being over his shoulder.

That's when Karan turned and saw it for the first time. A girl, maybe fourteen or fifteen, with a wild tangled mess of black hair, a white sari stained in dried blood, the corners of her mouth dripping with black tar, and traces of the same down her arms and throat.

"What is that?" Laila whispered, her fingers gripping his arm.

"Looks like a bhooth? An evil spirit of a woman who was wronged. We have to get—"

"Draupadi," the ghost girl said with a musical laugh. "I found you after all this time." Her voice became sinister, and she took a step forward, her head cocked in an unnatural angle.

Laila's grip intensified. "Did she say my—"

"Yup. Yes, yes, she did."

"What do we do?" she said, her voice going shrill, even as the locker room door closed behind them. There was a click, and Karan was pretty sure neither of them locked the door so they would be stuck with a supernatural being.

The ghost-being advanced, still humming that strange tune, then tilted its head back so far that it was as if its head had been broken in that direction, before it snapped in place. Its eyes began glowing a hollow red, and the sockets turned black.

"Cremation is the only thing that works," Karan whispered as he stepped between the ghost and Laila. "Or the spirit needs to feel justice."

The apparition let out a shriek that gripped him with bone-deep fear. He barely had a chance to throw up his hands to prevent an attack when flames erupted from Laila's hands in a column of blue and red fire and shot straight through the being.

It let out an ear-splitting shriek as it was cut in half by flame. Then it collapsed in on itself until all that was left was a lick of blue flame on tile.

The fire stopped just as quickly as it had appeared, leaving the pungent odor of acrid smoke. Karan walked over to where the being had been standing and stomped out the small flame that was left. That's when he realized that he was still wearing his shower flip-flops and barely covered in his towel.

"Please tell me that this is all a dream," Laila said from behind him.

"I wish," Karan said, adjusting his towel. "I'm a monster hunter, and somehow my life is still getting weirder and weirder by the day."

Laila kept her eyes above shoulder-level, which he had to appreciate. "We need to talk, and this time, without the ropes and punches. Ben said that you were working late when I texted if the national team was around. Then my palm started glowing and I just *knew* something was wrong." She rubbed the spot on her hand now, as if trying to erase the reminder.

"I have to finish getting dressed. Then maybe we can—"

The locker room door swung open without any warning, and an elderly white woman who resembled one of the Golden Girls with a curly helmet of stark white hair let out an ear-piercing shriek, then covered her eyes with gloved hands.

"The good lord did not bless me today!" she shouted in an accent so thick that Karan had to remind himself they weren't in some Hollywood movie about the American South. "I heard some yelling over here and did not expect these kinds of shenanigans! Playing hanky-panky in front of the world to see! I ought to call Ben right now to tell him that you two are doing the deed on his property like a bunch of hooligans."

Karan didn't hesitate. "I'll meet you outside," he said to Laila before she bolted out of the locker room and into the studio. The employee took one last look at him and shook her head like she was lecturing a five-year-old and followed Laila. Karan was alone again, the lights shining brightly in the large space, with someone's discarded shoes in one corner and a towel draped over the bench in the other.

It was as if nothing had happened in the last five minutes.

He checked behind locker corners, the showers, the bathroom stalls, and didn't take a breath until he was sure that the coast was clear.

Laila. If it wasn't for her serious firepower, then God knows what would've happened. They sure as heck didn't have a pooja ready to go with mantras to chant.

Karan rushed through another shower, washing off the rest of his cold fear sweat and training with the hopes that the few minutes he took wouldn't give Laila a reason to leave.

He got dressed, and with his duffel swung over one shoulder, he emerged from the locker room. There was a sound of an industrial vacuum in the distance, and he could feel his face grow hot at the thought of running into the employee again.

Instead, he saw just the Daughter of Draupadi, standing at the end of the hallway, arms crossed and clutch in hand. She turned to look at him over her shoulder, her lips pressed in a thin line, her hands clenched into fists.

"I almost expected you to leave."

"I saw a ghost," she said, matter-of-factly. "I don't trust you, especially after you tried to kill me. I don't know if what you're saying is completely true, but I know that whatever that thing was in there, it puts horror movies to shame. And then I burned her to a crisp!" She flexed her hand as if debating whether she dreamed the whole experience. "I have matching tattoos with a monster-hunter, and my aunts are aging, and I burned her to a *crisp*."

"Not here," he said to her. He wasn't sure if there was a chance someone would hear their conversation. Karan looked over her shoulder and scanned their surroundings. "Do you have your car here? Let's find someplace we can talk."

"I'm surprised it didn't try to come back," Laila continued. She pushed her braid over her shoulder and matched his strides as they followed the right wall of the large studio to Ben's offices and the back exit. "I mean, it just . . . *poof!* Have you seen something like that before?"

"Yes, and yes, I'm surprised too."

He glanced left and right, keeping an eye out for anything that could indicate someone else was present. "Look, let's go back to my cabin, and—"

Laila stopped in her tracks. "To the *murder* cabin? I don't think so," she said. She held her hand out like a traffic light. "I don't trust you, but you've brought danger to my doorstep, so I have no choice but to figure out what you're doing to get my life back on track. I can kill you, but you might have more answers alive than dead. Also, there are bigger things than finding your parents at stake here."

He felt his own anger burning now. "What could be more important than innocent lives?"

"The fate of the world, asshole," she said. "Because as the Daughter of Draupadi, my existence is the linchpin that keeps our universe going."

Karan gaped at her. "Holy . . . Okay, now you have my attention."

11. LAILA

Laila couldn't get the image of the hollow black eyes out of her mind as she drove Karan to the Skylounge Diner. She was raised by rakshasi. She saw them in their natural form, knew of their histories, as well as the stories of other demons and demonesses that permeated Hindu mythology.

But she had *never* come face-to-face with something like the ghost-being that was casually haunting the men's locker room in the archery studio. She'd reacted on instinct, channeling the fire that was in her. She felt it all the time now, and she wasn't sure how it worked, but in that moment, she was so grateful for it.

She glanced at Karan in her passenger seat, his duffel bag tucked between his legs, his black hair, slightly damp, combed back with impatient fingers. His legs were so long that his knees almost touched the dash. He looked a lot calmer than she did, but maybe that was because this was just another Tuesday for him. Based on the little she knew about him, people probably tried to kill him all the time.

She'd never met anyone else who skirted life and death the same way she had to.

"It'll pass."

She jerked at the sound of his voice.

"What?"

"The shakes? It'll pass," Karan said, then brushed the pad of his thumb along the angular line of his jaw. "The first few times I came up against an asura, I puked. Then you get used to it."

Laila jerked again at the word *asura*. She thought of her aunts, and it reminded her of why she needed answers from him in the first place.

"If anyone was in there with you, or if Jane had walked in minutes earlier, she could've gotten hurt," Laila said as she pulled into the diner's parking lot.

"Not likely," Karan replied smoothly. The sharp line of his jaw clenched. "The asura said 'Draupadi.' I think she was looking for you."

Laila threw her hands up in frustration. "Great. I am part of the universe's worst kept secret at this point."

She parked her car and reached for her door handle before Karan stopped her. His dark brown eyes scanned her face before he glanced out the window.

"Are you sure this is a good idea?"

"What, the diner?" she asked. "Where else are we going to go?"

"We could go back to my place or yours."

"No," she said. "I already told you. I'm not going to your murder cabin in the woods. The last time we were there, you tied me up and told me you planned on delivering my head to some occult collector."

He swallowed, and the muscles in his throat flexed. There was a faded purple bruise under his left eye turning a sickly yellow, and a molten purple discoloration along the bridge of his nose. "I'm sorry, Laila, I—"

"I don't want your apology," she said, cutting him off. "Look, the Skylounge makes some really fantastic onion rings and it's a public place. I know you're not going to try to kill me in public, and it's unlikely a ghost will come haunting us in front of the whole town. Hopefully."

This time he didn't stop her from getting out of the car. When she turned back, she saw him staring into space at the bright blue building with neon pink lights and yellow double doors.

"Are you coming?"

He glanced at her, then after another minute, finally got out of the car.

"Are you sure the food is decent?" he asked when he joined her in front of the car. "I find it hard to believe that a place as remote as this would know how to cook up a decent onion ring."

"Look, if you don't like it, we can always go to the next Michelin star restaurant on Main Street."

"Point taken."

They walked through the double doors together and received a few curious glances and stares. Skylounge Diner was a spot for locals with the occasional tourist group stopping by. Laila was used to being viewed as an outsider. She was the niece of wealthy brown women vintners in a predominately white community. For the most part, wineries and vintners were also white. But because her aunts' business was well respected, no one ever made her feel like she didn't belong. Thankfully, the diner was dark with hanging lamps illuminating each booth, so the stares would stop shortly, too.

"I wonder if our ancestors had to deal with small-town gossip," Karan said. He must've also noticed the way people stared.

"Our ancestors probably had to deal with worse."

"What can be worse than gossip?" he asked.

"The British colonization of India."

Laila smiled at Ms. Colleen, who pointed to one of the empty booths at the back of the diner. Thankfully it would give them enough privacy for their conversation. She led the way to the back, ignoring everyone she passed, including two classmates and a teacher, before she sat down on the vinyl plastic bench seat and scooted in. She did not expect Karan to sit next to her and usher her further into the booth. He was taller than her, with broader shoulders and longer limbs. His knee knocked against hers; his thigh, which she had seen a little too intimately, was pressed against hers now.

"What are you doing? There is a perfectly good bench on the other side."

He leaned on the table, then gave her a sideways glance. "And have my back to the restaurant? Yeah, I don't think so."

She hated that she would've done the same thing.

"Hi, chickadee," Ms. Colleen said as she plopped two plastic-covered menus onto the table. She smacked her gum and smiled enough for the thick layer of makeup to crease in happy lines. "Is this your new man?"

"No, this—"

"Hi, I'm Karan." He waved a hand, then his mouth curved in an easy smile.

Ms. Colleen clicked her tongue. "It looks like you like to tussle."

"I'm a member of the national archery team, and I accidentally hurt myself during my morning workout," he said as he motioned to the bridge of his nose.

Laila snorted, and Ms. Colleen raised a brow.

Karan looked like he was trying for a charming smile. "Laila has been saying how great your onion rings are, so I had to come and try them for myself."

Ms. Colleen beamed like a proud mom. "Of course! I'll put in an order for you to start. Laila, should I also bring your usual tea with milk on the side?"

"Yes, please," Laila said.

"Can I have one of those too?" Karan added.

"Coming right up," Ms. Colleen said with a smile. "I'll be right back with those and to take your dinner orders."

"Wow, this is a small town," Karan said quietly. "You have a usual order."

"The local population is small. It gets really crowded in the summer, but now that school is in session, we'll start to see things quiet. There is another surge of tourists during fall." Laila pushed a plastic menu in front of him and then flipped hers over to look at the burgers. If she was going to get fries, she should probably have a burger, too. Now that her adrenaline was dropping, she'd developed an appetite that made her ravenous.

Karan took his time, reading through each section. "This place has everything from gyros to bratwurst to jasmine rice, and a whole selection of breakfast."

"I wouldn't get anything but breakfast or burgers if I were you. For dessert, the pie is good, but I think the ice cream is from the grocery store down the street."

Karan nodded solemnly, but she could see that he wasn't sure what to make of the place. She remembered that he'd said he was studying in the UK but he was originally from India. That was definitely different from the Finger Lakes region. It was on the tip of her tongue to ask him what growing up where everyone looked like him was like before she stopped herself.

What was she doing? Making friendly conversation with someone who was probably why her aunts were aging? Someone who had lured her out on a date, flirted with her, and then attacked her and tied her up in a murder cabin? Someone who was probably the impetus for a ghost showing up at the archery studio?

Laila needed to remember that she hated him. She most definitely should not be leaning closer to smell his clean, evergreen musk.

"I feel like the fish and chips here at this diner won't be the same I get at Oxford, yeah?"

She twisted in her seat and, ignoring his question, said, "I want to make it clear if I haven't done so already: I don't want to be friends. I don't want to make small talk. I don't want you here in the Finger Lakes. But when you showed up, things started happening, so now I need to figure out why. That is the only reason we're sitting here together."

He nodded, then closed his menu. "Fair enough. Now can I ask you a question?"

She debated it for a moment, then nodded.

"Back in the studio, you said that your palm warned you that something was happening?" he asked.

Laila looked down at her hand, at the smooth skin where she remembered seeing the mark she wasn't able to read. It had gotten hot, and her palm glowed again. The symbol looked like a letter from the Sanskrit alphabet. A curled dash on top of a Y shape with two vertical lines on either side.

The fact that she'd felt it warm for the first time since she'd received it alarmed her. Was it a homing beacon of some kind? Now that she had a better look at it when it reappeared, she'd have to check the books in the library to see if there was any other reference to it in the past.

She tucked her fists back under the table, feeling the heat from the center. "It's just an educated guess, but I had this instinctual response that you were in some kind of danger, and I should go . . . check on you. Did yours burn?"

"No, not at all," he said. "Maybe it's one-way? The person who is not in danger is the one who feels it? It's only happened one time so we can't be sure." Karan leaned back against the booth and the strands of his drying hair glinted like highlights in the dim lighting of their small section in the back of the restaurant.

"I don't know what to make of all this," Laila said. "As someone who has been reading the vedas, the history books, and scriptures, for my entire life, this is something I have never heard of before."

Ms. Colleen returned a moment later with two saucers, cups, and Lipton tea bags. She set a small plastic basket in the center of the table that smelled of the fragrant, double-fried, freshly made onion rings with a side of ketchup.

"There you two are. Now. What can I get ya?"

Laila's appetite had died, but she still smiled up at Ms. Colleen, who had been giving her milkshake refills since she was ten. "I'll have the cheeseburger, please. Medium well."

"I'll have the same," Karan said.

Ms. Colleen smiled. "Good choice! You two sure look cute. I'll get that for you so you can keep on with your date."

"Thanks, Ms. Colleen," Laila said. When the woman left their table, Laila reached for an onion ring. "The hand symbol and the tattoo are two unknown variables. Then there are my aunts."

"Maybe it's time you told me more about your history," Karan said. "You already know about me."

Laila tilted her head to the side, debating how much he should know. She wasn't supposed to give him any information, but what if her past was a puzzle piece that he could fit into place? "What do you want to know?"

"You mentioned that you're a Daughter of Draupadi back at the archery studio," Karan said. "Draupadi was cursed to watch all her offspring die. Her husbands, on the other hand, all had other wives who birthed multiple children."

"There are stories about the first time Draupadi appeared in the Mahabharata," Laila said as she dipped another onion ring into a puddle of ketchup. "Most accounts say that she was made from fire into a fully formed adult. Did you know that?"

"There are versions of the myth—"

"There are versions of every Hindu myth," Laila cut in. "Some of them are rooted in almost cultish beliefs and some are rooted in truth. Draupadi was formed from fire. That's how she came into the world. That's the truth. So when she was told that her descendants would play a key part in protecting the good people left in the Kali Yuga realm, the realm of humans and evil that we live in today, she formed a daughter from the same fire."

There were four realms. The first was for the gods. The second was for gods and demons. The third was for gods, demons, and humans. And the fourth? Where humanity and depravity prevailed.

They were living a life that was literal hell on earth.

Karan drank his tea deeply, then bit into another onion ring before speaking again. Laila could practically see the wheels turning in his head. "Does that mean that as a descendant of Karna, there is a chance that my responsibility is similar to yours? That if I don't fulfill my duty . . . then I affect Kali Yuga as well?"

"Maybe? I don't know. Draupadi was a central figure in the Mahabharata that acted a linchpin. A negotiator." Laila knew that most people didn't view her descendant in quite the same way. To most, she was a princess won in an archery competition and then wed to five demigod brothers because their mother told them, "Share all your things." Laila read the diaries, studied all the records and histories. Draupadi was badass, and Laila liked to think that even though it was hard to understand her ancestor, that part of Draupadi's personality was relatable.

"As her descendant, I've been taught the tools that are supposed to be key as the end of the world approaches," Laila continued. "That could be when my child is alive, or when my great-times-one-hundred-grandchild is here. My responsibility is to have a baby, and to teach it everything I've been taught since birth, and to then record my major life moments in a journal to add to our history."

Karan's eyes widened. "You have to have a *baby*?"

Laila smiled ruefully. "Before my twenty-fifth birthday. But that's not your business. How my legacy intersects with your legacy is what we need to figure out. My aunts are immortal, but they began to age when you and I . . . fought."

His eyes bugged out. "Immortal? What are they, witches? Demons?"

Rakshasi were classified as demons by today's vernacular, but like hell she was going to tell him that. No, she'd keep the identity of her aunts a secret just like she'd always been taught she had to. "They aren't human, even though they look human," she said, vaguely. "They fought in the Kurukshetra War with the Pandavas. After the war, their . . . er, species, was going extinct, so Lord Krishna made a deal with them. If they protected the Daughters of Draupadi for eternity, they'd get to live just as long."

The onion ring slipped from his fingers and landed with a clink against his plate. "They fought in the *Kurukshetra War*?"

"Keep up, Buffy." She snapped her fingers in his face.

"You can't blame me if all of this is hard to believe."

"I don't care what you believe," she replied. "Your arrival has screwed up my life. Now tell me how we're going to fix it."

He pinched the bridge of his nose, wincing when he aggravated the healing bruise. "Look, my life was as normal as it can get . . . for a monster-hunter, anyway. Our legacy was to prolong human existence as much as possible by keeping the evil population down. I've honored my legacy since birth. Now my parents are missing, and the clues led me here."

Laila tapped her fingernails on the table in a quick, rapid beat. "You said your uncle was the one who gave you the information that you needed to find me."

"Uncle Satya and my cousin." Karan nudged the basket toward her, and Laila picked up an onion ring automatically. She took a small bite, feeling the soft crunch of it, but her stomach was starting to twist into knots.

"How did they know where to find me?" she asked.

"The details are a little hazy . . ."

"Hazy?"

"I don't think it's that important to be honest. Look, can I get access to your library to see if there are any references to information that might be familiar to me and my family?"

"Absolutely not," Laila said. Anyone in her library space other than her masis was forbidden. Well, there were no official rules other than the fact that the information was for the Daughters of Draupadi. "Tell me what you want me to look for, and I'll do the research. I already plan on searching for any clues on our tattoo and hand symbols."

She'd nearly forgotten about the markings on her body until she saw Karan reach for another onion ring and the swirl of a letter peeked out from under the sleeve of his T-shirt.

"You have to trust me if we're working together," Karan said.

Laila spotted Ms. Colleen walking down the aisle toward them with two stacked burgers and fries. "I don't think that's going to happen," Laila said. "But since we're born from the same epic myth, maybe our destiny will surprise us. While we eat, tell me everything else you know."

"Haven't I already done that?"

"No," she said even as she smiled at their waitress. "I want your origin story, Karan. I want your childhood, and information about your hunts. I want all the details, down to the flight number you took to the States. There must be something we're missing, and we're running out of time."

12. LAILA

"Will I see you at practice tomorrow?" Karan asked when she pulled into the archery studio parking lot.

Laila twisted in her seat to look at him. "I'll be here. Afterward, let's compare notes on any information we were able to find. Hopefully your uncle tells you something useful."

Karan's jaw clenched; his eyes narrowed. "He's a good guy. He's been a part of my life since I was a kid, and he's been on a ton of hunts with us in the past."

"I believe you think he's a good guy," Laila said. She just wasn't sure if she believed his uncle. How could someone so close to Karan and his family refuse to divulge information about his sources? The secrecy was suspicious.

Karan opened the door and was about to get out when he stopped, then turned to look back at her. The strong lines in his face were shadowed with fatigue and faint bruises. "Are you going to be okay alone tonight?"

No, she thought. *No, I hate being alone. But I have my cat, and I turn on the lights in the house and put my headphones on and listen to music on full blast until I fall asleep.*

"I'll be fine," she said.

He didn't look like he believed her, but he got out of her car anyway. Then he bent down to look through the open door and winked. His boyish grin was so charming that she felt like her brain cells were frying.

"You know, I always thought Draupadi and Karna should've worked together," he said. "The Kurukshetra War could've probably been avoided if she'd chosen him. I guess we'll now have a chance at rewriting our ancestors' story."

Laila snorted. "According to the Mahabharata, Karna was disrespectful to Draupadi and she never forgave him."

"That wasn't the way I remember their relationship," Karan said.

"Then you should read about what happened during the dice game," Laila replied. The infamous dice game where Draupadi's husbands gambled Draupadi away in hopes of winning back their kingdom. The die from that moment were more important than anyone could've ever imagined.

"I prefer my version," Karan said, then with another wink, he shut the door and crossed the empty lot to his car. It was a hot summer night, and in the parking lot lamp she could see the tiny bugs, flecks of white against an inky-black sky, floating toward the light.

He started his car, and with a wave out his driver's-side window, he pulled out of the lot and left. She smiled at that. He'd probably guessed that she'd be pissed off if he waited for her to go first.

She put her car in drive, then parked it again. Laila dropped her head back against the seat rest and closed her eyes. "What am I supposed to do now?" she whispered.

Laila wasn't sure what to make of her meeting with Karan. He had been open with her about his past. He told her as much as he possibly could about asuras and monster-hunting. And when he'd spoken about his parents, Laila could see the worry in his eyes. He was scared for them, scared for where they were or if they were even alive.

A part of her was beginning to soften, because she understood what it was like to want to find the people in her life who were so important to her. Her mother had died in a car accident. The car had caught on fire and Laila was never able to say goodbye.

But just because she sympathized with his position didn't mean that she could trust him.

Her mother's memory had her thoughts drifting to her aunts. She scrubbed her hands over her face as she thought about three shape-shifting rakshasi on a plane. Their magic was limited to shapeshifting and Giri Masi's kitchen magic, so they had to pack their Chanel bags and take first-class tickets to India. By now they should be in the modern state of Gujarat, which meant that she could call them when she got home.

Laila put her car in gear again when the roaring sound of a motorcycle vibrated through her windows. She watched in surprise as a bike turned into the studio parking lot. It was sleek and black, the type that was used for racing instead of leisurely joyriding.

The biker pulled up under the streetlamp, the glow creating a spotlight over his leather-clad jacket covering broad shoulders and fitted jeans tucked into worn black ankle boots.

Was he a tourist in the area? Was he lost? The nearest Finger Lake was fifteen minutes away from the studio.

Laila watched as he unhooked his helmet strap and pulled it straight off his head, revealing a thick cap of black curls. His skin was dark brown, his lips full and his jaw angular. He hooked the helmet on the handlebar of his bike, toed the kickstand forward, then reached into the pocket of his leather jacket to remove a pair of round black eyeglasses. He slipped them up the bridge of his nose, then swung one leg off the bike in a smooth, almost dancer-like motion. Then he turned slowly to face her. He lifted one hand and wiggled his fingers in a wave.

What was this, the invasion of hot Desi men in the Finger Lakes? Laila knew that this person had to be around the same age as Karan. More importantly, he looked at her as if he knew her. As if he had come here to the parking lot of the archery studio at night with every intention of finding her.

She rubbed a thumb over the center of her palm, the same one that had glowed when Karan was in danger. If this person was out to get her, then Karan would be turning around right now. Even though he had tried to murder her when they first met, she knew without a doubt that he believed working together was now the best option for them to figure out what brought them together. He would want to make sure she was alive.

Laila pushed open the door and with her hand still gripped on the handle, she stepped outside and stood. She put her hand over the slim digital watch she always wore and pressed the side button.

“Please tell me you’re not an asura,” she said.

He grinned, his teeth a brilliant white. Then he adjusted his glasses. “No, darling. I’m not an asura.”

The accent. It was as if each word sounded like it was from a different region of the world. South African? Australian?

“Then who are you?”

The man tucked his hands in the back of his dark-wash jeans. His leather jacket parted to reveal a crisp white button-down shirt underneath, which was tucked into his waistband. “Let’s just say that I’m a friend.”

Laila rolled her eyes. “Yeah, I’ve heard that before. Sorry, but I don’t believe you.”

“That’s too bad. I was hoping we could help each other.”

She braced her feet and gripped the car door that separated them. “Okay, *friend*. What’s with the dramatic entrance?”

He motioned to his bike. “Oh, this? You thought that was dramatic, darling? I guess I should be flattered. No, I’ve just come to check on you. To make sure that you were okay after today’s little demon attack.”

Attack.

The asura.

Her heart began to pound hard in her chest, her palms hot and dampening with a nervous sweat. “Friends don’t send friends demons as a hostess gift.”

The man shrugged, his leather jacket settling comfortable over his lean frame. “That wasn’t me, but I can understand why you’d think so. My arrival is a bit suspicious. From what I can gather, it's the universe testing you two now that your destinies have crossed."

Laila didn't respond. There was something about him that made her want to stay, that had her trusting he wouldn't hurt her, but that didn't mean she was going to have a besties heart-to-heart in the middle of the parking lot.

The man shrugged, as if to brush off her reaction, and began to circle his bike. At one point, he squatted to check the rims, his thighs bunching with the movement. He stood again, and turned to face her, his amusement on display in the overhead light.

"Have you figured out the tattoos yet?" he asked casually.

The fact that he knew had Laila's knuckles whitening as she gripped the car door jam. "Please don't tell me you're here because of that, too."

"Unfortunately," he said with a sigh. "Karan and you should've never met, and honestly, I shouldn't be talking to you either."

"Then why are you?"

"Because we're on the same side, and the longer it takes for you to figure out your path, the harder it will be for you to succeed."

"That's ominous."

The humor in his tone faded. "It's true. Your destinies should've never crossed. I don't want things to end before they've just gotten interesting, so I've come with some advice. Trust Karan."

Trust Karan? That was the last thing she expected to hear from a strange Indian apparition in her studio parking lot.

"Why?"

"Because his story may be the answer to some of the mysteries in your own past."

Great. Now she had more questions than she started with. Who was this guy and what did he mean when he said that hers and Karan's destinies should've never crossed? How did he know about the asura?

"Do you know what's happening to my aunts?" she blurted out.

She saw the humor on his face fade, and his jaw tightened. "No," he said. "I'm sorry. I know family is important to you."

"How?" she asked. Then she stepped around the car door so that she could face him. "How do you know that? How do you know me, or Karan, or that our destinies shouldn't have crossed? It sounds like you're the only one with answers right now, and it would be great if you could share some—"

"No," he said.

He'd cut her off so cleanly, so efficiently, that she gaped at him. "*No?* That's it? Just no? This is our lives we're talking about."

The man took his glasses off and squinted as he peered through the lenses for a moment, then he folded them carefully and tucked them back in his breast pocket. He picked up his helmet while simultaneously straddling his bike.

"We all have a role to play," the man said. "I've already done more than I should, more than I was supposed to. You see, I have rules too, and if I break mine, then all of our lives are at risk. Take my advice, darling. Karan is the best lead you have right now."

Before she could approach him, he'd put his helmet back on, kicked up the stand to his bike, revved once, then twice, and zipped out of the parking lot.

Laila heard his bike roar away until she was left in the soft quiet of night in front of the archery studio. She quickly got back in her car and stopped the recording on her watch. She hoped that it was strong enough to pick up his voice. She'd write down what he said and try her best to figure out what he'd meant. Then she'd go and tell Karan. Because if there was one thing she wasn't, it was a fool. She'd heard the man crystal clear. That Karan's past somehow had answers to her own.

Hopefully she'd stay alive long enough to figure out what it was, because at this rate, either she was going to have panic attacks that would kill her, or someone else was going to blow into town that she wouldn't be able to defeat.

13. KARAN

UNKNOWN NUMBER: Hi, it's Laila. I met some guy last night. He mentioned the asura then drove off on a motorcycle. He didn't approach me, or try to hurt me, but he definitely had a message.

KARAN: Are you okay? I know that you said he didn't hurt you, but are you feeling okay after that?

LAILA: Yeah, I'm fine. I'll see you at the studio later.

KARAN: Let me know if you need me to pick you up.

LAILA: I'm not helpless. The minute you think you're stronger than I am is the minute that both of us are at a disadvantage. Stop it, otherwise I will burn you like barbecue.

KARAN: I don't think your fire can work on me but noted.

KARAN: Circumstances have changed. Can you look into anything about Draupadi's daughters?

BOO: Draupadi didn't have any living children after the Kurukshetra War. She was cursed by a rakshasi to watch them all die.

KARAN: Except she created a daughter from blood and fire. It was the same fire that she was created from. That daughter then had a daughter and so on.

BOO: I don't believe you.

KARAN: I'm sending you an encrypted picture. Our asura is a descendant of Draupadi, Boo. The god Krishna himself helped protect Draupadi's lineage by granting her immortal protectors. I think these protectors are witches? Laila wouldn't say. She said that according to her ancestory, Draupadi was considered the impetus for the war, the communicator and negotiator in the way she managed the five demigod Pandava brothers who led the battle against their evil cousins.

BOO: What have you gotten yourself into, cousin? This is way bigger than just hunting asuras.

KARAN: I could use the help.

BOO: I'm on it.

KARAN: Great. I'm going to call Uncle Satya, too, to see what he says.

BOO: I have some advice for you that you may not like. Don't give him all the details. I know that you've known him since you were a baby, but it's really important for you to realize that he is going to have his own agenda and you have yours.

KARAN: Boo, he's like family.

BOO: No, he's wanted to be, but he's human. He has no claim to the legacy that is squarely on your shoulders. Remember that.

Karan stared at his cousin's text as he sat on the side of his bed, on the squeaking mattress in what Laila had dubbed "the murder cabin in the woods." He was trying to stave off the headache that was brewing behind his eyeballs.

Boo wasn't very skilled when it came to reading people. She was a genius, and she had incredible intuition about history, events, patterns in science. But people? In the short number of times that he'd spent in her company, he knew that she struggled with social cues.

Except there was something about the way that she read Uncle Satyapal that had Karan paying attention.

A flash of an image, of a familiar woman with black veins forming from an arrow wound in the center of her chest. Her eyes were rimmed with red.

Satyapal.

"Damn," he hissed and pressed his fingertips to his closed eyelids. There was a sharp pinprick of pain that made it difficult to focus.

It took him a few minutes before he was able to stand from the edge of his bed and retrieve his phone. If he didn't make the call now, then it would be too late in India. He had to get ready to go to the studio. There was an urgency humming in his blood now. He wanted to stay as close to Laila as he could. If there was another asura attack, he wanted to be there.

After tapping the name that appeared just under his parents' number in his favorites list, he pressed the phone to his ear and heard the first shrilling ring that often accompanied an international call.

Uncle Satya picked up on the second ring.

"Beta? Karan? Are you okay?" There was an edge in his voice, a desperation that Karan felt every morning he woke up knowing that he wasn't closer to his parents.

"I'm fine," Karan said softly. "I'm sorry if I worried you. Is this a good time for you to talk, Uncle Satya?"

There was the sound of a crowd in the background, muted and familiar at the same time. "I just finished my last evening class. I am walking into my office now." There was the loud squeak of the office door that Karan remembered hearing every time he'd visited his father and uncle on the school campus.

The sound was a vivid reminder of the life he left behind. He'd train with his father and uncle. He'd eat his mother's cooking as she pushed his hair off his forehead and complained that he needed a haircut like his father. There would be hunts, because there were always hunts. Then he'd go to school at Oxford and spend his nights with friends.

As he looked around his cabin, waiting for his uncle to get settled, he ached for the familiarity of home.

"Now, tell me if you have any news."

"Uncle Satya," he said. Then let out a long sigh.

As if he understood, Uncle Satya released a breath of his own. "I don't know how much longer I can delay the university before they terminate your father's contract," he said softly. "This sudden leave of absence due to a family death is an excuse that can only hold for so long. And there are the bills at home. I went to check on everything yesterday."

"We're close," Karan said. "We just need a little more time."

There was another creak. His uncle was probably leaning back in his faded mint green desk chair that always hit the cinder block wall behind him. "Beta, did you find the asura? Making a sacrifice and presenting it to one of my contacts may be the best way to get the information we need."

Karan's gut churned. "I think I found what you *thought* was an asura."

"'Thought'? What do you mean, 'thought'? Is my information incorrect?"

"Uncle Satya, where did you get your information from?"

There was a long pause. "What are you asking me?" There was the sound of the chair squeaking again, as if he was pushing his chair back.

Just stick with the plan. Don't tell him more than he needs to know. He'll . . . worry.

"I need to know where you got your information about the asura in America. What was said, and who said it."

"Beta." Uncle Satya's tone was almost as if he was comforting a child now instead of a twenty-year-old man. "You know that I have a network that I built with your father. These are people who hunt, just like you. They may not have godly blood, but their passion and purpose is often from experience."

"I know," Karan said. "But I think the information was wrong. I wanted to follow up with the resource myself."

"Oh, is that it?" Uncle Satya said smoothly. "Just tell me and I can coordinate with my contact directly."

"No," Karan said. He swallowed hard, bucking against the knee-jerk reaction that told him he should just defer to his elder, and trust the man who had always been there for him.

Except there was too much at stake to trust anyone without question. There were his dreams, his cousin, and of course, Laila's trust. He had to approach this situation like it was a hunt, and his uncle was a suspicious party, too. "I really would like to talk to them myself."

"No," Uncle Satya said. His voice taking on an impatient tone. "They won't talk to you. They trust me. They are my source."

"Uncle Satya," Karan said smoothly, "I thought we were supposed to share everything. I know Dad shared his resources with you. So have I. What is it about this source, this asura-hunter, that makes you want to deny the trust and the family relationship we have?"

Karan could practically hear the razor edge in his uncle's voice as he grew angrier. "There are certain things I'm not proud of that I have to do in order to get the information we need to complete our job."

In that moment, Karan wasn't sure why his uncle wanted to fight asuras in the first place. He sounded like he was burdened with the task, when this was a choice he made. Why would he put himself in danger or develop relationships with asura-hunters that were dangerous themselves, if this wasn't a calling?

Karan walked over to the window. "The longer it takes to find Mom and Dad, the more chances there are of them being killed. Uncle Satya, please. Be honest with me here. This is *our* family I'm talking about. This is the people that we love."

There was another long breath, another pause. Then his uncle spoke words that were so chilling, Karan shivered from the sound.

"It's necessary to work with dark magic, Karan."

"Satya Uncle, what—"

"Beta, I have done so rarely in the past when we've looked for the most dangerous, the deadliest of monsters, and I didn't hesitate to use it this time to try to find your parents. Demons. Their voices spoke to me and told me what I needed to know. It's like a voice whispering in my ear. And now I hear it in my sleep. It needs its payment. It needs the head of the asura before it tells me the rest."

Dark magic.

Karan knew that occult collectors existed. When he'd tagged along with his father, he'd encountered a few of his own. He'd believed Uncle Satya because the lie sounded so real, so convincing. He wished it was true.

"Uncle Satya, you know that's against the rules!"

"*Your* rules, beta. Your father's rules. But not mine."

Karan began pacing the small space in the bedroom. "Dark magic violates everyone's rules for karma. It requires a sacrifice, and sometimes that sacrifice is your soul. It's *dangerous*."

"There is nothing that forbids me, a regular human, from partaking in dark magic," Uncle Satya said. His voice was calm, coaxing again.

Karan swallowed the lump in his throat. Shit, this was bad. This was beyond bad. He'd read the stories, done his homework. He knew that dark magic had a way of manipulating people's realities until they were no longer the person they used to be.

He froze in the center of the room when he realized the implications of Satya Uncle's words. "Wait, does Dad know?"

"No," he said softly. "No, he doesn't, because he's just as honorable and rule-following as you are. Both of you are loyal like your ancestor. He would've told me not to do it too. He would've warned me just as you're doing now."

"Then why are you doing it?" Karan burst out. A part of Karan hated to think that Satya Uncle wanted to be just as destined as Karan and his father were. Was it jealousy? Greed? Or was he really meddling in dark magic because of a greater purpose?

"Your father is family and I'll do anything for him," Satya Uncle said. "Now tell me. Have you found the asura or not?"

Karan closed his eyes and rubbed at the crease between his brows. "I found something. But like I said, she's not an asura. She's another descendant."

"Of Karna?"

He hesitated.

"Karan!"

He shook his head. He couldn't tell him the whole truth. "No, not really. She's just different."

There was a sharp intake of breath, then a whoosh of air that was tinged with desperation, as if his uncle had been given life-altering news.

"You found her," he whispered reverently. "You found her."

"Found who?"

"The Daughter of Draupadi," he whispered. "I thought the lineage died over ten years ago, but it's alive. You've *found* her."

Karan felt chilled all over again. The desperation was palatable. It frightened Karan. Images from his dreams became more and more vivid in that moment. A rakshasi. His first kill.

She'd said his uncle's name, hadn't she? In that moment, Karan knew that there were more secrets that Satya hadn't shared. There was more darkness within his uncle than he'd let on. He should've trusted his gut, trusted his *cousin*, and kept all the information a secret.

"Draupadi didn't have any children," Karan said smoothly. "Uncle Satya, she's human. There is nothing special about her, and I've done a week's worth of surveillance."

"Then what aren't you telling me?" he demanded.

"My cousin Boo is working on the case," Karan said, hoping that the relaxed tone of his voice sounded convincing to Uncle Satya. "Boo said that there is a chance this . . . person is one of like fifteen different people who could be a part of the Mahabharata family tree in this region. There were so many characters in that epic mythology so it's undoubtedly going to take a long time."

"There's something you're not telling me," Uncle Satyapal replied. There was the sound of the chair crashing against the cinder block wall. "What aren't you telling me, Karan?"

"Nothing! Really, it's no big deal. Listen, Uncle Satya, I have to go—"

"Where are you?" he demanded. Satyapal's voice had taken on a hardened edge that Karan had never heard before.

"What do you mean? You're the one who sent me to America in the first place."

"Tell me your location, Karan. I'm coming to find you. I want to see this Daughter of Draupadi myself."

"I really don't know where she is—"

"You're lying to me!" Satyapal roared.

That was the moment that Karan knew his Uncle Satya was not the man he thought that Satyapal was. That his situation was most likely connected to the dark magic that he was involved in, and he had to protect Laila at all costs. His presence had already cost her the safety of her aunts. He wasn't willing to bring Uncle Satyapal to her door, either.

"I'll call you when I have more information," Karan said evenly.

"I can force you to tell me the truth," Uncle Satyapal said. There was a note in his voice that sounded wrong.

That sounded as demonic as the asuras they hunted.

That's when he knew that Satya Uncle was no longer family he could trust.

"I am telling you the truth," he lied. Before Satyapal could respond, he said, "I thought you were trying to help me find my parents. That's the only thing I care about, and the only reason why we're talking in the first place."

"You have no idea the power that you've come in contact with, you fool," Uncle Satyapal said, his voice changing even more, sending chills down Karan's spine. "Tell me where you are, boy, and tell me now."

"I'll talk to you when you've cooled off, and I have more information," he said. Then he hung up the phone. He had a hollow pit in his stomach.

All he knew was that he had to find Laila. He had to make sure that she was safe. She was his partner in all of this, and he needed to make sure that she was okay. Then he'd do what his father had taught him to do since he was a child: He'd prepare to fight.

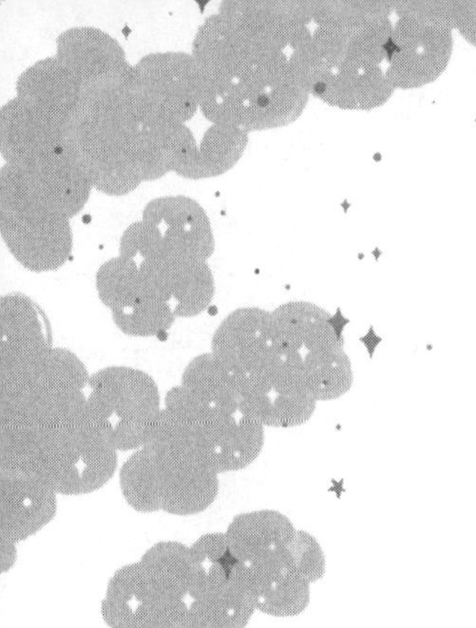

14. LAILA

KARAN: Where are you?

LAILA: Working a double shift today. Then I was going to head to practice. It's a late one so I won't be done until around nine. Why?

KARAN: I had a weird feeling.

LAILA: That sounds like a you problem.

KARAN: Probably. Look, I'm at the studio now but I have to run to Ithaca to do some research. I can meet you after practice. Just in case you need backup.

LAILA: Fine but try not to attract attention.

KARAN: Might be too late for that.

LAILA: What does that mean?

KARAN: I'll tell you about it later.

Five hours later

LAILA: Where are you? Are we meeting here, or am I going home?

Laila stood in the parking lot again, in front of the archery studio. There were a few cars left, but she knew that it would only be a matter of time before that changed too.

A mosquito bit her in the arm, and she scratched at it, ignoring the welt that was forming. It was still hot even though they were on the verge of sliding into fall.

She began to pace, glancing at her phone every few minutes. If Karan didn't text her back in the next five minutes, she was just going to get in her car and go home.

His words had haunted Laila as she finished practice and showered. There was an urgency in his text messages that had her on edge. If Karan had spoken to his uncle, did that mean he'd uncovered some information that could help them figure out what was going on?

No, it was probably safer that they didn't communicate over the phone. Either someone was going to try to find them and hurt them, or Laila would be institutionalized for talking about apparitions. If that happened there wasn't a lot they could do to help his parents and her aunts.

After practice, Laila had rushed through her shower and skincare routine while some of her teammates were still using the locker room. She had no intention of being stuck by herself where she could be caught by another creepy thing that went bump in the night.

But now she was dangerously close to being alone again. Her heart began to pound as the cleaning crew packed up their car and backed out of their parking spot.

Dammit, she hated being alone.

Finally, Ben stepped out of the studio, and with his musical assortment of keys, he locked the front doors. When he turned, Laila saw him squint in her direction.

"Laila? Is your car okay?"

"Everything's fine, Ben," she said. "I'm just waiting for a friend. We're supposed to leave together from here to go to the Skylounge Diner."

Ben ambled down the front stairs. He was surprisingly slow for being a champion archer and coach. Adjusting the strap of his duffel, and then his cap, he approached her until he was only a few feet away.

"I always liked their cheeseburgers. Helen has me on some sort of a diet, so I'm going to have to go home and eat some lean fish or something. We're headed to nationals in a few months and I'm taking her with me."

Laila smiled. "You'll have a good time," she said. "I'm sure of it."

She watched the indecision play out on his face and held her breath. She'd worked with him now for almost five years, and ever since the first time she'd hit all her targets at the same level of speed and accuracy as an adult professional, he'd suggested the same thing.

"You know, you could make it all the way. I don't say that lightly—you really could. And I know your aunts own the winery. You wouldn't even need a sponsorship to compete."

"I like archery," Laila said. It had been the one sport her aunts had permitted, because it was an important part of her training. "I'm really not interested in competition. But it means a lot to me that you think I'm good enough."

"You are," Ben said. Then, as if he was moving before he could second-guess his actions, he reached out and patted her on the shoulder. "If there is ever anything you ever need . . . if you ever need someone to talk to, you come to me, okay?"

She smiled. "Thanks, Ben. Seriously."

"Now I'll wait with you here for your friend to come—"

"Oh no, you don't have to do that," she said. "You know what? I may have mixed up our texts. I think I'm just going to head to the diner and meet them there."

Ben raised a brow at her. "If you're sure. I mean, I can stay if you'd like."

"I'm sure," Laila said. She'd been so cold, so tense since her aunts left for India. It was comforting to know that Ben cared about her even though he didn't know what was happening in her life.

He said goodbye one more time, then got into his car on the other side of the lot. When he sat idling for a few moments, she knew that he wasn't going to go anywhere until she left first. With a sigh, she climbed in behind the wheel and cranked up her latest Spotify playlist before she followed Ben's car out of the lot. He waved over his shoulder and turned right before she turned left.

She still hadn't heard from Karan, but she assumed that he'd gotten caught up in research. It wasn't until she turned onto the back road, the two-lane paved stretch that was nestled between looming trees and darkness, that her phone buzzed on the mount.

When she saw the familiar number, her heart began to pound in her chest. She immediately pulled over to the side of the road and threw her car into park to make sure she didn't lose the call. The interior of her Audi was plunged into darkness.

"Hello?" she shouted into the receiver. "Hello, Vika Masi?"

"Laila!" The sound was faded and hollow. "Laila, are you okay?"

"I'm fine!" The road was desolate at this time of night, which meant she could focus on her phone and not worry about erratic drivers side-swiping her on the shoulder. "Why haven't you called me since you've landed? What's going on? Have you figured out why you're aging?"

"We haven't aged any more than when you saw us last," Vika Masi said. "But something is happening, and we can't come back."

"W-what? What do you mean?"

Vika Masi's voice cut in and out again.

"Hello! Masi? Hello?"

"We can't talk," Vika Masi said. "You're in dang—"

"What? Masi? Hello?"

"Laila? Something's happened. Get back home now—"

"What? What is it?" Her heart began to pound erratically. Her masis were trying to tell her something was wrong, and they couldn't get the call through.

She shouted into the receiver again and again, but it was just her on the side of the road with enormous trees on either side, casting a shadow onto the pavement.

Then the call cut out and she was left in silence.

"Shit," she hissed. Then quickly typed a message into her phone.

LAILA: Where are you? What danger am I in? Are you safe? Come home!

Her heart was pounding so hard in her chest now that she didn't know if she could ever get it under control. Why did her masi call her? Was she trying to warn her about something? And how did she know that Laila was driving? Something was obviously very wrong with this whole situation. Laila twisted her key in the ignition and looked up through the front windshield for the first time since the call came through.

There was a woman standing in front of her car.

Not any woman, but her mother. For a moment, Laila thought that she was imagining her presence because she was so homesick for her family. But this wasn't a dream.

Her mother had the same floral dress she wore the last time Laila remembered seeing her, the day of the accident. There were pink peonies on the dress, and it fit along her slender frame. Her black hair was a riot of curls that framed her face and fell in waves down her back.

There was a trickle of blood under her nose, and her arm looked like it was dislocated.

"Laila?" The voice sounded as clear as if it was coming her passenger seat. The woman switched to Mauritian Creole, and each syllable broke her heart. "My baby, it's me. Your mother. You've gotten so big! How I've missed seeing you."

"This is a dream, this is a dream, this is a dream," she whispered to herself, her fingers clenched tight enough on her steering that her knuckles were bone white.

"Laila? You can come out now," her mother said. Her fingers curled as if calling her closer in that language she'd only heard in her sleep these days.

"I am not getting out of this car."

There was the soft arch of her brow, and the slight tilt of her head. "No? Okay, then I'll just have to come in there with you."

The woman in front of her disappeared from one blink of the eye to the next. She felt the breath on the back of her neck, then looked up in the rearview mirror.

Her mother . . . god, her beautiful, sweet, gentle-hearted mother who loved her for the first eight years of her life, was sitting in her back seat, her eyes black sockets with a red iris as small as a pin prick in the center. She smiled and her mouth was filled with teeth sharpened to a needle point.

"Hello, darling."

"Get out of the car, get out of the car, get out of the car," Laila chanted. She had her seat belt unbuckled and was diving out of the driver's seat before whatever creature was in her mother's form tried to grab her around the neck. She stumbled into the middle of the road, gasping for air.

"Holy shit," she gasped. She watched in horror as her mother appeared in front of her in the blink of an eye. The apparition cocked her head, cracking the bones in her neck before she started walking toward Laila. Her feet were bare, and blood dripped from her fingertips now.

"What are you?" Laila said in English, then in Creole as she stumbled back.

"I'm here because you've summoned us," the creature said. Her mother's voice faded into something that sounded more sinister. Deeper and darker.

"I didn't summon anything!" Laila snapped. Her heart ached at the sight of the familiar face. She wanted to scream at the universe. It wasn't fair, dammit. It wasn't fucking fair. Her palms began to glow, and she held them up like a stop sign, but nothing came out. Nothing worked, not when she was still looking at her mother.

"Mama," she sobbed, tears rolling down her cheeks even as the demon moved with lightning-fast speed now to stand inches from her.

Laila stumbled back and fell to the pavement. The grit and asphalt cut into her hands. She got back up and stumbled again, increasing the space between herself and her mother as much as she could, hating this version of a woman she'd preserved with such care in her mind.

"I will have you, Daughter of Draupadi," it said, and the words sounded deeper, almost as if they were coming from a man.

There was the screech of an engine and the roar of something powerful. Then a single headlight came speeding down the road, and Laila held an arm up to block the light. In her limited vision she saw the apparition shriek, then dissipate as a motorcycle cut straight through it. Her mother's form melted like mist as the motorcycle came to a screeching halt.

"Laila!"

The stranger from the studio parking lot jumped off his bike and kicked the stand into place. He rushed toward her and fell to his knees at her side. He wasn't wearing his helmet or his glasses. His eyes blazed with fury.

"Are you okay?" he said as he cupped her face in his hands. His fingers were cool on her skin, and she felt the hint of calluses. She recognized those calluses. They were the same ones she had on her draw fingers from archery.

"How did you know—"

"I'm here to protect you, and you're not making it easy." He got to his feet, and then hooked his hands under her arms and pulled her up to a standing position.

"Who are you?" she said, shrugging him off. "And how did you know that I'd be here?"

"Gopal," he said. "My name is Gopal, and you need to leave."

Just as he finished talking, there was a whoosh of air, a rustle of wind, and in the light of the single motorcycle headlamp, the apparition formed in front of them again. This time, Laila's mother's teeth were dripping with blood. She opened her mouth and her jaw cracked wide as her head nearly split in half.

"Move!" Gopal shouted, and shoved her toward her car. "Get back to the compound!"

"I'll drink from both of you," the creature screeched.

The apparition dove at Gopal, but he dodged her like a dancer, sliding smoothly out of reach of her claws. Laila's palms began to glow again, and she held them up one last time, in one more effort to kill the being, but nothing came. All she could think about was her mother's face. The mother that she had lost and who she desperately wanted to see again. Just not like this.

"Laila, now!" Gopal roared. Then he reached at his hip, and as if he was pulling a weapon from a sheath, he removed a brilliant glowing dark blue strand of light that formed a sword.

He spun it in a circle over his head and brought it down toward the demon. It dodged the strike, then turned to face Laila. The face changed again, and now it was the beautiful, flawless skin of her mother.

"Save me, Laila. You know it's me! Save me!"

Laila couldn't stand it anymore. She dove into her car again and revved the engine. Without looking back, she slammed on the accelerator and escaped the scene, tires shrieking. She glanced in her rearview mirror once and was only able to see the light of the motorcycle lamp before she disappeared over the hill and into the forest. Her phone buzzed a moment later, Karan's name appearing on the screen.

"H-hello?" Her voice sounded broken and hoarse as if she'd been screaming for hours.

"Where are you?" he said. There was an edge to his voice. A desperation that she'd felt herself moments before.

"Wh-what?"

"The symbol on my palm is lighting up like a Christmas tree," he shouted. She could hear the roar of his car engine in the back, the frantic tone of her voice that was as clipped as her beating heart. "I've called dozens of times and I couldn't get through. You're in trouble. Where are you? I'm going to come and get you now—"

"I'm fine," she said, then let out a deep breath. Her hands were still trembling so hard that she had to focus to keep the steering wheel steady. "I'm fine now. But I just saw my mother, and I watched the demon impersonating her die."

There was a long pause, and she knew that Karan was trying to process what she'd just told him.

"You're okay?"

"Now I am."

"Oh, Laila," he said softly. Then let out a deep breath. "I'm so sorry."

"I'm going home," Laila said. "I'll see you tomorrow. I think tonight's the first night I'm okay with being alone."

"We should talk about what happened."

"I'll make a note and tell you everything later."

"Okay. I have some information too. I'll see you soon."

Then she hung up the phone and settled into the quiet drive back to her masis' house. Her heart was breaking all over again.

15. KARAN

Karan was still thinking about Laila's words as he made his way back to the campground where he was staying. He'd taken a long drive to Ithaca to check the college library resource system. He didn't have the tools or information handy with his laptop and needed a larger network of information to access. He planned on driving straight to the studio to meet Laila, but he'd been stuck behind a tractor.

A tractor. On a two-lane road. Laila could've been killed because he was stuck in tractor traffic in this hellscape of a country.

If he'd been farther away and she'd needed him, then he didn't know what he'd do in that moment. With his Uncle Satyapal's dark magic and desperation, his parents still missing, and her aunts unable to protect her, he'd have to be more watchful.

They were a team, and they had to start working together as a unit.

He turned down the narrow path that led to private cabins along the tree line. He passed RVs, tents, and golf carts of vacationers who were enjoying the last vestiges of summer in the Finger Lakes, completely unaware that there were demigods and demons that haunted the woods.

One of the maintenance men who Karan had gotten to know was standing at the waste station, helping someone hook up their RV. He waved at Karan, who returned the gesture. It was good to know the few people who worked there, because they'd be honest about whether strangers were coming around.

After checking his mirrors and making a slow lap around the entire site, he turned left down a side road that looped around the back to the cabins. He was pretty sure that the road was more for the maintenance crew, but no one had stopped him from using it. After another slow perusal, he pulled into a small bush that he was able to use to cover the front and back plates of his car.

Karan had been careful to make sure no one followed him to and from practice so he didn't have any more run-ins with ghosts. But realistically, he knew that the period of peace would end soon, too.

After getting out and grabbing his duffel bag, he pulled two branches over next to his wheels to use as a security device. He'd know if someone was around if those branches were moved.

He approached the front door of the cabin and froze.

He'd left the small wire trigger covering the dead bolt, and it was now on the floor.

Someone had tried to enter his cabin.

Or someone was in his cabin already.

He carefully put down his duffel bag and crouched so that no one could see him through the small window next to the entrance. There was a back entrance, but he'd shoved the couch in front of it and covered it with debris so it looked like it was part of a wall. The intruder would have to do a lot of work to get through to the woods behind the cabin.

Which meant that all he had to do was bust down the door.

The problem with using bows and arrows as his weapon of choice was that they weren't exactly the most practical to carry around. He had a knife, but that was only good for close-contact combat.

It'll have to do.

He carefully removed it from his bag and stood, standing just off-center from the door. Then, after counting to three, he shoved in his key, and twisted the knob before pushing the door in.

"My goodness. This cabin is so unsecure that a draft opens the door."

The familiar voice had him straightening. "What the hell? Boo?"

He stepped in the doorway and was hit with a shriek so loud that he wouldn't have been surprised someone two states away heard the echo of it.

His sixteen-year-old cousin, wearing two French braids dyed blue and pink, stood at the small makeshift kitchen counter, eating his last Pop-Tart, holding a butter knife at him to his five-inch serrated blade. Her eyes were like golf balls behind thick frames.

"Oh my lord, you scared me!"

"What are you doing here?" he snapped, then quickly stepped inside the cabin and closed the door at his back.

Pop-Tart crumbs littered the chipped linoleum countertop. "What are you doing sneaking around with a knife?"

"It's my cabin!" he shouted. Then took a deep breath. There was a chance that the neighboring campsite would call security or maintenance on him if there was any more yelling.

"Boo, you're supposed to be working in Germany."

She put down the Pop-Tart. "Technically, I was working for an art history think tank that was funded by multiple heads of state." Her accent, a combination of what she had picked up from her childhood in Singapore and formative years at Oxford and in Heidelberg, was a mix of hard consonants and soft vowels.

Karan rubbed his hands over his face. "You can't just try to sneak away from your work. Those projects you're on are government funded. I already have ghosts trying to kill me. I don't need the American, German, and Singaporean governments after me too, thinking that I'm the one who stole their asset."

"Don't forget Russian."

"Boo!"

She rolled her eyes as if *he* was the unreasonable one, then brushed her hands on her jeans, sending crumbs to the floor. "Okay, I admit, sneaking into someone's cabin who has combat training is probably not the smartest thing I could've done, but the lock was pathetic, and I have my own reasons for being here. Can I at least get a hug for trying to surprise you, bhai?"

This was Boo. His bratty cousin. The only other person who knew his entire history, and the one person he'd called right away for help when his parents were taken.

He opened his arms and waited as she crashed against his chest, then wrapped her scrawny limbs around him. She was bony, just the way he remembered the last time they'd met a few years before.

"It's good to see you," he said softly.

"You too," she whispered back.

His heart rate began to slow. "Boo?" he said, holding her shoulders and pulling back so he could look her in the eye. "Why are you in New York? How did you get here?"

Boo wiggled her eyebrows. "I forged a letter from my parents that said there was a family emergency and I had to take a temporary leave of absence from my post to handle it."

"And your think tank just . . . accepted that?"

"It's not a prison, bhai. It's a job. And I've saved more money than most adults have in their lifetime. Money that I've used to buy a ticket, get some fake IDs, and fly from Germany to this place called Rochester. I had two layovers. Thank goodness for business class."

"And no one was suspicious about the sixteen-year-old flying by herself?"

"No, because I had a notarized letter and all the appropriate documents required for a minor to fly unaccompanied."

Karan looked around his cabin. "How did you get from Rochester to here? There is no public transportation available."

"I hired a private car." She answered him as if he was being unreasonable with his questions.

Karan balked. "Do you know how dangerous it is to get into a vehicle with someone who you don't know? Boo, have you lost your mind?"

"I think you've been watching too many true crime shows," Boo said as she crossed the small cabin to pick up her Pop-Tart again. "And I made sure the driver was a woman. Rebecca. She has two kids who are in middle school. Statistically, my chances of being murdered and dropped in a ditch are much less with a woman named Rebecca with two kids."

If this was what it was like having a little sister, then he wanted out. "Boo!"

"I'm just saying." She shrugged, scattering more crumbs along the way. "And I was safe! I had her drop me off at the entrance of the campsite, and I walked here." She motioned to her bags in the corner. Her bookbag was rich black leather with a structured back board that looked like it cost more than his cabin rent for the month. Then there was the hot pink rolling suitcase next to it.

Karan tried to process all this information coming at him. As much as he loved his cousin, her being here in his cabin when there was an active threat would mean that his attention would be fractured from Satyapal to Laila to babysitting Boo. She was a genius, but a sheltered genius. "I really don't have the time to play twenty questions right now. *What are you doing here?*"

Her smile faded, her lips thinning and her chin quivering ever so slightly. "You need my help and you're my family."

"But it's dangerous."

"So is crossing the road," she shot back. "But if you get hurt, then I wouldn't be able to forgive myself." Her lower lip trembled as she braced her fists on her hips.

Karan sighed, and some of his rage diffused. He tried to remember who this was. The first time he met Boo, she'd showed up at his dorm room in Oxford with a suitcase like the one that currently sat in the corner of the living room. She'd been so young and looked so scared. Her family tree led to Karan and that was all the reasoning she needed to pack a bag and meet him in person.

To Boo, family was important. Her parents had neglected her all her life, so when he'd taken her in, she'd instantly attached herself like a barnacle.

Having her close *would* mean that he'd be able to protect her easier than if she was on a different continent.

"I just don't want all these government investors knocking on my door," he said.

Boo shook her head. "I promise you; I was super careful. There is no way anyone could—"

There was a crash as a heavy object was hurled through the small window. Karan dove for Boo, taking her to the floor. Glass shattered at their feet.

"Ouch!" Boo cried out. She immediately struggled to a sitting position and rubbed her arms.

White phosphorus was starting to fill the room. It was a military-grade smoke shell that had been thrown through the window.

"Move!" he shouted.

He gripped his cousin by her elbow, hard, and dragged her to her feet before tugging her in the direction of the bedroom in the back of the cabin. He'd have to go through the hidden door. That would hopefully buy them time to exit by one of the escape routes he'd carved through the brush.

"My bag!" Boo shrieked. As they stumbled past the kitchen, she hooked an arm around her pack and dragged it behind her.

"Help me with the couch," he said as they made it to his room and approached the love seat pushed up against the back door. The smell of acrid smoke bomb began to fill the cabin. He stood on one end and shoved. Boo's added effort was enough to quickly move it aside. He unlatched the door and caught the heavy fall of branches that he'd lined up to cover the exit.

"We're trapped, aren't we," Boo said, her voice sounding slightly hysterical.

"No," he said. "Not yet." With a few quick pushes, he managed to make a pathway into the thick woods. This was why he'd chosen this location. The hidden escape route would buy them just enough time to get out.

Once they were in the brush, the door closed and the branches put back in place to slow down anyone trying to follow them, they dove behind a hedge and began to crawl on their hands and knees. Karan had Boo lead the way so he could cover her back.

There was the sound of leaves crunching. Of hushed conversation. They were coming for them, and they were coming fast. He wanted to pause, to try to catch whatever conversation he could. Their attackers were obviously human, and it didn't seem like they wanted Karan or Boo dead.

When the sound of tree branches snapping became louder, Karan decided that waiting wasn't worth the risk and nudged Boo forward so they could move faster down the path until they reached the maintenance trail that was partially hidden from the front of the house.

"Run!" he said, and hand in hand, they charged through the wooded area on the outskirts of the campsite, until there was only the quiet sounds of the forest and the barely visible waning light of dusk. Boo's heavy breathing cut through the silence.

They didn't stop until they reached a small clearing surrounded by beech trees.

"Oh my god," Boo said, gasping. "Oh my god, you're actually in danger. That was real. Like, I've seen military people, and clips and things like that in movies, but this is *real*. Oh my god, bhai. You took me to the floor, and my knee is killing me, and then there was smoke, and we were running, and I really should work out more, but oh my god."

He didn't want to remind her that it was likely Boo who'd brought the danger to his door since they were dealing with humans and not the supernatural. But Boo was a certified genius and probably knew that already.

"I don't know if they'll have someone waiting at the cabin for us to come back," he said quietly, thinking about all the research he'd hidden in the floorboards over the last few weeks. "My things are there."

"I guess we could go check if you want," Boo said, reluctance in her tone. "They can't still be at your cabin, right? We could—"

Karan cut her off with a quick wave of his hand. "There is no *we*. I'll go check, and you'll stay somewhere safe until I get back."

Even in the dark, he could see her eyes go wide. She gripped the straps of her backpack, which she'd put on halfway down the trail. "No way, bhai. What if they find me? I am not equipped to save myself in a physical altercation. All my superpowers are up here." She tapped her temple. "Even though I come from a far removed, remote branch of the Karna family tree, you're the fighter, not me. I can do other . . . things."

"Okay, then," Karan said, crossing his arms over his chest. "Put your brain to use. Even if I am able to get my things from the cabin, how do you plan on helping us out of this situation?"

She paused, then cocked her head. "I guess I can figure out where we're going to stay?"

"Oh yeah?"

There was a beat of silence before Boo began to smile. "I heard there was an asura that lived around here on some mountaintop. Maybe she'd be interested in taking in roommates."

16. LAILA

Laila pulled into the long driveway in front of her home with only one thought on her mind. Her masis were going to kill her.

No, scratch that. They were going to kill the two people in her car, and then they were going to kill her. Then Boo and Karan were both going to come back from the dead to curse her out for not telling them that she was living with three demons.

"You have a beautiful home," the young girl said from Laila's back seat. "Huge! It looks over thirteen hundred square meters. The privacy is great for resale value."

"Ah, thanks," Laila replied, as she nosed her Audi into the spot next to the front door. "Look, it's not exactly safe for you two, since my aunts—"

"Will cast a spell on us and rip our guts out?"

"Jesus, Boo," Karan said. He covered his face with his hands. "What did we talk about before Laila came to pick us up? We need her to like us, not turn around and dump us on the side of the road."

Boo shrugged. "If that was your plan, then you shouldn't have tried to kill her."

"Your cousin has a point," Laila said.

"I'm making conversation, bhai," Boo added. Her hands were clasped together on her lap, and she took in the scenery outside the windows as if she was on a comfortable drive instead of running for her life straight into danger.

Laila turned off the car and swiveled in her seat to look at the girl. "Just so I have this straight, you are a sixteen-year-old genius who was working an adult job in Germany for an art history think tank funded by multiple governments, some of them not so friendly?"

Boo nodded. "That is correct, yes."

"And because you wanted to help your cousin and for some reasons that are personal, you got some fake IDs, forged a sick note, and hopped on a plane to Rochester, where you got someone to drive you to the campground Karan had told you he was staying?"

"Also correct."

"But because you didn't pay attention to your safety, someone saw that you were traveling to New York and followed you to the murder cabin in the woods."

"That last part is an assumption," Boo said, holding up her hand. She flipped her pink and blue braids over her shoulders. "We don't know if the people after me were from one of those unfriendly government investors."

Laila looked over at Karan, who just shook his head as if to say, *Let it go.*

He didn't have to tell her twice. This night was strange enough as it was. She'd experienced her own attack, and now this?

She turned to face her house. The sleek modern lines of the building, the wide balconies that rarely got any use. The double doors that led to the marble foyer.

It was just a place for her to sleep and train and study without her masis. As much as she hated having strangers in her house, it would be nice not to be alone at night. Just knowing there were other people would help her get more rest.

As long as they weren't really out to kill her. She'd been wrong about Karan once. There was the chance that she could be wrong again, despite the advice from her mysterious knight in shining armor, Gopal.

She closed her eyes and dropped her head against the headrest. "Let's just go."

"Great!" Boo said, then opened her door. She dragged a big backpack behind her that was almost the size of her torso. "Bhai, can you grab my suitcase, please?" Then she was slamming the door shut and walking up the front steps.

"Hey," Karan said, and brushed Laila's arm with a fingertip. "We can stay somewhere else. You don't have to do this."

"Where else would you go?"

"A hotel maybe?"

Laila shook her head. "Karan, the nearest hotel is like forty-five minutes away. And a place with that many exits and entrances is not going to be safe. Not only do you have dudes after you, but there is also the chance you could have a recurring ghost. My house is really the only option for you and your cousin."

Those soft lips curved in a knowing smile. "Even after all I've done, you're worried about me?"

She rolled her eyes. "I saw the state of that murder cabin in the woods when I came to pick you up. It was ransacked. If you die, then so does any last connection I have to figuring out what is going on with my family and why I have a new body tattoo. You're lucky the owner of the campground was so understanding and let you leave."

"Can we please stop calling it a murder cabin in the woods?"

"I call it what it is," she said, holding her hands up in surrender. "And we haven't exactly had any leads since we called a truce. With your cousin here, maybe we'll have a better chance at figuring out why my immortal aunts are aging. Right now, I feel like I can't do anything to help them from here."

His jaw flexed. "And we have to find where my parents are located. There are too many coincidences for the two events not to be tied together."

"Right. That, too." Laila felt a twinge of guilt at forgetting that there were two lives at stake since her sole focus had been on her family. She had to change that.

Her mother would've wanted Laila to save as many people as she possible could.

She shivered at the memory of the version of the sweet woman she saw.

"My Giri Masi blessed the land," she said as she got out of the car. "There are protection charms around the house. We should be safe."

Karan nodded. "We'll get Boo caught up, and hopefully we can—"

"Guys?" The muffled cry from the front of the house interrupted their conversation. "I'm hungry. Can we have pizza? The last time I had it was in Italy when I was keynote at a conference."

Laila couldn't help but smile at that. She ascended the front stairs, cutting through the balmy heat of the late-summer air. "I hate to break it to you, Boo, but you're about to be very disappointed."

"Huh," she said, hip cocked. "That's a shame."

Karan took their suitcases and duffels from the trunk, followed by his bow bag. "Boo, I really need you to behave yourself."

She glared at him as she waited in front of the entrance. "Bhai, like that threat is going to work. Who are you going to call, my parents? They don't even know I left work. Dad is busy on his latest research project and Mom is being Mom."

"Well, behave anyway," he snapped.

Laila had to bite back a smile. Who would've thought that their bickering would help her calm down?

After she stepped aside and let Karan and Boo into the house first, she took time to lock the heavy metal doors as a precaution. She relaxed into its familiar shadows and silence once they were safely inside.

"Whoa," Boo said quietly as she looked at the vaulted ceilings. "It's better than the murder cabin in the woods, but it's also like the rich *Addams Family*."

"Boo!" Karan hissed.

"No, she's right," Laila said, amused. "That sums up my place perfectly. But then again, guardians who have been around for centuries are the ones that designed it."

"This is the best day of my life," Boo said spinning on her heels. "Where can we sleep?"

"Yeah, I guess it is getting late." Laila thought about where to put them, and since the only place that made sense was in her room, she led the way up the stairs into the west wing of the house, down a long corridor to the end.

"One of you will have to sleep on the pull out, and the other will have to use an air mattress in the TV room, okay?"

"TV room?" Karan asked.

She pushed open the French doors to her room and heard the soft intake of breath from Karan and Boo behind her. "This is my place," she said.

There was the large king-size bed next to the window. A vanity bench with her makeup on one side, a walk-in closet with built-ins for her bags and shoes. A smaller closet next to it with her weapons and workout gear. Then through a small corridor was her TV room with a couch, coffee table, and small beverage fridge. Off to the right side was the door to her en suite bathroom. Everything was in soft shades of pinks and creams. There were twinkle lights along the windows, and a bookshelf crammed with romance novels.

"Okay, this is definitely not *Addams Family*," Boo said as she walked further into the room. "Wow, Laila!" She walked straight toward the mini fridge and opened it to inspect its contents.

"I would give you both a guest room to stay in for privacy, but we don't ever have guests," Laila said. "And my aunts' rooms are off-limits even though they aren't here right now."

"This is great," Karan said. He brushed his fingers against the back of her arm, and when Laila turned toward him, she saw the surprise on his expression too as he examined her personal space.

It was strange seeing it through their eyes. To her, this room had simply been home.

There was an irritated meow, and Billi emerged from under the covers.

"A cat!" Boo said with a smile. "So cute."

"You have a cat," Karan said, motioning to Billi. "I guess that's clichéd enough for witches, right?"

She knew he was fishing for information about her aunts. A part of her felt like she should tell him, but this was the first rule she learned as a child. Tell no one. Her safety depended on their anonymity. "I don't think there are any cat myths for South Asians."

"Okay," he said. "Okay, then I guess that's fair." He stretched his hands over his head on a yawn, then rubbed the back of his neck. She couldn't help but track the languid movement of muscle, the T-shirt riding up over his hip and the peek of the tattoo that matched hers.

"Oh, fascinating."

At the sound of Boo's voice, Laila turned to see the girl scramble off the bed and approach Karan, her gaze fixed on his hip.

"What is it?" Karan asked. His hands remained suspended over his head.

"Can you take off your shirt?"

"Good lord, Boo."

"Bhai, just do it. I need to see the tattoo up close."

Karan shot Laila a look that was part exasperated, part heat, as if he knew that she was interested in looking at his body even though the last time they'd touched, really touched, had been right before he attacked her. Then he reached across his shoulder and tugged the shirt over his head.

"Happy?" he said, turning slightly so Boo could see the thin markings that trailed in a diagonal line across his body.

"Not quite," she mused. "Laila, can you remove your shirt, too?"

Laila was anticipating the question, and with a sigh, pulled her T-shirt off over her head. She wasn't shy about her body. She'd always been taught to treat it like a weapon and a haven. Nourish it and train it with equal precision. She had to wonder if Karan admired her form the same way she was interested in his, though.

Laila turned so that her back was facing Boo. Her sports bra had thick straps and a band underneath her breasts, but the tattoo was still visible.

"Now I need you two to hug," Boo said.

"What?" Karan said.

"Absolutely not."

Boo made an irritated, dismissive sound. "Don't be prudes," she said, and her tone was so authoritative, it made Laila think of her Usha Masi. "When you both turned at that moment, it almost looked like your tattoos weren't mirror images of each other but connected."

Laila looked at Karan, whose eyebrows shot up.

"I'll do it if you're okay with it," he finally said.

The thought of hugging him while they weren't fully clothed, especially in front of an audience, made her squeamish enough that it irritated her. "Uh, fine."

Without another thought, she stepped forward and rested her hands on his shoulders. His fell to the curve of her hips.

She could feel the heat of his body, the warm, heavy feel of his hand as it rested on her hips. She smelled the rich musk of his body wash and something that was uniquely him. And then she felt Boo poke her in the hip. She jumped a foot, her nose bumping into Karan's shoulder. She would've stumbled back if he hadn't tightened his hold on her hips.

"What are you doing back there?" Laila said in as modulated a tone of voice as she could manage. She couldn't look at Karan when they were so . . . close. "I've been researching the letters for two days now, and I can't find anything."

"That's because you're not reading it together as a set," Boo said. "It looks like the tattoo links. It's Sanskrit, dating back to three hundred BCE maybe? I'm not sure. I'm going to take pictures of it. If we had a copy of the original Mahabharata text, I have a feeling some of the symbols and letters at that time would help us decipher this."

Laila thought about the library but wasn't sure yet if she should trust them with all her secrets. Maybe there was time for that in the morning. If only she could get in touch with her aunts to ask them what they wanted her to do.

"We don't have a lot of time, Boo," Karan said softly. His words were like a caress across her neck, and she had to bite back a shiver.

"After my conversation with Uncle Satyapal, I know he's going to be coming for us too. And if he's involved in dark magic—"

"*Excuse* me?" Laila said. She pushed away from Karan so she could look him in the eye. The butterflies in her stomach were gone between one word and the next. "What did you just say?"

He glanced at Boo, then back at Laila. "We have a lot to talk about."

Laila picked up her shirt and put it back on. She waved off Boo's protests. "Great. You have dark magic and I have some guy who shows up on a motorcycle with a blue sword."

Karan and Boo gaped at her, and in chorus, shouted, *"What?"*

17. LAILA

Laila couldn't sleep. Not when she had two strangers on makeshift beds in the en suite room. She had pulled the partition wall closed to give herself some privacy and was grateful that the wall existed now even though she thought she'd never use it.

Then there were all the thoughts swirling in her head. Between Karan, Boo, and herself, all they had were questions without answers.

Why was she feeling the fire burning so strongly now?

What did a connected tattoo mean?

Why were her aunts aging, and Karan's parents missing?

What did Satyapal have to do with this?

She tried calling her aunts again before she went to bed, then she tried to meditate down in the temple room next to the library, the small marble enclave that her aunts made her use when she was younger and so angry about the world. It was to center her thoughts, and it almost always worked.

It didn't this time.

The longer she lay diagonal across her mattress, thinking about all the possible doom scenarios, the worse her anxiety about the unknown became. She had to do something.

It was three in the morning when she decided that it was time to get up.

Laila pushed the blanket away, then petted Billi once, feeling the soft purr under her hand before she slipped off the side of the bed. A book slipped to the floor, and she picked up her copy of *The Awakening.*

Laila would be a mother-woman. That was her destiny. But right now, she was going to be the woman Draupadi was, and try to do everything she could to save her family.

She tossed the book on the bed, and ignored the irritated meow from Billi before she grabbed a sweatshirt and shrugged it on. Laila tiptoed out of her bedroom and into the en suite room. In the dark, she saw Karan's sleeping form. He lay sprawled on his stomach, his arms tucked under his pillow. His broad shoulder muscles were clearly defined through the thin fabric of his shirt.

Then there was Boo, the strange but charming cousin that savored the pizza she'd ordered for dinner like it was Michelin star rated. She slept on her back, her arms at her side, and a satin bonnet protecting her brightly dyed hair.

Laila was about to walk past them when she spotted Karan's backpack at the foot of his bed. She'd watched him put his laptop in it earlier that day. Maybe there was something she could do, she thought. It was a huge invasion of privacy, but she was inviting strangers into her home, people she didn't know. Despite Gopal's advice to trust Karan, she had to figure him out for herself. If she could get some assurance that they were who they said they were, then maybe she'd feel better about partnering with them.

After all, Karan had mentioned that monster-hunting was his legacy. What would he do if he found out that her aunts were rakshasi?

Without making a sound, she tiptoed to his sleeping form and quietly picked up his backpack. She spun on her toes, and in a few quick moves, carried it with her out of the room and into the hallway. When she closed her bedroom door behind her with a soft snick, the hallway lights flickered on overhead and cast a warm glow from her room to the stairwell and down to the first floor.

She walked quickly, bag in hand, to the main kitchen, where she placed Karan's backpack on the counter. He'd know that she'd been looking through his things, but that couldn't be helped. Hopefully, she'd discover some sort of clue to his character before he woke up and followed her.

Laila looked over her shoulder, pausing to make sure that no one was coming yet, before she unzipped the big pocket. Rummaging through the bag, she found braces for archery, pocketknives, and car keys. There was a notebook, but most of the information in the pages of the book was written as shorthand markings that she couldn't decipher.

His laptop looked new. He'd used it earlier that day, and she'd followed his finger strokes to memorize his password. It was something Vika Masi had once taught her how to do.

Thank god for training, she thought. She never thought she'd need the skill, but it definitely came in handy.

"Five, four, six, nine, one, seven," she said in a whisper as she tapped the keys.

The screensaver dissolved, revealing Karan's desktop.

"Perfect," she whispered. Then she opened the browser and pulled up his email account, which he'd left logged in.

There were the normal number of spam messages. A few coupons for sneakers. Then there were emails from an official Oxford account. She opened one of the messages.

This email counts as an official acceptance of your temporary leave of absence from Oxford University.

At least he was telling the truth about school.

The fact that he was a college student, that he was able to go away for school and stay in a dorm room and have friends and go to parties, was a painful reminder of how different their lives were. Even though they were connected right now through magic and legacy, through a common enemy, Karan had the choice of going back to the way things were, while she would always have a responsibility to someone and something else.

Shaking her hands, as if that could help her shake off the jealousy, she scrolled through his email box to see if she could find any messages that told her that he was not who he said he was. Then she typed Satyapal's name in the search bar. At least the way she thought his name was spelled. The result came back with zero hits.

Okay, maybe Karan was too smart to email details back and forth with someone who was neck-deep in dark magic.

Laila got up, walked over to the chai machine, and filled it with milk and the masala mixes that she kept in mason jars in the base cabinet drawer. The machine quietly came to life and began to hum. While she waited, she went through his hard drive and searched the folders for documents or traces of information that might tell her that he was lying.

All her searches came up with nothing.

Just as the chai machine beeped softly that it was done brewing, she closed the laptop lid.

"Do you want to check my phone, too?"

She jumped out of her chair and threw the first punch right at Karan's throat before she stopped to register who it was. He caught her fist in one hand and held the other up in surrender.

"Sorry," he said with a soft chuckle. "I didn't mean to scare you." His voice was rough with sleep, his hair tousled and his eyes a soft, dreamy brown that had her heart fluttering with more than just the jump scare.

"You almost gave me a *heart attack*," she said, and stepped back from him.

He glanced at the counter, where she'd been going through his bag and computer, then back at Laila.

Okay, she felt a twinge guilty. "Can you blame me?" she said with a shrug. "I mean, we didn't exactly meet under the best circumstances."

"I don't blame you," he said softly. Then he pulled his phone out of his short pocket and held it out toward her. "Here. The password is the same as my laptop. Feel free to check messages, apps, whatever."

She looked down at the phone, then back at Karan before she took it. "Why are you okay with this?"

"Honestly?" he said, then rubbed the back of his neck. "I would be doing the same thing if I was in your situation. You're letting us into your home, and you're trusting us with your aunts' lives. Just like we're trusting you with my parents' future."

Laila glanced at the phone, up at his face, then down at the phone again before she took it from him. She tapped the screen and immediately went to his messages. She scrolled through the familiar names at the top. There was Boo, someone on his team asking about making plans for food, her messages, and someone back in Oxford checking in with him to see how he's doing. Then she saw Satyapal's name as "Uncle Satya" and opened the text chain. The information was vague, and usually ended with "call me for details."

She scrolled further down into his older messages until she reached the text chain with "Dad." She felt her heart crack when she read the last few messages from Karan. He sounded so desperate. The words were heartbreaking.

Tell me you're okay. I need you in my life, Dad.

She felt those same words herself when it came to her mom and aunts. She knew exactly what he meant.

She closed his messages and handed the phone back. If there was any information that she needed from him to prove that he was worth trusting, she'd just found it.

"I don't feel bad about how long it's taken for me to trust you."

He nodded. "I understand."

She took a step back and motioned to the contents of his bag on the counter. "Is there anything of mine you need to check?"

There was that quick, lightning-fire grin on his gorgeous face that gave her butterflies. "Are you going to hand over your phone?"

"Absolutely not," she said. Her aunts weren't exactly careful with their messages. "How about this? You can ask me anything that's on your mind."

She walked over to the chai machine and retrieved two mugs from overhead as he sat at the counter stool she'd just vacated.

"Okay," he said. He pulled out a stool in front of the counter and sat down. "What are you studying in school?"

Laila almost dropped the mugs. She turned to face him, gaping. "What?"

Karan tilted his head toward the stairwell and leaned on his forearms. His broad shoulders shifted as he settled in. "I saw the textbooks upstairs. Some history, some basic 101 courses. Do you know what you want to specialize in?"

Laila thought about her classes and winced when she remembered that she was a week behind in homework assignments. Then she felt sad at the reminder that it didn't really matter that much anyway.

"I'm taking whatever interests me. My life is different from yours. I can get a degree if I want, but I won't be able to pursue a career beyond what my aunts think is safe."

"Your aunts can't be *that* controlling."

"My aunts' life purpose is my safety. I wore a tracker until I was sixteen because they take their job so seriously. What do you think?"

"Yeah, point taken."

She smiled, enjoying the way he combed his fingers through his hair again. "Right now, I'm really liking my mythos and story class, and my accounting class," she admitted. "Mythos is just interesting, but the accounting credits are for the vineyard and winery."

He cocked his head, and Laila could tell that Karan's brain was working overtime. "Wait, do your immortal aunts really own a winery?"

She grinned and put the first mug under the dispenser spout. "They do. They bought it from a family when we moved here before high school. It basically keeps people from questioning who we are, who I am, things like that."

When the first mug was full, she put the second mug in place.

"Laila?"

"Yeah?"

"Are your aunts involved in any dark magic? Do they hurt innocent people?"

Laila she turned to Karan, her expression masked and firmly in place. She wasn't going to tell him the centuries they spent hunting humans for blood. No one ever died from what she was told, but humans weren't exactly willing participants either. "They've never been involved in dark magic."

"But they've hurt humans," Karan pressed.

"They were in a war, Karan. Before their immortality. Okay, fine, they were in more than one war if you count the fight against the British Raj and an accidental wrong place–wrong time moment in the French Revolution. But they now live like you and me."

Karan raised a brow.

Laila shook her head. "Look, the aunts are sort of like magical vegetarians. They saw *Twilight* and they changed their . . . ah, diet."

"Wait, your aunts are vampires? Are you serious?"

She put a cup of chai in front of him, and then lifted her own cup to her lips. The delicious hot liquid was warm and sweet. When she looked up from her drink, Karan was still staring at her.

"I promise you they're amazing parental figures," she said, then put her own cup down on the counter across from him. "I want to tell you. I mean, we've come so far that I should just tell you the truth. But I can't. I've been told since I was a kid to keep the secret, and it's the one rule that I have promised not to break. It could mean my safety and the safety of my children."

He watched her, the intensity of his stare so potent that she had to cup her hands around her mug to ward off the shiver.

"Okay," he finally said.

"Okay?"

"Yes," he replied. "Okay." Then he took a sip of his chai. His eyes widened, and a steam of curses in Hindi bloomed from his lips. She'd forgotten that was his native language, and the sound of his perfectly accented words were . . . sexy.

"This chai is literally the best I've ever had in my life," he said, switching to English. "Did it really come from a machine?"

Laila nodded. "The recipe is a family one. I drink it all the time."

"And it doesn't keep you up?" he said after taking a long gulp. "We still have a few more hours of darkness left. You can go back to sleep if you want."

There was something about the way that he openly appreciated her chai that was more comforting to her than the beverage.

"I don't think I could sleep if I tried," she said as she rotated the cup in her hand.

"Okay," he said. "Then I'll keep you company."

"You don't have to do that."

"After this chai, I won't sleep either," he said. Karan stood from his chair. "But it's worth it. Come on, let's get some workout clothes. I'm assuming you have a place to train?"

She gaped at him. "Karan, it's three thirty in the morning."

"Yeah?" he said. He chugged the rest of his chai before adding, "If we're fighting some dark magic and asuras, you're going to need to work on hand-to-hand combat. Your punches feel soft."

"My punches are not soft!" Laila propped her fists on her hips. The last time her aunts complained about her punches, she'd managed to put them all down in a sparring match. "Why would you insult me like that after I gave you the best chai in your life?"

"I'm just calling it the way I see it," he said. Then he walked around the counter and put the cup in the sink. He took a moment to use the sponge and soap to wash it, as if he was casually doing dishes in his own home.

He then put the mug in the drying rack, winked in her direction, and turned to stroll out of the kitchen and toward the stairwell.

"Are you coming or not?" he called out. "Unless you're worried about having your ass handed to you again."

She barely suppressed a screech. Then she drained her chai, slammed her mug on the island countertop, and stomped after him.

She thought of the dice game in the Mahabharata, and how the version of the myth from the original texts describes Karna taunting Draupadi when her husbands gambled her life for their kindgom.

Laila really hoped this time her firepower would burn Karan to a crisp because she was quickly learning that he was very much like his ancestor.

18. KARAN

The gym was connected to the main structure by a short tunnel, and after finishing their chai and scarfing down a banana, they walked side by side from the kitchen to the facility. After his initial shock at the size of the space, he led Laila through a quick warmup, they immediately made use of the equipment. They did drills and sparred for almost four hours until their limp bodies were soaked in sweat, and their lungs were working overtime.

When Laila tapped out of their last round, Karan helped her clean the mats before he followed her upstairs. Laila had opted to bathe down the hall in her aunts' wing and let him have her room to wash off.

It felt strange to get ready in such a feminine space. He was used to having his own small washroom at home, and then in boarding school, he'd shared with men. He'd been military neat, the habits drilled into him during boarding school and at university. But even then, the shared stalls and sink stations smelled of cologne and aftershave. Laila's space was a unique mix of jasmine and incense. Then there was the shower, a tiled monstrosity that looked like it belonged in a magazine or in a high-end hotel. There were river rocks in her drain, for god's sake. But after showering in the small tube-like space at his cabin, or in the locker room at the studio, it felt nice to have decent water pressure.

Although it was morning and he'd experienced a caffeine and adrenaline rush with Laila, he decided to lie back on the mattress to rest his eyes and ended up falling asleep to the sound of his cousin's soft snores, with the smell of jasmine perfuming the air.

He'd woken to the movement of the screen separating the rooms. He shifted to see Laila slip through the crack with her duffel bag in hand.

"Where are you going?" he whispered.

She jumped a foot and then made a shushing sound before pointing to Boo. "I am so late for work," she whispered. "Don't go anywhere but the common areas. I'm trusting you two to stick to that rule, otherwise I'm kicking you out. See you later." Her long black braid swung over her shoulder to her butt, and with a wave over her shoulder, she was out the door.

Karan struggled off the air mattress, tripped once over the comforter, twice over the cat, and then hurried to the door. Laila was already running down the stairs by the time he entered the hallway.

"Laila, will you just wait a damn minute? You can't go to work today!" He was very awake now, the sleep clearing from his eyes from one moment to the next as he caught up with her in the kitchen. Every possible bad thing that could happen to her was racing through his head as he thought of all the security checks he still hadn't performed on the house, her car, and her belongings.

She paused in the kitchen, shoving a reusable water bottle under the fridge dispenser. "What are you talking about? Of course I'm going to work."

"If you haven't noticed, there have been not one, but two ghostly attacks."

"Both of them happened when we were alone. I'll be careful. Besides, either you or our mysterious friend *Gopal* will show up."

Karan stepped in her path, then braced himself for a fight when her eyes narrowed on him. "We don't know who he is. He could be as bad as Satyapal."

"If he was as bad as Satyapal, he would've hurt me by now," she said, then nudged past him. "Remember what I said? You can't try to protect me; if you try, you'll just get in my way."

She was almost out the side door that he knew led to the garage when he called out, "Why do you have to go to work anyway? Isn't this more important?"

Laila froze in her tracks. She turned to face him. "Are you saying that I don't think this puzzle we're trying to solve, my aunts' lives, our lives is important to me?"

He winced when he realized how that sounded. "Laila, that's not what I—"

"If we stay holed up in this house," she said evenly, her duffel bag clutched under one arm, "then there is a chance we'll never figure out what we need to do to get our lives back. And if I don't get out into the world and do something normal like point people to where the winery tours begin, or tell people about the sales that we have, or shoot a few arrows with my team after work, then I won't have anything left to fight for."

Normalcy. That's what she was craving. She had so little control over her own life compared to his that he could understand why she was trying to follow her normal schedule. How was he supposed to tell her that he was afraid she'd get hurt if he couldn't back her up?

"Laila." He let out a sigh. "If you want some company for lunch, call me, yeah?"

She finally turned to glance at him over one shoulder. "Really?"

He shrugged. "I can't say it'll be the most romantic date, so I'll most likely have to bring my baby cousin along."

That's when Karan saw a hint of a smile. "If you have to go out, there is a key hook in the garage. You can borrow my Explorer. I rarely use it when the weather is nice, so you may have to fill it with gas. The chai dispenser is set for six cups. It'll stay warm all day. I picked up a grocery order a few nights ago so there should be food in the kitchen. I'll see you tonight."

Then she was slamming the side door shut behind her.

His shoulders slumped the minute he heard the side door. "Well, shit."

He heard the footsteps from the hallway before his cousin spoke. "Good job, bhai. Pissing off our host. What are we going to do if she kicks us out?"

Karan turned to face Boo. Her hair was sticking up at odd angles, and her oversize T-shirt that read *I'm smarter than Einstein* slouched off one shoulder.

"Thank you for that vote of confidence," he said mildly.

Boo yawned, then stretched her arms over her head. "Is there any coffee?"

"Aren't you too young to be drinking coffee? Doesn't it impact your brain development or something at your age?"

"God, I hope so. Being this smart makes everyone else seem boring," Boo said. She walked over to the chai dispenser. After inspecting it from one side to the other, she opened the nearest cabinet and removed a mug. Then she put the cup in place and pressed a button. Chai poured in a quiet stream into her mug.

"Can I get one of those?" he asked.

"If you promise not to piss off Laila again," she said over her shoulder.

"It wasn't intentional," he replied. He sat at the counter just like he had when he found Laila hours earlier. "It makes sense for us to stay here and work."

"No," Boo said. "It makes sense for me to stay here and work. Now that I have an image of your tattoo, I can begin decrypting it."

"We could help and make the whole process faster."

"I work better on my own," Boo replied. She slid a cup across the counter until he caught it in his cupped hands. "Besides, I'm the one with experience in classic languages. I've been working with texts like this since before your voice changed into that deep manly sound."

Was his voice manly?

He cleared his throat. "Fine, I understand if you work better on your own, but there must be something that we can do here."

Boo's eyebrow arched. "Are you really trying to make excuses so you can keep an eye on Laila and me?"

Guilty.

He'd usually have more time to prepare, more time to ensure that everyone would remain safe. That no one who wasn't supposed to die would get themselves killed in the process.

He watched Boo dispense the second cup of chai as if she'd been doing it her whole life.

"I really wish you'd consider going back to your job, love," he said.

Boo shook her head. "You don't get it, bhai. What's the point in being so smart if I can't help family?" She sipped the chai, then made a smacking sound as if savoring the taste. "Yes, this is delicious."

"This isn't a game," Karan insisted. "My parents are already missing. I don't want to put you in that position too." She'd never been on a hunt, never been pressed between a dayan and a cliff face, or a raging river, a cobra and a bhooth before. His duty was to maintain the balance in Kali Yuga. Laila's was to be the negotiator, the linchpin for this world. Boo was the sidekick, and the sidekick inevitably got murdered.

He refused to have more innocent deaths on his hands than he was already responsible for. Even though he wasn't sure why he believed he had caused an innocent being to suffer, the feeling was there.

Boo leaned against the counter, ignorant of his spiraling thoughts. "Bhai, I've never felt like I was welcomed or belonged anywhere. My parents think I'm a freak."

Her confession was like a slap in the face. He shook his head. "They love you, Boo—"

"How do you know? You've never met them."

He quieted. That was true. In the short time that Boo had been in his life, her parents had remained absent. When he realized that she intended to stick around, to be a constant presence in his world, Karan had called her father to find out if he had permission to take Boo home for holidays. There were three in total, and those phone calls were brief and emotionless.

"My employer thinks of me as a necessary evil," Boo continued, her assessment direct. "My friends? I have none, other than the geniuses I meet on the internet, and they still think of me as competition. You are the only person who never wanted anything from me other than to be family. If you're in trouble, this is where I'll be. And besides, you can't do this without me. Like I said, you're too close to the texts. It's my turn to bring a fresh perspective to this."

He sighed. Family was important to him, and he was important to Boo.

With a groan, he stepped around the island and pulled Boo into his arms for a hug. He pressed a quick kiss to the crown of her head, hating that she felt so alone. "You're as stubborn as a younger cousin should be," he said.

"I know," she replied, but she leaned against his chest for a moment, sagging as if in relief. Then she stepped back and pushed one brightly colored braid over her shoulder.

"Now go to practice or whatever it is you have to do. Better yet, find that guy that keeps bumping into Laila. He might have some information for you too. According to Laila, he shows up out of nowhere, and he disappears just as quickly. Maybe if you go to the last spot that she saw him, he'll show himself to you."

It wasn't a bad idea. Gopal hadn't shared much information with Laila that they could use, but if he asked a different set of questions, maybe Karan could get a different set of answers. "I think I will," he said. "From what it sounds like, he might be our best option."

Karan left Laila's house an hour later after he'd made Boo and himself breakfast and ensured that his cousin was set with her research. He also wanted to make sure that she had no plans to do any exploring of the rest of the house. Thankfully, she was occupied with work in no time, and he was able to hop in Laila's Explorer and leave.

Based on the information Laila had shared, he managed to find the stretch of road on the two-lane highway where she'd gotten stuck the night before. It was jarring to see the bit of asphalt that had tire burn marks, a clear sign of the Audi speeding away. He pulled over in front of the marks and looked both ways before he got out of the car.

Karan wasn't ashamed to admit that he felt uneasy about the spot. There was a lingering stench in the air. It was reminded him of the chemical-like burn smell that lingered after a successful hunt. Usually, the smell went away after a short period of time. However, the stronger the asura, the longer the smell stuck around. He'd walked across the highway twice in search of any other signs, grateful for the lack of traffic, when he heard the familiar sound of a motor.

He crossed back to his car to make sure that he gave the driver plenty of room to pass, and saw that it was a motorcycle coming. The man on top matched the description that Laila had given. Dark skin, tall build, and square-cut jaw.

She'd failed to mention that he wasn't exactly an ugly dude.

Karan's shoulders straightened as the driver slowed to a halt behind Karan's car. He flipped the kickstand forward and removed his helmet. "You know, you're just asking for trouble by standing around here," the rider said. He hooked his helmet over one handlebar, then slipped on a pair of black-framed glasses. "You're not even armed."

Karan kept the man in his line of sight as he reached inside the open window of the Explorer and pulled out his sword.

"I guess I was wrong." Gopal swung a leg over the back of his bike and stood with his hands on his hips. "I really hate being summoned like this."

"Summoned?"

He held up a hand and pointed at his palm. "You're not exactly the only one with a mark that burns hot if they're needed."

"How did you—"

Gopal held up a finger. "This stretch of road isn't safe anymore."

Karan looked out at the highway again. Other than the smell, there were no other signs of the asura. "If you know about Laila's history, then you probably know about mine. I know what I'm doing."

"This isn't your normal hunt," Gopal replied, his Australian accent morphed into something that sounded like Karan's own Delhi-based voice. "We can cleanse the ground, we can wash it, whatever you want to call it. But whatever evil Satyapal sends can come back to this very spot. Think of it as a thinning between worlds. It's easier for asuras to get through in this area, and each time they do, they'll arrive stronger and more powerful than before."

The thinning of worlds. Gopal had said that it was Satyapal who caused this, which meant that it could be stopped, too.

"I'm not going until I get some answers," Karan said, as he moved in front of Gopal's bike. "How do you know my uncle is behind this? Do you know what we can do to stop it?"

Gopol looked at Laila's Explorer, then back at his bike. He adjusted the cuffs on the leather jacket he wore despite the humidity that clung to the late-summer air. "I'll tell you what. I'll answer three questions. Just three. If you promise to do one thing for me."

"What's the promise?"

"I can't tell you until you agree to the deal," Gopal said. He held up his hands in feigned innocence. "I swear it's nothing nefarious. It's something that's well within your control. I'm safe to you since I'm human. Well. Sort of."

It was dangerous to agree to something without knowing all the details, especially because Karan still wasn't sure if Gopal was one of the good guys or the bad. But he didn't have any options. He needed answers.

"As long as your promise doesn't involve hurting anyone innocent, then yes," he said, "I agree."

Gopal's smile was quick, and sharp. "There was a reason why my ancestor always liked yours. That loyalty and honor to your destiny is an inherited trait."

Karan folded his arms over his chest. He wasn't going to be distracted by cryptic statements and messages. "Question number one. Who are you?"

Gopal shook his head and made a *tsk*ing sound. "What a waste of a question. You already know my name. I'm Gopal. I'm like you, but I have more of an advisory role in your destiny than a participatory role. I'm supposed to stay out of your path, and frankly, by being here and revealing myself to you, I've already bent the rules."

Karan was desperate to follow up his question with another. If he was like Karan, that meant he was a descendant of some kind. He'd revealed as much when he referred to their ancestors. But what rules was he talking about?

"Ticktock," Gopal said. He motioned to the road. "The longer we wait, the more dangerous our surroundings become."

"Question number two," Karan said. He paused, trying to make sure that he had the right words so he'd get the response he wanted. "Where are my parents?"

"They're somewhere safe," Gopal said, his voice soft. "They're doing fine, Karan. Right now, they are out of harm's way."

Karan braced his hands on his knees and let out a whoosh of air in relief. He'd been so wound up, so tight with worry, his entire body ached when he was finally able to take a deep breath. His lungs burned as he replayed Gopal's words in his head. His parents were alive, and safe. That would have to do for now. As long as he knew that he had a chance at seeing them again.

"One more question," Gopal said. "Time's ticking."

Karan stood to his full height. He was so desperate to ask where he could find his parents. Instead, he focused on Laila.

"Why do Laila and I have a matching tattoo?"

Gopal tilted his head to the side as if contemplating his response. Then he said, "You two were never supposed to meet."

"Yeah, we figured that part out."

"The thing is, if Kali Yuga is to eventually come to an end, the descendants of the great warriors from the Mahabharata have to fight to save the innocent. If they're going to win . . . shouldn't they follow their own path?"

"I'm not sure I understand," Karan said. His whole life he was told he had to accept the fate, accept the destiny that was decided for him. That was what Karna's descendants were all charged to do.

Gopal motioned to the highway, as if the asura attack could explain everything. "In the Mahabharata, the Pandavas won the Kurukshetra War by the skin of their teeth. If there will be another war for the fate of the universe . . . let's just say that if we have to fight, we should be doing things differently. That means that two descendants who are never supposed to meet should join forces."

"It sounds like you think that my coming here is a good thing," Karan said.

"It should be since I'm the one who brought you here." Gopal shoved his hands in his pockets. "I'm sorry about putting you two together in a difficult situation, but you seem to be handling things okay."

Karan gaped at him. "Wait, you're the reason why we're in this mess in the first place?"

Gopal didn't answer the question. Instead, he took his glasses off and tucked them back in his pocket. Then he refastened his helmet. "Now you have to do something for me. Prepare for Satyapal's arrival."

Karan felt like he had whiplash. One minute he wanted to deck Gopal, and the next he was stunned by the words coming out of his mouth. "Satyapal doesn't know where I am."

Gopal straddled his bike. "You made a promise, and it's your responsibility to complete it," he said. "I'll give you until the new moon. Three weeks."

Karan stepped in front of the bike with his arms crossed. "Is that all we're supposed to do? Wait for Satyapal? Why do I feel like this is just a game you're playing with us?"

Gopal's eyes flashed with fire. "Don't be a fool, Karan. By now you should be able to know when you're fighting good or evil."

Gopal revved the bike. He raised his voice over the sound of the powerful hum of the motor. "The only way to fight Satyapal is to meet him where Laila feels the most powerful. Your time is up, Karan."

Then he lurched forward, but Karan was prepared for it. He stood his ground, even though the front wheel of the bike came millimeters from grazing his knee.

Behind the dark tint of the helmet's visor, he saw the gleam in Gopal's eye. Then he was backing up his bike and making a sharp turn in the middle of the road. He was gone a moment later.

Karan didn't waste any time. He hopped in Laila's car and put the winery's location into his phone. He knew that she was working, but he needed to see her, needed to make sure that she was okay. They hadn't known each other that long, but there was something about seeing Gopal that made him think there was another attack on the horizon and that Laila was the target.

19. KARAN

"Thank you so much for visiting us," Laila said.

"Thanks, we had such a great time," the blond woman replied. She was beginning to slur, which was the typical state of the last bachelorette party group of the day. Usually, Divine Winery got the tail end of the tour groups, and at six p.m. everyone was hammered. The good thing was that the tour buses ran on a regular schedule, and this twenty-something with a sash that read *Ms. to Mrs.* would get back to her bed-and-breakfast safely, and with a whole lot of wine bottles to commemorate her trip.

"We're happy to hear that," Laila replied, and handed over her receipt and gift bag with a T-shirt and magnet. "Congratulations again."

There was a round of cheering from her friends who stood by the door, and when the group of women were finally gone and the tour bus pulled out of the gravel lot in front of the winery information center, Laila locked the glass doors. She leaned back against them, and turned to Denise, who was folding T-shirts in the merchandise section.

"Alone at last."

"I can't believe we still have so many people coming through the winery," Denise replied. "Aren't we supposed to be winding down for the season?"

"You'd think so, right?" Laila said. "Last year we had a rush in the fall because the weather was so nice. Maybe we should expect the same this year."

That was if she lived through the year.

Brenda poked her head out from the large opening in the back of the information center. "The tasting room is all cleaned up. I was told to ask you girls to finish inventory and lock the doors when you leave. Everyone else is gone from out back. Laila, Lucy asked if you could put the money pouch in the drawer in her office. You should know the key."

"Thanks, Brenda. Will do."

"Thanks, Brenda," Denise called out. She turned to Laila, her dark brown hair swinging in an arc. "I'm going to finish cataloging the inventory in the back. Are you okay closing out both registers?"

Laila thought about her promise to Karan. She'd be careful not to be alone. With Denise in the back room, she technically wasn't alone, right? "Yeah, absolutely," she said. "Hey, do you need a ride to practice after this?"

Her smile was wide and infectious. "I thought you'd never ask! As a treat, I can get you a burger on the way?"

"I'd never turn down a burger," Laila said with a smile.

"Great," she said, and clasped her hands together. "Thank you, Laila. Really. I'll call my boyfriend and let him know that he doesn't need to swing by."

When Denise had left for the back room, Laila let out a sigh of relief. A part of her had dreaded driving down the single-lane highway that cut through the mountains toward the studio, and she hoped that with Denise by her side, she wouldn't run into any other apparitions of her mother. That the demon sightings were just for her and Karan.

Laila began to busy herself with closing out the registers. Rarely did people use cash anymore, but there was still enough from merchandise sales that they had to go through a process. She loved the tactile aspect of working with cash. It felt real, and it helped her get out of her head when all day her mind kept wandering to her masis.

She missed them so much, but what she'd said to Karan that morning was true. She needed to continue to operate as if everything was okay. Because she refused to hide. She refused to fear what came for her. Her aunts taught her never to stand down from a fight.

Then there was the fire. She knew that none of her ancestors had ever had to suppress some serious rage-flames. For Laila, the fire that was an ever-constant presence in her was beginning to burn hotter, and she was afraid that if she didn't keep moving, she would combust.

Laila finished zeroing out the till and put the cash in the pouch for a bank deposit. She was about to run to the back office where she'd leave it in her manager's drawer when there was a knock on the glass door.

She went to motion to whoever it was that they were closed, but through the glass she saw that it was Karan standing there. In his jeans and fitted shirt, he looked like he'd fit right in with the bougie winery patrons, the guests on vacation that came in with a beautiful partner on their arm.

She rounded the desk, keys in hand, and unlocked the glass door to let him in.

"What are you doing here?"

His shoulders relaxed, as if just seeing her was validation that whatever worried him wasn't coming to fruition. "I just had an interesting run-in with your friend Gopal. I came to check on you because something about the moment made me think that you could be in trouble."

She gaped at him. "Did your hand burn or—"

"No," he said. "No, maybe I was just nervous or something."

"How did you see Gopal, then? Did something happen to you?" Her voice sounded reedy to her ears. He'd been worried about her this morning, but she'd never thought that he would put himself in danger.

Just like a man.

"No," he said slowly. "But there is a lot of information we should talk about."

She nodded and knew that it was probably a good idea to skip practice. She'd drop off Denise and then head home. It was one thing to want to live her life, to be out in the world and stop cowering, but it was another to be the fool in a horror movie who insisted on running into a dangerous situation when the signs were clearly there.

"Can you give me a hint at what's going on so I don't have to wait?"

"My parents are safe," he said in a rush. "Gopal said that my parents are safe, and he sounded very convincing of that fact."

"That's a good thing, right?"

Karan smiled with that easy slow curve of his lips that made him look young and carefree. "It's a great thing."

"Did Gopal say anything about my aunts?"

Karan's smile faded. "I'm sorry, he didn't. I should've asked."

Laila swallowed the lump in her throat. "It's okay," she said. "I mean, at least I got to hear their voice *once*. Now you have confirmation too."

He reached out and ran his thumb gently over the curve of her cheekbone. "We'll find them. Don't worry."

I really hope so, she thought.

Karan looked around the information center, the wide opening in the back that led to the tasting room, and then over his shoulder at the parking lot out front. There were only her cars left—the Audi she drove, and the Explorer that he'd borrowed from the garage.

"Why don't we go back to the house and we can talk some more?"

"I have to drop Denise off first," Laila said. "She's finishing up the inventory report for the day."

Just as Laila finished her sentence, there was a loud crash that came from the back of the building.

Both Laila and Karan bolted toward the sound. Laila ran first, making a left through the tasting room with Karan hot on her heels. They rounded the corner, down a hallway, past the stairs that led to the basement and the wine cellar to the stockroom where they kept the merchandise for the information center.

"Denise!" Laila called out. She expected to see her friend and co-worker. Maybe the sound was just a box dropping or a chair falling over.

It had to be. It had to be.

When they reached the doorway, Laila's hand burned red hot, and the symbol that had imprinted on it glowed. She looked from her hand to Karan, who held up his palm. Then she turned to the figure standing in the stockroom.

Denise stood between rows of shelves with her head cocked at a ninety-degree angle. The lightbulb overhead had burst and cast the room in dark shadows except for a few sparks from the exposed electrical. As if Denise had yanked the whole light fixture out of the ceiling.

Her eyeballs were black, and blood dripped in a steady stream from her nose.

She spoke an indiscernible language that chilled Laila to her bones, filled with *p* and *s* sounds that made her skin crawl.

"Karan?" Laila said, her voice pitchy. "What's happening to my friend?"

"Possession," he said, grimly. "Could be a ghost, could be a pisacha. With this kind of control and the black eyes, pisacha is my guess. They have their own language, which is why it sounds like nothing we've heard before."

"Have you ever—"

"Nope." His voice was almost singsong in tune. "They were technically supposed to have gone extinct after the Kurukshetra War."

"How do we—"

"No idea."

"Then I guess we better—"

"Run."

They began to back away from the doorway in tandem. Karan had gripped her arm to push her toward the hallway, but Laila hesitated. There was Denise in that body. There was her friend, her teammate, and the person she worked with. There was the funny, sweet girl who was the only person who shared a life like hers until she went off to college.

"Wait, we can't just leave her like this."

"You must die," the creature said in a twisted version of Denise's voice.

Then it lunged across the room and between one blink of an eye and the next, the being that had possessed her friend wrapped its hands around Laila's neck and slammed her into the far wall with enough force to crack the drywall.

Laila gasped for air, feeling the indescribable pain of the hold, of her airways closing, as she gripped Denise's hands. They were impossibly strong, stronger than her masis had ever prepared her for.

Karan came up from behind her, wrapped an arm around Denise's neck, and pulled back, but Denise wouldn't budge. The pisacha that controlled Denise's body didn't feel any hit, any pain.

Laila shoved hard and was able to swallow a gulp of air. "Karan!" she croaked. She was starting to see spots at the corners of her eyes. Even as she squeezed a knee between her body and Denise's to push back, the pisacha continued to apply pressure around Laila's neck.

And those eyes, those eerie, soulless black eyes stayed focused on Laila's face.

The grayness at the edge of her vision was beginning to spread, and her grip on Denise's hands were starting to slip. She felt her body going limp, her brain clouding even as she heard Karan's voice, a faint shout in the distance.

"Don't you dare lose your shit now, Laila!"

She vaguely made out his form behind Denise's body as he swung a large wine bottle over her head and crashed it against her skull. Denise's neck cracked, and the sound of bone crunching echoed through the room as her head bent sideways until her ear touched her shoulder. There was blood gushing like a geyser from a wound at Denise's neck.

Then the pisacha spoke again, first in that hissing language, and then again in Denise's twisted voice. "I'll find your precious protectors. Then I'll kill them and everyone you know. There will be no mercy. There will be nothing left. We will win the war."

Laila had almost nothing left thanks to her legacy. She was a vessel to the gods, a mother-woman whose family was taken from her. This was the only part of her life that she had claimed for herself, this friendship that she had protected, and it was being ripped away from her too.

The anger burned inside her, and with what little consciousness she had left, she pressed her palms against her friend's chest.

"I'm so sorry, Denise," she gasped, and the fire burned through her friend's body.

The pisacha shrieked, and its grip loosened enough for Laila to take a gasping breath. Laila let the burn inside her intensify until it poured out of her. The pisacha continued to scream, the sound morphing into Denise's voice before fading into a demonic undertone until the only sound left was the crackle of burning flesh.

Then the fire stopped, and Laila was curled on the floor sitting next to the charred dead body with licking flames eating away at what was left of her teammate and friend. She continued to gasp for air, fighting to breathe through the soreness in her throat as the reality of what she'd done began to set in. She'd killed an innocent person.

Karan found a sheet from somewhere, a moving blanket, and dropped it on top of Denise. He patted her remains until the remaining fire extinguished. In the back of her mind, Laila realized that he was able to touch the flames without getting burned.

She felt tears on her cheeks as she continued to suck in deep breaths. The trembling began seconds later.

"Get up," Karan said quietly.

She didn't move.

"Laila, get up," Karan snapped. Then he stepped over Denise, hooked his arms under Laila's, and pulled her to her feet. He then propped her against the wall, his hands cupping her face, so similar to the way Gopal had done it when she'd been with the asura that looked like her mother.

"Laila, look at me."

She shook her head, her eyes hazy with tears.

"Listen, you need to be strong right now," he said, his voice hard. "Are there cameras back here?"

She didn't understand what he was saying at first. Denise was dead. Denise was dead, and she'd been responsible. This was her only friend left. Everyone else had gone to college, and this was the one person who was part of her life that didn't involve legacies and having children and living for the gods.

"Laila!" Karan's voice was a roar now. "Are there fucking cameras in this room?"

"N-no," she said, her thoughts clearing enough to respond. Her voice was hoarse, and it hurt to speak, but she managed to qualify her response. "Tasting room, office, and front store. One outside. Not back here."

"Laila," Karan said, his voice even now. "I need you to be strong," he said. "We have to get rid of the body and delete the footage from the security cameras."

"D-Denise," she managed. "Her name was Denise."

"We have to cremate Denise's body. With rites. It's the only way to ensure she has a proper afterlife, okay?"

Laila tried to push past the shock, even as her fingers trembled and tightened into fists. "They'll think it's me," she said, hoarsely. "I'll be to blame. It's only us two working right now."

Karan pushed her hair back off her face that had come free from her braid. His fingers brushed against the sore spot on her neck, and she winced. Swallowing was difficult.

"We're going to have to burn the place down," he said quietly.

"W-what? No! Karan, are you—"

"Listen to me," he said, his lips pressed in a thin line. "We have no choice. We burn the place down. We leave so we can wash up, clean off the blood. We figure out what to do to hide your bruises on your neck. The cops will come. Before we go, we'll delete the footage."

"I won't do it," she croaked. "This is my *future*, Karan. This is the only thing I'll have!"

His grip on her arms intensified. "You won't have any future at all if you aren't alive, Laila. Come on, think for two seconds. Think how this is going to play out!"

Through the intense waves of shock, Laila understood that he was right. She knew that if she ended up in jail, she'd be a sitting duck, and there would be no way to save her aunts. She looked at the body under the sheet, and sobbed, one painful, deep heart-wrenching sob.

Karan led her toward the office in the back and pushed her into her manager's chair. And because she knew that she had no choice, she compartmentalized her grief in that moment as best as she could.

Laila knew the information for the security program they used, and how to log into the security system for the cameras. Even though Lucy handled all the details, her aunts wanted her to have complete access and control. She was grateful for it now as she worked quickly to delete all the backup footage for the last month.

Karan found Denise's phone and used the one uncharred thumb to unlock it. After a quick cursory overview of the text chain, he texted Denise's boyfriend that she needed a ride after all because Laila wasn't feeling well and had to go home.

Laila swallowed her nausea as she helped Karan as she performed a basic religious rites ceremony over Denise's body. Her palms began to glow, and fire licked at her fingertips as she tried to process what she'd done. Because of her, Denise was dead.

"Perfect timing," Karan said softly as they stepped into the hallway one last time.

Laila let out a sob, and then, holding her palms out, shot flames from her hands that spread over the walls like water. She pointed at the back office, the ceiling, the stockroom. It burst from her body like a release of energy. And then she was done. Her skin was slick with sweat, and the overhead sprinklers went off. The alarms blared from the tasting room and the front of the store. Black smoke billowed at the ceiling and spread like a storm cloud in fast-forward.

She knew Karan was worried about her, but she was strong enough to get into her car as he got into the Explorer. They raced out of the parking lot just as the windows burst in the building. With her heart pounding, they made it back to the house.

Karan helped her strip down to her underwear, and then guided her into the shower and left, closing the door behind him as she scrubbed frantically at her hair to get the soot out of her skin, from her nails. Giri Masi had made her shampoo that immediately dissolved the stench and grit and had her smelling like rose and jasmine again. She had never thanked her Giri Masi for her kitchen magic, and the salves and creams she made. It may save her life now, she thought.

Her cell phone was ringing when she got out of the shower, and she saw that it was Lucy. Karan held it out for her to answer, and clearing her throat, swallowing past the ache of her bruised vocal cords, she picked up.

"Hello?"

"Oh, thank god," Lucy said, gasping. "Laila, there has been a fire. Where are you? Are you okay?"

"Yeah, I'm fine," Laila said. "Did you say 'fire'?"

"Yes, the winery is in flames." There were sounds of sirens and beeping in the background, and Laila knew that the manager was at the location now.

Laila ensured that her voice sounded as close to normal as possible, none of the hoarse huskiness from before, none of the heartbreak. "I wasn't feeling great, so I left after I put the change purse in your office. Denise was at the winery, Lucy. I left at the end of my shift, and she stayed behind. She said she'd ask her boyfriend for a ride."

There was a long pause. "I don't know if I can get in touch with your aunts right now. Do you think you can ask them to call me?"

Laila cleared her throat. "They're on a religious pilgrimage. They won't be back for weeks, and they don't have internet access where they are. I'm coming down there. I can help you if you need me. How bad is it? Do you know what caused it? I mean we have sprinklers, right, so hopefully the damage is minimal."

There was another long pause. "Try to get ahold of your aunts for me. I know you're not feeling well, but you may have to come down and speak to the fire chief."

With one half-hearted goodbye and a promise to come to the winery shortly, Laila hung up the phone. Then she went down to the medicine pantry, where she smeared Giri Masi's cream on her neck to hide the bruises.

Laila used Vika Masi's car to go back to the scene, which was now crawling with cops and fire trucks. She was interrogated, and because she didn't have a trace of smoke or soot on her, she was let go. She held Lucy's hand and cried when Denise was declared missing.

And when she came back home at two in the morning, she crawled into bed and slept.

20. KARAN

"Is she doing okay?" Boo asked quietly.

They both stood in the kitchen in the same spots they had been in the morning before.

"I think she's in as good of space as can be expected," Karan replied. She'd watched her friend die. He couldn't imagine what that had been like for her. Although he'd had an idea of what she needed when it came to handling the adrenaline aftershocks from a hunt, this was personal. He'd never had anything so personal happen in his life before until his parents' disappearance. Karan wasn't sure how close Laila was to Denise, but he'd gathered that they'd known each other during high school.

She didn't talk when she got back from the winery. Her voice was still hoarse and the bruising around her neck was starting to show again through the cream that she'd applied before she'd left. She'd gone back in the smaller kitchen space that was hidden behind the larger industrial-size kitchen and returned with a jar of a mud-like paste that she'd applied in silence. Then she'd gone up to bed and closed the screen between her room and the en suite space.

After Boo had gone to sleep, he'd lain awake and heard the soft sounds of Laila's crying. He wanted to go to her but knew that she needed some time. His heart wrenched as he stayed awake, just in case she needed him, until the early hours of the morning.

Then when Boo woke, he'd gotten up, groggy and exhausted, and followed her downstairs.

He'd been a fool, he thought now as he sipped his chai. He'd been ridiculous not to prepare for casualties. Wars always had innocents that were caught in the crossfires.

"They were just supposed to come for us," he finally said into the silence.

"Says who?" Boo replied with a snort. She stood in an oversize T-shirt again with some sort of a mathematical equation on it, her pants so long that they pooled at her ankles. "There were always good people dying in our mythology, bhai. Denise is an unfortunate casualty, but you should expect more of this to happen until we figure out what's going on and put an end to it. That's why we're racing to find out what we can do to stop the demon sightings, or whatever it is that's happening."

"Yeah, I was afraid you'd say that."

Boo crossed to his side, then in a move so tender and unexpected, she wrapped an arm around his back and rested her head on his shoulder. "She's stronger than the fire that burns in her blood, bhai. And if she's anything like the Draupadi we know from stories, she has a vengeance streak a mile wide. Laila will be ready to kick some ass in no time."

"I hope so," he said quietly.

Then he twisted so he could wrap Boo in a hug.

"I'll keep you safe," she said fiercely.

He smiled against her temple. He didn't doubt that someone as strong as Boo wouldn't try to do just that. "That's my line."

"We'll keep each other safe, then," she said, then pulled back to look up at him. "Because we're family."

"We're family," he repeated. Karan patted Boo's hand, then drained his cup. "I'm going to go check on her," he said. He put the cup back in the dishwasher next to the sink, marveling that Laila's magical aunts wouldn't have a more efficient way to do dishes, before he headed up the wide grand-entrance staircase to the second level.

He stepped in the doorway of Laila's room and saw that the screen was still pulled between the bedroom area and the large living space that he and Boo had taken over.

Karan pushed the screen aside enough to peek through.

"Laila?" he called softly.

He saw her shift under the blanket, but she didn't respond. He pushed the screen open just enough to step inside, then closed it again.

Karan knew that she'd kick him out if she didn't want him in her space, but he also knew that she was too proud to ask him for comfort.

He thought about calling her name again, about asking her if she wanted something to eat or if she needed his help. Then he simply crossed to the other side of the bed on cold hardwood floors. He eyed the cat curled up on a throw next to her feet and decided that he'd chance her claws before he lifted the comforter and slid under the blankets.

Karan scooted across the king-size mattress until he could feel the warmth of her body against his. He tucked one arm under her pillow and wrapped the other over her waist. He shifted her braid between them and held her close.

Laila stiffened, but she didn't move away. She also didn't say a word as her lashes fluttered in a crescent moon shape against her cheek, and she relaxed degree by incremental degree until she was leaning back against him.

Karan was content to be there, to just hold her like that for as long as she wanted. He'd begun to think of her as a partner. He pressed his stubbled chin against the exposed tattoo that began at her shoulder. As her partner, he wished he could take away some of her pain. He'd wished that when they'd met, he'd known all the soft, vulnerable parts of her so that he didn't waste any time fighting her.

It wasn't too long before she spoke.

"Usually, I get a date before I invite someone into my bed."

He bit back a chuckle. "I'll owe you one."

They slipped into silence for a long time, lying side by side, barely an inch separating their bodies.

"I should have listened to you," she said finally. "Being around people is dangerous. I was so stupid to think that I'd be safe, but the attack happened anyway, and now Denise is gone."

"This wasn't your fault," he whispered. "I thought the same thing. That this fight, or whatever it is that's coming for us, it's ours and no one would get hurt. But, Laila, this was the pisacha's fault. It was whatever is doing this to us."

He pressed a kiss behind her ear because he knew that either she needed it, or he did. When had she become someone that he cared about? In such a short amount of time, Laila's feelings, her well-being became one of his priorities, and he had no idea how it happened.

"I should've stayed home," Laila said, interrupting his train of thought.

Karan squeezed her once as if to tell her to stop. "If you would've known, then you wouldn't have gone. But neither of us could have predicted that this pisacha would find you, would appear through a thinning between dimensions and time."

"Is that how it happened?" she asked.

Karan sighed. "I think so."

They were quiet again for a long minute. Laila shifted against him, her body warm and relaxed in his arms. "Denise was always so nice to me," she whispered. "When I started at the high school, I had an accent from growing up in Mauritius. She was the first person who really made me feel welcome."

"Were you close?"

"Not really," Laila admitted. "I can't really get close to anyone. No sleepovers, or vacations. I knew back then I couldn't go away to college. It wasn't safe for me or for my masis. My life would be here in these mountains hidden in the house between the trees. That didn't stop Denise from trying, though. She always asked about sleepovers or spending time with me, no matter what."

"It sounds like she was really great."

"Great" is really all you can come up with right now, Karan? Really?

Laila didn't seem to mind. She tilted her head back until the crown of her head was tucked under his chin. "Have you ever lost someone?"

"No," he said. "Well, my grandparents, but that happened when I was a baby."

She hummed, her voice sounding stronger now since the bruises had faded to only the barest hint of yellow around her neck.

"I lost my mother," she said. "Car accident. But I told you that already. I had four aunts who took me in. I was closest to my Usha Masi. She was so strong and comforting. When she held me, I knew that everything was going to be okay. We were living in . . . it doesn't matter. She was killed when she was out for a . . . run."

His gut churned at the thought that she had two losses in her very short life. And now there was Denise.

"I'm so sorry, Laila."

"Me too," she whispered. Then she shifted and turned in his arms. He could do nothing more than pull her close and smell the jasmine and rose incense in her hair. Their chests were pressed together, their foreheads resting against each other, their breathing falling in sync as she grieved.

"Did you know that Denise was going to go to college?"

"No, I didn't."

"She had plans," Laila continued softly. Karan closed his eyes and began rubbing in her back in smooth circles as she told him about the woman who'd died in the winery. "Denise couldn't afford it this semester, but she was going. She had a boyfriend who loved her but had no sense of time, so I usually drove her to practice."

Laila's voice cracked. "If her boyfriend was there, then she would've gone and she would've gotten away."

He heard her voice crack, and his heart clenched painfully at the sound. "Laila," he said, his voice gruff.

She tilted her face a fraction closer, and because he wanted her to know that he cared, and that she was important, he pressed a gentle kiss against the full bow curve of her mouth. He felt the soft intake of breath, and deepened the kiss for a fraction of a second before pulling back.

"If I could stop this from happening, I would," he whispered.

Her hand came up to press against his cheek, her eyes meeting his from across the pillow, and she leaned forward to kiss him again.

He swore he could feel her fire burning him in that moment before she pulled back.

Magic.

"Thank you," she said as she sat up.

"You're welcome," he whispered back as he brushed a stray curl off her cheek. He tried not to cringe. Who said "you're welcome" after a first kiss? Especially one that packed such a punch? He was pretty sure his heart had skipped a beat.

Then Laila cleared her voice, and Karan could see that she was compartmentalizing her grief and the moment they shared. She was moving forward so that she could fight whatever was coming for them, just like Boo said that she would.

"I can't let Denise's death be for nothing," Laila said, her voice calmer this time. Louder. "I want to find out why we have a tattoo.

And I want to find out why your uncle is dabbling in dark magic and what that has to do with me."

"About that," Karan said as he sat up by her side. "We didn't get to talk about it yesterday, but Gopal said we should prepare for Satyapal's arrival."

She watched the shock on her face, and then her eyes narrowed. "Gopal?"

Karan nodded. "I don't trust him, but out of all the options we have, he's our best one."

"You sure?"

Karan nodded again.

She slipped out of bed and then walked to her closet. "Then we better get ready," she said. "If Satyapal wants to come here, and he's had experience hunting people like me, people like my masis, then I want to be prepared for him."

Karan rubbed the back of his neck as he watched her pull out those fitted workout sets with the shorts and the matching cropped tank that she preferred to wear. "We can always start tomorrow, Laila. Why don't you take today to rest? I mean, you were almost choked to death."

"Giri Masi's paste fixed it," she said. Then she pointed to her neck, where there was barely a bruise left. "My voice is almost back, too. Besides, I feel, I don't know, hot."

"I'm not going to make the obvious statement here," he muttered.

She had walked into her closet in that moment then stuck her head back out. "Did you say something?"

"Nope," he called back. Then he pushed off the comforter. He'd always been the first person to take his mission seriously. He'd never shied away from a fight. "I guess I'd better get ready too. If we're fighting my uncle, then we're running drills."

"With fire," Laila called out from her closet. "I need to learn how to control my firepower, and since you don't feel the burn from it, you'll have to be my target."

"Wonderful," he said. It wasn't like she made him hot enough.

He groaned as the thought crossed his mind. The fire jokes had already begun.

21. LAILA

Laila knew that something had changed in her relationship with Karan. She wasn't sure how to describe it, but there was a new awareness between them now because of that one, confusing, spectacular kiss. It was supposed to be a gesture of comfort, but she was afraid that it had the opposite effect. She was anything but comforted now. In fact, she was itching to kiss him again. She wanted to know how it would feel to be with Karan when she wasn't hazy with grief.

Laila knew that Karan felt the aftereffects of their kiss, too. He watched her over their brief dinner conversations, or their chai breaks in the morning. He'd cock his head when she walked into the room wearing her workout gear. Regardless of his heightened interest, he never did anything more than look.

In the two days since Denise's death, they sparred regularly in the training gym. The constant physical contact was supposed to take her mind off of every distraction, but instead, it just continued to fray her nerves.

Paired with the consuming thoughts she had about Denise, and fears for her aunts, Laila was beginning to feel the frustration and soreness all the way to her bone marrow.

"Again," Karan shouted, after she finished a rep, and her fire still wouldn't come from her hands. It was inside her: She felt it burning in her heart, in her abdomen. She felt it singe her fingertips, but it wouldn't come out.

"This isn't working, Karan," she shouted.

"Then try again. If Satyapal shows up like Gopal said, you have to be prepared. He knows you're the Daughter of Draupadi."

"The fire will come when I see him."

"Or you'll curl up in the fetal position and cry."

Laila narrowed her eyes at his taunting. Then she took her position and did the combination again. Her muscles burned, sweat streamed from her face, and her palms glowed.

Karan stood in front of her, his hands stacked behind his back, his own body gleaming with sweat. "Not good enough," he said. "Again."

Laila put her hands on her hips. "I know how to fight!"

"You had your ass handed to you three times now."

"Hey," she snapped. "You were also handed your ass in two of those situations!"

"Which is why I'm training with you," he said. "Let's do it again. This time, more firepower, Sparky."

"Sparky?" she said, her voice sounding shriller than she intended. "One day I'm going to burn your ass." She stepped back, then ran through the combination again. Her palms continued to glow with no result.

"Laila," Karan said with a sigh. "You are literally a descendant of a woman who was formed from fire. Draupadi's daughter was made from blood and fire. You couldn't even light a candle at the rate you're going."

"I can't control it," Laila snapped. She was so tired of his smug expression, his condescending tone, his . . . shiny muscles. "I've read through all the journals before, and none of my ancestors ever talked about having firepower unless they were in extreme danger or stress. It always culminates around eighteen and practically disappears after giving birth to the next Daughter of Draupadi."

To be fair, Laila was also the only one who had the fire ability come earlier than most of her ancestors. She was also the only one who'd lost her mother at such a young age.

As if Karan read her mind, he said, "Your life is different from your ancestors." He stepped closer to her until only inches away. The bubbling awareness between them was intoxicating, and she almost swayed forward until she caught herself.

"What we're doing doesn't change the fact that I can't command the fire at will," Laila said. She held his gaze, taking in the deep brown of his eyes framed by thick black lashes.

"You have to learn."

"How, by doing combo drills for two days? I told you, it's not working, Karan."

"Okay, then let's try something else that does," he replied, his voice stubbornly reasonable.

"Like what?"

"You need motivation. Something that makes you feel like you can channel some of the fire that burns within you," he replied.

He moved closer to her, his shoulders rolling in a way that had her thinking about their kiss again.

"I don't need more motivation than I already have," she said. "My family. My aunts? People are affected and we have no idea what's going on. Instead, we're in here doing combo drills."

She was almost shouting when she finished, and Karan's smug expression only made her want to shout even louder. Why did she want another kiss even more now that he was irritating her?

Before she could step around him and storm out of the gym, his hand shot out and gripped the back of her neck. She realized in that split second that he had been just as worked up, just as focused as she was on embracing again. His lips crashed down onto hers, and the feel of his kiss had all the aching, uneasy parts inside of her erupting in flames. Her eyes slammed shut as she felt her palms erupt, a column of fire engulfing them. Then Laila wrapped her arms around Karan's neck, their bodies slick with sweat as they pressed together.

This had been brewing between them since he held her after Denise's death. No, this started when they went on their first date.

The frustration and anger roared through Laila, along with the hurt at not being able to do anything but want this man. The selfishness of taking this moment ripped through her just as Karan's hands coasted down her back. He slid them under her butt and hoisted her up so that she could wrap her legs around his waist.

Her fingers tunneled through his hair, and before she could pull away, before she could beg him to take her to the mat, she was hit with a hard spray of icy-cold water. It hurt like needles jabbing her side, and she released her hold on Karan and held her hands up to protect her face.

"What the hell?" she heard Karan call out. "Boo! Cut it out!"

The spray stopped, and both Laila and Karan stood soaked in the center of the gym floor. Against the far wall, Boo stood with a hose in hand that she'd pulled off the wall mount. Her hand was still on the nozzle.

"Is this what you two do when I'm stuck in the main house actually working on figuring out where your families are?"

"No, we were just—"

"Of course not, we were—"

"I bet you didn't even know that you were on fire, did you?" she said, and pointed a finger at them like a schoolteacher ready to issue out detention notices. With her plaid skirt that fell past her knees and her Mary Jane shoes, that was a real possibility.

"Look at the floor! That is a *fire* hazard," she snapped.

Laila looked down at the perfect burn circle that surrounded both herself and Karan.

Boo stumbled as she hoisted the hose nozzle over her head and fit it back against the bracket. When she finished, she brushed her hands against each other.

"This is irresponsible training," she said when she faced them again. "Fire is really dangerous, and we are in the middle of the woods where it hasn't rained in four and a half days. You cannot reenact scenes from *Carrie* without proper precaution!"

Karan combed his fingers through his wet hair, while Laila squeezed her drenched braid as they listened to Boo rant for another minute.

"I will meet you back in the main house," she snapped, and then spun on her shoes. She stormed out of the gym, leaving Laila and Karan alone again.

"I, ah, should go change if we're getting another lecture," Laila said.

He touched her arm to stop her. "Laila."

"Look, if we're going to talk about the kiss—"

"Laila, the fire came," he said. "The fire came easily to you that time. It's there, you just have to let loose and let it go."

She smiled now, leaning in just a bit to his touch. She watched his eyes narrow, his gaze drop to her mouth, then back up. "What do you think, I'm supposed to kiss you every time I need to access the fire?"

He gave her one of his quick grins, the flash of happiness that was so rare between them. "You probably just have to think of me." Then he winked and strode past her.

"Wait, I want to shower first!" she called out, then ran past him. The house was cold, and she did not want to be caught in a thin workout outfit with cold boobs. She'd reached her max embarrassment for the day.

Karan bolted after her, and as they ran through the kitchen, they heard Boo's voice follow them up the stairs. "For god's sake, stop running indoors, too! I swear, I'm working with infants."

22. KARAN

Karan finished changing into clean clothes and hurried down to the dining room, where Boo sat at the end of a very long mahogany table. The dining room, or as Boo had begun to call it, the command center, had filigree wallpaper, vaulted ceilings, and crown molding that reminded him of some of the British estates in parts of India.

When he walked in, he saw Laila sitting in a pair of her leggings and a hoodie now, her damp hair in a tightly wound braid perfectly in place. He remembered their kiss, and the soft feel of her mouth against his, the press of her body, and thought about how he desperately wanted to do it again.

Instead, he walked to the other side of the table, on Boo's left, and pulled out a chair. Both Boo and Laila were drinking chai, and thankfully they had set a third cup on the table in front of the seat he was now occupying.

"He's here," Laila said, turning to Boo. She pulled her knees to her chest and cupped her chai in both hands. "What's the exciting news?"

"I can't believe it took me so long to figure it out," Boo said. Then she motioned to her laptop. "All the clues were right there. He practically told you himself."

"Who told us what?" Karan asked.

"Gopal is Krishna."

"What?" Karan and Laila said at the same time. Chai sloshed out of their cups as they put them back down on the table.

Krishna. The last god to walk the earth. The last avatar of Vishnu. Powerful strategist and mastermind in love and war.

"I'm pretty sure it's true," Boo said. "He's either Lord Krishna, or he's a descendant of Krishna. I'm leaning toward descendant because he's told both of you that he's human."

"Can you walk us through how you came to that conclusion, Boo?" Laila asked. "Because if he is, then that changes . . . a lot."

"Why do you say that?" Karan asked.

Laila looked over at him, her hands cupped around her chai again. "If a god is involved, and it's more than just tattoos and throbbing palms or missing family members, it could mean—"

"It could mean what?"

Laila looked at Boo, then back at him. "It's just that our prophecies are tied to the fabric of the universe. If we don't fulfill our responsibilities . . ."

"The end of humanity is coming sooner than it was supposed to?" Boo said, finishing Laila's sentence.

Karan laughed, but when Laila and Boo didn't laugh with him, the expression on his face fell into one of confusion.

"You're joking, right?"

Laila didn't say anything.

"Look, the thinning veil between mortality and demon realms, the rise in demon attacks, even the existence of immortal rakshasi I believe . . . but the end of the world?"

"Makes sense to me," Boo said with a shrug.

Karan balked. Laila had admitted that if she didn't fulfill her prophecy, it could mean the end of Kali Yuga. With Gopal's presence, her confession felt even more real.

"Maybe we need to think less about what would happen if we don't fulfill our destiny and about what we *can* control," Laila said. "Boo, can you tell us why you think Gopal is the one descendant out of all that has godly blood from one of the big three instead of from a demigod in the Mahabharata?"

Boo nodded. "First, his name. Gopal is one of the hundred and eight names of Lord Krishna."

"There are a ton of people named Gopal," Karan argued. "That doesn't mean he's a god."

"That reeks of jealousy," Laila said, sounding amused. "Worried about some competition?"

He grinned, and because he couldn't help teasing her, he winked in her direction. "Based on the way you were climbing all over me, I don't think I have much to worry about—"

"Nope!" Boo shouted. She held her hands in a T-shape. "Absolutely not. We are not going there. As I was *saying*." She glared at Karan. "After the Kurukshetra War, there was a period of peace. Krishna went into the forest to meditate, and an archer saw an eye in the foliage, thought it was a deer, and ended up shooting Krishna's weakest part. His soul, which was on the bottom of his heel. The records are complicated after that. Some stories said that he just disappeared, while others claimed that his body and soul ascended after death together."

Karan remembered the Krishna myths. He'd heard them from his father and from Uncle Satya hundreds of times. The death of the last god on earth was the start of Kali Yuga, or the fourth realm of existence. That was where humanity prospered and evil thrived.

"Didn't Krishna have hundreds of children?" Karan said.

Boo held up a finger, her eyes bright with excitement. "Yes and no. The stories that are in the various editions of the Mahabharata claim that Krishna did procreate a lot with his hundreds of wives. But yesterday I was able to connect with a colleague from school who now works at the Indian national archives."

"From school?" Laila asked. She looked at Karan and then back at Boo. "Which one?"

"Oxford," she said, blinking owlishly behind her glasses. "I wasn't the only Indian there, you know. There are quite a few of us who are geniuses."

"I don't doubt it," Laila said. "What did your friend at the national archives say?"

"Well, it's more of what he was able to show me. There are these texts that haven't been translated yet. He sent pictures. They're the same language as the new markings on your backs. The texts talk about Krishna's family and that there were only two sons. One was born from his wife, Rukmani, and one born from his love, Radha. They in turn had one child who had one child, and so on. Their legacy was to be the advisor to the next crop of leaders who fought for humanity at the end of Kali Yuga."

Karan thought back to his interaction with Gopal, to all the answers he received. Then he gulped his chai like it was alcohol.

"Okay," he said as he set the mug down. He leaned over the table. "Gopal is stronger than all of us. He has the full-god bloodline. That confirms why he knows more than us. But why bring us together when we were never supposed to meet? And why is he showing his face if he's supposed to stay in hiding?"

Laila held up a finger. "He said that he's here to protect me. In the Mahabharata, Krishna was very close to Draupadi. They were friends and had a sibling relationship. When she was in trouble and her husbands didn't save her, Krishna came to her rescue. Maybe things are heating up in a way that he didn't anticipate so he had no choice to step in."

"In all the years that my father trained me, not once did we ever consider that there were descendants from other lineages who were also destined to follow a specific rule book," Karan mused. He nodded at Laila. "What about you?"

Laila shook her head. "My aunts always told me that there was only one daughter of Draupadi fighting against armies of evil. That's why I never bothered to look for other descendants. I wonder if they told us all that we were alone in our quests, so we didn't go looking for each other."

Boo picked up her pen and made a note on the small pad next to her computer. Then she gasped so loudly that both Laila and Karan jerked in their seats.

"What is it? What happened?" Laila said. "Are you okay?"

"I had an epiphany!" Boo shouted. "Specifically about Gopal's role in your lives. What if Gopal is here because your aunts can't be with you right now?"

"What do you mean?" Karan asked.

She turned in her chair to face him. "We just established that Krishna protected Draupadi. What if he's here to protect Laila if her aunts can't be? I mean, Laila, didn't you say that the aunts got their immortality *from* Krishna? That Draupadi's safety was incredibly important to him?"

"If he was here to protect Laila, then where was he when she was being choked to death?" Karan said. A cold chill raced up his spine as he remembered the way her eyes bulged in fear, her cheeks reddening, then her eyes going hazy in that moment as he frantically tried to do something, anything to stop the pisacha.

"I'm with Karan," Laila said. "My aunts are on my case twenty-four seven. There have been multiple attacks now, and he showed up to one."

Boo tapped her pen against her pad in a rapid beat, as if she were doing code or a sequence of numbers as she thought through Laila's and his comments. "I think that the circumstances at the winery happened so quickly, there was no way to come in time," she said. "Especially if he's still limited by a human body and can't just teleport in or something."

"Something is still not adding up," Laila said. She sat back in her chair, and crossed her legs, folding her lithe body onto the seat with ease. "He's not being honest with us. Why not just come to my door and say, 'Hey, let's work together? I'm on your side'? I feel like there is a piece of the puzzle that's still missing."

Karan's brain didn't work quite as fast as his cousin's, and he didn't have the type of information from his family history like

Laila, but he was beginning to get a better picture of Gopal's character. "What if," he said softly, "Gopal is doing exactly what his ancestor was responsible for doing back in the Mahabharata?"

"What's that?" Laila said, her eyebrow raised.

"Krishna was a trickster his whole life. He used riddles to share life lessons, and he got his way by convincing people to do the one thing that resulted in exactly what he wanted in the end. Then during the war, he'd taken a vow not to lift a single weapon himself. He was only able to work as an advisor. As the charioteer of Arjun and the confidant to the Pandavas."

"You think he has to play mind games to obtain an objective role," Laila said. "Maybe those are the rules he has to follow according to his destiny."

"That's a good deduction based on what we know so far," Boo said. She put her pen down and crossed her arms over her chest. "Now if only we can figure out the rest. Your tattoos, Satyapal, all of it."

Every time Satyapal's name came up, Karan felt a twinge of betrayal. He still couldn't understand how his own uncle would do anything to hurt him or his father. A part of Karan hoped that he was wrong, or that Satyapal was possessed by a power that was easy to explain away. He also knew that he'd have to accept the truth that there were too many signals pointing to dark magic.

"We have to figure out the tattoos soon," Karan finally said. "Gopal gave us a timeline."

Laila looked back and forth between Karan and Boo. "What would help you figure out the tattoos faster?" she asked.

Boo shrugged. "I need the copies of the original texts. It's the fastest way to decode. The documents I got from the national archives are only partial alphabets and I had to interpret a lot of it to get the general meaning."

Laila took a quick glance at Karan and looked back at Boo. There was indecision on Laila's face.

"What is it?" he asked gently.

"Draupadi was considered the linchpin in the Mahabharata because her thirst for justice fueled the ambition and motivation in a lot of the key players in the war," Laila said. "But she was also incredibly well read, and an excellent negotiator."

"You mentioned that earlier," Boo replied. "She had to persuade her husbands to do better, to be better than they were."

"Because she was more perceptive than even Yudhishthira, the most intelligent Pandava brother, After the Kurukshetra War, the sages and Krishna entrusted her with a gift she was destined to protect. That I now protect."

Karan wanted to reach out and touch her hand. To tell her that she could trust them. Boo was not that subtle.

"I hope this buildup that you're doing won't be a disappointment," she said.

"Boo, lay off," Karan said. He knocked on the table in front of her. "Come on, when she's ready she'll tell us."

Laila met his gaze and nodded. "I don't know if I'll ever be ready to tell you. I'm not supposed to. But this may be our only choice." She pushed away from the table and motioned toward the back exit of the dining room. Karan looked at Boo and shrugged. They got up and followed close behind. They cut through the kitchen, the sunken living room with wide deep couches and an archway. Then in the wide hallway before the kitchen, Laila walked over to a simple shelving unit and opened a cabinet door to reveal a keypad.

Karan's adrenaline kicked in, and his senses went on high alert.

Laila keyed in the code, and a wall panel snicked open like a door.

"Oh my god, a secret passageway!" Boo squealed. She clapped her hands together in delight. "Where does it lead?"

"Follow me," Laila said with a deep breath. "It's been blessed by my masis, so I hope you both will be able to enter after me."

Karan let Laila go first through the opening, then Boo followed. He took up the rear as they descended through a dark corridor of unadorned stone. A spiral staircase narrowed as they walked down one flight, then two flights of stairs. When they reached the base, there was a large statue of Ravana, the most famous rakshasa in Hindu mythology.

Karan shot Boo a look, but she shook her head. She had no idea what this place was either. But a Ravana stone statue was definitely sending a message. His fingertips itched for a knife, for any weapon.

They stopped in front of a set of double doors, and when Laila pressed her hand against the panel, the carvings in the stone shimmered in gold before they swung open. He stretched an arm out in front of Boo even as his cousin gasped in excitement.

Here, there was a large tapestry of names stitched in neat columns. "My ancestors," Laila said softly. "These are the names of all the mothers who came before me." Karan wanted to reach out and touch the soft fabric but knew that it wasn't for him to do. He'd be respectful of Laila's family heirlooms and keep his distance.

As they turned the corner, there was a soft ping and overhead lights flicked on one at a time, illuminating a long wide staircase that stretched into a lower level. Section after section after section was illuminated in the lower level, creating a long corridor with shelves on either side. A wooden table lined the center of the bottom floor, and at the end of the corridor were four marble columns carved in the shape of rakshasi that framed large wooden doors with Sanskrit etched into the paneling. There was a large gold padlock on the door.

"It's a secret library," Boo said reverently.

"This," Laila said quietly, "is the library of Vyasa."

Vyasa. The author of the Vedas, the Puranas . . . and the Mahabharata.

Karan's heart began to pound. They descended to the lower level and Karan walked over to the nearest shelf and scanned the scrolls laid at an angle with a handle on each side. Next to the scrolls were new volumes of books. "It can't be," he said.

"I'm going to pass out," Boo said as she swayed on her feet. "You can't mean, this is Vyasa's *actual* library. This was lost centuries ago! It was buried under the rubble and dust of wars and invaders!"

Karan pulled out a heavy wooden chair from the long table and propped it behind Boo. She collapsed into it, her mouth still gaping like a fish's.

"This is the secret you've been keeping," Karan said to Laila.

She shrugged. "A girl has to have some mystery."

"You are the coolest person ever," Boo cried out. She pressed her hands against her temples and repeated her outburst in three different languages.

"I think I got all that," Laila said. "Boo, everything that you may need to figure out the language tattooed into our backs should be in here." She motioned to the racks to the left. "I started looking before you showed up, but I couldn't find anything. Then when you took over, I assumed that you wouldn't need any of this information. I was hoping you wouldn't need access to any of this information," she corrected.

"Laila?" Boo pointed to the locked doors at the end of the corridor. "What's behind that?"

"The diaries of my ancestors," she said. She stood between the double doors and Karan and Boo. "You can't access those. My aunts' diaries are also included in there, and their secrets are not for me to share."

"No-access zone," Boo said. Then she gave Laila a salute. "We absolutely respect your boundaries. Right, bhai?"

"Right," he said. He spun in a slow circle, taking in all the scrolls and books. "I don't think we'll have time to worry about the no-access zone anyway. This is a lot."

Karan stepped forward, and even though his cousin was already making gagging noises, he pressed his hands against the curve of Laila's hips and pulled her closer. "Why didn't you want to show us this sooner? Because you still didn't trust us?"

Laila hesitated before resting her hands against his shoulders. "No one is supposed to be down here other than the guardians and the Daughters of Draupadi. This is my legacy, and the legacy of my masis. Information is power, and the original Vedas, Puranas, and teaching of the strongest sage in the Dharma religions are very powerful tools. I am asking you to accept responsibility for protecting this library the way I have to as well."

She didn't sound like herself, he thought. Laila was so direct, her words cutting. But now, they were heavy with the same responsibility that he had heard most of his life.

"We understand," Karan said.

"I am a genius," Boo said as she adjusted her glasses. Then she got to her feet. "I would be an absolute idiot if I told anyone about this space when I could literally access all the information for myself."

Laila smiled. "You're welcome to it," she said. "There is a bit of an order to it, and since this is my hell every summer when my masis make me study, I can tell you where to find everything."

Boo's smile was infectious, her excitement contagious. "Then let's do this," she said. "Bhai? Can you get my laptop? Laila, maybe you can show me what you were looking at before I came. Then I'm going to need anything you have on Krishna. Have you thought about a digital cataloging system? I can program one for you."

23. LAILA

Laila stared at the marketing textbook in front of her. It had been a full week since Boo had been able to identify Gopal, and they'd fallen into a restless peace that only made the fire harder to control. She knew that they were so close to finding the answers that they needed. She was uneasy with awareness, the heat from the fire coursing through her blood made her skin hot. It didn't help that now, whenever she looked at Karan, she was . . . distracted.

But she didn't push for more than the kisses they'd shared, even though a part of her was reckless and drunk on the sensation. Instead, she'd put her copy of Kate Chopin's book on top of her bedside table as a reminder of what she'd lose if she fell for a man too quickly.

Karan looked like he wasn't doing any better than she was. They had two more weeks before the deadline Gopal had set for Satyapal's arrival. As they trained, and they studied, and they ate in silence together at the dining table before Boo broke the ice with a random factoid, Laila could see the tension in the lines of his face, the way that his jaw would clench when he looked out the window. She couldn't imagine what it was like to know that the person they were about to face was family.

She hadn't known Karan very long, but it wasn't difficult to see his sense of loyalty, his dedication to the people he loved. Laila just hoped that Karan's loyalty had a breaking point unlike his ancestor Karna, who some believed followed his friend, his king Duryodhana, to his death.

Thankfully, Boo was the one who kept the faith. She was starting to put the pieces together, like a puzzle snapping in place.

"Hey."

The sound of Karan's voice had Laila's head jerking up to look at him. She'd been on the same page in her book for almost forty minutes. The recorded lecture was paused on her laptop in front of her.

"Hey," she said. She rolled her aching shoulders, feeling the sore muscles in her back from training earlier that day.

"How is it going?" Karan asked as he motioned to her books.

"Not that great," she said. Then she tucked her pen between the pages of her textbook and closed it. "It's hard to concentrate when the winery is in ashes, my friend is dead, and I'm two weeks behind on homework while we prepare for an asura-hunter who uses dark magic. I feel like we're already losing."

He looked down at her, a curl sliding over his hair and flopping onto his forehead. It was a little less militant from the crew cut he'd shown up with, she thought. A little unruly.

"The people we love are safe," he said. "We have to believe Gopal. *I* have to believe Gopal. If we focus on that, maybe we can figure out the rest."

"I hope we're right that he's not just playing us," she said.

"If he is, then it's a long game," Karan replied.

"Right," she said. Then she scrubbed her hands over her face, feeling the grittiness in her eyes. Her triceps and biceps burned and ached from the workout that they had done the previous day and then again that morning. It was a good ache, though. She felt stronger physically than she had in a long time. Karan had teased her that her aunts had been going easy on her, and she had to believe now that he was right about that.

"Listen," he said slowly. "I have a surprise for you. I was wondering if you wanted to come down to the lake with me."

She leaned back in her chair. "A surprise? What kind of surprise could be at the lake?" She'd never had a man give her a surprise before. She felt flutters in her belly as she saw Karan's slow, easy smile.

"You'll just have to see," he said.

It had been a while since she'd visited the lake. Not since her aunts had left for India. The water would be cold now, but with the way she was constantly burning, it didn't seem like that would be a problem.

"There's a bit of a chill in the air," he continued, his accent a little sharper than it had been since he'd moved into her house. "You can wear a jacket, but a sweatshirt should be enough. With a long-sleeved shirt underneath."

"I don't know," she said softly, even though every cell in her body wanted to scream yes. "If this doesn't have anything to do with research or training, I might have to pass. I feel like I need to be productive right now."

"Rest is productive," he said. "I won't keep you for long, but we need to take a breath." Then he cupped her chin, his callused fingers brushing against her skin. "I can see that you need to take a breather or you're going burn up."

"But the tattoo," she said, and as she spoke, his thumb grazed against her lower lip. The delicate touch fried her concentration.

"No one will fault us if we take a moment to forget."

Forget, she thought. She'd never really had the luxury of forgetting.

Or pretending to be normal. Now she didn't even have the luxury of the normal she once had before she met Karan and her aunts began to age. There were moments when all she wanted was to feel her aunts' hugs and hear them laugh at her human jokes while they trained in the studio.

Karan touched the bridge of her nose, then her jaw, and she strained against his palm, closing her eyes as he finally cupped her cheek.

"You're so . . . hot."

Her eyes popped open. "Uh, thank you?"

Karan laughed. "No, Laila. Your skin is burning. This reprieve might help."

And that was the most convincing reason for her to step away from the house, to walk down to the lake in the cool fall night breeze. "You're making it hard to say no."

"I'll meet you down there in a few minutes," he said quietly. Then his hand fell away and he was gone.

After she heard the door open and close, Laila fanned herself. The stress and tension, the way that she was pulled toward Karan, was like jumping into a barbecue. She was sizzling, and at this point, definitely not safe in the house.

Laila dressed warmly in jeans and a sweater. She felt foolish when she combed her hair and took the time to put it in a loose braid. She tied a ribbon at the end, crimson red and delicate. As she took a few deep, meditative breaths through which she focused all her energy on the center of her palm, she forced the powerful burning inside of her to that one spot.

She stepped out of the house into the cool night air. The fall winds had come in fierce and strong, whipping through the trees and rattling the leaves until only the strong were left clinging to dried branches. But as her power pulsed, a small flame the size of a candle bloomed from her lifeline and flickered toward her fingertips.

Cupping the flame, she used it as her guiding light, keeping her energy focused solely on it as she walked down the small stone path between the grove of trees toward the water.

When she reached the clearing, she could see the partial moon reflected on the surface of the lake. She immediately looked toward the wide plank dock. Normally shrouded in the same darkness that covered the forest, the dock was lit with a brilliant flicker of string lights that draped from post to post to post. In the center of the dock, Karan stood in front of what looked like a blanket and containers of food.

It was the most romantic thing anyone had ever done for her.

Because she was too busy sighing, she lost her concentration and the flame flickered out. It didn't matter. She was able to see clearly with the moonlight now, as she walked across the bank and ascended the dock.

"When did you have time to do all this?" she asked, delighted to see a whole picnic spread at his feet.

"I snuck out a bit earlier today to pick some things up."

"Karan," she said, her words frigid. "You know that's dangerous."

"I ordered a lot of these items in advance so I didn't spend long in the stores."

Laila walked up the two steps onto the dock, and took in the checkered red picnic blanket, the flicker of tea lights around the blanket and on the edge of the dock, as well as the bottle of wine from her aunts' winery.

"This all feels very adult," she said, and couldn't help but let out a giggle.

"Adult?" he said with a grin.

She shrugged. "You have to remember that I've lived a very sheltered life, and the guys that I'm used to meeting still require a ride from their mother to the movie theater."

"Well, if you're impressed, then I did my job," he said. He held out a hand to lead her onto the blanket on one side of the food he'd laid out for them. She toed off her shoes and sat cross-legged in front of one of the plastic cups. Karan sat on the other side of the blanket and began uncovering trays of food. There was a cheese and charcuterie board, finger sandwiches, and mini brownie bites.

"Have you tried your aunts' wine?" he asked as he picked up the bottle at the edge of the picnic spread and carefully removed the cork. He'd done it before, she noted, and she wanted to know the story behind his first bottle. The first sip he ever took, the people he was with, and the friends he was closest to in the moment.

"A couple of times," she replied absently, feeling so much hunger for all the memories he had of a life different from hers.

"What do you think?"

"I like it," she said. "Wine isn't exactly the beverage of choice for my aunts, so they want me to taste the stuff every once in a while, to share my opinion." She smiled as she remembered the blood-bag fridge she'd managed to keep hidden behind a locked cabinet door in the walk-in pantry. "What about you? Wine drinker?"

"I feel like in India, all my friends enjoy spending time together with alcohol, but I never got into it. When I moved to the UK, most of my peers were from wealthier families. They preferred spirits over wine, which I've learned to enjoy."

"Spirits?"

"Bourbon, whiskey, scotch whiskey. You know, liquor. Preferably in a tumbler made out of crystal if we're talking about Oxford friends."

"That sounds ridiculously bougie."

"Speaks the girl who has her own apartment in a house with two kitchens and an attached gym. Your closet has a motorized rotating hanging rack, and your shoe shelves have underlighting. Let's not forget the secret library that has an incantation to open doors."

"Guilty," Laila said cheerfully as she loaded up a cracker with a wedge of cheese and prosciutto. "To be fair, you can accumulate a lot of cash in centuries of living." She popped the cracker in her mouth and closed her eyes on a moan.

"Good?"

"Great," she said after she chewed and swallowed. "I don't think I've ever tasted that combination before."

"Of wine and cheese?"

"Sheltered Daughter of Draupadi, remember? We used to eat quite a bit of Indian food before I pitched a fit and we started getting food service. The aunts had to learn how to feed me because even though they had trained my ancestors, I was the only one in a long time they needed to raise. But they did a good job. I never felt unloved, and I always knew that they did their best because they wanted me to feel like I was important. Not for the role I played in the larger story of the universe, but because I was Laila."

"They sound like really great parent figures," he said as he chewed on a grape. Then he plucked one off the stem, leaned forward, and slowly slipped it into her mouth. Her eyes went wide at the gesture. She chewed and swallowed before speaking.

"I can feed myself," she said ruefully.

"I know, but I just like the idea of feeding you." He smiled, and the flickering lights around them enhanced the sharp lines of his jaw and cheekbones. The fire was building at the base of her spine, eager to burst from her hands.

"And since this is our second date," he continued.

"Wait a minute," she said, holding up a hand. "How is this our second date?"

"I bought you burgers and fries and we sat next to a waterfall the first time. Now I made you a cheese spread and we're sitting outside with candlelight and string lights in front of the water."

She shot him a bland expression. "You tried to kill me on that date."

"We all make mistakes," he said.

And then she laughed, and felt a little bit lighter, the stress a little bit easier to manage. She stacked another cracker, took a sip of the crisp white wine, and then motioned toward Karan. "What was your childhood like? Tell me your stories."

He hummed. "A little bit different, I guess. My father was like the Indian Indiana Jones. Always holding maps of remote parts of the country under one arm and a cup of chai in the other. He would unfold them carefully because so many of them were printed a hundred or two hundred years ago of the original landscape. He'd lay one out on our cherrywood dining table. He had this pencil that he tucked behind his ear that was barely two inches long, and he'd stick it between his teeth when he was contemplating his next move. I used to get him a new pencil every year for Diwali. Almost like a joke. And he'd wear that one down too until the next year."

"And then you would hunt," she said.

"And then we would hunt," he replied slowly. "Like all of Karna's descendants had. Our job was to keep the balance between humans and the supernatural, and we were good at it, too." He smeared brie on the edge of a cracker and topped it with apricot jelly before he held it out for her mouth. He was relaxed now, lying on his side propped up on his elbow, the lights flickering against his hair and the soft breeze lifting the curls in his hair. She leaned forward, her eyes on him, and bit into the cracker. He watched her in silence. And when she pulled back, he tucked the rest of the cracker in his mouth and licked the pad of his thumb.

"What about your childhood?" he asked casually. "Every time I bring it up, I feel like I never get a straight answer from you."

She chewed on a cut strawberry and contemplated his words. "That's because there really is nothing more to tell."

"Come on, there has to be one embarrassing story you're willing to share."

"You first."

"My mother gave me a bowl cut," he said easily. "I was ten and people didn't stop laughing at me until my father finally convinced her to let me go to a stylist."

Laila balked. "Okay, that is bad." She tried to imagine him as a child with a terrible haircut, and she couldn't fathom what it looked like.

"Yeah, it wasn't my finest moment," he said. "No, tell me.

"There's nothing to tell," Laila replied. "My mother died, I was raised by immortals, I studied, I fought, I practiced archery, and I went to school. Then I started working at the winery at the information booth. My aunts had purchased it when we moved to the area because they didn't want to attract attention with their big house and their reclusive nature without reason."

He moved closer, scooting on his elbow. "Let me ask you this question. If you weren't the Daughter of Draupadi, what would you do?"

"I'd go to college," she said. "I'd take classes in person, and stay in a dorm or an apartment, and I'd get drunk on Saturday nights, and listen to bad open mic poetry nights and argue with students in class about South Asian history. But you already know that."

She licked her finger again and watched as his gaze followed her every move. It was powerfully exciting to know that he was attracted to her in a way that she'd never felt from anyone.

"Tell me more," he said softly. "Do you ever wish you could change your life so you could be the Laila that goes to college and gets drunk on weekends?"

"No," she said. She was so sure of her answer that she didn't have to think about it before she spoke. "I can't really separate out what makes me who I am from the life that I have. As much as the training and the scripture and the fighting sucked when I was growing up . . . it is part of me. And the only reason I can't go to college and live a more open existence is that my mother is not here to protect me. I have to live with immortals who have to stay hidden. I don't resent them. If anything, they are just like mothers to me too."

He leaned forward and brushed the corner of her mouth, releasing a tiny crumb that had clung to her frown. She felt a burst of heat straight to her lower back, and she tensed, trying to control the surge. Sometimes it felt like it was going to explode from her pores.

"Can I make you a promise?" he said quietly.

"Ohh? What would that be?"

"If we make it out of whatever situation we've found ourselves in . . . with our tattoos and our missing families and these fucking weird apparitions that are showing up out of nowhere. I want you to apply to school in the UK and come back with me. I will be your protector. I will be your sword. I will be your bow. I will be the person who makes sure that the Daughter of Draupadi is safe, but also that Laila is free."

His words were so softly spoken, but they landed like an arrow piercing through the softest center of her heart. She felt the fire rise within her until her fingers tingled with heat. He looked down at her hands and smiled.

"You believe me?" he asked.

"Yes," she whispered, her voice trembling. "Yes. If we make it out of this, I will . . . apply to college. There is no way I'm going to get into Oxford, though. You know that, right?"

"I'm sure your witchy aunts can figure something out," he said with a wink.

Right, she thought. He still thought they were witches.

Laila picked up a chocolate-covered raisin. "After college, what would you want to do? Would you want to be a monster-hunter professor like your father?"

"It's in my blood," he said.

"But do you *want* to do it?" she asked. "Would you choose it as your future if you didn't have to?" She had to know.

"No," he admitted, "but my fate is the same as yours. I wouldn't be who I am if that part of me didn't exist."

She took two deep, measured breaths to suppress the flames.

"Laila?" he said, his voice filled with concern. "Are you okay?"

"F-fine," she said, trembling. "It's just been a rough week. Hell, a rough few weeks. I just have to work on my control. I can't feel anymore without wanting to explode, but the deep breathing helps."

"Then maybe you should explode," he said softly.

"What? What do you mean?"

He sat up. "I mean maybe you should explode." He got to his feet, and then held out a hand to pull her to hers. Their food was left half eaten, their wineglasses still two-thirds full. They carefully stepped over the remnants of their meal on the blanket and walked closer to the edge of the dock.

Karan reached over his shoulder and yanked his shirt off over his head, revealing smooth dark brown skin marred with the lines and curves of the Sanskrit-like language.

"We're going in," he said.

"What are you talking about? It's freezing. I'm not jumping in the water."

"It wouldn't be the first time you've gone skinny-dipping," he said.

"*What?*" she burst out. "How in the world do you know that?"

Karan had the decency to wince. "I was doing surveillance from the other side of the lake and saw you the day we met. But in my defense, I looked away. Plus it was dark, and I couldn't really make out anything other than a figure."

The heat rushed to her cheeks, and she punched him in the arm. Hard. "Creeper. The barrier my aunts erected should've kept you out."

"Well, maybe it didn't see me as a threat," he said. "Look, your fire won't be that intense if you're in the water when you let it go. If anything, based on the size of the lake? It'll feel like bathwater in a minute. I had hoped that taking some time for yourself would help, but maybe this is a better solution."

He unbuckled his belt, and she turned away as he shoved his pants down his legs. She heard the clink of the metal against the planks. "I'm coming in with you," he said.

"Karan."

The soft rustling of his shorts followed. She saw the color around his ankles from the periphery of her vision.

"Don't be chicken," he said smoothly. Before she could respond, she felt the planks under her feet give as he jumped and vaulted himself off the edge of the dock.

"Oh my god, Karan!"

Then there was a loud splash, and she turned to see his head emerge from the surface of the water. Karan was a shadow barely visible because the dim light couldn't illuminate all his features from this distance.

"It really is cold," he said with a short barking laugh. "It would be great if you could get in here now."

Seeing him in the water, knowing that he was naked, knowing that he wouldn't be hurt from her flame, she debated it for a moment, and then the surge inside of her, restless and bubbling, answered the question for her.

"Will you just turn around and close your eyes?" she shouted to him. She saw him bobble in the distance, and then turn until he was facing the rest of the lake.

"Come on! Before I freeze to death."

"It's not that cold," she muttered. At least she wouldn't be that cold. Sweat was beginning to bead against her forehead.

Laila made quick work of shrugging out of her sweater and pushing her jeans and panties in one fell swoop down her leg. She toed off her socks, pulled off her T-shirt and bra, and then, without thinking, without taking another moment to process what she was about to feel, she dove off the dock headfirst into the water.

"Holy shit," she shouted as she surfaced. The water was frigid. Although the air was a cool sixty degrees, the water felt significantly colder. The icy chill seeped its way through her skin and threatened to defuse the flames inside of her. And then Karan was in front of her, treading so close that his legs brushed against hers.

"Are you okay?" he asked.

Even in the shadows, she could see that his lips trembled.

"It is freezing. You are absolutely insane for suggesting this."

She was acutely aware of their nakedness. Of the smooth muscled length of him that dipped into those hip muscles she'd seen when he'd stretch. And of her breasts, which were sensitive to the chilly water, the cool lapping making her nipples ache.

"Let go." He motioned to the lake. "If you want to swim further out, I'll swim with you. And then just let go."

She shivered. "I think it's too cold for me to concentrate."

The words were barely out of her mouth before he reached out for her. His arms wrapped around her waist and pulled her close until her naked chest was pressed against his, their legs tangled as they both treaded water and their mouths fused together in a familiar salty wet kiss filled with all the heat and desire that she'd had for him. And as his fingers dove into her hair, the water lit like a candle, and she embraced the feeling as the fire skidded across the surface.

He tore his mouth away and she felt how aroused he was for her, how much he wanted her, pressed against her thigh, and in that moment, she wanted nothing else but to lose herself within him.

"Let go," he whispered.

And this time she wrapped her legs around his and let him carry them both. When the fire erupted out of her, she poured everything she had into it as they both sank below the surface, clinging to each other until there was no other thought but how perfectly they fit.

24. KARAN

When Karan came downstairs the next morning, he saw Laila in the same position she'd been sitting in the day before. She was perched on the stool at the counter with her textbooks in front of her. He paused, just to look at her and drink in the sight of the long, muscled line of her back.

Their relationship had permanently changed the night before. When they were at the dock, he felt her soft skin under his fingers as they embraced shoulder to knees, fire raging around them. He'd never felt like he was in danger when the flames were coming from her. He'd reach out and touch them and feel as though it was a unique part of her.

And then they'd had sex under a moonlit sky.

No, that description didn't feel personal enough for how he felt about her.

They'd . . . made love. Without protection.

He'd had casual girlfriends before. The type of girl who was important in the moment, but whose life moved on while his continued on a destined path. He'd never neglected protection, though. And with Laila, it was so much more important.

But she'd told him that part of the curse was that she got to choose when she'd have her child as long as it was before her twenty-sixth birthday. He believed her, because he couldn't imagine Laila would lie to him. Not about this.

Thank god for divine birth control.

Literally.

As he watched her now, he realized that there was something about her that looked more centered. He crossed the room, and when she looked up at him, he cupped her face to kiss her mouth. When he pulled back, he could have sworn that he saw the fire reflected in her eyes.

"Good morning," he said softly as he brushed his thumb pads over her cheekbones.

"Good morning," she whispered back.

"How are you feeling?"

"Tired," she said. Her cheeks reddened. "A little sore. But oddly rested? Less anxious and nervous."

"Then the trick worked," he said.

She smirked. "Yeah, it did."

It was his turn to blush. "Shut up," he said. "I meant releasing some of your pent-up firepower." He then pressed another soft, quick kiss against her upturned mouth.

"I guess it did," she said, smiling.

After they had gotten out of the lake, he'd carried her back to the house. Her body had been exhausted from releasing that much energy. He knew now that she was affected physically from the flames.

After he walked her back to the house, he'd returned to the lake to clean up their food and the lights he'd strung around the dock for her. He'd returned just as exhausted as she'd been, and he had desperately wanted to crawl into the bed with her to hold her all night.

But Boo was with them. He was going to respect his cousin even though he was craving the safety he felt with Laila to the point where his bones felt as hot as Laila's flames.

As he strode over to the chai machine to fill his cup, he knew that he was even more determined to figure out the mess they found themselves in. Not only was he desperate to get his family back, to stop the strange supernatural occurrences that had happened over the course of the last few weeks, but he wanted to find a place of normalcy where he could spend time with Laila and explore the relationship that was beginning to form between them.

He turned to speak to her and caught her staring. There were flames in her eyes again, and he froze, watching them flicker. *What in the world?*

She blinked, and they were gone again. "You're staring," she said. "Is everything okay?"

"Yeah," he replied. He probably didn't get enough sleep. "Maybe we need to take a rest day and go down into the library with Boo."

"Okay," she said. She motioned to her textbook. "I'm almost done with this."

No sooner had she spoken than there was the sound of footsteps on the stairs. Then, a loud, jaw-cracking yawn. Boo strolled into the kitchen a moment later, her hair wet and slicked back off her face and braided down her back.

Instead of her pressed outfits or slouching sleepwear, she had on a pair of unfamiliar jeans and a sweatshirt that said *Varsity Archery* on it.

"I borrowed your clothes," she said to Laila in greeting. "I have to do laundry, but I realized I've never done it before."

"I'll help you," Laila said. "My masis aren't ones for laundry either."

"Thanks," she said.

Karan took his cup and crossed the kitchen so he could give it to his cousin. "You look like you need this first."

"Brilliant," she said, taking the cup, "but we really need to get coffee here too."

"You're too young for—"

"Don't," Boo said, and held up a hand. "I was doing Calculus Three while you were still in diapers."

"Actually, I don't think that's true," Karan said, amused.

"The sentiment remains." She sipped from the cup, then sighed.

"Did you get anywhere yesterday?" Laila asked.

Boo nodded, taking a seat next to her at the counter. "I went all the way to the beginning. I decided to go to the roots of your stories and started with the Mahabharata. There is a lot of reference to the dice game in the books you have in your library, Laila."

"Ah, yeah," she said, and glanced at Karan. "I always thought that was Draupadi's origin story. The moment when she came into her feminine rage."

Boo snorted. "I can't blame her. The husbands that had sworn to protect her, all five of them, looked away while she was offered up in a game of dice in exchange for a kingdom. And Karna was in the room, taunting her to sit on his lap—"

"That is *not* the version of the story I remember," Karan said. How many times did he have to defend the honor of his ancestor? He had been a flawed figure in the Mahabharata, but Karan had to believe he wasn't that much of an asshole . . . right?

"Believe what you want," Boo continued. She turned back to Laila. "I'm through volume five at this point. I'm starting to find that some of the letters are similar to your tattoo as I translate them."

"That's great!" Laila said. "Have you been able to make out any of the words?"

"Some, but it still doesn't make sense yet," Boo said, huddled over her cup like it was a cauldron and she was a witch hovering over her latest potion. "The words *souls, destined, parted, reunited* are all separated by shorter words. I don't know what order to read them, but we're almost there."

Souls. Destined. Parted. Reunited. Karan glanced at Laila and saw her cheeks reddening before she looked away. He reached over his shoulder to touch the very top of his tattoo that was supposed to connect with hers. Were their souls destined to be together? His from Karna's and hers from Draupadi's? If that was the case, then why did Gopal say they were never supposed to meet?

As if Boo was reading his mind, she said, "You know, there was a Maharashtrian story about the Mahabharata that makes sense in this situation. Karna was supposed to be better than Arjuna Pandava at everything. As a warrior, a strategist, as a freaking human being. The only reason he was stuck fighting on the wrong side of the war was that he wasn't royalty, despite being half-brothers to the Pandavas."

"Casteism, right?"

"Exactly," Boo said. "Anyway, the Maharashtrian story says that Draupadi had approached Karna once and said that she wished she'd married him. That she'd know he'd protect her, he'd love her the way she deserved to be loved. Karna had feelings for her too, but he was honorable even in that version of the history. They . . . pined for each other at a distance."

Karan rubbed the back of his neck. The reality of his feelings for Laila was starting to seem like a mirror to the fated stories of their legacies.

"The thing about interpretations is that it's more of what the people want to believe than the actual truth," Laila said.

"I don't know about that," Boo replied. "History is written by the victor. Interpretations have truth because they're written by the quietest characters, right?"

They descended into silence, and Karan had to wonder what version of the stories they should believe. Vyasa's library, or the ones from their family histories?

"Instead of training today, why don't we figure out the rest of the translation?" Laila said. She looked pointedly at Karan. "That way we can know for sure we aren't pawns in the hands of the gods."

She knew, he thought. She always knew. She understood in a way that no one else possibly could. He smiled at her and nodded. If he was fated to love Laila, then he'd accept it. He refused to believe that he was influenced by any godly intervention. No, those feelings were real, and his.

Just as he was about to offer to make a robust bowl of oatmeal for all of them before they got to work, a phone buzzed on the end of the counter.

Laila's eyes widened and she lunged across the granite to grasp her device as fast as possible. She quickly picked up the phone and held it up to see the screen.

"It—it's an unknown number," she said. "Looks like it's from out of town."

"You're supposed to hear from the insurance adjuster for your aunts' vineyard," he said gently. "This could be that call. We don't have to jump to conclusions."

Laila nodded. He watched her, keeping an eye out to see if her fingertips began to glow, but she looked like she was coolly in control. She cleared her throat, then answered and put the phone on speaker. "Yes?"

"Hello, love."

The sound of Gopal had all of them freezing, eyes wide.

Boo almost upended her chai cup. "Is that him?" she mouthed.

Laila and Karan nodded.

"How did you get my number?" she said coolly.

"Never you mind that," he said. "You need to get to the archery studio."

"What? Why?"

"No time to explain, but when I have a feeling, it's generally spot-on. And not in a good way. Bring Karan. And be prepared. I can't take this beast on my own, unfortunately, and you have no idea how much it pains me to admit that."

"Okay, we'll head out—"

"Now," he said, his voice sharp. "This is not a test, love. I can't hold him off by myself while you chitchat in your safe little home."

The line went dead, and Karan was already moving. He ran upstairs, Laila hot on his heels. They were dressed in combat gear in seconds.

A trip to her weapons closet in the gym loaded them with enough artillery that he felt like he'd have a fighting chance this time against whatever was coming.

They were in his car in under five minutes and speeding toward the studio.

"What could it be?" Laila asked.

"The question is, why is something happening again when we're not even there?" Karan replied.

They made it to the studio in under ten minutes, and the skies began to pour as they exited their car. They made a break toward the entrance as rain came down in torrential sheets.

"Do you see his bike?" Laila called out.

Karen glanced around and shook his head. Just as they were about to get to the front doors, they burst open and students spilled out, screams erupting from their throats. Laila and Karan were almost knocked over on their feet as the stampede pushed past them and many dove into cars.

She looked back at him, her eyes wide with surprise. The flames that he saw looking at her irises had returned, and this time he was sure that he saw them.

"You should stay here while I—"

There were more screams and this time they couldn't wait. They both burst through the double doors and into the large open studio space.

They heard the clash of the sword before they saw the rakshasa in the center of the room: four arms, talons dripping with red blood that sizzled when it hit the mat. Sharp, elongated canines and a forked tongue. It was over eight feet tall.

"Rakshasa," Karan said, his voice thick. A flood of memories cascaded through his mind, memories that felt like watching a new movie while knowing it was vaguely familiar. He felt the same sickening rise of stomach bile, the same urge to vomit at how terrified he was in that moment.

He turned to Laila, but she wasn't looking at the rakshasa. She was staring at the body at its feet. Ben's bent, lifeless form looked like a rag doll next to the monster, his head bent in an angle that showed his neck had cracked. His abdomen had been torn open—the jagged edges of his flesh folded back, revealing intestines that had been pulled out of the cavity and tangled like pink and red yarn.

"Ben," Laila gasped.

Just as Gopal deflected a swipe of talons and the curved blade in his meaty fist, the rakshasa spun to look at Laila.

"Watch the talons," Gopal said sharply. Karan saw the trickle of blood from his ear and his nose. From the corner of his mouth. The sweat against his forehead. Then he remembered how fast his blood had worked the first and only other time he'd seen a rakshasa.

He ran over to the rack of compound bows and grabbed a fistful of arrows.

Laila remained frozen in place, her chest rising and falling as she looked between Ben and the rakshasa. He couldn't focus on her right now, couldn't go to comfort her. Gopal was starting to lose ground, his strength wavering.

Karan retrieved a knife he'd tucked in his ankle holster and nicked himself on his hand. Then he rubbed the tip of an arrow across the blooming redness before he nocked it.

"I need an opening!" he called out.

Gopal swung his sword in an arc and then hit the floor, lying flat on his stomach. The rakshasa lifted one foot as if to step on Gopal, then moved in Laila's direction. Karan released the arrow on a breath.

It lodged in the center of the rakshasa's forehead.

The demon monster began to scream, the pained wail sounding like a thousand souls being released from a pinprick in a balloon.

Karan did the same with the second arrow and released it so it lodged in the rakshasa's chest, right into the heart.

It screamed again, stumbled to the side, first left, then right, swaying in a drunken dance before it fell to its knees.

Gopal was up on his feet, now standing at a distance, his sword tucked against his back, disappearing from one blink of an eye to the next as it melded into his skin.

Karan soaked the third arrow in the blood welling at his cut and launched it. That's when the rakshasa fell face-first into the ground.

Karan stepped up to him, close enough for him to hear, far enough so that a careless swipe of talons didn't kill him.

"Where did you come from?" he said, repeating the sentence in formal Hindi.

The words were faint, and Karan couldn't make them out. Gopal had stumbled to his side by then. He said something in what sounded like a variation of the Sanskrit that Karan knew how to read.

"Why are you here?"

We came for you.

And then steam, smelling of acrid smoke, erupted from the wounds as it collapsed, its corpse shriveling up like a raisin.

When there was nothing left but ash and smoke, Gopal turned to Karan.

"Took your sweet fucking time, didn't ya?" he said, his accent even more pronounced.

"How did you know there was an attack?" Karan replied.

"I've been following the rakshasa for days. It's been here for a while, assuming a different form. It attacked today hoping to lure you out, since yours and Laila's smells are all over this building."

Gopal motioned with his chin. "You may want to take care of your lady love."

Karan turned to Laila and saw that she was kneeling next to Ben's head, tears racing down her cheeks.

"Laila," he said, his heart breaking for her.

Before he could move toward her, Gopal stopped him with a hand on his arm. "Word of advice? Until this is over, you should refrain from telling her the truth about your first kill."

Karan's eyes narrowed. "What are you—"

"It's for your own good," Gopal said. Then he brushed the back of his hand against his nose, smearing the blood and sweat. His breath was still fast, his hair slicked back. "Now get out of here. I'll take care of the rest."

Karan knew when to argue and when to walk. "We need to talk," he said.

"Not yet," Gopal said. "You have a week to face Satyapal. Then once you do, I'll find you. Don't forget what I said."

Karan heard the soft whimper from Laila and saw that she was rocking back and forth now, her trembling fingers brushing over Ben's shining head.

Karan dropped the compound bow at his feet and crossed the room to her. He rested his hands against her shoulders, and when she turned to look at him, her eyes were that same dark brown that he'd begun to fall in love with.

"Challo," he said softly. "We have to go."

When she didn't make a move to get up, he tucked his forearms under her armpits and hefted her to her feet. She began to struggle.

"No! I am not leaving Ben," she said. "I am not leaving!"

Gopal was in front of her a moment later, sandwiching her between himself and Karan at her back.

"Love, you are in a war," he said softly. "You cannot avenge his death if you fall apart now. Go with Karan. I'll make sure Ben has the last rites of a king."

"Gopal," she said, her eyes filled with tears. "What is going on?"

"You'll find out soon enough," he said, his eyes soft when he looked down at her. "The police are on their way, and you cannot be here."

Karan didn't waste any more time. He looped an arm under her knees and lifted her in one easy movement. She was built with muscle and strength, and she could conk him in the head if she didn't want to be carried, but she let him hold her until they reached the entrance of the gym.

"Put me down," she said as they passed through the double doors. "Put me down, Karan."

Taking a chance and trusting her not to run back inside, he placed her gently on her feet. She turned back and for a brief second, he saw that she was thinking about it.

"Laila."

She shook her head, and then jogged down the steps. "We have to trust Gopal," she said.

He breathed a sigh of relief and ran toward the driver's seat.

In a moment of déjà vu, they were down the road, far enough away not to be seen, before they heard the sirens.

25. LAILA

"Laila, it's time for you to wake up."

"No, silly! Don't wake her up, then she can't hear us."

Laila turned away from the brilliant crystal blue waters that she used to play in as a child. Her toes dug into warm sand so fine, it was like dust. There was a breeze that smelled as sweet as the air she used to breathe in Mauritius. When she turned to look over her shoulder, her three masis stared back at her, standing in a huddle on a sand dune.

Laila's eyes welled with tears.

"Oh my god, you're here," she whispered.

Then she was on her feet, and embraced by the human arms of her aunts. Vika Masi pressed a series of rapid kisses on the crown of her head. Giri Masi patted her hips, as if checking to make sure that she was eating. Rashmi Masi was petting her hair, pushing it back off her face and out of the breeze.

They looked young again. Vibrant. The way they had for thousands of years.

"Where are you? Where are we?"

"Dreaming," Vika Masi said as she cupped Laila's cheek. "This is the only way we could communicate."

"Why can't you come back?" she asked. She couldn't let go of them, couldn't stop holding on to her family that she missed so much. She had never been away from them for more than a night, and after Denise's and Ben's death, all she wanted was to curl up in their arms.

Vika Masi was the first to speak. "We believe that we began to age because the prophecy for the Daughter of Draupadi has been broken. Our immortality is based on the protection of your lineage. We are only safe and protected in the lands that used to belong to the god of the Rakshasa. If we leave India, we become a part of mythology too."

Her heart was in her throat now. "So, what, my lineage is broken because of something that I did? Is it going to end with me? Can we set the clock back? I'm sorry about all the times I complained when you made me study. I swear I'll never do it again if we can just go back to the way things were."

They glanced at each other, then back to her. "It's now in the universe's hands. We are protected here, but if we leave . . ."

"We die," Rashmi Masi said.

Laila felt her heart squeeze. "Are you saying I'll never see you again?" she whispered.

"We're going to come back to you," Giri Masi said fiercely. "We are going to find a way. But right now, we just need you to stay alive. You have to stay alive."

Laila nodded. In the studio, she'd frozen, transfixed by the rakshasa that looked so like her masis but wholly different. He had killed Ben. Her masis never would've done the same.

"Some things have happened while you're gone," she said. "There have been . . . attacks. And the winery . . ."

She felt the sand shift under her feet. Her masis gasped. Their grips tightened on her arms, and the frantic panic in their eyes had her fighting to hold back her fear tenfold.

"Don't trust anyone!" Vika Masi yelled. "Protect yourself, Laila. You know how. We're counting on you."

"Laila?" She felt two small, strong hands grip her arm and shake. "Laila, wake up."

She turned under the comforter to see Boo's face, ashen in color, her eyes wide.

"Boo? What's wrong? What happened?" Her head was still foggy with dreams, and she tried to focus. The weight of Ben's death pressed heavy on her heart as she remembered where she was and what had happened that day. Another person who she knew, who'd she let close, was now dead.

"I figured it out," Boo whispered, her voice shaking. "I figured out the text, and . . . and the rest. Can you come down to the library?"

She looked at the clock on her bedside table and saw that it was one in the morning. If it couldn't wait, then it meant not only should she get up, but she had to hurry.

"Yes," she said. "Give me a second."

Boo nodded. She stood, hands linked together, watching as Laila got out of bed. She was scared, Laila thought. But Laila's dream, the one that she'd just been yanked from, had given her strength that she hadn't had in a while.

When she slipped on the sweatshirt that she'd discarded by the bedside table, she looked past the screen divider to Boo and Karan's space.

"Where is Karan?" she asked. "Is he already downstairs?"

Boo nodded, her expression solemn.

Instinctively, Laila knew that he'd been the one who helped her into bed.

"Is everything okay?" she asked.

"We should talk," Boo replied.

"That doesn't sound good."

Boo hesitated, then sat at the edge of the bed. "I'm not very good at this," she said quietly.

Laila cocked her head. "Good at what?"

She watched the indecision play on Boo's face.

"Worrying," she finally said. "It's easier on my own, but now I have Karan and I haven't stopped worrying."

Laila was very aware that she hadn't mentioned her parents. Boo almost never talked about them. Her heart went out to this strange, generous, brilliant person. She remembered her dream and like the way her Vika Masi had touched her cheek, Laila reached out and cupped Boo's face. "And now you're worried about me, too."

Boo froze at the touch, then as if she was a bird, hesitant to trust affection, relaxed against Laila's hand. "Yeah," she finally said. "Now I'm worried about you, too."

"We're the descendants of demigods," Laila said, then stood. "We're going to be fine."

Boo followed her out of the room. "This isn't exactly a kids movie about kids on a quest," she replied. "If the Mahabharata has taught us anything, it's that the universe demands what it's owed, and in a war, everyone loses."

"Is that all? Sounds like a piece of cake," Laila said easily, more for Boo's benefit than her own. They walked down to the main level of the home.

The kitchen was empty, and the dining room had a dim light in the corner next to where Boo normally sat.

"We have to go to the library," she said.

Laila's heart began beating in rapid succession as they descended the spiral staircase into the stone underground, and through the open doors enchanted and protected by rakshasi for generations. There, she saw Karan pacing with his arms crossed, the small crease between his brows visible, in front of the long table.

The news couldn't be good if Boo had to wake her up, and Karan pacing. She swallowed hard, bracing herself for the worst.

"Just rip it off like a Band-Aid," Laila said. "Just tell me what the message says and we can deal with it together."

Boo stepped up in front of a large book propped on a wooden reading mount that angled the pages toward her. The open book was at least two feet long and a foot wide, but it was one of the slenderest volumes of texts in the library, pages handwritten with ink steeped in the magic from the sages and bound in leather.

"This had the key," Boo said reverently.

"Why did you pull the book of myths and legends?" Laila asked.

Boo and Karan looked up at her at that moment, their heads jerking in unison.

"You know it?" Boo said.

Laila nodded. "I know all the Smriti texts," she said, and motioned to the volumes on the left of the library. The volumes that were authored by specific individuals, versus the vedas, which were collective knowledge. "When Vyasa dictated the Mahabharata to Lord Ganesha, who wrote the epic using his tusk, he completed nineteen volumes. Except the nineteenth volume was never released."

"Why not?" Karan asked. "Is it because of the significance of the number eighteen? The war was for eighteen days, there were eighteen books, and that number comes up again and again and again during the epic."

Laila shook her head. "Technically there are only eighteen books that cover the full story of the Pandavas, the Kauravas, and those connected to the warring factions. The nineteenth volume is about the future of those who survived, and their legacy. Less story, and more like a guidebook. Humans didn't need to know it, so it was never published. The myths and legends volume in front of you is the only text in existence."

"That explains a lot," Boo said quietly.

Laila scanned the open pages from her position on the opposite side of the table. Next to it was a yellow legal pad and a ballpoint pen. The notes that Boo had scratched in tiny barely legible text looked like the ramblings of a mad person compared to the even lines from the book she had been referencing.

Karan wouldn't look at her. He remained on the opposite side of the table with his arms crossed over his chest and he paced in the small space he'd carved out for himself.

"Karan?"

"Just hear her out," he said.

Laila looked over at Boo. She was so young. At sixteen she spoke like she was in her thirties. And here she was, day after day, struggling to find answers for them.

And now she was in her element. Boo adjusted the frames on her nose and read the text that she had printed on the legal pad next to the book of myths and legends.

"From shoulder to hip on Laila, and then from hip to shoulder on bhai it reads: 'The two souls destined to love, damned to be parted, reunited to begin the end of it all.'"

The end of it all.

Laila pulled out a chair and fell heavily into it. "Please tell me I do not have a dark omen for the apocalypse tattooed on my back." For the first time since it had appeared on her skin, she felt like she wanted to claw it off, to remove it as quickly as possible. Most days she forgot it existed, but now? It was all she could think about.

"I'm afraid you do," Boo said. "Both of you do."

The signs of Kali Yuga ending, she thought. Even though she'd known that it was a distinct possibility in her lifetime that if she didn't fulfill her duty, she could create a ripple effect in the universe, but to have it tattooed on her back?

That was like rubbing her nose in her mistake.

"And this is because we touched?" Laila asked. She remembered the moment she'd first seen Karan, and then they'd shaken hands. The burst of energy that spread through the archery studio and made the lights flicker and their palms glow. "This means that Gopal knew we were going to trigger the end of Kali Yuga. Son of a bitch!"

"There's more," Karan said. He still wouldn't look at her. His gaze remained focused on his cousin. "Boo, tell her the rest."

She went back to the book in front of her, the book of myths and legends that had been seemingly insignificant. The one Laila's aunt hadn't even tested her on because they always said that her history was in her family legacy books and not in this volume specifically about the two warring factions.

"There is a small section here that looks like it has been ripped out. But I was able to figure out what parts were missing from the text." She flipped the page and revealed a tear where half of the page was missing.

"Strange," Layla said. "I don't remember ever seeing that. My aunts are insane about keeping the texts pristine. Was it intentional?"

"Laila," Boo said gently. "I don't know your masis, but it's probably because they didn't want you to know the whole story of what I think it all means. They wanted you to feel like you had some control over the partner that you chose to have a child with."

"Some control? What are you talking about?"

Boo glanced at Karan, then back at her notes. "I think it says that the Daughter of Draupadi is destined to continue to cultivate a lineage with the descendants of the Pandavas to maintain the balance of good and even in the universe. That even though the lines are diluted centuries after they began, in some way or another, the blood of a Pandava is to connect with the blood of Draupadi. And destiny sets the course. Your ancestors had the same fate before you and you're supposed to step in line."

Laila was going to be sick. "I feel like that's a little incestuous, don't you think?"

Boo shook her head. "Draupadi had five husbands who all had other wives and birthed other children. The lines are so diluted that the closest you could probably get was like an eighth cousin."

"Still, a little gross."

"You're viewing this through the lens of your American upbringing," Boo said. "Through colonialism. Eighth cousin was no big deal when the gods decided your fate. You have to view it through their experience."

Laila clenched her fists. "I'm viewing it as a person who has been told her entire life that her main responsibility is to have children and carry on her bloodline. I'm viewing this as a person who has spent her entire life in hiding. I'm viewing it as a person who now has the responsibility to have a child but doesn't even have a say in who she wants to have a child with."

"I'm sorry," Boo said quietly. Her voice trembled. "I'm really sorry. Don't shoot the messenger here."

"You're right," Laila sighed. "I'm sorry. It's not your fault."

"I need a minute," Karan said. The words were so quiet and fierce that she hadn't even known that he'd spoken them at first.

Then he turned and he walked out of the library. Laila could hear his footsteps on the stone staircase as he ascended to the main level, and then there was quiet. She was left alone with Boo sitting in front of the one text that she had a feeling her aunts never wanted her to find.

Laila scrubbed her hand over her face and tried to think beyond the anger, to think practically about her situation. Maybe a part of her always knew that the idea of finding a person to have a child with was never really a free experience. Nothing in her life was free. But she couldn't change that. That wasn't going to bring her aunts back. They'd already gone past the point of no return, and she either had to accept a fate that would make her miserable to save Kali Yuga or be doomed with everyone else.

Doomsday didn't sound like such a bad situation, to be honest.

Thoughts of her aunts and the dream she'd had fogged her mind, and she was beginning to think that she had all the pieces and that now they just had to start putting the puzzle together.

"Boo, over all the centuries, do you think this is the first time that a descendant of Karna met a Daughter of Draupadi? There has to be something that was put in place to make sure that Draupadi would never cross Karna's bloodline."

Boo nodded. "I was thinking that too, but I haven't found anything in the text."

"Okay, then let's go back to what we do know," Laila said. "Gopal was the one who instigated Karan's quest. We have to assume that when his parents went missing, he'd go to his uncle who would dabble in dark magic that would somehow lead to me."

"Okay, I'm following," Boo said.

"If Gopal knows that I'm supposed to be with another Pandava, then why would he intentionally disrupt the narrative when he's supposed to be on our side? When he's supposed to protect Kali Yuga from ending early? Why would he play this big elaborate game so I end up meeting the person I needed to stay away from the most?"

Boo shook her head. "I don't know. But he has to have a reason. And if he was in that studio trying to stop the rakshasa this morning, then he may have anticipated all these spirits coming and had to take the risk that this was a by-product of the plan. He is playing with fate and destiny."

"That means he wants us to fight Satyapal for a reason, too," Laila said as she leaned forward. "We're still not finished with the game."

"That's what I'm afraid of," Boo said.

Laila got up and walked around the table. She held her arms out and Boo looked at them, then back at her face, before she accepted the embrace. She rested her head against Laila's chest and sighed.

"I thought that this would be an interesting intellectual challenge that I could pursue while helping my cousin," she said, and her thin, nervous body trembled with the words. "I'm scared how real this is."

"We'll figure it out," Laila said quietly. She rubbed a hand down Boo's back. "We'll figure it out, I promise."

Then she let her go and brushed a stray tear off the soft curve of her cheek. "Why don't you go to sleep? You've done a lot today. We can't do anything more right now, so take some time to rest."

Boo looked down at the book. "What about bhai?"

"I'll go get him," she said. Either he was in the kitchen pacing, or he'd headed out to the gym. Her bet was the gym at this time of night.

"Boo, Billi is neglected lately," Laila said, mentioning her cat. "She's probably in need of some cuddles too."

Boo sniffled. "Okay. For the health of the animal, of course."

"Of course," Laila said with a smile. She followed Boo, and before she walked through the library entrance, she glanced at the temple at the end of the corridor. The one protected by the image of her four rakshasi masis. Then she closed the library doors and walked up to the main level. No matter how many people told her that she didn't have a choice, she was going to figure out a way to choose her own destiny. If Laila had to fight to protect her happiness, to protect Karan, then she'd cheerfully find a way to burn down the world for him.

26. KARAN

Laila was never meant for him. They were just cogs in a machine, and she was supposed to be with someone else. She was supposed to fall in love and have a family and have memories with a Pandava. Because centuries after Karna's existence, the bloodline was still not good enough. His soul was damned.

And wasn't that a wakeup call if he'd ever had one?

After he walked into the gym, he paced restlessly before he rolled out the large punching bag. His father had been the first person to tell him never to get into the habit of using physical aggression to get out anger or heightened emotions. To instead meditate and let the emotions run through him before they dissipated. But right now, all he wanted to do was punch something. To curse the fate that had scarred him in ink that had seeped deep into the layers of his skin.

He had feelings for Laila. She was so damn smart, and she understood him on a level that he'd never been able to connect with another person before. He wanted more moments on the dock with her. He wanted moments to laugh with her and be with her as they trained. And he wanted to find his parents so he could introduce her to them. Maybe that was a foolish thought. Maybe his dreams of taking her away to college, of protecting her and making sure she was safe, were foolish fantasies.

Karan lashed out against the punching bag. He used the mixed combat art form from Kerala that his father and uncle had once taught him as a boy, hating that the one time he was by himself, he'd fallen into a path that put his entire legacy at risk.

He still felt like he was grieving for the uncle he had once known, coming to terms with the fact that this history was a lie, only to find out that the life he had made for himself with the woman he was developing feelings for was something that he could never experience.

Karan pulled his T-shirt over his head, tossing it aside and revealing the naked chest gleaming with sweat already from the brief burst of energy that pulsed through him.

He had been running through drills and combinations he'd learned in his youth, alternating between lessons from military school and childhood, when he saw the flash of color at the corner of his eye at the room's entrance.

Laila was still wearing her sleep pants and the sweatshirt that she'd left at the edge of her bed. He remembers seeing it before she'd gently closed the panel between her room and the sleeping quarters.

"I'm really not in the best space for a conversation," he said as he rounded on the bag and continued a series of combination hits. Each hit caused the padded bag to rattle against its base, swaying from left to right with a *thwack*.

He moved left to right. Punch, kick, grapple. Punch, kick, grapple. Over the head, and then an undercut. When he had run through the drill, his chest heaving as he gasped for air, he felt the soft featherlike touch of her fingertips against the tattoo on his back. The tattoo that damned both of them.

"Why aren't you more upset about this," he said quietly.

"Because I'm more mature than you?"

He said the words before he could stop himself: "Draupadi came from a royal bloodline, from the blood of the fire goddess herself."

"Yeah, that's not new information," Laila said.

He turned to look at her over his shoulder. "She was married to royalty. Her legacy belongs with the descendants of the same royalty. My legacy is that of a warrior. A guard. Even though I have Kunti's and Surya's blood in me, my ancestor's role, my role, has always been less than yours."

Laila stepped around him, her fingers tracing over the hard ridges of his abdomen until she was standing inches away, her head tilted back as she looked up at his face. "Are you trying to tell me that you're not good enough for me?"

His jaw flexed and he clenched so hard he could swear that his teeth cracked at the impact. "Do you think that, too?"

"Karan," she said, softly. "I will never and have never thought that you were anything less than the honest, dedicated, intelligent person that you are. I've already accepted the fact that we can't undo what we've already done. We've met, we've touched, and now we've been together." She stood up on her toes, her fingers gripping his shoulders and digging into his muscles, easing some of the tension there. She stood on her toes and pressed a soft kiss to the underside of his chin.

The brief feather-light touch helped him relax a fraction. His hands went to her waist and entangled in the ends of her long hair, which she'd left loose.

"Just because a bunch of people who are no longer with us have said that the descendants of your ancestor are not good enough to touch me, that doesn't mean that I believe the same thing," she whispered. Then she pressed another kiss, this one along his jaw line, and he bent his head so that he could smell the soft scent of her hair, the nape of her neck.

A part of him wondered if she had been numb after seeing the death of her archery coach the day before. That this was all too much for her. But when their eyes met, all he saw were the deep, dark pools. Her skin was cool to the touch and her fingers didn't burn.

"What do we do?" he asked, his voice raw. "Even though Gopal had a hand in us meeting, we've played right into his hands and royally screwed up."

"For someone who's so uptight about honor and legacy that must suck for you," she said. Then her arms were around his waist, and they were pressed against each other. His hand slipped under the hem of her sweatshirt so he could touch the bare skin and trace his fingertips against the dark mark that scarred them both.

"Not funny," he muttered even as his gaze focused on her mouth.

Then with her head tipped back, her mouth parted, she said, "I want you. I only want to be with you. There are so many parts of ourselves that we have yet to share with each other, but this is one that I know for sure. I choose to give my body to you. To give my . . . my heart to you."

His own heart squeezed. Her words were like a precious gift that branded her deeper than the curse that tattooed both of them ever could.

Karan kissed her, and the soft press of her lips was as electric as the first moment that their hands met in the archery studio. It was like lightning and fire raced under the surface of his skin, and he felt alive with the feel of her in his arms.

With quick hands and desperate lips, they lowered to the mat, eager to be with each other. Eager to touch each other and hold each other and explore each other's bodies and the brief moment of pleasure that they could give themselves. And each other.

They had gone back to the bedroom shortly after they . . . made love. He had to get used to thinking of sex with Laila that way. It was too important, too vital, to be anything else. Their fingers linked and palms pressed firmly together where the mark glowed whenever one needed the other. Boo was sleeping soundly on the makeshift mattress in the living area in Laila's suite, and out of respect for her, Karan moved to sleep on his makeshift mattress.

"No," Laila said softly when he let go of her hand. "Sleep with me. You don't have to do anything but just sleep with me. We'll close the screen and, in the morning, you can go back into the bed."

He nodded because there wasn't anything he wasn't able to give her. Maybe it was a part of who he was. After all, Karna had been the most virtuous and giving figures in the Mahabharata. When someone asked for something, he had to provide it. He had even given his armor away to Lord Indira. Karan was unable to deny Laila the same way.

They settled under her blankets, and he curled around her back the way he was becoming accustomed to doing, so that they were pressed tightly together, chest to back, legs tangled, his arm underneath her pillow and his hand twined with hers as she pressed their joined hands against her chest.

Just as they were drifting off, she turned to him and asked a question that had every muscle in his body tensing.

"Can I ask you something," she said, her voice thick with sleep.

"Anything."

"I was so focused on Ben, but I saw you make that shot. You dipped your arrow in your blood. You knew exactly how to kill the rakshasa."

He pressed a kiss against the curve of her shoulder. "Monster-hunting is what I do."

"How did you know that your blood would do that?" she asked, followed by a yawn.

He thought about his first asura hunt. When they got back to India, and he tried to recall the details, he couldn't remember anything. His father and uncle had told him it was the adrenaline rush. However, the longer he'd stayed with Laila, the more he was able to remember of that night in Indonesia.

Like a blood-tipped arrow.

Wait a minute. She'd said something. What had she said to him? What was it about that conversation that, he had a feeling, was so important to remember now?

"Karan?"

"Yeah, I learned it on my first hunt," he said absently.

Laila hummed, then closed her eyes. "That's good to know."

"Why, are you planning on slaying any rakshasa?"

There was a soft, sleepy chuckle. "No, silly. The exact opposite. I'm going to protect them. That's what you do with family."

His eyes widened and he held his breath, waiting until hers evened out. When she was fast asleep, he slipped out from the other side of the bed, his heart racing. Her masis. Were her masis rakshasi? He turned to look at her over his shoulder from his position at the edge of the mattress.

The Daughter of Draupadi with fire in her eyes.

The woman he loved was raised by monsters.

He stood and put on his T-shirt again. He quietly made his way downstairs, through the kitchen, then through the panel and into the library.

The lights flickered on, and then he walked for the first time to the double doors all the way at the end of the library corridor.

He hadn't paid close attention to the statues that guarded the room at the end of the library. There was something about them that made him anxious, a little nervous.

Behind the closed doors was Laila's family's legacy.

He tilted his head to the side, examining the narrow waists, the big breasts, and the wide hips covered in a layered skirt to the knees.

His eyes widened at the subtle indentation of the carving. If he stood at just the right angle, he could see that the women were rakshasi.

There were four rakshasi that protected the Daughters of Draupadi, and four rakshasi carvings that literally protected the written legacy of the daughters.

It was right in front of him this whole time.

But there were four of them.

Karan remembered that Laila said one of her aunts had died.

He walked parallel to the doors until he reached the one at the far end. His memory was hazy, blurred from fear. He reached out to touch the door, and when his fingertips grazed the arm of the rakshasi, they began to burn. He immediately jerked back, swearing at the bolt of pain.

Do not go near her.

Satyapal.

Do not go near her.

Floaters blurred his vision, and he blinked them away. Then he stumbled back into the edge of the table, looking up at the rakshasi.

"Oh my god," he whispered. The night he'd killed the rakshasi became crystal clear between one heartbeat and the next. He could smell his own sweat, feel the heat, hear the buzz of insects in the rainforest.

She is divine.

He ran back to the myths and legends book that was laid open on the table. And then looked at the notepad sitting next to it. He read the translation of the text on his back again. Two souls loved, two souls damned, two souls parted.

Gopal's warning made so much sense now.

Karan quickly made his way back upstairs, and mindful of the soft sounds of sleep, he was able to retrieve a pair of jeans, a T-shirt, and a sweatshirt before slipping out of the suite once more.

Before he entered the garage, he sent a quick text message to Boo and Laila, letting them know that he was heading to the winery because he wanted to check the site again as a precaution. He hoped that the lie would hold them over while he searched for Gopal.

Had he really been the one responsible for killing Laila's aunt? Had their destinies been intertwined this whole time?

27. KARAN

Karan backed out of the open bay onto the driveway before he made his way to the end of the long serpentine pavement path and through the sensor-responding metal gates. Night was still hovering over the trees, moments away from crawling back into the shadows under dawn.

He made a left onto the single-lane road and was headed toward the same stretch of road where he'd first met Gopal when his phone pinged with an incoming message.

Karan glanced at the unknown number and narrowed his eyes before he decided to take a chance and open it.

UNKNOWN: Next time you go down that road, you won't like what you encounter.

He quickly typed a text back with one hand before returning the phone to the mount.

KARAN: Who is this?

UNKNOWN: Gopal, you idiot.

KARAN: It's not like I have you in my phone, dude. Where are you?

UNKNOWN: Meet me at Flume Falls. Where you and Laila had your first romantic getaway.

Karan made the turn down the next road so that he could loop around and drive in the opposite direction. His palms began to sweat against the steering wheel.

Ten minutes later, he almost missed the small turnoff in the dark where he had to park to access Flume Falls. He slowed, his lights cutting through the grayish early morning, and came to a stop in the center of the lot. It felt like it had been eons ago when he met Laila for their first date alone, when in reality they had covered just a few weeks.

Karan stepped out of the car, and in the distance, hidden between the bent branches of a tree, he spotted the wheels of a bike. It was hidden away so well, he would've missed it if he wasn't looking for the black and silver vehicle.

He pulled out his phone and tried to text the number that had sent him the message, but he was in a dead zone. There were so many spots in the Finger Lakes where the signal was poor. This was one of them, unfortunately.

"This better not be a trap," he murmured to himself before he strapped his bow with four arrows to his back, then grabbed his hunting knife and holstered it at his thigh. He removed his night-vision goggles from the bag that he'd retrieved from the foot of his bed and tossed in the car just in case he needed it.

Then, with his senses sharpened, and tense with alertness and adrenaline, he stepped onto the path into the woods that he'd once taken to meet the Daughter of Draupadi.

"Gopal?" he whispered. "Is this to get back at me for the time that I jumped Laila?"

He was almost at the falls when he heard a rustle in the trees.

Then there was the soft sound of singing.

The sound was melodic, and vaguely familiar.

Then he recognized it as the humming grew louder. It was an old Hindi song.

Eecheka dana peecheka dana, dane upar dana, eecheka dana.

"M-Mom?"

His heart began to pound at a rapid rate. He moved quickly down the path to the sound. "Mom!"

Someone body-slammed him in his side and took him to the ground between the trees. He rolled and was about to jump against his attacker when he saw the familiar glow of the blue sword.

"Gopal, what the hell—"

"Shhh!" Gopal hissed, a finger to his lips.

The singing started again, and Karan was about to lunge toward the trees when Gopal stopped him a second time.

That is not your mother, he mouthed.

Karan didn't know how to process all of the emotions so fast, from acknowledgment to sorrow to pain and anger.

What is it? he mouthed back.

Gopal adjusted his glasses. In the dark and with the help of his goggles, Karan saw his mouth move to form a word.

Dayan.

He'd fought witches before, but none of them had the ability to mask their voices into the sound of a woman who he loved and admired and desperately wanted to be with.

The singing started again, and it was growing closer.

It was so achingly beautiful, and it called to him like a siren song.

He crouched behind the trunk of a tree next to Gopal. They listened for any movement, any subtle shift in the tree line. His father had told him that a dayan was a woman who had been wronged and murdered in life who haunted trees and forests near villages. They sucked the life force out of men by drinking their blood, and walked on backward feet. They went after the men who harmed them first, then all the men in their families, before they razed villages. And lastly, they'd attack any man who had lied to or wronged a woman.

So many villages in India still believed in dark magic, and branded innocent women dayans. But this one? This was real.

And after lying to Laila in bed when he'd implied that his father had taught him how to kill a rakshasa, then texting her the wrong location, he'd almost been lured to his death.

"What is a dayan doing in the Finger Lakes?" he whispered, his voice barely audible over the rustle of trees.

"Trying to kill you," Gopal said, pointing to Karan's chest.

Karan rolled his eyes as he removed his knife.

The sound was growing closer, the haunting sound of his mother singing the children's song. It sounded so real.

He felt his palm began to glow, and swore. Laila was about to find out what he was up to, and that was the last thing he wanted.

There was the sound of laughter, innocent and sultry at the same time. Karan looked up. The movement came from the tree limbs above them.

Karan looked at Gopal, eyes wide, before they both dove backward, rolling away from the spot they'd occupied, just as the dayan landed on feet twisted complete around, a bloodstained white nightgown, black hair tangled around a pale face, and black holes for eye sockets.

Karan had his knife held out in front of him as the dayan turned in his direction.

"So young," it said in Hindi. "So handsome." Then she launched herself at Karan, mouth open with black and bloodstained teeth. She lunged at his neck.

"A little help!" he called out.

Gopal's blue sword flashed behind them and cut through her neck in one slice, metal severing bone and carotid artery.

Except the head stayed on the body.

"It didn't work," Karan cried as he blocked blow after blow.

"I can see that," Gopal replied in a singsong voice. "But it should work. Every asura dies with the sword."

Karan managed to avoid the swiping talons and used his knife as a shield. "Dayans aren't asuras!" he shouted.

"Oh," Gopal said, his voice filled with curious awareness now. "Then I guess that makes sense."

Karan dodged another attempt to bite into his neck. "Are you going to do something or not?" he shouted.

"Will your blood work?"

Karan kicked out, giving him a second to respond. "It won't! Just works with the rakshasi!"

"Then I guess we just have to do it the old-fashioned way," Gopal said. He sliced through the neck again, and then did a roundhouse kick.

The dayan stumbled forward, then in one slow move, turned to face Gopal.

"Do you think I fear a god?" she hissed. Karan watched as the dayan lunged at Gopal, who danced away from the attack.

They looked like they were in a waltz. The dayan had single-minded focus to bite, her jaw working overtime like the mouth of a piranha, while Gopal barely made it out of reach. Karan dove for the bow and arrow he'd dropped, nocked the arrow, and released it into the head of the dayan moments later.

The arrow lodged in the skull, and there was a screech, a hiss, as the dayan whirled on him. She yanked the arrow out, which made a popping sound like the cork out of a glass bottle.

"Well, that was . . . weird," he said.

The dayan stumbled across the clearing and screeched when she stepped into a triangle of light that filtered through the trees. She scurried back, screeching again.

Karan and Gopal looked up at each other.

The dayan couldn't survive in the light.

They immediately circled the dayan, forcing her closer and closer to the clearing, where dawn had spilled through the tree canopy. Then Gopal and Karan struck, each blow meant to keep her in place until she was hissing and screaming from the pain of sunlight.

Just as her skin began to steam, she lashed out with her black nails, long and dipped in poison. Gopal and Karan dodged the attack, which gave her just enough time to break free and run into the darkness.

They moved into the light, breathing heavily from the exertion.

"Should we go after her?" Karan said, whipping off his night-vision goggles. The sun had risen enough for him to see in the forest.

"No," Gopal said. "I've been tracking her. She'll be the hardest one to kill."

"How many more are there that you know about?" Karan asked.

"She's the last one," Gopal said. Then he turned to look at Karan. "For now. They've come in the places that you both have a signature. A life force imprint. That's where the veil between yugas is the thinnest and they can come through."

Yugas. The four realms of life. The first was only the gods. The second was gods and demons. The third was gods, demons, and humans. And Kali Yuga? The one they lived in now was only humans. The yugas weren't stacked on top of each other like he'd always envisioned but aligned next to each other like books on a shelf.

Karan thought back to all the attacks. The studio. The winery. The road between the studio and the house. Flume Falls.

He braced his feet, facing Gopal. "You knew this was going to happen, didn't you?" Karan said. "You knew these attacks would happen, so you're here, and my parents are out of the picture, along with Laila's aunts."

Gopal's sword shimmered, and he lifted it over his shoulder, as if holstering it. The moment it touched his back, it was gone.

"If we're going to fight a centuries-old war for the second time and win, don't you think we should do something different instead of the same thing that the other side is going to expect?"

Draupadi and the Pandavas.

His relationship with Satyapal made sense then. His loyalty to Satyapal was the same loyalty that Karna had to the head of the Kaurava army.

If history repeated himself, then he would've killed Laila if he had the chance. Instead, he fell in love with her.

"Did you know that we would trigger the end of Kali Yuga when we met?"

Gopal shook his head. "I can usually . . . predict a lot of things. I thought that I was helping Laila, but this was something that I wasn't prepared for."

But that could all fall apart. "Tell me," he said hoarsely. "Tell me the truth, Gopal. The rakshasi I killed in the forest all those years ago."

Gopal sighed. His shoulders slumped. "That shouldn't have happened. Satyapal had been playing with dark magic for some time at that point. He'd gotten farther than any human has in centuries because of his relationship to your father. He was tracking Laila's guardians."

Which meant that Karan had killed Laila's aunt.

"Oh my god," he whispered. She'd never forgive him.

Karan brushed a thumb against the aching center of his palm, which continued to glow.

Gopal tracked his movement, his eyes widening.

"Karan, why is your palm glowing?" he said.

"It's been aching since I first stepped into the forest," he said. "Does it go away—"

Gopal pushed past him toward the parking lot beyond the trees. "It should've stopped the minute the dayan left."

"Then why is it . . . Oh no."

It was Laila who was in trouble now.

No, he thought. No, he wasn't going to let this happen. He wouldn't let anyone hurt her. Even if she never wanted anything to do with him again once she found out the truth.

28. LAILA

Laila woke to the feel of her palm burning. She bolted in an upright position and glanced over at the other side of the bed. "Karan?"

She was alone, and when she touched the empty spot, the sheets were cool.

"Shit," she hissed as she stumbled out of bed. Karan was in trouble.

Laila put on a sports bra and pants, socks, and sneakers, and strapped the knife sheath to her thigh before she bolted out of her room. Boo wasn't in her bed. Her blanket was also pushed off to the end of the makeshift mattress.

"Boo!" she called out as she raced down the hall toward the stairs. Her palm continued to pulse, and her heart was in her throat at the thought of Karan being in danger. Where did he go? Why did he leave after they had just faced off with a rakshasa at the gym?

"What is it?" The sound of Boo's voice put her at ease as she rounded the corner and entered the kitchen. Boo was sitting at the counter reading Laila's textbook for school while she drank a cup of chai. She looked up at Laila, startled, when Laila entered the room. "What happened?"

Laila held up her palm. "Where is Karan?"

Boo's eyes bulged. "I don't know. He wasn't down here when I woke up. The door to the library looks like it's still closed too."

Laila knew that the property was protected and that there was no way for him to get hurt while he was on the grounds. Which meant that he had to have left the house. She ran to the entrance of the garage and opened the door, praying that she would see all the cars in their respective bays. But when she yanked the door open, she saw only her aunts' vehicles and her Audi. Her Explorer was missing.

Laila ran back into the kitchen and found her phone where she'd left it charging on the island.

KARAN: Headed to the winery to see if we missed anything.

"Dammit!" She quickly called his number and heard it ring once before it went straight to voicemail.

"Karan, you absolute idiot!" she shouted. Why was his phone off?

Boo stood from her spot at the counter, her hands trembling as she linked them together. "I remember he said that Gopal told him if he went back to any of the previous spots where there had been an attack, there was a good chance that he would get attacked again."

Her hand was still throbbing. She needed to go to him. All she had to do was get in her car and drive.

But first she rounded the counter and stopped in front of Boo. With her hand on the young girl's shoulders, she leaned in to say, "You're going to be okay. I'm going to bring him home, Boo."

Her eyes welled, and she nodded. "I can't be alone again," she said, her voice trembling. "I want both of you to come back. Please."

"I'll make sure that Karan is with me when I get back to the house," she said softly. And then she grabbed her keys and phone and dove into her car.

She raced down her driveway, through her barely parted gates, and out onto the road. Laila made a hard left, trying to focus on the pulsing in the center of her palm. Her firepower was under control. She felt it cool and contained inside her.

"If you die, I am going to be very mad," she muttered as her car soared over a bump and landed with a hard thud before screeching around the corner.

Her heart ached as she saw the familiar crossroads of the winery and she remembered Denise's face, twisted with the rage of the pisacha that possessed her. She turned into the lot before she registered the other car parked next to the burned remnants of the winery, the charred broken half walls that were a breath away from collapsing.

That wasn't her Explorer, but it was familiar.

It was the same vehicle Karan had used when he'd first arrived in upstate New York, the same car that should've been damaged and turned in to the rental agency. It was now in front of the yellow Caution tape and the Condemned signage.

"What the hell?" she said. Her palm cooled, as if it was telling her Karan wasn't in danger. Then why was his old rental car in the lot?

She stayed in the car, watching for movement, when finally a middle-aged white man with broad shoulders and a kind smile stepped out from the driver's side.

He stood at a distance, his gait awkward.

He held up a small badge. "Hello?" he called out. She could hear him through the windows. "I'm Ron. I'm the insurance adjuster for the property. I was told I could come and inspect the outside myself."

Insurance adjuster? That's right. She was supposed to get a call from the adjuster. But why had he just shown up at the property instead of calling her? And why was he in the familiar car that shouldn't be driveable? It was also barely seven in the morning.

Something is wrong, she thought. Something felt off.

And then her palm began to glow again.

"Oh shit," she said. She shoved the gearshift and put the car in reverse before she slammed her gas pedal. The car jerked backward, but in the rearview mirror she saw the exterior gate closing.

"Come on, come on, come on!" she screamed. But her car slammed into the gate, and she jerked forward, crashing her forehead against the steering wheel. She felt blood ooze out of her forehead, and stars flashed in front of her eyes.

She shoved her car door open and stumbled outside. Then braced her feet apart.

Ron was no longer the white middle-aged man she'd seen when she'd first driven into the winery parking lot. He'd transformed into an older Indian man, whose fitted jeans and black tunic did nothing to conceal the weapons strapped to his body.

"How did you—"

"Concealment magic, my dear," he said conversationally, his accent the same as Karan's, but harder, with thick vowels and consonants that felt like bullets. “The monsters you call your family protect you with the same type of magic.”

Laila pressed a hand against the cut on her forehead, her palm heating and hopefully helping the wound to seal.

He took one step toward her, then another. “My, my, my. I have been looking for you for ten years, Laila Bansal.”

“Really?” she said, trying to sound conversational even as her stomach turned. “I’ve never met someone so old who was obsessed with me. I don’t even know your name.”

The man tsked as if he was just biding his time. He removed a blade from his shoe and then examined the sharp edge. If he threw it at her, would she remember her training enough to dodge it? She was still disoriented, her body aching from the impact of hitting the gate.

“You know of my nephew, but right now, I’m not sure he deserves to be called that. He’s a traitor, after all. Very unlike his bloodline. I can only assume it’s your influence.”

Satyapal. He’d found them.

She tried to ignore her aching forehead as she moved to the left, to distance herself from her opponent and make it to the small path that wrapped around the side of the gate. If he had dark magic on his side, her chances of escaping were slim.

No, that was a defeatist attitude, and her aunts would’ve been horrified if they knew she was accepting defeat so soon. Laila knew she could do this. She had been training for this her whole life.

“I don’t know where Karan’s parents are,” she said, hoping that if she could misdirect his attention, she’d buy herself time to figure out what to do. “You’ve made the trip for nothing.”

"Oh, I don't care where they are, frankly," Satyapal said coldly. He flipped the knife in his hand, as if measuring the weight of the hilt. "They are my family, but there are things in this world that are more important than transient relationships. There is legacy."

Keep him talking. Keep him talking.

"Legacy? What are you even talking about?"

"Like you would understand," he said. The bitterness in his voice was hard to miss. "Like you would even know what it was like being a human with middle-class parents. If I die, no one will remember me. No one will read about my name in history books. Unless I change the course myself. Now Karan. People will remember him and his father. His life has meaning even if he doesn't deserve it. Even if he doesn't respect it the way that someone like I would."

"What does that have to do with me?" she said. She moved again when he took a step closer. They were like boxers in a ring, circling each other now.

"It has everything to do with you, my dear," he said, his words sounding as sinister as she'd expect from a middle-aged Indian man on a power trip. He stopped, straightening, as he looked her up and down. "You're just as beautiful as your mother."

Her mother? Laila froze. "You knew my mother?"

"I wanted to know your mother," Satyapal said. With one hand tucked in his pocket and the other twisting the blade, he shook his head. "Such a shame she had to die so young. When you were so young."

Laila felt like she was going to be sick. Bile rose in her stomach. Did he have something to do with her mother's accident?

Before she could ask, he moved faster than she'd ever anticipated. His hand was around her throat, the knife point digging into her abdomen. With one sharp jerk, he could gut her.

"When I learned she died, I was going to raise you as my own," he said softly, as if he was comforting a child. "And then I was going to plant my seed in your body, and the next Daughter of Draupadi would have my blood."

Okay, I'm definitely going to throw up now, she thought as he held her in his grasp. The idea that this man would ever touch her made her sick and, for the first time, afraid. Is that what he'd wanted this whole time? To mix his bloodline with hers? To create a legacy?

No wonder men were the ones who started wars.

Because they were absolutely ridiculous.

"How did you find me?" she said, gulping for air. Just another minute. If he could keep his eyes on hers.

"The asuras answer to me," he whispered, his face inches from hers. She could smell the fetid breath from his lips, see the chipped front tooth, and hear the hiss of the venom that coated his tongue. If she didn't hate him before, she sure as hell hated him now. How could this man have anything to do with her Karan?

"Do you die like the asuras do?" she whispered. Her fire blasted out toward him and he stumbled back two full steps.

But he didn't burn.

Satyapal brushed at his steaming shirt as he laughed. "You're stronger than your mother was. Good! I want a strong daughter from you. Then my blood will be woven into the fabric of the universe."

He lunged for her again, but this time she was ready. She kicked his knife out of his hand, thrusting a fist in the center of his chest. He cried out, jerking back, and then she felt an invisible shackle on her wrist, wrenching her arm behind her back. Her knees folded under the pressure and the pain sang through her body as she hit the gravel.

Her skin heated and she focused all her attention on her wrists before the shackles released, but it was too late. Satyapal slammed a fist against her cheek and she went flying. She hit the ground hard enough that it took a moment for her to orient herself.

For the love of god, Laila, don't pass out. You were trained by rakshasi.

As if her aunts had given her the strength to move forward, she shot another bolt of flames toward Satyapal, forcing him back before he could hit her again.

"You're a fool if you think that your fire could hurt me," he shouted. "I'm just a mortal and Draupadi's fire is an illusion."

"Did you kill my mother?" she said hoarsely.

"You're mother was *weak*. She couldn't protect you any better than those rakshasi have."

"Did you kill my mother?"

"Yes," he hissed. "And I *relished* it."

This son of a bitch. For the first time in her life, Laila knew exactly what Draupadi was feeling during the dice game. This was her moment of feminine rage, and she felt the fire burn inside her like an inferno.

She stumbled to her feet. "I can't believe that you had anything to do with Karan," she said as her hands became engulfed in flame.

Satyapal tossed his head back in laughter. “Really, little girl? You think Karan is the innocent one? You should ask him who his first kill was. Then you’ll know that we’re not so different after all.”

“What are you talking about?”

This time, he flung out a hand, and the invisible pressure gripped her lungs. Her flames dissipated and she pressed her palms against her chest as she struggled to take a deep breath.

Just as she fell to the ground gasping, a car crashed through the gates, narrowly missing her vehicle.

Gopal and Karan jumped out and ran toward her.

Gopal skidded on his knees until he wrapped an arm around Laila’s waist and hauled her to her feet.

“Satya Uncle,” Karan said. He was frozen in place, and when Satyapal dropped his hand, Laila could finally breathe. She leaned into Gopal’s side as Karan and Satyapal faced each other.

“Karan,” Satyapal said, his voice friendly and filled with joy, as if he was seeing his son again on a visit home from college. “You’re looking well, my boy.”

“What were you doing to Laila?” He walked over to stand between her and his uncle.

Laila wanted to go to him, to stand by his side, but Gopal’s hold was iron strong. He pulled her back toward her car even as she struggled against him, gasping for air.

“I’ve come to finish the job that you haven’t been strong enough to do on your own,” Satyapal said, his voice hardening. “Now let’s go. You have much to catch me up on.”

“No,” Karan said. “This is wrong, Uncle Satya.”

"Karan? What are you doing aligning yourself with an asura?"

"We both know that she's not an asura." His legs spread to brace himself. "And we know that I will fight you if you try to jump her again."

Satyapal tilted his chin up, his brows raising to his hairline. "I see. So that's how it is." He shoved his knife back in his sheath at his thigh. "Then you have become my enemy instead of like a son to me. And this isn't over. You'll die in the crossfire. You've never been good enough for this work."

"I'll take my chances," Karan said. And in a move that had Laila gasping, he removed his knife and tossed it straight at Satyapal's forehead.

Instead of lodging between his eyes, it whizzed through the air and landed at a distance. Satyapal and the car were gone.

Karan turned back toward Laila and ran to her side. He took her in his arms, cradling her against his chest. "Laila, oh my god, are you okay? Did he hurt you?"

Laila replayed her conversation with Satyapal in her head. She pulled back and looked up at Karan. Her vision in her left eye was blurry, and it felt like needles were being shoved into her skull, but on this one thing she was clear.

"Did you kill my masi?"

29. LAILA

"I think so."

The words were said with such quiet regret that she felt it with the same strength as Satyapal's fist.

Karan, the man she'd been with, the man she'd started to fall in love with . . . for the first time in her life, the man who encouraged her to dream of having her own individuality while carrying the weight of her legacy, was the reason why she didn't have her Usha Masi.

Her death was seven years ago, which meant he had been only thirteen years old.

How had a thirteen-year-old killed a rakshasi with incredible strength and agility?

Laila looked down at his hand and saw the cut from the day before. It was still red, a raw wound that hadn't had time to heal.

Her Usha Masi didn't have a chance.

"I'm going to be sick," she said as her stomach heaved. She pressed a palm to her abdomen and braced herself on her knee.

What else hadn't he told her? What else had he done that he'd neglected to tell her?

More importantly, did he know that her fire didn't work on Satyapal?

Gopal moved forward, standing between them like a referee. "We can't stay here. Go back to your home in the mountains. It's safer for you behind the protection barrier that your aunts have built for you."

Laila turned to him. "You're coming with us. We're past games at this point, Gopal. You got us into this mess, which means you have to help us get out of it."

He looked down at her, his expression solemn. "You both have your responsibilities, and I have mine. I've already interfered more than I'm allowed."

"Then you can interfere some more," Laila snapped. "We're running out of time and it's clear that we can't figure out the answers to what Satyapal wants and what he's up to on our own."

Gopal sighed. He looked like he was deliberating the end of the world.

Laila shook her head. That was probably the worst analogy she could come up with in this moment.

"I can't say no to you, love," he replied softly in his accent edged with a dozen cultures. "But I can't stay for long. I have to go back to Flume Falls tonight."

"We just need to talk," she said. Then she winced as she felt the pain vibrate through her cheek. "I'm going to have to fix my face first. That son of a bitch sucker punched me."

"God, I am so sorry," Karan whispered.

He looked like he wanted to reach out and touch her again, but she turned away from him, the word *traitor* flashing in her mind.

They left Laila's Audi in the winery parking lot and drove back in the Explorer. The short trip was made in silence. Laila sat in the back, her head resting against the doorframe, her eyes closed as she tried to breathe through the pulsing pain that ached with every heartbeat.

She felt a rush of relief when they pulled onto her driveway and Karan drove into the empty bay in the garage. A part of her appreciated that they had a safe place where they didn't have to worry about attacks and could sleep with both eyes closed. Another part of her resented the house because it was beginning to feel like a prison. Her masis hadn't wanted her to ever leave either.

Laila didn't want to ever be trapped. The next time she had a run-in with Satyapal, and there would be a next time, he was going to pay for all of the heartache that he'd put her through. He was going to pay for both Denise's and Ben's death. And for being the reason she had to give up what little autonomy she had.

"These are some excellent vehicles," Gopal mused as he got out of the car. "Who would have thought that rakshasi would develop such elite taste from the gaudy hoarders of gold that they used to be?"

Laila refused to acknowledge the look he shot her. Somehow, he knew exactly what was behind the locked doors in her library. She'd ask him about it later, but right now, there were more pressing questions.

She walked through the door connecting the garage to the house and kicked off her shoes in the mudroom before she headed straight for the kitchen. She heard the low buzz of conversation from Karan and Gopal behind her, but she couldn't make out what they were saying.

Boo was pacing in front of the sink, a phone clutched in hand. When she saw Laila, her eyes widened like saucers behind her glasses. "Oh my god, you're back. Laila, you're hurt!"

She rushed forward, hand outstretched as if she was looking to touch the bruise blooming on her cheek. Then she saw Gopal enter, and her jaw went slack.

"Oh my god. Literally." Her voice was breathy and reverent.

Gopal laughed, his voice deep and rich. "Hello, chickie. You must be Badhuri."

Then with phone in hand, she folded her palms together and tried to curtsey at the same time. Gopal moved as gracefully as a dancer and as quickly as a leopard until he was standing in front of her. He closed his palms over her folded hands.

"No need for formalities, chickie. I'm technically human like you."

"Oh," she said, her cheeks reddening. "Sorry. I don't think there is an etiquette guide for this. I'm sort of making it up as I go."

"Aren't we all?" he said, and it was then that she could see he was distracting Boo, keeping her calm by being charming.

Laila turned to Karan, and she realized that he was watching her, his arms crossed, his gaze steady. "You need help with that cheek?"

"No," she said. But she pulled out a stool to sit and faced him. "I'll take care of it, but I need some answers first."

He didn't reply.

"What's happening?" Boo whispered.

"They're about to get into it," Gopal whispered back. His mouth was set in a grim line.

Laila ignored them, her rage burning again. "Did you know?" she asked. "Did you know that you killed my masi when you came here in my house to stay with me?"

"No, of course not," he said. "God, Laila, is that what you really think of me after all this time together? That I would do that to you?"

She tasted iron in her mouth, and it made her nauseous. "Then when," she said.

"Last night. You asked me how I knew about the blood-tipped arrow for the rakshasa in the archery studio. Then when I asked you why you needed to know, if it was to kill rakshasa on your own, you said that you were planning on doing the exact opposite. Look, the night of my first kill is . . . foggy. I didn't remember the details until I went down into the library and touched the door at the end of the hall. Then there was this weird zap, and all these memories came flooding back."

"It sounds like Satyapal didn't want you to remember," Gopal said. "Probably because Laila's aunt tried to warn you away from your uncle."

Her forehead creased and the small movement in her face caused a fresh wave of pain. She ignored it, ignored the swelling, as grief flooded her veins. Even if Karan hadn't known, he'd killed one of the most important people in her life, and there was a part of her that wasn't sure she'd ever be able to forgive him for that. How could she love someone who hurt her?

"Laila, I swear, if I had known from the beginning, I would've never come here. I hate that I'm the reason you lost a family member, I hate even more that looking at me now you're reminded of it."

"What did she say?" Laila said softly.

"What?"

"What did my masi say?" She looked over at Gopal, but he was staring at the floor while Boo was staring at him.

"She said she knew Karna," Karan said softly. "She said that he fought valiantly. And not to touch *her*. That 'she is divine.' Then she said Satyapal's name, as if she knew it. I didn't know what that meant, and I was so fucking scared. I left when I heard screams, these terrifying sounds, and she told me to run."

Laila needed time to process, to think about what Karan was telling her. About his final moments with Usha Masi. They had been living in Indonesia at the time and she was trying to understand English and Hindi and shedding her constant use of Creole that no one else understood while learning Indonesian. She missed the water, missed her mother.

It would be so easy, she thought. It would be so easy to go upstairs and crawl under her covers and pull out her copy of *The Awakening*. To forget her need for feminine rage that Draupadi wore like a badge of honor.

"I need a minute," she said quietly.

"Laila, I am so—"

"Sorry," she said. "Yeah, I know. I'm sorry, too. I'm sorry that my aunt is dead. That my firepower doesn't work on the one guy who may be responsible for my mother's murder. And I'm sorry that I trusted you when both of us together is the reason why Denise and Ben are dead."

Then she slid off the stool and walked around him toward the second kitchen. She pulled the pocket door closed and let out a deep, shuddering breath when she was alone.

The aches from her bruised skin were now overwhelming, and she slid to the floor, her back to the lower cabinets. She didn't know how long she sat there before the pocket door slid open again.

She glanced up to tell them to leave her be when she saw Gopal enter. He closed the pocket door gently behind him as he looked around in the space.

"Very *Practical Magic*," he said. "With the high ceilings and butcher-block island? I'm liking this space. All the metal and granite and marble out there is a bit much, if I'm being honest, but this is the cottagecore I think suits you."

"It's my masis'," she said quietly. "Gopal, I really need to be alone. I'm pissed at you too since you're the one who decided now would be the perfect time to start Kali Yuga."

"I told your lover out there the same thing I'll tell you. That was definitely not something I thought would happen. So—"

"Sorry? Is that seriously what you're about to say?"

"Sadly, that's the best I can do in the moment." He sighed, and then slid to the floor next to her. Their shoulders touched, and he bent his knees and rested his folded arms on top of them. His long, lean body dwarfed hers.

"Can I tell you something?" he asked.

"Are you going to tell me anyway?"

He chuckled, the sound gruff and deep. "Yes," he said. "Laila, Karan has the same legacy you do. He was thirteen years old, and his father and uncle sent him into a very dangerous situation to train him. If your masis asked the same of you at thirteen, wouldn't you do it?"

In a heartbeat, she thought. In a heartbeat. She owed them her life, and they loved her like she had come from them.

Laila rested her head against her knees. "What does this all mean?" she said quietly. "What is going on that we just don't know?"

There was a long, drawn-out pause. "Satyapal started something that he doesn't have the capacity to understand," Gopal said. "He grew up with Karan's father and over time began to resent the fact that he didn't have the gifts, the abilities that made Karan's family so vital to the fabric of the universe. Karna's legacy is the ability to see military strategy from a bird's-eye view. His marksmanship. His unwavering loyalty and protection skills. Karan possesses all those qualities, too."

"That's why all of the texts, all of the books tell us that we can't get too close to humans," she said softly. "That we have to keep our secrets close. Because people like Satyapal are seeking what we have."

"Exactly," Gopal said.

"After Satyapal grew resentful, he used dark magic to make himself a vital figure," Laila said quietly as the pieces began clicking in her head. She was starting to get a full picture of the very evil that they were fighting. "Or he's trying to."

"He's no longer what he once was," Gopal said. He reached in his breast pocket and removed his glasses. Then he slipped them on his nose. "Satyapal as a man has been consumed by malevolence. Now he's using dark magic and wanting to have a child."

With me. She tasted metal and fear whenever she thought of his lust-filled expression, not for her but for what she could make that had his blood.

"He's been hearing whispers from the ghosts of the past. And if he can have this child he desperately wants, it'll trigger the collapse of everything we know that exists today. There will be wars, climate change, famine, disease, until we consume each other, and nothing is left."

Laila shifted so she could look at Gopal directly in the eye. "How do you play into this?" she asked.

"I have a legacy of my own," Gopal said quietly, and for the first time since she'd met him in the darkness, his eyes filled with memories of horror. "I am supposed to be the one who guides you to the right match. We're never supposed to meet. Because the closer we get, the harder it is for me to see your future and protect you."

"Oh my god, you have precognition abilities?" She gaped at him.

"It's no longer . . . clear," he said, his voice filled with frustration. "I think I've crossed a line, and nothing is making sense anymore. All I wanted to do was even the scales against Satyapal. This has never happened in history, and I knew that we couldn't operate the same way we'd been going for centuries if we had a fighting chance."

This time when she turned to look at Gopal, she could see that he was wrestling with the same uncertain future that she and Karan had spent the last few weeks connecting over. That he was just as pressed as she was to find a solution and move on.

"Where are you staying?" she asked.

The corner of his mouth quirked. "Who do you think called the authorities about Boo? I'm staying in the cabin."

Laila shook her head, then punched him in the arm. "You are worse than an auntie matchmaker," she said.

He chuckled. "Well, it worked."

They paused, their heads leaning back against the cabinets now. He wasn't a bad guy, after all. No, he was one of the good ones, and if she could forgive Karan for trusting the people he loved, then Laila could forgive Gopal, too.

"Gopal, if you can't see the future anymore when it comes to us," she said quietly, "don't you think that it makes sense for you to stay here at the house?"

He looked at her, bewildered at the thought of moving in. "You're joking."

"I'm not," she said. "You've done something to protect our families and I'm grateful for that, but now we need everyone to work together if we're going to beat Satyapal at his own game."

There was a longer pause, and then he nodded. "That mattress is absolute rubbish," he said. "It would be nice to actually sleep on a bed."

"I can't guarantee a bed since no one is allowed in my masis' rooms, but I can guarantee an endless supply of chai."

"Accepted," he said with a laugh.

Gopal got to his feet, then reached down to help her up. She winced at the pain in her side, then cupped her cheek. It was still hot, and it felt swollen.

"Let's get you taken care of," he said gently. Then he gripped her hips and, in one easy move, sat her down on the countertop. He began opening cabinet doors and taking out the same jars that Giri Masi would use to combine the ingredients and make a salve. "My mother taught me this," he said. "Apparently your masi taught her."

There were still so many unknowns, so many questions she had for him, that she desperately wanted to know, especially if his life had somehow intersected with hers. But she listened in silence now to his deep voice, soothing and gentle, almost melodic in nature, as he combined a paste and began applying it to her cheek.

When it was time to put some of the salve on her ribs, she lifted her shirt and tilted to the side to give him access. He was quick and efficient, but his fingers lingered on the edge of her tattoo.

"The universe has its way of taking a pound of flesh, doesn't it?"

"I guess it does," she said quietly.

He put the dishes in the small workstation sink, and then helped her off the counter. "There," he said. "Now you should rest a bit. Then we'll talk about Satyapal."

The mention of his name, the reference of what they still had to do, reminded her of a crucial fact she'd forgotten when she'd learned about Karan and Usha Masi. "Oh my god, the fire," she said. Then she snapped her fingers, and the flame came easy to her before she snapped them again and the flame went out. "It doesn't burn him."

Gopal's eyebrows formed a V shape. "Impossible."

"You don't think I would've fried him like barbecue if it had before he punched me?" she said. "I'm not helpless, you know."

"I never said you were," Gopal replied, opening the pocket door for her. "But the flames should work . . ."

"Unless?"

Before Gopal could answer, Laila felt a sharp pain shoot through her palm. She yelped and looked down at her hand. The symbol began to glow.

She gasped, then looked up at Gopal. His mirroring expression of horror was enough to have her pushing through the door and running through the house.

"Karan!" she called out. Karan was in trouble.

30. KARAN

Karan had never felt the weight of his legacy as much as he did in that moment when Laila shrugged him off and walked away asking for some time. She'd become a vital part of his future. He couldn't see a way back to his old life without her being a part of it. Even though they had only spent a few weeks together, it was enough.

It was enough.

But now they were two souls who loved, and she would never trust him again because of what he'd done when he was thirteen. He knew that it was unfair to compare his life with that of some other twenty-year-old bloke from Oxford, a South Asian from Delhi working at a university. But damn, he wished for that easier life.

"I'm going to go check on her," Gopal said into the silence. He looked directly at Karan. "Do not leave the house." Then he was gone, and Karan was alone in the kitchen with his cousin.

A sharp stab of jealousy pierced his heart, but he knew he had no right to follow Laila when she'd discovered how fundamentally he'd changed her life.

But damn, he should be the one comforting her and holding her.

"I'm not exactly sure what to do in this situation and it's making me uncomfortable," Boo said finally. Then she walked over to the chai dispenser and put a cup under it before pressing the start button.

Karan didn't know what to do in this situation either. "I need some air," he said. He turned to the back doors.

"Hey, didn't our resident god just tell you not to go outside?"

"The grounds are part of the house," Karan said to his cousin as he walked out of the kitchen to exit the back of the house.

"Suit yourself," she called out after him. "I'm going to go down to the library. This tension is feeling a bit suffocating for me."

Karan stepped out into the cool air wearing a sweatshirt, jeans, and the sneakers he hadn't taken off when he'd entered the house. He let out a deep, shuddering breath. "Move forward," he said to himself. "Assess, plan, execute. Move forward."

He'd always wanted to follow his legacy, to bring honor to his family name. As ridiculous as that sounded, he'd romanticized a future where he was the Indiana Jones, and his father was the absentminded professor father with harebrained ideas.

Now, he wanted that dream with Laila.

As if his body was acting out his directives, he lifted one foot in front of the other and began walking the perimeter of the house, cutting through the grove of trees toward the lake.

He'd earn Laila's trust back. He didn't know how just yet, but he'd do what it took to earn her trust back.

Karan reached the dock and stepped out onto it. He took a deep breath and tried not to think of Laila and the time they shared a few nights ago.

Then he admitted to the secret part of his heart that he felt like a traitor to his uncle when he saw him again today. He felt like for all the times that they shared together, he'd thrown it out because he'd fallen in love with a woman with a similar destiny as his.

Karan knew he'd do it again, though. It was only right.

"It's the right thing to do," he whispered.

"Is it?"

Karan whirled, nearly stepping back into the water.

There, at the end of the dock, Satyapal stood in the black trousers he always wore, his button-down shirt tucked into the waistband, and a holster with a knife. The hilt looked like was wrapped in a mesh cloth and tucked under his armpit.

"How did you—"

"Get through the magic barrier?" Satyapal said, amused. "It's not meant for humans, Karan. And I am still human."

He glanced back at the water, then at his uncle. If he jumped in, would he have a better or worse chance of survival? Uncle Satya wasn't a strong swimmer. That's what he'd always said, anyway. Maybe he could take his uncle with him.

Satyapal held up his hands in surrender. "I come in peace," he said as he stepped onto the dock. "I had to follow you here and was hoping that sooner or later you'd come outside on your own. I just want to talk to my best friend's son. The man I helped raise. What happened, Karan?"

"What do you mean?" Karan said as he watched Satyapal take another step closer.

"I mean, when did you turn your back on the legacy your ancestors worked so hard to protect? You were never supposed to meet the Daughter of Draupadi. Your souls are forbidden. Even I had no intention of you meeting each other. I just wanted *her*."

"Why didn't anyone tell me?" he burst out. "Why didn't I know about this part of our legacy?"

"Someone did," Satyapal said as he cocked his head. "Don't you remember what the rakshasi said to you in the forest?"

Karan's blood ran cold. "Maybe the better question is, how did you know what the rakshasi told me?"

He adjusted the cuff of his shirt, the pointed end of the knife shifting as it pointed downward behind his back. "I knew that you had a secret, so I read your memories the night we returned to the hotel in Indonesia. Then to give you some rest, I took the one about the message."

He'd been dealing in dark magic for so long, he didn't even see how dangerous, how wrong that was for him to do to someone else.

Satyapal took a step closer and continued crafting his story. "You don't know what it's like," he said. "You were born with your life planned for you, beta, but I was just as good, just as smart, if not smarter than your father. I *deserve* the right and freedom to have a legacy too."

And then, between one blink and another, his eyes had gone black, then returned to their original color.

He had reached the center of the dock. Karan stood his ground, his hands curled into fists at his side. "And you think taking Laila is going to give you that legacy."

"Your father and you don't understand the responsibility you carry. You've taken it for granted," he said in a singsong voice. "I plan to have a child, to raise a child to be strong and powerful."

"You'll cause another Kurukshetra War," Karan said. Satyapal's obsession was beginning to make sense and the future he had planned was coated in blood. "Millions of people will die. The universe will swallow us whole, and Kali Yuga will finish."

"Karan," Satyapal chided, as if Karan was still a child. He carefully removed the mesh cloth from the long dagger at his side. The hilt looked like it was solid gold. "I plan on bringing the war to us. Don't you remember your scripture? Those who survive the great battle at the end of Kali Yuga will live among the gods."

His eyes went black again, this time flashing the depths of malevolence for longer. "I will *be* among the gods, Karan. I will be a god."

Satyapal pulled the dagger out of its sheath and Karan could see the curved hilt, the polished platinum blade, the emerald-and-ruby-encrusted hilt. "I convinced your father to let me hold this once," he said conversationally. "He never realized that I had replaced it with a forgery and kept this one as an insurance policy in case you or he ever turned your back on me." He took another half-step forward.

"What is it?" Karan said as he shifted back until his heels met the edge of the dock. The sound of water gurgled below.

"Oh, that's right," Satyapal said with amusement. "He hasn't given it to you yet. On your twenty-first birthday, he planned on presenting you with the angalikastra."

Angalikastra.

He knew his scripture backward and forward. The celestial weapon created by the goddess Indra. A short sword that was the only tool that could kill Karna. It had caused his death when Arjuna rammed it into Karna's neck. His father had it this whole time?

He thought of their humble two-bedroom flat in Delhi.

And then he thought of Satyapal living in the next building over, close, just as he'd been when his father and Satyapal were growing up as boys.

"I don't know why you had to take out the fancy sword," he said even as he prepared to jump. "I'm literally human. I can die by a regular sword."

"Ah, but then I'd have to contend with your father," Satyapal said. "If I use this, every last person alive from Karna's legacy will die."

Karan's blood went icy. How had he ever called this man his uncle? How had he ever let him close? He was about to jump when Satyapal lunged at him, yanking him back onto the dock.

Karan blocked the next hit, then landed a solid kick in Satyapal's abdomen.

Satyapal sliced out with the angalikastra, the sword glowing in a purple and red hue as it sliced through the air.

There was a rustle coming from the trees, and his heart jumped in his throat at the thought that Laila would come to his rescue, that she'd be in Satyapal's path.

The moment of distraction was enough for Satyapal to jump him, to grasp him around the neck and hold the angalikastra against his throat, the one vulnerability that Karna had also possessed. Invisible bands tightened around his wrists and his hands tugged together behind his back, wrenching hard enough for him to feel a sharp shooting pain through his shoulders.

His feet were glued to the dock, and he stood, facing the edge, where both Laila and Gopal stood, twin expressions of horror on their faces.

"So good of you to join us," Satyapal said conversationally. His voice was as cultured as Karan's father's, thanks to years of foreign education and classroom presentation.

"It's the angalikastra," Gopal said to Laila.

She gaped at Karan, their eyes meeting. He wished he could tell her that he loved her, that they most likely will die and they have so little time, but in the fleeting moment of their existence, she was the bright, shining star that he'd been pulled toward this whole time.

"Let him go," Laila called out.

Satyapal's laugh had the edge of a hiss in it. "Not likely."

Laila shrugged. "Honestly, it seemed like the thing to say at the time. What do you want, Satyapal?"

"I thought I made my intentions obvious," Satyapal said, his words echoing in Karan's ear as he shouted across the distance. His breath feathered over his neck. "I want my child. With you. But I'm willing to make a trade. Karan's life for yours."

"No—"

"Shut up," Satyapal said, his accented words hitting hard like bullets as he gripped Karan's shoulder and pressed hard on a pressure point. Karan almost went to his knees, and stars flashed before his eyes.

"Walk slowly toward us," Satyapal said. "When you reach my side, I'll let Karan go."

Karan opened his mouth to tell her no again, but Satyapal anticipated his intention and pressed again on the pressure point. Karan's vision became hazy and darkness clouded the edges of his sight.

Please don't. I love you. I don't want him near you, let along touching you.

"Fine," Laila said. She stepped onto the dock, and in slow, easy steps began walking toward them.

"It'll never work," Gopal said in a singsong tone behind her.

Karan could feel Satyapal's entire body stiffen. "What are you talking about."

"Gopal, shut up," Laila hissed.

"What?" he said, feigning innocence. "Satyapal wants a child. He wants his bloodline to mix with Draupadi's, and then manipulate the child through dark magic to end Kali Yuga. Do I have that right?"

"My reasons are not your concern, *boy*."

"Here is the thing," Gopal said, as he adjusted the cuffs of his jacket. "Laila has to *choose* you as the one to father her child. If you force her now, then she'll never submit. And knowing Laila? She'll burn every building you put her in. You'll be stuck with a raw end of the deal."

"Gopal," Laila snapped. "Whose side are you on?"

Gopal raised his hand in surrender. "Hey, I'm a descendant of the Lord Krishna. I don't take sides. I just share information."

At that revelation, Karan felt Satyapal take in a deep, almost gasping breath. Then his grip tightened on Karan's shoulder and Karan almost went to his knees.

"If she does not submit, then I'll just kill Karan. And I'll kill you."

Karan could see energy practically crackle around Gopal. "You could try to kill me, but you'll only piss off a lot of people who are stronger than you'll ever be. Satyapal, look. The only way your baby plan is going to work is either if you convince her to accept you, or if you win her in a game that she accepts the terms of willingly."

"Gopal, I will kill you," Laila snapped.

Karan's mind raced as he thought about what Gopal was trying to do. What game was *he* playing in the moment?

Dice. The origin of Draupadi's feminine rage.

Of her firepower.

"Dice," Karan said. "A dice game."

Satyapal's grip relaxed a fraction. "Dice." said smoothly. "Chausar."

Chausar. In the Mahabharata, the dice game was played with rigged die that obeyed whatever Shakuni asked for. The Pandavas had gambled Draupadi in that game. They lost their kingdom first and then their wife. Krishna had been the one to save her.

"You know what's in your favor here?" Gopal said conversationally as he tucked his hands in his back pockets and rocked on his heels. "We have the descendant of Yudhishthira sitting in the house. The oldest Pandava. Yudhishthira had lost the original game of Chausar, you know. We can ask her to roll the dice as a neutral party. And the dice themselves? Well, lucky for you, like Karna's family lineage protected that angalikastra sword, Laila has the original dice used."

"Gopal!" she snapped. "You're not supposed to *know* that."

The dice are cursed, Karan thought. They were cursed so the Pandavas would lose. Why would Gopal offer them?

"You want to play a game of Chausar," Satyapal said slowly. Then he let out a laugh so loud and filled with confidence that Karan began struggling against his invisible ties again, careful not to nick himself on the blade at his throat.

"A modified version," Gopal said. "Because who has hours to play a full round? Call a number, and roll the dice. Closest roll wins. Best two out of three."

"You'll lose," Satyapal said, his voice filled with confidence and amusement. "That is your destiny. If you play the dice, Draupadi and her bloodline lose."

Laila met his eyes again, and he shook his head in a barely perceptible movement. Just enough for her full mouth to press in a thin line.

She then looked over his shoulder. "I'll do it. I'll risk it. And if you win, then I can't say no to you. You get what you want. Even though the idea of sleeping with a gremlin like you makes my skin scrawl."

Karan's heart began pounding, his pulse racing as he began to struggle in earnest.

"Fine," Satyapal said, his tone amused. He didn't even seem phased by the gremlin comment. "Tonight—"

"No," Gopal said, his voice sharp. "You play with magical dice, then you play under the new moon," he said.

"What does the new moon have to do with the dice?" Satyapal said. "This better not be a trick. Otherwise, you die too."

"No trick," Gopal said, holding his hands up. "In twenty-eight hours. It's going to take that long to get the dice out of the vault."

There must have been something in his tone that had Satyapal dropping the blade to his side. "Fine," he said. "I'll be accommodating."

Then Satyapal pointed the tip of the sword at Laila. Karan could still feel his strength behind him, the honed skills of a fighter that had trained Karan and taught him everything he knew. "There is a clearing in the woods between your home and the woods, Laila."

Laila knew exactly what he was talking about. It was just on the other side of the perimeter that protected her lands. "I know it."

"We'll meet there tomorrow night at six p.m. Bring the dice, and your player." He then pointed the sword at Gopal. "But you are not permitted near the game. I don't know what kind of interference you can do. If I sense you nearby, the game is off."

Laila nodded.

Gopal nodded.

"Karan, what do you think? Your life for the life of the woman you've had feelings for? The woman I plan on having a baby with?"

Karan swallowed hard, the taste of bile thick in his throat. He turned his head just enough to meet Satyapal's gaze, the blade grazing his skin, but not close enough to cut. Satyapal's eyes were human again, but still carried rage. "I'll enjoy watching when she kicks your ass, old man."

Satyapal *tsk*ed and shook his head. "Who says you'll be awake to see? I plan on keeping you with me for insurance."

He lifted the hilt of the angalikastra and slammed it against Karan's temple.

His vision went black and then there was nothing.

31. LAILA

Satyapal winked out of existence as quickly as he had left in the parking lot of the winery. This time, he took a slumped Karan with him.

"No!" Laila screamed, and she ran to the edge of the dock, wishing, no, hoping that she could catch them. Except there was nothing but air and water at her feet. Karan. He'd taken Karan, and now there was a very real chance that she'd never see him again.

Gopal stood at the edge of the dock, his arms crossed. "He made it past the perimeter. That means he still has some human left in him."

Laila couldn't stop thinking of the fear in Karan's eyes, the worry for her, and then the rage when he looked at Satyapal. She stormed off the dock, back toward Gopal. "Why didn't you do something? Obviously you have some sort of magic power situation that could've handled him!"

"I can't swim."

She paused at that, then shook her head. "We were on the *dock*."

"Laila, you know that if I interfere—"

"But you have, Gopal," she interjected. She knew that she sounded desperate, that her words were bordering on shrill now. "You already have."

Gopal pressed his lips together. Then he inched forward, almost as if he was standing at the edge of a cliff instead of on a stable dock. He extended a hand for her. "Come on. We have to check on Boo. There is a lot we need to do before tomorrow night."

Laila ignored his hand and stormed past him toward the house. A house that was no longer safe the way that her masis had intended it to be.

Her thumb passed over the invisible mark on her palm, the marking that had tied her to Karan since the moment they first met.

Live for me, she pleaded. *Live long enough so I can kick your ass myself.*

Laila strode into the house, toeing off the shoes she'd haphazardly worn when she'd gone after Karan and went straight to the library doors. She ran down the spiral staircase into the sealed tomb for Vyasa's library that the Daughter of Draupadi was destined to keep. When she reached the double doors at the base of the staircase, she found them sealed shut, the rivulets of gold magic shimmering.

"Boo?" she called out. She pressed her hands against the door in the way that her masis taught her to open them. "Boo!"

Gopal appeared a moment later. He looked up at the doors then back at her. "The library sealed shut when it perceived that there was an intruder," he said quietly.

Laila's pulse raced as she touched one of the curved stone carvings in the door that was lined with a pulsing glow. "Boo is in there. I'm not leaving her in there."

Gopal took his black frames out of his pocket and slipped them on his nose. He stepped closer to the door to examine it. Then in the place that Laila had put her palm, he pressed his fingertips and pushed.

There was a loud boom, and the sound of a crack, almost as if the doors were powering down like a giant computer on the fritz.

"Bloody hell," he muttered.

"What is it?" she called out. "What happened?"

"I may have broken the spell. My ancestor and the rakshasa race weren't exactly on the best of terms in their lifetime, so it makes sense that we undo each other's power. There is no way to protect the library now other than with guards."

He grabbed the handle and pulled, the stone doors opening inch by inch by inch as they scraped heavily across the floor. Laila grabbed the other handle and began tugging.

Together, using the strength they had, they got the doors open wide enough for both of them to slip through the opening.

"Boo!" Laila called out.

The lights were still working, so that was a plus. The doors at the end of the library were still pulsing with a glow. Thank god that was sealed, too. That was her legacy, her curse in a physical form.

Laila walked to the wooden table, to the spot where Boo had set up her computer, her notebooks, and a neglected cup of chai. "Boo, come out! It's safe."

"Laila?"

The name was said with such hesitancy, such fear, that Laila's heart clenched. She got to her hands and knees and saw that Boo had curled herself into a ball, and was rocking back and forth under the table.

"Hi there," she said softly. "Come on out."

Boo's eyes welled with tears, but she crawled from under the table and rushed Laila, wrapping her arms around Laila's waist. A soft sob erupted from her mouth as she held on tight. And because Laila needed the hug too, she squeezed back hard.

"What happened?" Boo cried. She pulled back enough to look up at Laila. "I was sitting here reading when there was a blast of noise. All the shelves rattled, then the doors slammed shut and I couldn't get out! My body felt like it was on fire then, and I think I passed out. When I woke up, I was on the floor in front of the doors. I just crawled under the table and stayed there because that's protocol for a hurricane."

Laila rubbed her back. "The library was protecting itself. Satyapal made it past the perimeter." That didn't explain why Boo's body was on fire, but stranger things have happened in her life. She probably mistranslated something in the library.

Boo's eyes went wide. She looked over Laila's shoulder at Gopal, then back at Laila. "Where's bhai?" she asked.

When Laila didn't respond, Boo gripped her shoulders and shook as hard as her slender frame could manage. "Laila! Where is bhai?"

Gopal stepped forward then. "Chickie, Satyapal isn't going to hurt Karan. He's the insurance policy. Tomorrow night we're going to fight for his life. Both Karan's and Laila's. But we're going to need your help."

"He took Karan?" She gasped. "Laila!"

Laila's hold on her tightened at Boo's panic set in, as it grated against her own. He had become her family, too. Then she held

Boo as she cried, as she raged the same way Laila wanted to do. She gripped the trembling girl in her arms and felt her own eyes well. She forgot how young Boo was sometimes.

When the sobs subsided, Gopal was by their side a moment later, his hand on Boo's shoulder. She seemed to calm at the touch.

Boo looked up at him, and Laila. "What are we going to do?"

"We're going to play Chauser," he said.

Laila could practically see the wheels turning in her brain. "Dice. Why are you . . . wait, did you make a bargain?"

"Gopal technically made one," Laila said ruefully.

Boo's eyes went wide. You're recreating the dice game from the Mahabharata. From when the Pandavas bet their wife and lost her to the Kauravas."

Laila swallowed hard. "Yes," she said. "Boo, I know we never talked about it, but it's important that we talk about it now. How are you and Karan cousins?"

Boo wiped her eyes with the back of her hands. Her lower lip continued to tremble. "I was doing a genealogy chart for my family, and it shows my lineage intersects with his because his great-grandfather had six children instead of one. I am a product of an offshoot of his family history. The others each had one or two children, but I didn't look into it."

"And how far back were you able to go with your line in particular?" Gopal asked.

She cocked her head. "Why does this matter? Bhai is missing. Shouldn't we focus on him and not me?"

"It's important," Laila said gently.

She reached under the collar of her shirt and scratched at her shoulder. "I was only able to go back to the mid-1800s. The records aren't clear after that since so much genealogy in India was oral or saved in the family home. With British occupation, and so many home raids, it's impossible to authenticate anything past that."

Gopal extended a hand and touched the collar of her shirt. Boo's eyes went wide in shock, and she froze. He slowly pushed the collar aside until a small corner of a mass of black ink on her skin was visible to Laila. That was where Boo had been scratching.

"Oh my god," Laila whispered.

"She's part of this now," Gopal said to her. His hand fell away. "If she's rolling the dice, then she's part of it."

"Me?" Boo said, then shook her head. "No way. I am your research person, not a warrior. I get nervous holding a butter knife."

"We'll protect you," Laila said gently. Then she cupped Boo's face in her hands. Her palms were warm, and Boo relaxed against the touch. "Boo, you have a tattoo on your back now. It matches ours."

"No," she said, the word quick and sharp.

"I'm going to take a picture of it with your phone while Gopal goes upstairs, okay? And then we have to talk."

Boo's lower lip trembled, and her swollen eyes filled with tears again. "No," she said again. She shook her head, and her frizzing ponytail slid over her shoulders. She backed away from Laila now, creating space between them. Then she cupped a hand directly over the part of her shoulder that she'd been itching. "No, no, no."

"We need you to stay calm, Chickie," Gopal said gently.

"Stay calm?" she cried out. Then she switched into German and then into Hindi. "This is not a time to stay calm! I have a tattoo. My parents are going to kill me! This is worse than the time I hacked into the United States Pentagon mainframe."

"The universe is going to end before your parents can ground you for a tattoo if we don't do something," Laila said. "Boo, we need you to roll the dice—otherwise Satyapal will kill Karan. You're part of this now, and we need you. We need you to leave this library and come with us into the woods tomorrow night to do it."

"Why tomorrow night?" Boo said as she rubbed her palms over her thighs. "Why do we have to wait instead of getting Karan back now?"

"Tomorrow is the new moon," Gopal said. He looked up at Laila, his eyes solemn. "Laila is more powerful during a new moon than any other time in the month."

She turned to him, her arms crossed over her chest. "How do you know that?"

"Because Draupadi's rage always burned brightest in the darkest of times," he said quietly. "So will yours."

There were few moments in her life where she understood her ancestor, the queen born from the fires of the god Agni, and the prayer of a mother unable to have children on her own. This moment, when she felt rage, was one of them.

"And me?" Boo said. "How am I playing into this? I still don't understand why I have a tattoo. Is it because I'm related to Karan?"

Laila turned to Gopal and motioned for him to tell Boo all of it. She wasn't exactly sure herself how he knew, but there were secrets that Gopal still hadn't shared, that she doubted he would until he was good and ready.

"You don't think that your entire father's history is filled with genius IQs because of natural selection, do you?" Gopal said to her. "How else are you able to understand the Mahabharata and the language so easily?"

"Holy shit," Boo said softly. "I'm a descendant of the most intelligent Pandva? But I thought I was a part of Karna's lineage."

"You have both," Gopal said softly. "Descendant of Yudhishthira, you have a chance to correct the mistakes of your ancestor. Instead of gambling the Daughter of Draupadi away, we are hoping you'll be able to save her."

Boo looked at Laila, then back at Gopal. She pushed her glasses up the bridge of her nose, then sniffled again. "I just want to put it on record that I think this is a very bad idea, but tell me what I have to know so I can try to get my cousin back."

Gopal turned to Laila, then glanced at the doors at the back of the library. "First, we need the dice."

32. LAILA

Laila didn't normally go into her family vault. She'd had no choice but to spend time there when she was young and studying her family history, but since she'd passed the exams that her aunts had created to test her knowledge back when she was sixteen, she'd avoided the space.

Now, at the age of eighteen, she stopped in front of the double doors in the empty library. Gopal had taken Boo upstairs to distract her and to walk her through a dice game. They were going to practice with fake dice that he'd gone out to purchase at the local Target. Not that the dice looked the same, but it was a good starting point.

Laila was alone. She had to do this alone.

She touched the door handles of the back room and watched as a stream of light shot around the frame of the door like the lights on a pinball machine. Then with a loud groan and a rumble of the cavernous library, the doors opened toward her, revealing a room encased in marble, diamond, and gold.

Laila thought back to Gopal's comment about rakshasi hoarding gold.

Her aunts still loved the precious metal, but they were a little subtler about it now. How they managed to secure the library and transfer it from Indonesia where they were protected for centuries after the Kurukshetra War, to the United States, still flummoxed her, but she remembered it had taken all their strength and power to do it.

Laila stepped inside on bare feet, the marble cold to the touch. In the center of the room was the Garbhagriha in a square twenty-by-twenty structure. A Shikhara formed on top of the Garbhagriha, a spire reaching for the heavens even this far underground. And then there was the Mandapa, the small platform in front of the Garbhagriha with a single white cushion in the center.

Around the square Garbhagriha was gold and platinum shelving with scrolls and books: centuries of diaries from the Daughters of Draupadi.

Personally, she preferred writing down her thoughts on an app in her phone, but she figured one day she could download all the data and just print it or something to add to the collection.

As Laila walked into the room, candles around the perimeter burst into flame. The doors creaked closed behind her. Her heart pounded at the thought of being shut inside, but right now that didn't really seem like such a bad idea.

She walked up the two steps into the Mandapa portico, where she sat cross-legged on the white cushion. In front of her, protected by the Garbhagriha, the sanctum made to house Hindu deity statues, was a pedestal with a red cushion. On the cushion were two dice wrapped in the tattered shreds of a red sari, the same red sari that Draupadi had worn that day, that continued to unravel and protected her dignity when the Kauravas tried to undress her in public. She'd called for help and Lord Krishna had listened.

She had Lord Krishna's descendant in her house. She needed someone who understood her. Who loved her.

Closing her eyes and taking a deep, even breath, she tried to summon a dreamlike state, the same one that she'd first been in when she spoke with her aunts. Just like she'd been taught her entire life, she focused on calming her thoughts, on narrowing her energy to this one task of talking to her masis.

Breathe in, breathe out, breathe in, breathe out.

She didn't know how long she sat cross-legged, meditating, trying to clear her head. It wasn't until she heard the soft crinkle of a potato chip bag that her eyes popped open.

There was a person sitting across from her, less than three feet away. They were also sitting cross-legged, their hair in a half bun on the crown of their head, the rest in long, thick waves to the floor, where it trailed along the marble tile.

Their jaw was pointed in a sharp angle, and they had high cheekbones. Their shoulders were wide, arms muscled and bare. A white lungi wrapped around their waist, and the tail tucked between their legs and into the waistband of the long cloth. Their skin was a deep reddened brown, their black eyes rimmed with gold and lined with smoke.

They radiated with heat. Like a furnace that was turned up on high. The energy was warm, almost like a fireplace on a cold night.

In their hand was snack-size bag of Flamin' Hot Cheetos.

"This is the best invention that humanity has made," they said, their voice deep and amused as they tossed another Cheeto in their mouth. They used traditional Hindi, like Laila's masis.

Laila pressed her hands together in prayer. Then said, "I . . . I don't know if I should bow."

Agni's thick black brow quirked. "You recognize me. Not many humans do. For that, you can remain where you are."

"Oh . . . ah, okay. Wow . . . you're here."

"Consider this a literal godly intervention," Agni replied, amused. They extended the bag of Cheetos out to Laila. "Want one?"

"Uh, no thank you?"

Agni's eyes seemed to flash. "When the god of fire is giving you a gift, it's in your best interest to accept it."

"Then I'd love one, thank you," Laila said quickly and took one out of the bag. She prayed that this wasn't going to burn her mouth. As much as she was a fan of Indian food, and could produce fire, her spice tolerance was shit.

With a deep breath, she bit off the end . . . and tasted sweetness.

Agni must have been watching her face, because they chuckled. "I'd like to think I'm full of surprises. Like showing up here when you were expecting your masis."

Laila finished the Cheeto, then wiped the powder cheese residue onto her leggings. "I was hoping for their advice."

"Will you take mine instead?"

"Yes, ah . . . my lord?"

They shrugged. "I accept. We appear in a form that is the most relatable to our subjects, which means that we have to accept the language our subjects use, too. Why don't you tell me what's on your mind?"

Laila let out a deep breath. "A few weeks ago, the friends I made in high school started college. I signed up for some online classes, but it's not like I can really do anything with it more than run the small winery here in the Finger Lakes."

"The one you burned down?"

"Uh . . . yeah." She had to assume that the gods were all-knowing. Depending on the mythology or the text, Agni was technically one of the most powerful. They were the messenger that communicated between the humans and the gods. And they were here. "But then Karan showed up. And our hands touched, then we were marked."

"And then you fell in love, didn't you?" Agni said as they ate another Cheeto.

"Despite what he did when he was thirteen, what he brought to my door, there is no one that I would trust by my side the way that I trust Karan." It felt like a form of betrayal to her Usha Masi to admit that, but when she saw him at the end of the dock with Satyapal, she knew the truth. Her Usha Masi would've forgiven her. She would've forgiven Karan, too.

"Mm-hm," Agni said as they chewed. "So, what is the problem?"

"The problem is destiny? Legacy? Satyapal? The end of Kali Yuga, which feels strange to say because right now, I'm just trying to get Karan back. I feel like there's so many things happening right now."

"You read that English book," Agni said slowly. "The one the American writer wrote at the turn of the twentieth century. The duty of a mother and a woman is the same."

They were referencing *The Awakening*, she thought. She thought of her tattered book, hidden in her bedside drawer. "Yes, my lord."

Agni chuckled, their broad shoulders shaking with amusement. "You resent that you, the daughter of fire and blood formed from my daughter, Draupadi, must have a child so they may have a child and so they may have a child after that until the end of time as you know it."

"Yeah, pretty much," she replied. She propped her elbows on her knees and rested her chin against her fists. "Draupadi didn't have any autonomy when she was given to five brothers to marry all of them. She didn't have any autonomy when she was told that her husbands had gambled her away in a dice game. She didn't have any autonomy when she was cursed to see her sons die in the Kurukshetra War. And I now have no autonomy either. I must have a child to carry on my legacy. I need to stay at home for my safety. With Satyapal, I have to watch while Boo plays dice and pursues her own path."

Agni nodded, humming as if they were following along and commiserating with her struggle. They folded the Cheetos bag and set it to the side before folding their hands together in front of them.

"Laila, you were born into this life because you were chosen. You were born to have these unique opportunities because you have the tools to create a space for choice and individual agency on your own."

"I can't see a way out," she said quietly. "I can't see a way to create my own life."

Agni nodded, then brushed a finger against the corner of their mouth as if to remove a crumb. "You know what's so powerful about fire?"

Laila shook her head.

"It doesn't just destroy," they said, then snapped their fingers, making a flame appear. "It can also purify." Agni looked up, their eyes flashing red, then blue, then orange and gold before returning to a dark amber ringed with gold. "Maybe what you really need to do, daughter of my daughters, is to embrace the legacy you've been given. Let it burn through you. Once it purifies your soul, you can begin to start seeing a new path."

Laila wasn't sure she understood what Agni was talking about, but the thought that the fire could purify . . . there was something about it that triggered an idea. It wasn't fully formed yet, but the seed was planted.

Agni let out a booming laugh. "I see that you're starting to think on your own. Think beyond the help of your little sister, beyond the help of Krishna's blood. You're beginning to think like your ancestor. I'll leave you to it."

"Ah, thank you," Laila said. "Thank you for . . . ah, giving me a chance. For helping me."

"You were always a good child, Laila," Agni said. Their voice softened. "I'm sorry that the ones you loved left you so soon. I wasn't supposed to come. Gods aren't to interfere. But some of them have broken the rules, and I want you to know that you're never alone."

Laila swallowed. "My mother? My Usha Masi?"

"They've moved on," Agni said. "I'm sorry, but anytime you dream of them, it's made up of what you've heard them say to you, or what you believe they would say. Their souls are living a new life. Happy lives. I promise you that much."

"Thank you," Laila said again, as her eyes filled with tears. "Thank you."

"You're welcome, Laila. Just remember, this is only the beginning. Don't lose the first battle in the war."

Before Laila could ask them what they were referring to, Agni reached out and touched her forehead with their thumb.

She woke up seconds later, sprawled across the marble floor. She saw the discarded Cheeto bag sitting next to where Agni had appeared. Her hand closed around cool stone, and she sat up to look at the dice that lay in her palm.

They were four inches long and had black circles marking the numbers. Laila quickly got to her feet and looked at the pedestal in the Garbhagriha.

"What in the world?" she mused. When she got closer to the strip of red sari, she saw that the dice that were inherited as part of her family legacy were still there.

She looked down at the ones in her hand, and then smiled.

Lord Agni had said gods have interfered more than they should. [illegible] had said they needed to switch things up. Her plan was [illegible]her.

[illegible]ntial and respectful bow, she picked up [illegible] and walked out of the inner sanctum, the mandapa, and out of the back room into the library. The doors had opened as she approached, and they quickly shut behind her.

Then she strode out of the library, which closed on its own as well. The doors glowed as if their power of protection had been restored.

Laila heard Gopal and Boo talking in the dining room, but she didn't go to them yet. She carried the dice with her upstairs into her bedroom and walked straight to her bedside table.

She picked up her copy of *The Awakening*, and right there next to her rumpled bedsheets and the discarded clothes she'd tossed on the floor, she held the book tightly in one fist and burned it.

The flames licked the edges, consuming the copy of the text until there was nothing left but ash at her feet.

Satyapal was going down.

33. LAILA

Laila waited until they had ten minutes to spare before she laced up her boots and pocketed her knives. Then she held Boo's hand in hers as they stepped out into the chill night air.

"You're not coming with us?" Boo said, turning to Gopal.

Gopal shook his head. "No, Chickie, this is one I can't interfere in, no matter how hard I try. No matter how much I want to."

Laila met his gaze, seeing the worried yet solemn expression in the dark eyes behind his glasses. "You'll be here when we get back?"

Gopal didn't answer except for the barely perceptible movement of his head.

"Gopal—"

"You'll be late," he said, then motioned to the woods. "This has always been your battle, Laila. This has always been about Satyapal and the Daughter of Draupadi."

"I know," she said quietly. Then she let go of Boo's hand for a moment, and quickly crossed to Gopal, and wrapped her arms around his neck, pulling him in for a hug. She felt the tentative touch of his fingers at her waist before he returned the quick squeeze.

"Egypt had Cleopatra," he said quietly, his face inches from hers. "Greece had Helen of Troy. And India had Draupadi. Know how powerful you are."

"I do," she said quietly. Then she turned on her heels, gripped Boo's hand, and began walking toward the dark grove of trees. A path would veer off and head toward the edge of the perimeter around the house, and just on the other side of it was the clearing in the woods.

"I know this is a bad time to tell you this," Boo said quietly. "But I'm so scared that I think I'm going to pee."

Laila snapped her fingertips and the flame erupted like a torch from her skin. It hovered just above her palm, forming a column strong and bright. "Boo, if you pee your pants? No one is going to question why."

Her palm grew sweaty in Laila's hand. "Great," she said. "I have something to look forward to now. That is, if I survive."

"We'll survive," Laila said as she veered to the left down the path. They walked quickly, moving through the trees, the light pushing away the dark. "We're going to thrive. Or, I don't know . . . do something that sounds less toxic girlboss."

"I'll settle for survive," Boo said.

Laila heard the rustle of movement before they entered the clearing. Once they stepped past the tree line into the circular grove, she was surrounded by trees. The forest created an enclave where branches bowed over a perfect circular-shaped flat landscape covered in moss. Satyapal stood at a distance in the shadows. At his feet was a bound and gagged Karan. There was a bruise on his face, but he looked alive. His eyes flashed with concern when he saw them.

"And I was so sure that you'd allow Karan to die," Satyapal said, his voice reeking of malevolence.

"You never deserved him," Laila said, hating that the man she'd come to learn, to love, was tied to a villain like Satyapal. Then with a flick of her wrist, a rush coming straight from her chest and bursting down her arms and out of her fingertips, she set the clearing ablaze. A ring of fire formed around them, brightening the forest until she could see the wariness in Satyapal's expression.

"Clever," he mused.

They could see Karan clearly now. He looked like he was struggling to breathe, his body coated with sweat. Suspended above him was the angalikastra, twisting and twirling in the air with the blade pointed at Karan's neck. Laila's heart seized at the sight, and she had to tamp down on the urge to burn Satyapal to a crisp.

Not yet, she told herself. *Not yet.*

"Bhai!" Boo called out. She stepped toward the center of the clearing, but Satyapal raised a hand.

"Na-ah," he said in a singsong voice. "One move that I don't like, and I kill him. Understood?"

Boo looked back at Laila, who nodded. Then she turned to Satyapal. "I have the dice."

"Let's see them then," he said.

He came closer, and this time it was Laila who stopped him. "You can stay right there," she said. "We'll toss the dice to you. Then you can inspect them."

Satyapal looked irritated at that, like he was not only going to argue but end their whole game. Boo retrieved the dice, two long log-shaped items made of bone and marked with dots, from her pocket and hurled them at his feet.

"I do believe I'll enjoy killing both your friends, Laila," he said smoothly. "I'm glad you listened and didn't bring the third; otherwise, we wouldn't have even gotten this far."

He retrieved the dice and held them out to the firelight from the closest flame. The replicas were made of the same ivory, painted from the same animal ink.

Laila felt the centuries-old rage burning inside her. "You can't do anything with them," she said smoothly. "You're only human."

"Silence," he roared, his hands fisting over the dice. "Or do you not care that your friend's life hangs in the balance?"

"If you kill him, then what makes you think you can ever have me?" she replied. "And as a *human*, there isn't much you can do about it."

From a distance, she could see that his eyes began to darken. His voice deepened. "Insolent child."

"No, I'm the Daughter of Draupadi," she taunted, burning with anger. "Karan's legacy is that of Karna, one of the greatest warriors. And Badhuri here is a daughter of Yudhishthira and Karna. Which makes her even more important than both of us. We brought the dice, but unless you have power, then you'll never be able to win. So let's just get this over with."

"I have been wielding magic for twice your age," Satyapal said. The wind whipped through the clearing and sent her flames flickering, threatening to snuff out. Then, as if he was swallowing screams, Satyapal raised his hands to the sky, the dice pointed upward, and a black cloud wrapped around the objects then poured into his waiting mouth, straight into his body.

He swallowed the darkness, then cracked his neck left to right before he held out the dice again. His hand was burning. The celestial magic of the dice was hurting him because he was now filled with so much darkness.

Perfect.

"The dice of Shakuni," he said, then let out a belly laugh that rattled the trees. "Such fools to have trusted dice that were sworn to never roll in the favor of a Pandava. Especially a *child*."

Boo pointed at herself, as if waiting for him to confirm that he was talking to her. "Look, I really just want to get back to the house," Boo said. "There is ah, some age-appropriate TV show that I'm excited to watch. I'm here against my will, too."

"Then we'll try to make this quick," Satyapal said.

Boo glanced at Laila as if looking for approval. Laila just motioned to the clearing between them.

"Okay, great," Boo continued. "Mr. Evil, are you ready to roll?"

"Losers can set the rules," he said, his words almost amiable. He sounded like a typical uncle at a family barbecue playing an outdoor game.

Karan let out a muffled sound, rolling forward as if trying to get them to stop.

Laila ached for him, desperate to go to his side, but she knew there was no way she could move without revealing all her cards.

"We're not playing a full game of Chausar, because it could take hours," Boo said. Her voice wavered, then steadied again. "Instead, we call a number, roll the dice, and the person with the closest roll wins the round. Best two out of three."

She took a few tentative steps forward then and, using her sneakered foot, dragged her toe in the soil to make a line.

"We throw over the line. We don't have a Chausar board or anything, so we do what we can with what we have."

"Rudimentary," Satyapal said. "And almost an insult to our ancestors. But I'm willing to play." Then he looked up at Laila, his tongue licking at the corner of his mouth. "I'll have you tonight, Daughter of Draupadi."

She was going to be sick. The thought of being forced to give her body to a man who wanted to have a child, then to steal that child and infect it with evil. Laila refused to let him see her disgust and stood vigilantly at Boo's side.

"Round one," Boo called out. "Mr. Evil. You can go first since you have the dice."

He took a step toward the line, then before he called out his number, Laila spoke.

"I wonder what will happen to the dice since they're being handled by a normal human," Laila said loudly, delivering the first remark. Then nudged Boo.

"I'm not sure," Boo replied. "Not everyone descends from royalty, but maybe he'll get lucky."

"Satyapal?" Laila scoffed. "The unluckiest guy ever. He sat alone in his room with some sort of a crystal ball, because he was super jealous of his best friend, you know?"

"Silence!" Satyapal roared, and the trees rattled like skeletons. The fire closest to him snuffed out. Laila lit it again, holding her ground.

There was a whisper in the trees, a cackle, and Satyapal sucked more darkness in through his mouth, his nose, his eyes, the shadows crawling like little insects into his body.

"Eight," he said, his voice growing deeper.

He rolled the dice, and they landed on eight at Boo's feet.

Satyapal laughed, his eyeballs pitch black now. "Throw the dice!"

Boo scrambled forward and picked up the dice.

Laila rested a hand on her arm, hoping that it gave her strength.

"You know," Boo finally said, her frail form trembling, "He's sucking up demons like he's in one of those cheesy horror movies, but does he know that just means that the demons are strong and he's just their lackey?"

"Human," Laila and Boo said in unison, because they both knew that only a man would be dumb enough to assume that he was stronger than gods and demons.

The ground trembled. "I will relish watching you all die," Satyapal said.

"Trash talking is actually an important part of the game of Chausar," Boo said. "In the first version of the text there are tons of references to all the trash talking that happened. Oh, but that's our family history, not yours—"

Satyapal looked like he was ready to lunge across the clearing, but before he was able to react, Boo called a number.

"Four!"

The dice rolled and rolled, and slowly tipped on their side.

Twos appeared on each die.

"No!" Satyapal roared. The trees rattled again. "No, how can that be? You did something to the dice! You tried to trick me!" He lunged forward, but he was unable to cross the line that separated them in their game. He pounded on the invisible barrier. "What is this? What have you done to divide the clearing?"

"We're playing with magic dice, Satyapal," Laila called out. "What did you think would happen? Once you start the game, you can't stop."

"This is sorcery!" he shouted. From her position on the other side of the barrier, Laila could see a trickle of blood drip down his nose.

"No," she said calmly. "We just knew we were better than a human." She moved to stand at Boo's side. "The Mahabharata also showed that the Pandavas had a win at one point. It's not out of the realm of possibility, you know."

"Your turn," Boo said. She was standing so strong, Laila thought, even though she looked like she was ready to bolt and run.

Satyapal snapped his fingers and the dice appeared in his hands. "Two for the win," he called out. The wind around them howled, the darkness a dome over her ring of fire, threatening to extinguish all her flames.

Boo didn't bother with heckling this time. She called nine, and each die complied.

Laila looked over at Karan, who stared at her, his eyes focused on hers.

I forgive you. I love you. I'll save you.

"Satyapal, one last thing before you roll," she said conversationally. "You will *never* be as good as any of us. You are a lonely, creepy old man with no power other than what you are forced to take."

Satyapal roared, and this time the wind sounded like screams. "Twelve!"

He tossed them with one flick of his wrist, and the dice rolled and rolled and rolled until they landed.

Six.

Two.

"No!" he screamed.

Laila turned to Boo. "Run," she said.

Boo turned and bolted for the trees, cutting down the same path that she'd come from before, past the perimeter into safety from any of the malevolent forces that Satyapal had swallowed.

"I will have you!" he said, his voice mutated and mutilated from what he'd once been. Blood rushed from his ears, from his tear ducts and his nose. His nails grew to daggered points, and he snatched the angalikastra out of thin air.

Karan rolled forward just as Satyapal tried to stab it through his throat. Then Laila shot fire out of her hands, covering Karan with the flames until she could see that the invisible binds that tied his hands and wrists had burned free.

He kept rolling until he was in the middle of the clearing before he staggered to his feet.

Laila helped him up, carried his weight as he leaned against her side. "Are you okay?" she said.

He gripped his wrists, rubbing where he'd been bound. "Fine. The angalikastra. I don't have any weapons against it."

"You don't need any," she said as Satyapal moved forward, his body struggling under the weight of the demonic forces he'd summoned for aid. The sound of the damned pierced through the thin veil between worlds.

Then she moved in front of him to face Satyapal, her hands glowing with flame.

"How many times do I have to tell you that you're a loser before you give up?" she said.

More blackness poured from the night sky, seeping into every pore until she couldn't tell if Satyapal was even alive under the weight of it all.

"The Daughter of Draupadi," a voice responded. "I will plant my seed in you."

Then Satyapal lashed out with the angalikastra and she danced away. Taking a chance, she envisioned a blade in her hand, and formed it with fire. She stared at the fire sword, gaping at it as it appeared between one second and another.

"Oh my god, this is so cool," she said, momentarily stunned that her anger could be a physical weapon.

Satyapal lunged again, and she blocked it with her fire sword. It clashed as if metal hit metal. Then she jumped as he kicked out, taking a chance, and kicked him in his nuts.

He didn't so much as flinch.

Karan spoke from behind her "He should've—"

"I know," she called back. "Not yet!"

Then they fought with steel, and hands, and feet. Any time she felt him try to bind her limbs with his invisible power, she was able to quickly burn it away. She heard his sounds of frustration, saw his face covered with blood, saw him cough until it poured from his mouth. Then she kicked him hard in the chest until he stumbled back all the way across the clearing.

"I am the Daughter of Draupadi," she said, hoping that with her was not only Lord Agni, but her masis, the memory of her mother and her Usha Masi, and Draupadi herself. Channeling her power, she made a wide arc with her hand until it formed a bow. Then she created an arrow out of fire.

"You are *nothing* but a woman," the spirits inside Satyapal hissed as he struggled to stay on his feet. "You are nothing but a mother figure. You are no *fighter*."

"No, bitch," Laila snapped. "I come from the woman whose thirst for vengeance fueled a war. I am the linchpin in this whole battle, and I'm the last face you'll see before you die."

She let go of her control, and a funnel of flame shot out of her palms, piercing Satyapal's chest. He screamed and fell to his knees. His body burned, and he was trapped in the flames. His body went limp.

The bow and arrow disappeared, and this time she was the one leaning against Karan's side as she felt all her energy drain out of her until her knees weakened.

They watched in silence until finally there was nothing left but a hollowed-out carcass of a man and a pile of ash.

"We need to do a proper burial," Karan said, his voice heavy and thick. "We don't want Satyapal to come back to haunt us."

"Definitely not," she said.

"I got the shovel!"

Laila and Karan turned around to see Boo step back into the clearing with Karan's night goggles on, a shovel in one hand, and a kitchen steak knife in the other. "I was hoping you'd be done by now. Hi, bhai!"

She dropped the shovel and knife and ran toward Karan. He was barely strong enough to open his arms and catch her hug. He pressed a kiss against the top of her head and stroked a hand down her back. "You did well, Boo. You did so good."

"Thanks, bhai," she said, as her breath caught.

Then Boo was hugging Laila with the same ferocious strength. "Oh my god, our mean girl routine was so good."

"Yes, it was," Laila chuckled. "Yeah, it really was."

In silence, they worked together to give Satyapal his last burial rites, and underneath the tree, they buried the last of his remains. Laila torched them to purify the space.

Because not only did fire kill, but it also had the ability to cleanse.

And it was time to start fresh. It was time to start over.

34. KARAN

Karan hadn't remembered what occurred over the last twenty-four hours. He was pretty sure that Satyapal had put him in a trance, a dreamlike state. One minute he was standing on the dock, and the next he'd been bound and gagged at Satyapal's feet in the clearing, the angalikastra pointing downward at his neck.

It was now wrapped in burlap tucked under Boo's arm along with the dice that Lord Agni had given Laila.

They crossed the lawn and entered the house from the back. Daylight was still a few hours away, and all he wanted to do was shower and hold Laila. But they had so much to talk about first. There was so much to do.

"Laila," he said when they entered the kitchen.

"I'm going to go put this in the library for now," Boo said, motioning to the angalikastra. "Technically getting cut by it could kill me too, since I have some of Karna's blood as well, so I'm not going to take any chances."

She was gone in a flash, leaving Laila and Karan alone.

"Wait, let me go find Gopal," she said, her fingers grazing over his arm. "He should be waiting for us."

She called his name, and then walked through the main level. There was no response.

Boo appeared a moment later. "Was Gopal downstairs?" Laila asked.

She shook her head. "No, but the magic has been restored to close the doors."

"He's gone, isn't he?" Karan asked. "He completed what he came here to do."

"I think so," she said. There was a flash of regret in her expression. "But it feels . . . unfinished. I feel like there is something we're missing that we haven't quite completed yet. Gopal is the only one with the answers."

"When it's time, I'm sure he'll show up," Boo said. "Right now, we have to figure out if it's safe for me to return to Germany yet. And Karan, hopefully we can find your parents now that Satyapal is gone. He was the immediate threat, right? The big bad wolf that Gopal was hoping we'd all get rid of?"

Karan wasn't so sure. In an effort to remove Satyapal from their path, they'd also created a host of other problems. The first being that there was still a chance every asura known to man was gravitating toward their location.

In freaking America.

"Whether or not Satyapal was the problem doesn't matter to me right now," Laila replied. "My aunts should be able to come home, too. They may not know as much as Gopal, but they are the OG. The last survivors of the Kurukshetra War. I know with their help—"

"And mine," Karan said. He faced Laila, bruised and battered, covered in sweat, despite the cool night air. "And my help," he repeated.

"I'm . . . ah, going to go shower," Boo said. "I think I'll even go to bed early with Billi. Maybe we'll watch that age-appropriate TV show. We can deal with the rest in the morning."

Then she was off, running toward the stairs. That left Laila and Karan alone in the kitchen again.

His heart began to pound in his chest. She was so damn beautiful with her hair disheveled, her jeans torn at the knee. In such a short amount of time, she'd become so important to him. Despite the hours of conversation and time they spent together, there was still so much he didn't know about her, and so much he wanted to discover. "Laila—"

"You may not have had time to process," she said as she crossed the room toward him. "But I have had a day, and I think it all makes sense," she said. Then she wrapped her arms around his waist. He breathed a sigh of relief, relishing the feel of her soft skin under his fingertips. He leaned his forehead against hers.

"I love you," he whispered as he pulled her close. "And I am so sorry."

"I love you, back," she said. "And I forgive you."

She forgave him. He let out a shuddering breath.

She forgave him.

"I swear on my heart," he whispered. "I swear on my soul that I will be the sword by your side. I will be your partner and protect you no matter what happens next."

There was a long pause. "God that is so cheesy, Karan. Did you seriously just say that to me?"

He snorted. And there she was, calling him on his bullshit. "I thought it was romantic."

She lifted her mouth to his, and he kissed her, feeling the warmth cascade through her, calming his racing heart, his racing pulse.

He felt complete after so long. Not because he was looking for, or because he needed Laila in his life as a reason for living, but because she gave him purpose. She gave him strength, and he wanted more time with her to know what they can be together. But if they created a thinning in the fabric of the universe . . .

Karan pulled back. "That's it," he said softly.

"What?"

"Gopal said that together, we created a signature, a way for those who crave your power to come through the thin parts of the fabric of the universe. If we're together, then there is a chance more people can die."

"I don't think that's true anymore," Laila said slowly. "At least, it won't be just us who creates chaos. A tattoo formed on Boo's back when Gopal told Satyapal that she was going to roll the dice in the dice game. I think the concentrated power signature that we created is . . . diluted. Boo thinks that all the descendants should be . . . ah, alerted."

"Which means they're all in trouble?" Karan asked.

Laila shook her head. "I don't know."

He felt his heart pound hard in his chest, but he took a chance. "I know I have a duty to uphold my legacy, but, Laila, I choose to stay with you. As long as I can keep you safe, I want us to say fuck all to the universe, and let's fight it together."

Her eyes began to tear. "Yeah," she said. "Yeah, that works for me."

They embraced again, and he lifted her off her feet, twirling her in a circle. He was loved, and he felt loved by this incredible, complicated woman.

"We should go on a date again," Laila said when he put her down. "I want to know everything. A date like the one by the dock, not the one where you tried to kill me."

"Ha, ha," he said, and pulled her close. He hoped that they had so many more dates together where she'd be able to make jokes like this.

Because they were exhausted, adrenaline running high, they showered together, then dressed. Karan combed Laila's hair and he watched her braid it. Then they stayed up until dawn talking about their plans. They were going to look for his parents first thing in the morning. Her masis were safe for now, but once Karan could find his mother and father, they'd try to bring the masis home.

If they could ensure their future. Karan knew that there was still so much left for them to uncover about their entwined legacies, but they could do it together.

When they walked down to the library the next morning, Boo was already sitting in front of the books. She had taken one of the kitchen

steak knives with her, and it sat at her elbow. She looked like she hadn't slept at all. There were dark shadows under her eyes, and she rocked back and forth in her chair like she'd had too much caffeine.

"We can get you a compact one," Laila said as she approached the table. She pointed to the knife. "This way you don't have to raid the cutlery drawer. Something with a better grip."

"And I'll teach you how to use it," Karan said as he rubbed her shoulders. She was so frail. They'd have to make sure she was eating enough. Boo had a tendency to forget to eat.

Her mouth was set in a grim line when she looked up at him. "Good, because I'm going to need it. I can't be the weakest link."

"What do you mean?" Laila asked.

Boo glanced at Karan, then motioned to the book that she'd been reading. The nineteenth volume of the Mahabharata that was never released to the world.

"It says here that there is more than just one descendant that will be called to fight."

Laila rushed forward. "What are you talking about? I've read that book backward and forward, and the only person who had a destiny that I was sure of was me."

Boo motioned to one of the pages in the back of the book. "It's written in code," she said. "It's in the same dialect that makes up the text of our tattoos."

Karan watched as Laila scanned the page

"Well shit," she said, stepping back. "I missed a whole section in the text when I had to study it, and that section just happened to be the most important part!"

"What does it mean, though?" Karan asked.

Laila tapped Boo's notebook. "It means that if you're a descendant of Karna, and Boo is a descendant of Yudhishthira, there are four other players we're missing. The four other Pandava brothers."

"We can't discount the other side," Boo said ruefully. She pointed to a line of text. "The descendants of the major players in the war were all gifted one element from the Kurukshetra War for safekeeping. There are three hundred and twenty-four items total. From arrows to knives to amulets, to clothes."

"Okay?" Karan asked as he sank into the chair next to Boo. "Do the items have any significance?"

"If anyone who is not a descendant received these objects and begins to collect them, and if they gather nineteen total, then they can, at will, open up pockets of dimensions in the universe so that asuras in the demon realm can enter at will."

"A literal hell mouth," Karan said. Just what they needed. "Are you serious?"

"It's been centuries that these items have been out in the world," Laila said as she sat at the table across from Boo. "We just killed Satyapal. He's one guy who had one item. It would be impossible for one person in their lifetime to capture nineteen."

Boo rubbed her shoulder at the same spot where Laila's and Karan's tattoos began. "I shouldn't have been marked, Laila. Or if I was, then it should go away by now. Something isn't right. There is more to the story that we're missing."

"Then we'll have to figure out what it is," Laila said. She turned to Karan, who nodded. Yes, he thought. For however long it took.

Their path was different than those who came before them, but that didn't matter. This was family they were talking about. He'd do whatever it took to keep them safe.

His phone buzzed in his pocket. Although he hadn't received a text or a note from his mates in ages, he still carried it just in case.

When he looked at the screen, he gasped. Then he answered before the second ring. "Papa?" he said.

Laila and Boo stared at each other, their faces brightening.

"Beta," he heard the heavy sound of his father's voice say. "I'm so glad to hear your voice."

"Papa," he said, his voice croaking. He nearly doubled over at the sound. His throat felt like it closed up, and tears burned behind his eyes. His father. This was really his father. "Are you okay? Is Mama all right?"

"She is. We're both back home in the flat."

Karan got to his feet and began pacing the library. "What happened to you? Were you safe?"

"Your friend Gopal took us in the middle of the night," he said. "I knew that something bad was happening, and I didn't want to go, but he . . . insisted."

There was rustling on the other end, and then his mother's voice joined the line.

"Karan!" she said, her voice bright. "I'm so glad you're okay, beta."

"Mom, I'm fine." Her voice was way too cheerful for them being held up in a safe house. "Where were you?"

"We were on a world cruise!" she said, her voice filled with excitement. "We just couldn't call you or talk to you. Those were the rules. It was for your own safety. But oh my goodness, beta, we saw *penguins*."

Great, he thought. His parents were seeing penguins while he was losing his mind over whether they were even alive.

There was more rustling on the other end of the phone before his father's voice filtered through the line again. "Karan? We need to talk. Where are you?"

"Ah, I'm in America right now, Papa. I don't know when I'll be back in India."

"Then I'll come to you," he said.

"It's not safe," Karan replied. He glanced back at Laila, who was having a conversation with their cousin. "Let's talk later tonight over here, first thing in the morning for you. We have a lot to catch up on."

"Okay, let me get Satya to—"

"No," Karan said, his heart hurting for his father. "No, Papa. This is just for us. I'll explain it all later."

There was another long pause. "Okay, beta. I'll talk to you soon."

Karan didn't want to say goodbye, didn't want to stop talking to this man who was such a huge part of his heart, but he hung up the phone and turned to Laila again, who had her own cell out. "If Gopal is gone, in theory, my aunts should be home soon too. Between your father and my masis, there has to be someone who has more knowledge than what we have to work with."

As the words left her mouth, there was a cry from upstairs.

"Yoo-hoo! We're home!"

Laila's eyes goggled. "Oh my god. Masis!"

She ran for the front door, leaving Karan standing in the kitchen.

The rakshasi were here. Holy hell, he was about to face her aunts.

Boo got to her feet, then she brushed her hands on her thighs. “I don’t know if I have it in me twice to play dice and save your life, bhai.”

“Then I hope Laila can handle this on her own,” he said quietly.

He straightened his shoulders, then walked up the steps until he reached the kitchen. There was commotion at the front of the house in the foyer.

“You’re not allowed to kill him!” Karan heard Laila shout. “I want you to swear on my head that you won’t kill him or Boo, or their families. Do it!”

There were grumblings, and a prickling sensation tickled the back of his neck.

Three women, towering over six feet, hair black as a raven, eyes rimmed with gold, strode into the kitchen. They stood side by side as they assessed Karan from behind Laila’s body.

“We will love you as long as you love our Laila,” one of them said.

“But if she so much as cries a single tear,” the second one added.

“We will enjoy sucking your eyeballs out of your head and eating them,” the third one said. “While you’re still alive and screaming to feel the pain.”

“Rashmi Masi!”

“He should know the stakes,” Rashmi Masi said simply. “Now. Care to tell me why you have moved a man into our house while we’re stuck in India?”

"He's not just any man," Laila said as she extended a hand for Karan to take it. "He's the descendant of Karna. And we have a lot to talk about."

The masis hushed, as they looked at each other then back to Laila.

Boo appeared a moment later. She adjusted her glasses, then wiggled her fingers in a wave. "Hi, my ancestor was Yudhishthira, in case anyone was interested."

There was another gasp, a cry, and to Karan's ears, the masis began speaking to Laila in French. She responded in kind, the words sounding harsh and sexy as she pronounced soft vowels and harsh consonants.

"We have a lot to do," the one named Vika Masi said in English. She looked at Karan, her red-rimmed eyes focused on him with an intensity that had his blood go cold. "There is so much at stake. If you have your marks, then the others have awoken with marks, too. And they are all in trouble."

35.

Gopal stood on the beach, the stormy Atlantic raging with whitecaps, and clouds kissing the shoreline. He'd made a fire. Not the way that Laila could easily do, but with matches and logs. Then he'd thrown rice, and flour, and butter into the flames. He'd offered milk and sugar. He'd given the flames the five elements.

And then he'd waited.

"You've done well."

He turned to his left to see an older Indian man, a bun on the top of his head, his long black hair draped over his shoulders. He wore a long coat and a suit. He leaned heavily on the cane from the injury he'd sustained in human form centuries ago.

A hunter had shot him with an arrow on the bottom of his foot. His soul, a marking in the shape of an eye, had been mistaken for a deer. He'd disappeared after that, and Kali Yuga, the universe as it existed today, began.

"I tried my best, ancestor, but they barely survived," Gopal said.

"You've done well," Lord Krishna said again. Then he clasped Gopal on the shoulder, the weight of his hand heavy. "But I warned you about getting too close."

Gopal nodded. "I couldn't see. And she almost died. Karan almost died."

"If fate demands their life, then it would've taken it," Krishna said. "But they're still alive. They're still on this new quest."

"Is my journey over?" Gopal asked. He desperately wanted it to be. He desperately wanted to know what life was for himself. He wanted someone like Laila to look at him the way that she looked at Karan. He'd wanted a woman as strong, as resilient, and as soft as she was to love him, too.

"Your journey has just begun, the son of my sons," Lord Krishna said. He left his hand on Gopal's shoulder as they watched the ocean. The touch was comforting. They stood in silence, until the god spoke again.

"You'll be tested, Gopal," he said. "Satyapal wasn't working alone, and now the others need your help."

Gopal nodded. "Yes, ancestor."

Lord Krishna shifted so he stood in front of Gopal now. The wind whipped at his hair, and the lapels of his coat fluttered. "You can't go back to see her, Gopal. Even if you stand at a distance. She's with her fated mate now. And you . . . your responsibility is elsewhere. If you insist on remaining close, all your power will disintegrate until you're left defenseless. Promise me, son of my son. Promise me that you won't ever see Laila Bansal again."

Gopal swallowed the hard knot in his throat. "I promise, ancestor." Then he pressed a fist to his heart and bowed his head. "I'm ready for my next task. I'd prefer to get started right away."

"Good," Lord Krishna replied. "Then let us begin."

Author's Note

I have been researching the mythology and folklore that has made its way into this story for years. However, I am definitely not an expert. Instead, I relied on the support of scholars who are. For those who are familiar with South Asian mythology and folklore, as well as the stories in the Mahabharata, not everything you read will be exactly as you were taught. Some facts came from regional variations of the myths, and others were from oral traditions.

Instead of a true depiction of the mythology that existed in the pages of Smriti texts, *Illusions of Fire* takes poetic license, and is inspired by the stories that resonated with me the most. If you are looking for a more authentic version of the mythology, *The Illustrated Mahabharata: The Definitive Guide to India's Greatest Epic* (DK) and the ten-volume Penguin Classic Mahabharata box set (translated by Bibek Debroy) are my favorites.

Acknowledgments

I started writing this book in 2009. It was previously titled *The Chosen Warrior*, which felt fitting for early 2000's paranormal fantasy romance. After I finished the draft, the same year that I graduated law school, I found an agency that was just as excited as I was to pitch the story. Except at that time, no one wanted it. In early 2011, every editor we went to said one of three things: they weren't sure where to place the book because they didn't have any comps for it, they already had a South Asian author, and it was too difficult to understand. I still have copies of these rejections because I made my agent send me every single one. By 2012, we shelved the project. When authors began publishing South Asian "high fantasy," my agent went out again with a revised version of the manuscript. This time the rejections were a bit worse. The most honest one read "it's easier for readers to understand South Asian fantastical elements in made up worlds than it is to understand them in the real world." My agent and I never lost sight of the book, though.

When I was done with my adult rom-com contract in 2022, I realized that with the rise in romantasy, and the way that the industry had shifted, I should revisit my manuscript. I changed the name, made it darker, and after over a decade of working as a writer, I heavily revised the story to reflect the improvements I'd made in my craft. Suzy was the first one who jumped on the story, and for the first time ever, I received a compliment for a novel that had been with me for the entire length of my professional career. "It reminds me of Buffy," she said.

So Suzy, the first thank-you is to you. Thank you for understanding my story, for working with me on this book, and for your trust in delivering a manuscript worthy of publication.

Thank you to the Union Square team. You've been incredible support and given me a gorgeous cover, patience, and an opportunity to share a very personal narrative with my readers.

To my incredible agent. Because Joy, I always need to thank you for being my partner in crime. Thank you for always remembering this story over the years, and for supporting me even though I know I don't make it easy.

To my South Asian writer friends who understand, in solidarity, early publishing for BIPOC authors, and for the newbies whose excitement reminds me why I love this job. Roshani Chokshi, special shout out to you for publishing your South Asian YA high fantasy in 2016 and cracking open doors for so many that followed.

Lastly, this one is to my parents. This is the only book my mother has read, and this is the one story my father has been my sensitivity reader. Thank you for humoring me as a child and telling me bedtime stories about the Pandavas, demons, and warrior princesses. This book is possible because of you.

About the Author

Nisha Sharma is a YA and adult contemporary romance writer living in the Philly suburbs with her Alaskan husband and a plethora of animals named after characters in literature. Her books have been included in best-of lists by *The New York Times*, *Entertainment Weekly*, *Cosmopolitan*, *The Washington Post*, *Time*, and more. Before she left the corporate world, Nisha spearheaded DEI initiatives at billion-dollar companies. She has continued her advocacy work by fighting for marginalized authors in publishing. When she's not writing about people of color experiencing radical joy or teaching about inclusivity, Nisha can be found hitting the books for her PhD in English and Social Justice. You can find her online at Nisha-sharma.com or on TikTok and Instagram at @nishawrites.